Grace Livingston Hill

Marcia Schuyler

BARBOUR
PUBLISHING

© 2000 by R. L. Munce Publishing Co., Inc.

Edited and updated for today's reader by Deborah Cole.

ISBN 1-59310-677-7

Published by Barbour Publishing, Inc., P.O. Box 719, Uhrichsville, Ohio 44683, www.barbourbooks.com

Our mission is to publish and distribute inspirational products offering exceptional value and biblical encouragement to the masses.

Member of the
Evangelical Christian
Publishers Association

Printed in the United States of America.
5 4 3 2 1

Chapter 1

*T*he sun was already up and the grass sparkling with dew when Marcia stepped from the kitchen door. She wore a chocolate calico with red and white sprigs scattered over it, her hair hung in smooth brown braids down her back, and the flush on her round cheeks reflected the rosy light in the east. Her face was as untroubled as the summer morning and her eyes as dreamy as the clouds that hovered on the horizon.

She walked lightly through the grass until a rail fence stopped her. She mounted it as if it were a steed to carry her onward and sat looking at the beauty of the morning. Her eyes took on that faraway look that annoyed her stepmother when she wanted her to hurry with the dishes or finish a long seam before getting supper.

She lingered only a moment, for her mind was full of business, and she wished to accomplish a great deal before the day ended. Swinging easily down to the other side of the fence, she moved on through the meadow, over another fence, and through another meadow, skirting the edge of a cool strip of woods that lured her with its green mysterious shadows, whispering leaves, and twittering birds. She glanced wistfully into the sweet silence; then, turning away, she sped on to the slope of Blackberry Hill.

It wasn't a long climb to where the blackberries grew, and she was soon at work, the great luscious berries dropping into her pail almost with a touch. But while she worked, the vision of the hills, the sheep meadow below, and the river winding between the neighboring farms melted away, nor did she see the ripe fruit before her. She was planning the new dress she'd buy with the berries. It was pink and white; she'd seen it in the store the last time she went for sugar and flour.

The past weeks at the house had been busy. Kate, her elder sister, was to be married in a few days.

It had taken a whole year to prepare: spinning and weaving and fine sewing. The smooth white linen lay ready, packed between rose leaves and lavender. The two girls had made yards of tatting and embroidery for the trousseau, and the village dressmaker had spent days at the house, cutting, fitting, shirring, till now gorgeous apparel was piled high on the bed and chairs and hung in the closets of the large spare bedroom. But—they were for Kate!

Of course that was right. Kate was to be married, not Marcia, who was scarcely more than a child, barely seventeen. No one thought of anything new for her, and she didn't expect it. But in her heart she longed for a new dress amid all this finery for Kate. She had her best one, of course. It was pretty and nice enough to wear to the wedding, and her stepmother was relieved Marcia would need nothing during the rush of getting Kate ready.

But friends of Kate and her stepmother were coming to the house every day, especially in the afternoons, to see Kate's wardrobe and talk things over. Marcia couldn't wear her best dress all the time. And *he* was coming! That was how Marcia always referred in her mind to the prospective bridegroom.

His name was David Spafford, and Kate often called him Dave. But Marcia could never bring herself to breathe the name so familiarly, even to herself. She held him in great awe. He was so fine and strong and good, with a face like a young saint in some old picture, she thought. She often wondered how her wild, bubbly sister dared to be so familiar with him. She ventured the thought once when she watched Kate dressing to go out with friends and preening herself like a bird of paradise before the mirror.

"Kate, you'll have to be very different when you're married," she said with conviction.

Her sister turned about with an amused look on her face and asked why.

"Because *he* is so good," Marcia replied, unable to explain further.

"Oh, is that all?" said the sister, wheeling back to the mirror. "Don't you worry—I'll soon take that out of him."

But Kate's indifference never lessened her younger sister's awe of her prospective brother-in-law. She listened to his conversations with her father during his brief visits, and she watched his face at church while he and Kate sang, "Rock of Ages, cleft for me, let me hide myself in Thee," a new song just written. And she mused upon the charmed life Kate would lead. It was wonderful to be a woman and be loved as Kate was loved, thought Marcia.

So in all the hurry, no one seemed to think much about Marcia, but she wasn't satisfied with her brown delaine afternoon dress. Truth to tell, it needed letting down, and there was nothing left to let down. She felt like last year in it with her slender ankles plainly seen. So she set her heart on the new chintz.

Now, with Marcia, to decide was to do. She didn't speak to her stepmother about it, for she knew it would be useless. Nor did she think it worthwhile to go to her father. Both his wife and Kate would find out and charge her with useless expense when the money was needed elsewhere, and they were anxious to have it all flow their way. So she took the time that belonged to her and went to the blackberry patch that belonged to everyone.

With nimble fingers she finished her task before the sun was high and turned happily toward the village. The pails wouldn't hold another berry.

Her cheeks glowed with the sun and exercise, and little wisps of wavy curls had escaped about her brow, damp with perspiration. Her eyes shone with her purpose, half fulfilled, as she hastened down the hill.

Crossing a field she met Hanford Weston with a rake over his shoulder and a wide-brimmed straw hat like a small shed over him. He was on his way to the south meadow. He blushed and greeted her as she passed by shyly, then paused and looked admiringly after her. They'd been in the same classes at school all winter, the girl at the head, the boy at the foot. But Hanford Weston's father owned the largest farm around, and he felt that didn't matter so much. He'd rather see Marcia at the head anyway, though there was never the slightest danger of his taking her place. He felt a sudden desire to follow her. It would be a pleasure to carry those pails as if they were mere featherweights.

He watched her steps for a moment, considered the sun in the sky and his father's command about the south meadow, and then strode after her. It didn't take long to reach her.

With sudden hotness in his face and a tremor in his throat, he haltingly asked if he might carry her burden for her.

Annoyed, Marcia stopped. He was attractive—sometimes the girls even called him "handsome Hanford"—but she'd forgotten all about him. She was planning exactly how to make the pink sprigged chintz and which parts to cut first to save time and material. She didn't wish to be interrupted and certainly not by a schoolmate she could see every day and could so easily "spell down." She summoned her thoughts from the details of mutton-leg sleeves and looked the boy over, to his great confusion.

"Weren't you going somewhere else?" she asked sweetly. "Wasn't there a rake over your shoulder? What have you done with it?"

The young man blushed more deeply.

"Where were you going?" she demanded.

"To the south meadow," he stammered.

"Oh, well, then you must go back. I'll do quite well, thank you. Your father wouldn't be pleased for you to neglect your work for me, though I'm much obliged, I'm sure."

Was there some foreshadowing of her womanhood in the decided way she spoke and the prim set of her head as she bowed good morning to him and continued on her way? The boy didn't understand. He only felt abashed and half angry she'd ordered him back to work—and in a tone that forbade him to take her memory with him. Nevertheless, her image lingered and haunted the south meadow as he worked.

Marcia, unconscious of stirring the young man's admiration, went her way quickly. Her spirit was one with the sunny morning, her body light with anticipation, for a new dress of her own choice was an event in her life.

Many times during the long hours she'd spent putting delicate stitches into her sister's wedding garments, she wondered how she'd feel if they were being made for her. She had whiled away many a dreary seam by imagining how she'd put on this or that if it were hers, go here or there, and have people love and admire her as they did Kate. It would never come true, of course. She never expected to be admired and loved like Kate. Kate was beautiful, bright, and lively. Everybody loved her, no matter how she treated them. It was a matter of course for Kate to have everything she wanted.

Marcia felt she could never attain to such heights. In the first place, she considered her own serious face with its brown eyes as exceedingly plain. She couldn't catch the lights hiding in her eyes when she talked with animation. Indeed, few saw her at her best, because she seldom talked freely. Only with certain people could she forget herself.

She didn't envy Kate. She was proud of her sister and loved her, though there was an element of anxiety in the love. But she never thought of her many faults. They were excusable because Kate was Kate. It was as if you should find fault with a wild rose because it carried a thorn. Kate was set about with many thorns, but amid them all she bloomed, her fragrant pink self, as apparently unconscious of the many pricks she gave, and unconcerned, as the flower itself.

So Marcia never thought to be jealous that Kate had so many lovely things and was going out into the world to do as she pleased and lead a charmed life with a man who was greater in the eyes of this girl than any prince in a fairy tale. But she saw no harm in imagining herself the beautiful, admired, elder sister instead of the plain younger one.

But this morning on her way to the village store with her berries, she thought no more of her sister's things, for her mind was on the material she'd purchase with the price of the berries and then go home and make.

She had a whole day to herself, for Kate and her stepmother had gone to the neighboring town to make a few last purchases. She'd told no one of her plans and was awake early in the morning to see the travelers off, eager to have them gone so she might carry out her plan.

At the edge of the village, Marcia put the pails of berries by a large flat stone and sat down. One shoelace had come untied, and her hair was rumpled. After tidying up, she was soon on her way again.

Mary Ann Fothergill waited by her gate till Marcia came, and the two girls walked on together. Mary Ann had stiff, straight, light-colored hair and high cheekbones, with pale eyes and lashes, all tucked under a checked sunbonnet. Her dull, tanned complexion was a contrast to Marcia's pink and white skin. She was tall and awkward and wore a linsey-woolsey dress as though it were a meal sack temporarily appropriated. She had the air of always trying to hide her feet and hands. Mary Ann had some fine qualities, but beauty wasn't among them. Beside her,

Marcia's delicate features showed clear-cut like a cameo.

Mary Ann regarded Marcia's smooth brown braids enviously. Her own sparse hair barely reached to her shoulders, straggling about her neck helplessly and hopelessly, in spite of her constant efforts.

"It must be lots of fun at your house these days," said Mary Ann with a sigh. "Are you 'most ready for the wedding?"

Marcia nodded, her eyes bright. She could see the sign of the village store and knew the bolts of new chintz were displayed in the window.

"My, but your cheeks do look pretty," said Mary Ann impulsively. "Say, how many of each has your sister got?"

"Two dozen," said Marcia, conscious of a little swelling of pride in her chest. Not every girl had such a setting out as her sister.

"My!" sighed Mary Ann. "And outside things, too. I s'pose she's got one of every color. What are her dresses? I've been up to Dutchess County and just got back last night. But Ma wrote Aunt Tilly, and Mis' Hotchkiss said her dresses was the prettiest Miss Hancock's ever sewed on."

"We think they're pretty," admitted Marcia modestly. "There's a muslin delaine and a blue delaine and a blue silk—"

"My! Silk!" breathed Mary Ann. "And what's she going to be married in?"

"White satin," answered Marcia. "And the veil was Mother's— our own mother's, you know."

Marcia spoke it reverently, her eyes shining with a faraway look.

"Oh, my! Don't you just envy her?"

"No," said Marcia slowly, "I think not. At least—I hope not. It wouldn't be right, you know. She's my sister, and I love her dearly, and it's nearly as nice for her to have pretty things and a good time as to have them myself."

"You're too good," said Mary Ann. "But I'd envy her. Mis' Hotchkiss told Ma there wasn't many lots in life so all honey-and-dew-prepared like your sister's. All the money she wanted to spend on clo'es, a nice set out, and a man as handsome as you'll find anywhere, and he's well off, too, ain't he? Ma said she heard he kept a horse and lived right in the village, too. That's what I call luxury—a horse to ride around with.

"And then Mr. What's-his-name? Oh, yes, Spafford. Everybody says he won't fuss if Kate has a good time. He'll just let her do as she pleases. Only old Grandma Doolittle says she doesn't believe it. She thinks every man, no matter how good he is, wants to manage his wife, just for the name of it. She says your sister'll have to change her ways or there'll be trouble. But that's Grandma! Everybody knows her. Ma says Kate's got her nest feathered well if ever a girl had. My! I only wish I had the same chance!"

Marcia held her head a bit high when Mary Ann touched on her sister's personal character, but they were nearing the store, and everybody knew Mary Ann was blunt. She meant no harm and was only repeating the village gossip. Besides, Marcia must concentrate on sprigged chintz. She had no time for discussions if she was to accomplish her purpose before the folks came home that night.

"Mary Ann," she said in her sweet, prim way that always made the other girl stand a little in awe of her, "you mustn't listen to gossip. It isn't worthwhile. I'm sure my sister will be very happy. I'm going in the store now—are you?" And the conversation was suddenly concluded.

Mary Ann followed meekly, watching with wonder and envy as Marcia bargained with the merchant and selected her chintz. What a delicious swish the scissors made as they cut through the width of cloth, and how delightfully the paper crackled as the bundle was being wrapped!

"Oh, my! Ain't you afraid to make it yourself?" asked Mary

Ann. "I would be. It's the prettiest I ever saw. Don't you cut both sleeves for one arm. That's what I did the only time Ma ever let me try." Mary Ann touched the package under Marcia's arm with a sigh.

At the bend in the road, Mary Ann turned to go home. "Well, good-bye! Will you wear it next Sunday?" she asked.

"Perhaps," answered Marcia breathlessly and hurried home, her cheeks bright with excitement.

In her room she spread the chintz on the bed and with trembling fingers set about her task. The shears clipped the edge and tore off the lengths exultantly as if in league with the girl. Birds sang across the meadow, and the sun mounted to the zenith and began its downward march, but still the busy fingers worked on. It suited Marcia's scheme that the fashion of the day was simple, with few tucks and plaits and little trimming required; otherwise her task would have been impossible.

Her heart beat rapidly as she tried on the new chintz at last. She went into the spare room and stood before the long mirror in its wide gilt frame resting on two gilt knobs that stood out from the wall like giant rosettes. She'd made the skirt a little longer than that of her best dress. It was almost as long as Kate's, and for a moment she lingered, sweeping back and forth before the mirror, admiring herself in the long, graceful folds. She caught up her braids in the same style Kate wore her hair and smiled at her reflection.

How funny to think she'd soon be a woman like Kate. When Kate was gone they'd call her "Miss" sometimes. But the present seemed enough; she didn't care to look ahead. She had so wrapped her thoughts in her sister's new life that her own seemed stale in comparison.

The second distant hay wagon on the road reminded her the sun was close to setting. The family carryall would soon be coming up the lane. She must hurry and take off her new chintz and be dressed before they arrived.

Marcia was so tired after supper that she was glad to slip away to bed without waiting to hear Kate's voluble account of her day in town.

She lay down and dreamed of the next day and the next and the next. She awoke during the night and found the moonlight streaming into her face. Then she laughed and rubbed her eyes and tried to sleep again. But she couldn't, for she'd dreamed she was a bride, and Mary Ann's words kept going over in her mind: "Oh, don't you envy her?" *Did* she envy her sister? It troubled her to think of it, and she tried to banish the dream, but it came again and again with a strange sweet pleasure.

She wondered if a time of joy like Kate's would ever come to her and if the spare bed would ever be piled high with clothes for her new life. How wonderful to be a woman and be loved!

The moon dropped lower, the bright stars paled, and dawn stole up through the edge of the woods far away and awakened a day that would transform Marcia's life.

Chapter 2

*B*ecause of her hard work and her midnight awakening, Marcia overslept the next morning. Her stepmother called her sharply, and she dressed in haste, not even glancing at her new chintz in the closet. She dared not mention it yet. There was much to be done, and not even Kate had time for an idle word with her. Marcia was called upon to run errands, sew on lost buttons, and do things no one else had time for. The household had suddenly realized only one more day stood between them and the wedding.

Late in the afternoon Marcia ventured to put on her frock. Even then she felt shy about appearing in it.

Madam Schuyler was busy in the parlor with callers, and Kate was locked in her own room where she'd gone to rest. No one would notice if Marcia dressed up, and she'd likely escape much notice even at the supper table, since everyone was so absorbed in other things.

She looked wistfully at herself in the mirror. She was pleased with the dress and her appearance in it, but there was something disappointing about it. It had none of the style of her sister's garments, newly come from the village dressmaker. It was girlish and showed her slight form prettily in the fashion of the day, but she wanted to look older. She found a bit of black velvet in her drawer and secured it around her throat with a pin containing the miniature of her mother. Then she pulled her long braids up in loops and fastened them about her head. The style suited her well, and the change astonished her. She decided to wear them like that and see if others noticed.

She drew a quick breath as she descended the stairs.

Her stepmother and the visitor were just entering the hall from the parlor. They both stopped talking at once and stared at her. A look of dismay crossed Madam Schuyler's face. She suddenly realized Marcia was no longer a child; she'd blossomed into young womanhood. She wouldn't have chosen now for such an event, with so much going on and Marcia still in school. She had no desire to steer another young soul through the various follies that beset a girl from the time she puts up her hair until she's safely married to the right—or wrong—man.

She'd been relieved to think of having Kate settled. Kate had been hard to manage with her strong will and a pretty way of always having it. She had no reverence for the old customs and was lectured to many times for unseemly behavior.

"Why!" exclaimed the visitor. "Is this the bride? How tall she looks! No! Bless me! It isn't, is it? Yes—well, I declare. It's just Marsh! What do you have on, child? How old you look!"

Marcia flushed. She didn't like having her young womanhood questioned and in such a familiar, patronizing tone. She also disliked the name "Marsh," especially on the lips of this sort of second cousin to her stepmother. She wished her stepmother could have inspected the new dress without witnesses, but it was too late.

If Madam Schuyler was disturbed, she wouldn't show her visitor. As it happened, Marcia's ordeal may have been less trying with another person present.

"That looks very nice, child," she said matter-of-factly.

Though Marcia had gone beyond orders in purchasing and making a garment without her stepmother's knowledge, the neatness and fit reflected well upon her training. It was, on the whole, a very creditable piece of work, and Madam Schuyler grew more reconciled to it as Marcia neared them.

"Make it herself?" asked cousin Maria. "Why, Marsh, you

did real well. My Luellen does all her own clothes now. It's time you were learning. It's longer than what you've been wearing them, isn't it? But you'll grow into it, I daresay. Your hair's a new way, too. I thought you were Kate when you first started downstairs. You'll make a good-looking young lady when you grow up; only don't be in a hurry. Take your girlhood while you've got it—that's what I always tell Luellen."

Luellen was well on to thirty and showed no signs of taking anything else.

Madam Schuyler smoothed an imaginary pucker across the shoulders and again pronounced the work good.

"I picked berries and got the cloth," confessed Marcia.

Madam Schuyler smiled benevolently and patted Marcia's cheek.

"You needn't have done that, child. Why didn't you come to me for money? You needed something new, and that's a very good purchase—a little light, perhaps, but very pretty. We've been so busy with Kate that you've been neglected."

Marcia smiled and entered the dining room, wondering what power the cousin had over her stepmother that she would overlook this digression from her rules so sweetly—even with praise.

At supper everyone encouraged Marcia about her changed appearance. Her father looked from one lovely daughter to the other and said the bridegroom would hardly know which sister to choose when he arrived. He praised Marcia for doing the work so neatly, inwardly admiring her courage to get the money on her own instead of asking for it. Later, as she was removing the dishes from the table, he walked through the dining room and handed her a crisp five-dollar note. It had occurred to him that one daughter was getting all the good things while the other was getting nothing. His eyes held a tender look, as though he recognized her rights as a young woman. Marcia's heart was light. For some reason her new dress was having a strange influence on people.

Even Kate treated her differently. During supper she sat staring quietly at her sister. Marcia wondered about it later. Was she just realizing she was leaving home forever and wondering how things would be after she left, with Marcia as older sister? Was Kate sad about going so far away from them or suddenly feeling the responsibility of the new position she was to occupy and the duties that would be hers?

No, that couldn't be it, for surely that would bring a soft expression, a sweet anticipation, and Kate's expression was perplexed, almost troubled. If she were not her sister, Marcia would have added the word *hard*.

It was a lovely evening, still twilight, as she stepped from the low piazza that ran the length of the house bearing another above it on great white pillars. A drapery of wisteria in full bloom festooned across one end and half over the front. Marcia stepped back across the stone flagging and driveway to survey the graceful purple clusters and thought how beautiful the house would look when the wedding guests arrived the day after tomorrow. Then she turned onto the gravel path, box-bordered, leading to the gate. On each side dahlias, peonies, and roses bloomed luxuriantly. The yard had never looked so pretty; the flowers had done their best for the occasion.

Tomorrow the children would return from Aunt Eliza's, where they had been kept safely out of the way for a few days—and *he* would come. Not later than three in the afternoon, Kate said, though he might come in the morning; but she wasn't counting on it. He was driving from his home to Schenectady and, leaving his horse there to rest, would continue on by coach.

Then he and Kate would go back in fine style to Schenectady in a coach and pair, with a coachman. At Schenectady they'd take their horse and drive home, a long beautiful ride, thought

Marcia enviously. What endless, delightful talks they might have about the birds and other sights they passed—except Kate didn't like to talk about such things. But then she'd be with David, and he talked beautifully about nature and everything else. Kate would learn to love it if she loved him.

Did Kate love David? Of course she must. Why else would she marry him? Marcia resented the thought that her sister might have other objects in view, as Mary Ann Fothergill had suggested. Of course Kate would never marry any man unless she loved him. That would be dreadful. Love was the greatest thing in the world.

Marcia looked up at the stars, awed over the great mysteries of life. Would life ever open for her in some great way? Would someone come to love her, someone she could love in return?

She'd often dreamed such dreams before, as girls will, but never had they come to her with such vividness as that night. Perhaps it was because the household had recognized the woman in her for the first time. Or perhaps the vision she saw reflected in her mirror that afternoon opened the door of the future a little wider than ever before.

She stood by the gate where the syringa and lilac bushes arched the way and the honeysuckle climbed about the fence.

The sidewalk outside was brick, and when she heard footsteps coming, she stepped back into the shadow of the syringa and was hidden from view. She was in no mood to talk with anyone.

She could see the horses and carryalls as they passed on the dusty road and recognized the occasional laughter of a friend from the village. Others strolled along the sidewalk, with fragments of talk floating back. Almost everyone commented on the wedding as they neared the gate, and if Marcia had been in another mood, it would have been interesting and gratifying to her pride. Everyone had a good word for Kate, though many disapproved of her in a general way for principle's sake.

Merry voices mingling with many footsteps came down the street and paused beside the gate. Marcia knew the voices and again slid behind the shrubbery; not even a thread of her light dress was visible. Three or four girlfriends of Kate's and a couple of young men trooped in.

Marcia thought how much they'd miss Kate and wondered if the young men who constantly came to see her felt no grief that their friend and leader was leaving them. Then she smiled. She seemed to be saying good-bye to the old friends, home, and life in Kate's place. But it wasn't her life, so why should she feel this sadness creeping over her for someone else?

Was it because she was losing her sister? No, Kate was never much of a companion to her. She always put her down as a little girl and emphasized the difference in their ages. Marcia was the little maid to fetch and carry, the errand girl, and an unselfish, devoted slave in Kate's life. Her manner toward Marcia was never protective or elder-sisterly. At times Marcia felt this keenly, but she never expressed this lack; afterward her devotion to her sister was greater, to compensate somewhat for this reproachful thought.

But Marcia couldn't shake off the sadness. She wondered again how she'd feel if day after tomorrow were her wedding day and she were leaving home and friends and all the scenes she'd known since babyhood.

Would she mind leaving her father? Yes, he'd been good to her, loved her, and was proud of her. But one doesn't lose one's father no matter how far one goes. A father is a father always. Mr. Schuyler wasn't a demonstrative man. Thus Marcia felt that her father wouldn't miss her deeply, nor was she sure she'd miss him so very much. She'd read to him a great deal and talked politics with him whenever he had no one better nearby, but aside from that she'd lived her life much apart from him.

On the other hand, she was used to looking to her stepmother for direction and would miss her as one misses a perfect mentor and guide. She knew she had a will of her own and would like a chance to exercise it; yet she knew that in many cases, without her stepmother she would be like a ship without a rudder. And she loved her stepmother, as a young girl loves a good woman who has been her guide and helper, even though no great tenderness lay between them. Yes, she'd miss her stepmother, but she wouldn't feel so sad over it.

Harriet and the little brothers? Oh, yes, she'd miss them; they were dear little things and devoted to her.

Then there were neighbors, schoolmates, and people of the village. She'd miss the dear old minister and his wife. Many times she'd gone with her arms full of flowers to the parsonage down the street and spent the afternoon with the minister's wife. Her smooth white hair under its muslin cap and her soft, wrinkled cheek were dear to the young girl. She'd shared her innermost thoughts with this friend more freely than with anyone else. Oh, she'd miss the minister's wife very much.

Her schoolmates came to mind: Harriet Woodgate, Eliza Buchanan, Margaret Fletcher, her three closest friends. She'd miss them, of course, but how much? She could scarcely tell. Margaret more than the other two. Mary Ann Fothergill? She almost laughed at the thought of anyone's missing Mary Ann. John Middleton? Hanford Weston? She wouldn't miss a single boy in the school, she told herself with conviction. Not one of them realized her ideal. There was much pairing off of boy and girl in school, but Marcia, like the heroine of "Comin' thro' the Rye," was good friends with all the boys and intimate with none. They all counted it an honor to wait upon her, and she didn't give a farthing for any. She felt herself too young, of course, to think of such things, but the man in her daydreams bore no familiar form or feature. He was a prince, and these were only schoolboys.

The lively chatter of the young people in the house floated through the open windows, and Marcia could hear her sister's voice above the others'. Chameleonlike, she was all laughter and fun now since her seriousness at supper.

They were coming out the front door and down the walk. Kate was with them. Marcia caught glimpses of the girls' white dresses as they came nearer. Her sister was walking with Captain Leavenworth. He was a handsome young man in his uniform. He and Kate had been close friends for two years; it might have been more than friendship if Kate's father hadn't intervened. He didn't think as well of the young captain as Kate or the United States Navy did. Squire Schuyler required deep integrity and strong moral character in any man aspiring to be his son-in-law. The captain didn't possess much of either.

A short, sharp contest ended in young Leavenworth's departure from the town some three years before, and Kate plunged into a brief season of tears and pouting. But soon her laughter was heard again, and her father thought she'd forgotten. About that time David Spafford appeared and promptly fell in love with the beautiful girl, and the Schuyler mind was relieved.

So when the captain reappeared wearing the insignia of his first honors, the squire received him graciously. He even felt he might be more lenient about his moral character and told himself Leavenworth might not be so bad after all; he must have something in him, or the U.S. government wouldn't have honored him. It was easier to think so now that Kate was safe.

Marcia watched her sister and the captain go laughing out into the street. She wondered how Kate could go out tonight when it was almost her last evening at home and why she'd walk with Captain Leavenworth when she belonged to David now. She might have gone with one of the girls. But that was Kate's way, and her ways weren't Marcia's ways.

Marcia admitted to herself that in many ways her sister's absence would be a relief to her. She recognized the power of her sister's beauty and will over her. At the same time she felt oppressed sometimes by the strain she was under to please and wearied of the constant, half-fretful, half-playful faultfinding.

The footsteps and voices died away, and Marcia ventured forth from her retreat. The moon was rising as a glorious burnished disk and silhouetted her face. She chose to be alone tonight and let her imagination wander. The beauty and mystery of a wedding were upon her, touching her deeper feelings.

The thought came to her then that if her wedding day were the day after tomorrow, she wouldn't have gone off with a lot of giggling girls or walked with another young man. She would have stood by the gate—and she moved toward her favorite arch of lilac and syringa—thinking how it would be when he'd come. She would have watched for David a week before the time he set for coming, for who knew if he might come sooner and surprise her? She'd have rejoiced that tonight she was alone, excusing herself from everything else to come down there in the stillness. She'd hear his step echoing down the street and lean over the gate to listen and watch. At last he'd be by her side, his wonderful surprise for her in his eyes. But if David really tried to surprise Kate by coming that way tonight, he wouldn't find her waiting or thinking of him at all, but off with Captain Leavenworth.

With a passing pity for David, she returned to her own dream. The delayed evening coach rumbled up to the tavern not far away and halted. Real footsteps came up the street, but Marcia noticed them only because they made her thoughts more vivid. The steps drew nearer until suddenly they halted and someone appeared out of the shadow. Her heart stood still, for form and face in the darkness seemed unreal, and the dreams had been most vivid. Then two strong arms were flung about her, and her face was drawn close to his across the vine-covered gate until her lips touched his. He gave her a long, tender kiss and held her head close against his chest for just a moment while he murmured, "My darling! My precious, precious Kate, I have you at last!"

Marcia's dream was shattered, the spell broken! She screamed and sprang from him with horror and a wild but holy joy mingled in confusion. She put her hand on her heart, marveling at the sweetness on her lips. Trying to recover her senses, she faced the eager man who opened the gate and stepped quickly toward her, as yet unaware he'd been talking with someone other than Kate.

Chapter 3

*M*arcia stood there trembling. In an instant she realized David Spafford had come a day earlier than expected to surprise Kate, and Kate was off having a good time with someone else. He mistook her for Kate. Her long dress and her pinned-up hair had deceived him in the moonlight. In her earnestness to make things right, she forgot her natural timidity.

"It isn't Kate," she said gently. "It's only Marcia. Kate didn't expect you till tomorrow. She had to go out—that is, she's gone with—"

The truthful young sister paused. In her opinion it was a calamity that Kate wasn't there to meet David. She should at least have been in the house ready for a surprise like this. Wouldn't David feel the omission keenly? She mustn't tell him about Captain Leavenworth, if possible. There was no reason he should feel bad about it, of course, and yet it might annoy him. But he stepped back, laughing at his mistake.

"Why, Marcia, is it you, child? How you've grown! I never would have known you!" said the young man pleasantly. He'd always had a serious tenderness for Kate's little sister. "Of course your sister didn't know I was coming and doubtless has many things to do. I didn't expect her to be out here watching for me, though for a moment I did think she was at the gate. You say she's gone out? Then we'll go up to the house, and I'll be there to surprise her when she comes."

Marcia turned with relief. He didn't ask where Kate had gone or with whom.

The squire and Madam Schuyler greeted the arrival elaborately. The squire also seemed annoyed Kate had gone out. He kept fuming back and forth from the window to the door, asking, "Why did she go out tonight? She should have stayed at home!"

But Madam Schuyler was satisfied now. The bridegroom had arrived; no further hitch could come in the ceremonies. He arrived a day before the time, but he hadn't found *her* unprepared. As far as she was concerned, with a few extra touches, the wedding might proceed at once. No one could find a nut or bolt loose in her household machinery.

She bustled about, giving orders and laying a bountiful supper before the young man. The squire sat and talked with him while Marcia waited on him, admiring the wave of his hair, tossed back from his forehead. She took a kind of pride in possessing this handsome face—the far-removed possession of a sister-in-law. His sunny smile could bring joy to a bleak December day. His hands were clean and firm. The vision of Hanford Weston's hands, red and bony, appeared before her. She hadn't known she looked at them that day when he stood awkwardly asking if he might walk with her. Poor Hanford! He couldn't compare with this cultured, scholarly man who was ten years older, though with ten years more, Hanford might have proved quite worthy of the admiration of any village girl.

The fruitcake, raspberry preserves, doughnuts, and other foods Madam Schuyler ordered for her guest were eaten. David and the squire talked about the news, touching on politics; the squire laughed a bit at the man who thought he'd invented a machine to draw carriages by steam instead of horses.

"There's a good deal to it, I believe," said the younger man. "His theory is all right if he can get someone to help him carry it out."

"Well, perhaps," said the squire, shaking his head, "but it

seems like a wild scheme. Horses are good enough for me. I wouldn't like to trust myself to an unknown quantity like steam, but time will tell."

"Yes, and the world is progressing. Something like it is sure to come. It has in England. It would make a vast change in our country, binding city to city and practically eradicating space."

"Visionary schemes, David, visionary schemes, that's what I call them. You and I will never see them in our day, I'm sure of that. Remember that this is a new country and must go slowly." He was half laughing, half in earnest.

During the talk Marcia slipped out. It occurred to her the captain might return with her sister. She must warn her. Like a shadow in the moonlight, she stepped softly down the gravel path once more and waited at the gate. Didn't that sacred kiss placed upon her lips by mistake bind her to this solemn duty? Wasn't it given to her to see as in a revelation, by that kiss, the love of one man for one woman, deep and tender and true?

In the darkness she wondered about Love, the marvelous. With the insight of one with years of marriage, yet without those years, Marcia understood the possibility and joy of sacrifice that made even sad things bright because of Love. She saw instantly how Kate could give up her life, her home, her friends, everything she held dear, so she might be by the side of the man who loved her so. But with this knowledge of David's love for Kate came a troubling doubt. Did Kate love David that way? If Kate had received that kiss, would she have returned it with the same tenderness and warmth with which it was given? Marcia didn't try to answer this. It was Kate's question, not hers, and she must never let it enter her mind again. Of course she must love him that way, or she'd never marry him.

The night crept slowly for the anxious watcher. Had she been sure where to look for her sister, she'd have started on a search at once. But she must wait as patiently as she could for her. Moreover, Kate might be walking even now in some secluded, rose-lined lane arm in arm with the captain, saying a pleasant farewell. It was Kate's way, and no one would oppose her.

Marcia's dreams as she stood there an hour earlier returned. The kiss had fitted into the dream. Then all at once conscience told her it was Kate's beloved, not her own, whose arms had encircled her. And now she felt a strange unwillingness to go back to the dreams at all; instead, she longed for the joys she glimpsed. She withdrew from all thoughts and tried to close the door on them. They seemed too sacred to enter. Her maidenhood was just begun, and she had much yet to learn of life. She was glad for Kate that something so wonderful was coming to her. Kate would be sweeter, softer, now. She couldn't help it with a love like that enfolding her life.

At last she heard footsteps! Two people—only two! Just what Marcia expected. The others had turned off or gone home. Kate and Captain Leavenworth were alone. They were walking slowly and talking in low tones, and the captain's head was bent over his companion in an earnest, pleading manner. Marcia couldn't bear to look and didn't wish to see more. Kate wouldn't be glad to see her sister at the gate. This last thought came with sudden conviction, but Marcia didn't falter.

"Kate, David has come!" Marcia said in low, almost accusing tones—at least, so it sounded to Kate—before the two hardly reached the gate.

Startled, Kate sprang away from her companion, an angry look on her face.

"How you scared me, Marsh!" she exclaimed. "What if he has come? That's nothing. I guess he can wait a few minutes. He had no business coming tonight anyway. He knew we wouldn't be ready for him till tomorrow."

Kate was recovering her self-possession as she realized the situation. That she was vexed over her bridegroom's arrival, neither of the two witnesses doubted. It stung her sister for David. He wasn't getting as much in Kate as he was giving. But there was no time for such thoughts; besides, Marcia was trembling from head to foot, partly with her own daring, partly with anger at her sister's words.

"For shame, Kate!" she cried. "How can you talk so, even in fun! David came to surprise you, and I think he had a right to expect to find you here so near your marriage."

Her young eyes flashed, and her chin lifted with conviction for the truth she spoke, giving her a new dignity even in the moonlight.

Captain Leavenworth looked at her in lazy admiration. "Why, Marsh, you're developing into quite a spitfire. What do you have on tonight that makes you look so tall and lovely? Why didn't you stay in and talk to your fine gentleman? I'm sure he'd have been as satisfied with you as your sister."

Marcia gave one withering glance at the young man and then turned her back on him. He wasn't worth noticing. Besides, he was to be pitied, for he evidently still cared for Kate.

But Kate was fairly white with anger. Perhaps her own accusing conscience encouraged it. She drew herself up haughtily and pointed toward the house.

"Marcia Schuyler," she said coldly, facing her sister, "go in the house and attend to your own affairs. You'll get into serious trouble if you meddle with mine. You're nothing but a child and should be punished for your impudence. Go!" she exclaimed, stamping her foot. "I'll come in when I get ready."

Marcia went, not proudly as she might have gone a moment before, but covered with confusion and shame, her head drooping like a crushed lily on a bleeding stalk. Fierce indignation and shame rushed through her—for her sister, for David, for herself. She didn't stop to analyze her feelings, nor did she stop to speak to those in the house. She fled to her room and, burying her face in the pillow, wept until she fell asleep.

The moon shadows grew longer about the arbored gateway where the two stood talking in hushed tones, glancing furtively now and then toward the house, then withdrawing into the covert of the bushes by the walk. But Kate dared not linger long. She could see her father's profile by the candlelight in the dining room. She didn't want further rebuke, so in a few minutes the two parted. Kate ran up the path, humming a sweet old love song cheerfully as she tripped by the dining room windows and thus announced her arrival. She guessed Marcia would have gone right to her room and said nothing. Kate intended to be surprised. She paused in the hall to hang up her wrap, called good night to her stepmother, and said she was very tired and was going straight to bed to be ready for tomorrow. Then she ran lightly across the hall to the stairs.

She knew they'd call her back and all come into the hall with David to see the effect of his surprise upon her. She planned exactly which stair she could reach before they got there, where she'd pause and what pose she'd take with her round, white arm stretched to the handrail, the sleeve turned carelessly back. She had her expressions ready—sleepy indifference, then pleased surprise, with a climax of delight. She carried it all out, this little bit of impromptu acting, as well as if she'd rehearsed for a month.

They called her, and she turned, one dainty, slippered foot, with its crossed black ribbons about the slender ankle, just leaving the stair below. She held her blue gown back enough for the white frill of her petticoat to show. She read well the admiration in the eyes below her. Admiration was Kate's life: She couldn't do without it.

David stood still, his love in his eyes, gazing upon the vision of his bride, and his heart swelled within him that such a great treasure should be his. Then straightway they all forgot to question where she had been or rebuke her for going at all. She knew they would. She possessed the power to make others forget her wrongdoings when it was worth her while.

The next morning, things were astir even earlier than usual. The sound of the beating of eggs, the mixing of cakes, and the clatter of pans could be heard from the wide, stone-flagged kitchen.

In spite of her cry the night before, Marcia was fresh as a flower as she arose to new opportunities for service. She was glad with the forgetfulness of youth when she looked at David's happy face, and she thought no more of Kate's treatment of her.

David was never more than a few moments out of Kate's sight, though it seemed to Marcia that Kate didn't try hard to stay with him. When afternoon came she dismissed him for what she called her "beauty nap." Marcia was passing through the hall at the time and caught the tender look on his face as he touched her brow reverently and said she had no need for that. Her eyes met Kate's as they were going upstairs.

In spite of what Kate had said the night before, Marcia couldn't refrain from saying, "Oh, Kate! How could you when he loves you so? You know you never take a nap in the daytime!"

"You silly girl!" said Kate pleasantly enough. "Don't you know the less a man sees one, the more he thinks of her?" With this remark she closed and fastened her door after her.

Marcia pondered these words for some time, wondering whether Kate really did it for that reason or whether she didn't care for his company. And why should a man love you less because he saw you more? In her straightforward code, the more you loved people, the more you wanted to be with them.

Kate came from her "beauty nap" with a feverish restlessness in her eyes, an averted face, and ink on one finger. At supper she scarcely spoke, and when she did, she laughed excitedly over little things. David watched her proudly, wondering even more over her beauty, and Marcia, seeing the light in his face, watched for its answer in her sister's; not finding it, she was troubled.

She watched them from her bedroom window as they walked down the path where she'd gone the evening before, decorously side by side, Kate holding her light muslin frock back from the dew on the hedges. She wondered if it was because Kate respected David more than Captain Leavenworth that she never seemed to treat him with as much familiarity. She didn't take possession of him in the same sweet, imperious way.

Marcia hadn't lighted her candle. The moon gave enough light, and she was weary, so she undressed in the dim room. Out in the moonlight were those two who'd be one tomorrow, and here she was alone. She'd never felt such loneliness. Was it sadness at parting with Kate or the inevitable partings of all human relationships and the aloneness of every living spirit?

She stood beside her window in her white robe. Gazing up into the full moon, she wondered if God knew the ache of loneliness in the souls of His human creatures and if He was prepared to satisfy them with something. Then her meek soul bowed in her faith, and she knelt for her evening prayer.

She heard Kate and David come in early and go upstairs, and she heard her father fastening the doors and windows for the night. Then stillness settled over the home, and she fell asleep. Later, in her dreams, the sound of hastening hooves echoed far down the deserted street and over the old covered bridge. But she took no note of any sound, and the weary household slept on.

Chapter 4

$\mathscr{T}$he wedding was set for ten o'clock in the morning, after which there was to be a wedding breakfast and the married couple would start immediately for their new home.

David drove the day before with his own horse and chaise to a town some twenty miles away and left his horse at a tavern there to rest for the return trip. Kate insisted they must leave the house in high style, so the finest equipage in town was secured to bear them on the first stage of their journey, with a portly driver and everything according to the highest customs. Nothing Kate desired in the arrangements had been left undone.

The household was up by half past four. The family breakfast was to be at six so that all might be cleared away and ready for the various aunts, uncles, cousins, and friends who'd arrive early from the country. Madam Schuyler would never have gotten over it if anything were amiss when a single uncle or aunt appeared on the scene, or if there seemed to be the least evidence of fluster and nervousness.

The rosy sunlight in the east was mixing the morning with fresh air when Marcia awoke. The sharp click of spoons and dishes, the maids' voices, and the sizzle, sputter, and odor of frying ham and eggs mingled with the early chorus of the birds, calling to life all living creatures, like an intrusion upon nature. It didn't seem right to steal the morning quiet so rudely. The thought flitted through the girl's mind, and in an instant more, a panorama of the day's excitement lay before her. She sprang from her bed and dressed quickly. She knew she'd have no further time beyond a moment to slip on her best gown and smooth her hair.

Marcia hurried downstairs just as the bell rang for breakfast. David, coming down smiling at the same time, patted her cheek and greeted her with, "Well, little sister, you look as rested as if you didn't do a thing all day yesterday."

She smiled shyly back at him, and her heart filled with pleasure over his new name for her. She was conscious of feeling glad he was to be so nearly related to her. She imagined what it would be like to say to Mary Ann: "My brother-in-law says so-and-so." It would be grand to call such a man "brother."

All were seated at the table but Kate, and Squire Schuyler waited with pleasantly frowning brows to ask the blessing on the morning food. Kate was often late. She was the only member of the family who dared to be late to breakfast, and being the bride, she was granted more leniency this morning.

Madam Schuyler waited until everyone at the table was served ham and eggs, coffee, bread and butter, and steaming griddle cakes. Then she looked anxiously at the clock and said, "Marcia, perhaps you better go up and see if your sister needs any help. She ought to be down by now. Uncle Joab and Aunt Polly are sure to be here by eight. She must have overslept, but we made so much noise she's surely awake by this time."

Marcia left her half-eaten breakfast and went slowly upstairs. She knew her sister wouldn't welcome her, for she'd been sent on similar errands before. The brunt of Kate's anger then fell upon the hapless messenger, wearing itself out there so she might descend all smiles to greet her father and mother and smooth out the situation.

Marcia paused before the door to listen. Perhaps her sister was almost ready, and she needn't perform the distasteful errand. But no sound came from the closed door. Softly she tried to lift the latch and peep in. Kate must still be asleep. It wasn't the first time Marcia found that to be the case when sent to bring her sister.

But the latch wouldn't lift. The catch was firmly down from the inside. Marcia peeped through the keyhole but could see only a dim outline of the window on the other side of the room. She tapped gently once or twice and waited again, then called softly: "Kate, Kate! Wake up! Breakfast is ready, and everybody's eating. Aunt Polly and Uncle Joab will be here soon."

She tapped and called, growing louder with no answer. Kate would often keep still to tease her. Surely she wouldn't do so on her wedding morning!

She called and shook the door, not daring, however, to make too much noise lest David should hear. She couldn't bear for him to know his bride's shortcomings.

But at last she grew alarmed. Perhaps Kate was ill. At any rate, whatever it was, it was time she was up. She worked for some minutes trying to loosen the catch that held the latch, but to no avail. She was forced to go downstairs and whisper the matter to her stepmother.

Madam Schuyler, excusing herself from the table, went upstairs, with determination in every footfall. Bride though she be, this time the girl had gone too far. Company and a fiancé and the approaching wedding hour were things not to be trifled with even by a charming Kate.

But Madam Schuyler returned in minutes, puffing and with heightened color in her face. She interrupted the squire without waiting for him to finish his sentence to David.

"I can't understand what's wrong with Kate," she said to her husband. "She doesn't seem to be awake, and I can't get her door open. She sleeps soundly, and I suppose the unusual excitement has made her very tired. But I'd think she'd hear my voice. Perhaps you better see if you can open the door."

Her face belied the calmness in her voice. She was worried Kate might be playing one of her pranks. She knew the girl's careless, fun-loving ways. She was more concerned that everything should go smoothly than that Kate should even be perfectly well. But Marcia's white face behind her stepmother's ample shoulder showed a dread of something worse than a mere indisposition.

David took alarm at once. He set down the silver jug of maple syrup and pushed back his chair.

"Perhaps she's fainted!" he exclaimed.

Both father and fiancé started up the stairs, the father angry, the fiancé alarmed. The squire grumbled all the way up that Kate should sleep so late, but David said nothing. He waited anxiously behind while the squire worked with the door. Madam Schuyler and Marcia followed them, with the two maids standing curiously behind. They all loved Miss Kate and were deeply interested in the day's events. They didn't want anything to interfere with the well-planned pageant.

The squire fumbled nervously with the latch, meanwhile calling his daughter to open the door. Then in his wrath he placed his solid shoulder and knee in just the right place, and with a groan and a wrench, the latch gave way, and the solid oak door swung open, propelling the anxious group somewhat suddenly into the room.

Almost at once they realized no one else was there. David stood with averted eyes at first; then he looked wildly about.

They saw at once the bed hadn't been slept in. The room was in confusion, but perhaps not more than expected when the occupant was about to leave the next day. Pieces of paper and string littered the floor, and one or two garments lay about as if cast off in a hurry. David recognized the purple muslin dress Kate wore the night before and put out his hand to touch it where it lay across the foot of the bed, vainly reaching after one who wasn't there.

Father, mother, sister, and fiancé stood in silence, taking in every detail of the deserted room. Then they looked blankly at one another, and in their eyes a terrible question dawned: Where was she?

Madam Schuyler recovered her senses first. "Who saw her last? Was she downstairs this morning?" She looked straight at Marcia, but the girl shook her head.

"I went to bed last night before they came in," she said, looking questioningly at David. A sudden remembrance and fear seized her heart, and she quickly turned toward the window.

"We came in early," said David, trying to steady his voice, as he remembered her good night to him. Surely nothing dreadful could have happened overnight—in her father's house! He looked around again for the everyday things to help drive out the thought of possible tragedy.

"Kate was tired. She said she was going to get up very early this morning and wash her face in the dew on the grass." He braved a smile and looked at the anxious group. "She must be out somewhere on the place," he continued, gathering courage with the thought. "She said it was an old superstition. She has maybe wandered farther than she intended and perhaps gotten into some trouble. I'd better search for her. Is there anyplace near here where she might be?" He turned to Marcia.

"But Kate would never delay so long, I'm sure," said the stepmother firmly. "She's not such a fool as to go traipsing through the wet grass by the kitchen pump. I know Kate."

Marcia's face crimsoned at her stepmother's words, but she looked at David with a troubled expression and tried to answer him. "There are plenty of places, but Kate has never cared to go to them. I can go and look everywhere."

She started to leave the room, but as she passed the bureau, she saw a bit of folded paper under the corner of the pincushion. With a smothered exclamation she walked over and picked it up. It was addressed to David in Kate's handwriting, fine and even, like copperplate. Without a word Marcia handed it to him and then stood back where the window draperies would shadow her.

Madam Schuyler, with sudden awareness, took alarm. Noticing the two maids standing with mouths agape in the hallway, she stepped into the hall, half closing the door behind her, and cowed the two handmaidens with her glance.

"It's all right!" she said calmly. "Miss Kate has left a note and will return soon. Go down and keep her breakfast warm and not a word to a soul! Dolly, Debby, do you understand? Not a word of this! Now hurry and do all that I told you before breakfast."

They went downstairs with disappointment on their faces, but she knew they wouldn't say a word. Madam's word was law. Therefore, with remarkable discretion they masked their wondering looks and did as they were bidden. So while the family stood solemnly in Kate's room, the wedding preparations moved steadily forward below. Only two somber maids, of the helpers that morning, knew a tragedy was hovering in the air and might burst upon them.

David had grasped for the letter eagerly and fumbled it open with a trembling hand. But as he read, the expectant smile froze on his lips, and his face grew ashen. He grasped the mantel shelf to steady himself as he read further, but he didn't seem to take in the meaning of what he read. The others waited breathlessly, while Madam Schuyler was impatiently patient. The long delay would disturb her arrangements. She should know the whole truth at once and be put in command of the situation.

Marcia stood quietly behind the curtain, staring at the carpet, while over and over the echo of a horse's hooves in a silent street sounded in her brain. She knew intuitively what had happened and dared not look at David.

"Well, what has she done with herself?" said the squire. Now that they had word, he wanted to know at once and return to his unfinished breakfast. The sight of his daughter's handwriting relieved him. She'd done some crazy thing, of course, but then she'd always done crazy things. She was wrong to frighten them, and he'd tell her so when she returned, even if it was her wedding day. But Kate would be Kate, and his breakfast was getting cold. He had the horses to look after and orders to give the hands before the early guests arrived.

But David didn't answer. He stood as one stricken dumb all at once. He raised his eyes to the squire's—pleading, pitiful. His face was haggard.

"Speak out, man—doesn't the letter tell?" demanded the squire. "Where's the girl?"

This time he managed to utter two words, "She's gone!" Then his head dropped forward on his hand that rested on the mantel. Great beads of perspiration stood out on his forehead as the letter fluttered to the floor.

The squire reached for it and, putting on his spectacles, drew near to the window to read, his heavy brows gathered in a frown. But his wife didn't need to read the letter, for she, like Marcia, had divined its purport; already she was prepared to face the predicament.

The squire with deepening frown was studying the girl's letter, scarcely able to believe his daughter could be so heartless.

The letter began—written hurriedly, as if at the last moment, as indeed it had been.

Dear David,
I want you to forgive me for what I'm doing. I know you'll feel bad about it, but I was never really the right one for you. I'm sure you thought me all too good, and I never could have stayed in a straitjacket; it would have killed me. I'll always consider you the best man in the world, and I like you better than anyone else except Captain Leavenworth.

*I can't help it that I care more for him than anyone else,
though I've tried. So I'm going away tonight, and when you
read this we'll have been married. You're so good that I
know you'll forgive me and be glad I'm happy. Don't think
ill of me, for I always cared a great deal for you.*

*Your loving
Kate*

True to her character, she demanded David's love and loyalty to the bitter end, false and heartless though she was. The
coquette in her played with him even now in the bitter pain
she must have known she was inflicting. She spoke no word of
contrition but, as always, took her deed as her prerogative. She
didn't even spare him the loving salutation customary in her
letters to him. She didn't hint at any better day for David or
give him permission to forget her; indeed, she bound him to
her, as she knew she would by those words, "I like you better
than anyone else except. . . !" They sank into the young man's
heart as he stood there those first few minutes and faced his
trouble, his head bowed on the mantel.

Meanwhile, Madam Schuyler's keen vision spied another
folded paper beside the pincushion, smaller than the other and
evidently placed farther out of sight. It was addressed to Kate's
father. Her stepmother opened and read it with her lips
pressed together and a steely look in her eyes.

Could the girl, in her treachery, have enjoyed the thought of
her stepmother reading that note and facing the horror of a
wedding party with no bride? Knowing her stepmother's vast
resources, did she think she'd at last brought her to a situation
to which she was unequal? An unseen, unspoken struggle for
supremacy had always existed between them. It was friendly,
for the girl seemed to be testing the woman's powers, with
some admiration mixed with amusement. But there was no
fear for the stepmother who was uniformly kind and loving

toward her, and for whom she cared, perhaps as much as she could have cared for her own mother. The note read:

> *Dear Father,*
>   *I'm going away tonight to marry Captain Leavenworth. You wouldn't let me have him in the right way, so I had to take this. I tried very hard to forget him and get interested in David, but it was no use. You couldn't stop it. So now I hope you'll see it the way we do and forgive us. We're going to Washington, and you can write us there and say you forgive us, and then we'll come home. I know you'll forgive us, Daddy, dear. You know you always loved your little Kate, and you couldn't really want me to be unhappy. Please send my trunks to Washington. I've tacked the card with the address on the envelope.*
>
> *Your loving girl,*
Kate

A terrible stillness filled the room, broken only by the crackling of the paper as the notes were turned in the hands of their readers. Marcia felt as if centuries were passing. David's soul was pierced by one awful thought: *She is gone!* Life was a blank for him stretching out into interminable years. Of her treachery in doing what she did as she had, he had no time to take account. That would come later. Now he was trying to understand this one fact.

Madam Schuyler handed the second note to her husband and skimmed the first one. Indignation arose within her. If she could have brought the erring girl back to face her disgraced wedding alone, she would have gladly done so. She knew that on her would likely rest the rearrangements, and she was already calculating the number of messages that must be sent to stop the guests from arriving. She waited anxiously for her husband to finish reading so she might consult with him as to the best message to send, but she was scarcely prepared for the outburst that followed.

The squire crushed his daughter's note in his hand and flung it from him. He respected and loved David, and seeing him broken in grief by his daughter's deed roused great anger in him. His voice shook, but a deep note of command in it caused Madam Schuyler to wait. The squire had arisen to the situation, and she deferred to him.

"She must be brought back at once at all costs!" he exclaimed. "That rascal shall not outwit us. Fool that I was to trust him in the house! Tell the men to saddle the horses. They can't have gone far yet, and there aren't so many roads to Washington. We may yet overtake them, and married or unmarried the girl shall be here for her wedding!"

But David raised his head and steadied his voice. "No, no, you mustn't do that—Father—"

The name came from his lips almost tenderly, as if he'd long considered using it with pleasure, and now he spoke it as a tender bond meant to comfort.

The older man started, and his face softened. A flash of understanding and love passed between the two men.

"Remember that she said she loves someone else. She could never be mine now."

David spoke the words sadly, and his voice broke.

Madam Schuyler turned away and took out her handkerchief, an article she seldom used.

The father looked hopelessly at David and took in the thought. Then he, too, bowed his head and groaned.

"And my daughter, my little Kate, has done it!"

Marcia covered her face with the curtains, and her tears fell.

David went and stood beside the squire and touched his arm.

"Don't!" he said pleadingly. "You couldn't help it. It wasn't your fault. Don't take it to heart!"

"But it's my disgrace. I brought up a child who could do it. I can't escape from that. It's the most dishonorable thing a woman can do. And look how she's done it—brought shame upon us all! Here we have a wedding on our hands and little or no time to do anything. I've lived in honor all my life, and now to be disgraced by my own daughter!"

Marcia shuddered at her father's agony and drew closer to him.

"To be deserted and dishonored by my own child! Something must be done. Stop the wedding!"

He looked at his wife who started toward the door to carry out his bidding, but he recalled her immediately.

"No, stay!" he cried. "It's too late to stop them all. Let them come and find out! Let the disgrace rest upon the one to whom it belongs!"

Madam Schuyler stopped. A wedding without a bride! Yet she knew it was serious to dispute with her husband in that mood.

"Oh, Father!" exclaimed Marcia finally. "We couldn't! Think of David."

Her words touched the right chord, for he turned toward the young man with tender pity in his face.

"Yes, we're forgetting David! We must do all we can to make it easier for you. You'll want to get away from us as quickly as possible. How can we manage it for you? And where will you go? You won't want to go home just yet?"

He paused, suddenly aware of David's part.

"No, I can't go home," said David simply. "The house will be ready for her and the table set. The friends will be coming in, and we're invited to dinner and tea everywhere. My friends will be coming to the house to welcome us. No, I can't go home." Then he added, "And yet I must—sometime I must go home!"

Chapter 5

The room was very still as he spoke. Madam Schuyler forgot the coming guests and the preparations out of concern for David and his grief. Marcia sobbed softly by her father's side, and he involuntarily placed his arm about her as he stood in painful thought.

"It's terrible!" he murmured. "How could she inflict such pain! She might have saved us the scorn of all our friends. David, you mustn't go back alone. You mustn't bear that. There are many lovely girls elsewhere. Find another one and marry her. Take your bride home with you, and no one in your home need be the wiser. Don't grieve for that cruel girl. Don't give her the satisfaction of feeling your life is broken. Take another. Any girl might be proud to go with you for the asking. If I had a dozen other daughters, you could have your pick of them, and one should go with you, if you'd condescend to choose another from the home where you've been so mistreated.

"But I have only this one girl," he said, looking down at Marcia. "She's still a child and can't compare with what you thought you had. I don't blame you if you don't wish to marry another Schuyler, but if you will, she's yours. And she's a good girl, David, though she's a child. Speak up, child, and say if you'll make amends for the wrong your sister has done!"

The room was so still one could almost hear the hearts beating. David raised his head and searched her face sadly, as if to find Kate's features there. Yet it seemed to Marcia that he didn't see her. He was looking beyond her, facing going home alone and the empty life that would follow.

She'd matured rapidly in the last few days. She understood and pitied, and her woman-nature longed to comfort. But she shrank from going unasked. This sudden situation thrust upon her was terrible; yet she was willing to sacrifice if she felt sure he wished it.

But David didn't seem to know he must speak. He waited, looking earnestly at her, through her, beyond her, to see if heaven would grant this small relief to his sufferings.

At last Marcia summoned her voice. "If David wishes, I will go."

She spoke the words solemnly, her eyes lifted slightly above him as if she were speaking to One higher than he. It was almost like an answer to a call from God. It seemed to leave her no room for drawing back, if indeed she'd wished to. Other considerations weren't present. She desired only to make amends in some measure for the wrong that had been done. She felt a family responsibility for it, perhaps even the shame and pain her father felt.

She'd step into the empty place Kate left and fill it as far as she could. Her only fear was of being unacceptable and unworthy to fill such a high place. She trembled over it, yet she couldn't hold back. She stood thus in a kind of sorrowful exaltation waiting for David. Her eyes lowered again, looking at him through the lashes. She felt as if she were pleading for a chance to help him.

Her voice broke the spell. David looked down upon her kindly, a pleasant light of gratitude flashing through the sternness and sorrow in his face. Here was comradeship in trouble, and his voice acknowledged it.

"Child, you're good to me, and I thank you. I'll try to make you happy if you'll go with me, and I'm sure your going will be a comfort in many ways. But I wouldn't have you go unwillingly."

Marcia felt an unexplainable dull ache in her heart, but she was conscious of being glad to be accepted, young though she was and child though he called her. His tone was kind— the same kindness that had won her sisterly love when he started visiting her sister. She remembered that answer for many long days and lived on it when doubts and loneliness came upon her.

But she raised her face to her father's now and said, "I will go, Father!"

The squire bent over and kissed his little girl for what might be the last time. Perhaps he realized that from this time forth she would be a little girl no longer and he'd never look into those child-eyes again, unclouded with life's sorrows and filled with the wonder of a rosy future. Both father and daughter felt as if she were renouncing her own life forever and taking up one of sacrificial penitence for her sister's wrongdoing.

The father then took Marcia's hand and placed it in David's, and the betrothal was complete.

Madam Schuyler, whose reign for the time being was set aside, stood silent, half disapproving, yet not interfering. Her conscience told her that this wholesale disposal of Marcia was against nature. The new arrangement was a relief to her in many ways and would make the day's solution less trying for everyone. But she was a woman and knew a woman's heart. Marcia wasn't having her chance in life as her sister had, as every woman had a right to have.

Her face hardened. How had Kate used her chances? Perhaps it was better for Marcia to be well placed in life before she grew headstrong enough to make a fool of herself as Kate had. She was certain David would be good to her. Perhaps it was all for the best. At least it wasn't her doing. And only the night before, she'd looked at Marcia and worried because she was becoming a woman so fast. Now she'd be relieved of that care and could enjoy life until her own children were grown. But the voice of her husband aroused her to the present.

"Let the wedding go on as planned, Sarah, and no one, except the minister, needs to know until the ceremony's over. I'll go and tell him. There'll only need to be a change of names."

"But," said his wife with alarm, as the suddenness of the whole thing flashed over her, "Marcia isn't ready. She has no suitable clothes for her wedding."

"Not ready? No clothes?" demanded the squire. "Where are all the clothes that were made in these past weeks and months? What more preparation does she need? Did the girl take her wedding things with her? What's in the trunk?"

"But those are Kate's things, Father," said Marcia gently. "Kate would be very angry if I took her things. They were made for her."

"And what if they were made for her?" answered her father, scowling. "You're close in size. What will do for one is good enough for the other. And let Kate be angry, but not one rag of it will she get. She is no daughter of mine from now on. That rascal has beaten me and stolen my daughter, but he gets a dowerless lass. Not a penny will ever go from the Schuyler estate to either one, and no trunk will ever travel from here to Washington for that heartless girl. I forbid it—do you hear?" He brought his fist down on the mahogany bureau, jangling the prisms on a candle stand in front of the mirror.

"Oh, Father!" gasped Marcia and turned in fear to her stepmother.

But David stood with his back toward the rest looking out the window. He'd forgotten them.

Madam Schuyler was now in command again. For once, the squire anticipated his wife, and the next move was planned without her help, but it was as she'd have it. Her face beamed with satisfaction beneath its mask of grave perplexity. She was relieved the ordeal of a wedding without a bride had changed to something less formidable.

At least the country around them couldn't pity, for who was to say David was as well suited with one sister as with the other? And Marcia was a good girl; doubtless she'd grow into a good wife—far more suitable for such a good, steady man as David than pretty, imperious Kate.

Madam Schuyler began to issue orders.

"Come then, Marcia. We have no time to waste. It's all right, as your father has said. Kate's things will fit you nicely, and you must go at once and get everything ready. You'll want all your time to dress and pack a few things and get calm. Go to your room right away and pick up anything you want to take with you, and I'll go down and see that Phoebe takes your place and then come back."

David and the squire went out like two men who had suddenly grown old and hadn't the strength to walk rapidly. No one thought again of breakfast. It was half past seven by the clock on the stair landing. Soon Aunt Polly and Uncle Joab would be driving up to the door.

If Mistress Kate Leavenworth could have looked into her old room an hour after her flight was discovered, she'd have been astonished beyond measure, for preparations were moving ahead as if nothing had happened.

Poor bewildered Marcia stood in her own room. She looked at her bed and realized she'd likely never sleep in it again. She gazed out of the small-paned window with its view of the distant hills and river and thought she was bidding it good-bye forever. She walked to her closet and reached out her hand to choose what to take with her, and her heart sank. There hung the short faded ginghams, scorned just yesterday; yet her heart clung to them. She almost would have put one on and returned to her happy, carefree school life. The new life frightened her. She must give up her girlhood all at once and not keep a vestige of it, for that would betray David. She must be Kate from morning to evening.

Suddenly she remembered she'd envied Kate, and now God had given her the punishment of being Kate. Only there was a great difference: She wasn't the chosen one, and Kate was. She must forever bear in her heart the thought of Kate's sin.

Her stepmother's voice warned her that her time alone was almost over. Out on the lawn she could hear the voices of Uncle Joab and Aunt Polly who had just arrived.

She dropped on her knees and poured out her soul in distress to God, in the breath of a wordless sob. Then she arose, dashed cold water on her face, and dried away the tears. She hastily gathered a few things from her closet and drawer.

She took one last lingering look around her room. Then she shut the door quickly and walked down the hall to her sister's room to enter her new life. She was literally putting off herself and putting on a new being as far as it was possible to do so outwardly.

There on the bed lay the bridal outfit. Madam Schuyler had just brought it from the spare room to avoid suspicion from going back and forth through the halls. She was determined to prevent any excitement or opportunity for gossip among the guests at least until the ceremony was over. She was satisfied no one outside the family, except the two maids, suspected anything amiss, and she felt sure of their silence.

Kate had taken very little with her, evidently to elude discovery, and had no doubt her father would relent and send her trousseau as she requested in her letter. She had, for once, forgotten her fineries and escaped with only two dresses and a few other necessities in a small handbag.

Madam Schuyler was relieved to the point of genuine cheerfulness, despite the cloud of tragedy that hung over the day. She talked to Marcia as if she were Kate, as she smoothed down this and that article and laid them back in the trunk. She told her the blue gown would be best for church and the green silk for fine places, teas, and the like. And she must wear the cream undersleeves with the Irish point lace with her silk gown as they set it off to perfection. She recalled how little experience Marcia had in the ways of the world. So while the girl was being dressed in the dainty bridal garments, she instructed her carefully in the art of succeeding in society.

By then Marcia felt that the green fields and the fences and trees to climb and the blackberry picking and the joyful games of the boys and girls were slipping away from her. She could even welcome Hanford Weston as a playfellow in her near future if only a little fresh air and freedom of her girlhood might remain.

Nevertheless, an elation stole over her. The soft garments, the delicate embroidery, the excitement lest the white slippers wouldn't fit her, the difficulty in styling her hair like Kate's— her stepmother insisted she look as nearly as possible as Kate would have looked—all these drove sadness from her mind. She began to delight in the pretty clothes, the great occasion, and her own importance. The vision in the mirror, too, told her that her own face was lovely and the new attire not unbecoming. She had seen something of this the night before when she put on the new chintz. Now the change was complete, as she stood in the white satin and lace with her mother's string of seed pearls tied about her throat.

She thought about the tradition of the pearls that Kate's girlfriends had laughingly reminded her of a few days before when they were looking at the bridal garments. They'd said that each pearl a bride wore meant a tear she would shed. She wondered if Kate had escaped the tears with the pearls and left them for her.

She was ready at last, even to her mother's veil that was her mother's before her. It fell in rich folds, yellowed by age, from her head to her feet, with its rare beautiful handiwork, transforming the girl into a woman and a bride.

Madam Schuyler arranged and rearranged the folds and

finally stood back to look with half-closed eyes at the effect. She decided few would notice the bride wasn't the one they expected until the ceremony was over and the veil thrown back. The sisters had never looked alike, yet there was a general family resemblance that was now accentuated by the dress. Perhaps only those nearest would notice it was Marcia instead of Kate. At least the guests would have the good grace to wonder to themselves until the ceremony was over.

Then Marcia was left alone with trembling hands and wildly beating heart. What would Mary Ann think? What would all the girls and boys think? Some would be there, and others would be standing along the shady streets to watch the carriage as it drove away. And they'd see her going instead of Kate. Perhaps they'd think it was all a great joke and she was going to be married all the time and not Kate. No—the truth would soon come out. People wouldn't be astonished at anything Kate did. They'd say it was what they expected from her and pity her father and pity her perhaps.

But they'd look at *her* and admire her, and for once she'd be the center of attention. The pink of pride rolled up into her cheeks; then, realizing what she was thinking, she crushed the feeling down. How could she think that way when Kate had done such a dreadful thing and David was suffering so terribly? Here she was actually enjoying being in Kate's place. Oh, she was wicked! She mustn't be happy for a moment in Kate's shame and David's sorrow.

She didn't think of her future with David, for her thoughts were full of the day's events. If the future crossed her mind at all, it was always that she was to care for David and help him. She knew she must grow up quickly, remember the hard things her stepmother taught her, and order his house well. But that didn't trouble her now. She was more concerned with the ceremony and the many eyes on her. She was relieved when she heard a tap on the door, and the dear old minister entered.

Chapter 6

*H*e stood a moment by the door surveying her, half startled. Then he walked to her side and looked into her
upturned, veiled face.

"My child!" he said tenderly. "Is this my little Marcia? I
didn't know you in this beautiful dress. You look like your
own mother when she was married. I remember perfectly, as
if it were yesterday, her face as she stood by your father's side.
I was a young man then, and it was my first wedding in my
new church, so you see I couldn't forget it. Your mother was
a beautiful woman, Marcia, and you are like her both in face
and life."

The tears came into Marcia's eyes, and her lips trembled.

"Are you sure, child," continued the old man gently, "that
you understand what a solemn thing you're doing? It isn't a
light thing to give yourself in marriage to any man. You're still
so young! Are you doing this quite willingly? Are you sure?
Your father is a good man and my dear old friend. But what's
happened has been a terrible blow to him and a great humiliation. It's perhaps unnerved his judgment for the time. No one
should have pressured a little girl like you to marry against
your will. Are you sure it's all right, dear?"

"Oh, yes, sir!" Marcia raised her eyes. "I'm doing it quite on
my own. No one has made me. I'm glad I might. It was so
dreadful for David!"

"But, child, do you love him?" the old minister asked,
searching her face closely.

Marcia's eyes shone out radiant and innocent through her

tears. "Oh, yes, sir! I love him, of course. No one could help loving David."

There was a knock at the door, and the squire entered. With a sigh the minister turned away, his heart troubled. The girl too frankly confessed her love. It wasn't as he'd have things for his daughter, but it couldn't be helped, of course, and he had no right to interfere. He'd like to speak to David, but David hadn't come out of his room yet. When he did, they had only a moment alone.

"Mr. Spafford, you'll be good to the little girl," he managed to say, "and remember she's only a child. She's been dear to us all."

David looked at him with wonder. "I will do all in my power to make her happy," he said earnestly.

The hour had come, and all things, just as Madam Schuyler had planned, were ready. The minister took his place, and the impatient bridesmaids were in a flutter, wondering why Kate hadn't called them in to see her. Slowly, with measured step, as if she'd practiced many times, Marcia, the maiden, walked down the hall on her father's arm. He was bowed with his trouble, and his face bore marks of the sudden calamity that had befallen his house. But the guests thought it was for sorrow at giving up his lovely Kate, and they said to one another, "How much he loved her!"

The girl scarcely felt the presence of the guests she'd dreaded, for to her the ceremony was holy. She was giving herself as a sacrifice for the sin of her sister. She was too young and inexperienced to know all that would be thought and said as soon as those present understood, nor did she yet dread what followed afterward. She also felt secure behind that lace film. It shut her in from the world, protecting her. She passed through a wide hall, and the day was bright; but the waiting bridesmaids shaded the windows so that the light didn't fall on her fully. Thus it wasn't strange they didn't know her at once.

She heard their smothered exclamations of wonder and admiration. One, Kate's dearest friend, whispered softly behind her, "Oh, Kate, why did you keep us waiting, you sly girl? How lovely you are! You look like an angel straight from heaven."

Marcia heard other whispered words sadly, without pleasure. The words were for Kate, not her. What would they say when they knew all?

David stood in the distance waiting for her. How fine he looked in his wedding clothes! How proud Kate might have been of him! How pitiful his pale face looked! He had summoned courage and put on a mask of happiness for the eyes of those who saw him, but he couldn't deceive Marcia. Not since the days when Jacob served seven years for Rachel and then lifted the bridal veil to look upon the face of her sister, Leah, did a sadder bridegroom walk this earth than David Spafford that day.

Down the stairs and through the wide hall they came, Marcia not daring to look up, yet seeing familiar glimpses as she passed: two nervous little hands and a neatly folded pocket handkerchief on a green silk lap belonging to Sabrina Bates; a round lace collar fastened by a brooch with a colored daguerreotype about Aunt Polly's neck. Beyond were Uncle Joab's Sunday boots, and next were little feet covered by white stockings and slippers fastened with crossed black ribbons, some child's. She didn't raise her eyes to identify whose now, for she had to focus on the great things in front of her. She wondered at herself for noticing such trivial things when she was walking up to the presence of the great God, and there stood the minister with his open book!

Now, at last, with most of the audience behind her, still protected by the lace film, she raised her eyes to the minister's familiar face, took David's arm without letting her hand tremble too much, and listened to the solemn words being read. They seemed intended for her alone. She knew David's heart was crushed, and it was only a form for him. She must take double vows for the sake of the wrong done to him. So she listened carefully.

"Dearly beloved, we are gathered together"—how the words thrilled her!—"in the sight of God and in the presence of this company to join together this man and woman in the bonds of holy matrimony." A deathly stillness rested upon the room, and the bride could hear only her heart beating. She was glad she could look straight into the minister's face. Had her mother felt this way when she was being married? Did her stepmother understand it? Yes, she must, in part at least, for she'd bent and kissed her tenderly on the brow before leaving her. It was a sentimental thing for her to do, and it touched Marcia deeply. She was fond of her stepmother.

She waited breathlessly, looking down, while the minister demanded, "If any man can show just cause why they may not be lawfully joined together, let him now declare it or else hereafter hold his peace." What if someone recognized her and, thinking she'd usurped Kate's place, spoke out and stopped the marriage! How would David feel? And she? She'd sink to the floor. But she must listen now. It was a solemn, holy vow she was taking upon herself for life. She brought herself sharply back to the ceremony.

The minister was talking to David now. "Wilt thou love her, comfort her, honor and keep her, in sickness and in health, and forsaking all others, keep thee only unto her, so long as ye both shall live?"

It was hard to make David promise that when his heart belonged to Kate. She wondered that his voice could be so steady when he said, "I will." Kate's white glove, a bit large for Marcia, trembled on David's arm as the minister turned to her.

"Wilt thou, Marcia"—ah, it was out now! The sharp rustle of silk and stiff linen showed that all present were aware at last of who the bride was. But the minister went steadily on. He didn't care what the listening assembly thought. He was talking earnestly to his little friend Marcia—"have this man to be thy wedded husband, to live together after God's ordinance in the holy estate of matrimony? Wilt thou obey him and serve him, love, honor, and keep him, in sickness and in health"— the words of the pledge continued.

It wasn't hard. The girl felt she could do all that. She was relieved to find it was no worse and to know she was no longer acting in a lie. They all knew who she was now. She held up her head and answered in a clear voice that made her few schoolmates gasp in admiration.

"I will!"

And the minister's wife, sitting in her soft gray poplin, white kerchief, and cap of book muslin, smiled at the music in Marcia's voice and nodded approval. She felt that all was well with her young friend.

Those astonished people waited till the ceremony was concluded and the prayer over, and then they burst forth. Brows lifted and looks passed from one to another, questioning and disclaiming any knowledge in the matter. And as soon as the minister turned and took the bride's hand to congratulate her, heads bent together behind fans, and the buzz of whispers began.

"What does it mean? Where's Kate? Did he change his mind at the last minute? . . . How old is Marcia? . . . Mercy me! Nothing but a child! Are you sure? Why, my Mary Ann is older than that by three months, and she's no more able to become mistress of a home than a nine-day-old kitten. . . . Are you sure that's Marcia? Didn't the minister make a mistake in the name? It looked to me like Kate. . . . Look again. She's put her veil back. . . . No, it can't be! . . . Yes, it is! . . . No, it looks like Kate! Her hair's done the same, but, no, Kate never had such a sweet, innocent look like that. Why, when she was a child, her face always had a sharpness to it. . . . Look at Marcia's eyes, poor lamb! I don't see how her father could bear it, and she so young. . . . But Kate! Where can she be? . . . You don't say! Yes, I did see that captain again last week or so. . . . Do you believe it? Surely she never would. Who told you? . . . Was he sure? Maria and Janet are bridesmaids, and they didn't see signs of anything. They were over here yesterday. . . . Yes, Kate showed them everything and planned how they'd all walk in. . . . No, she didn't do anything strange; Janet would have mentioned it. Janet sees everything. . . . Well, they say he's a good man, and Marcia'll be well provided for. Madam Schuyler'll be relieved about that. Marcia can't ever lead her the dance Kate has among the young men. . . . How pale he looks! Do you suppose he loves her? . . . What on earth can it all mean? Do you s'pose Kate feels bad? Where is she anyway? Wouldn't she come down? . . . Well, if 'twas his choosing, it served her right. She's too much of a flirt for a good man, and maybe he found her out. She's probably got just what she deserves, and I think Marcia'll make a good little wife. She always was a quiet, grown-up child, and Madam Schuyler trained her well. . . . But what will Kate do now? . . . Hush! They're coming this way. . . . How do you suppose we can find out? . . . Go ask Jane; perhaps they've told her or Aunt Polly. Surely she knows."

But Aunt Polly sat with pursed lips. She hadn't been told, and it was her prerogative to know everything. She always arrived early at funerals and weddings, especially in the family circle, to learn the utmost details, which she dispensed at her discretion to latecomers in fine whispers.

Now she sat silent, miffed, unable to explain a thing. She'd never liked Sarah Schuyler. Well, wait until her opportunity came. If they didn't wish her to say the truth, she must say something. She could at least tell what she thought, which was that Sarah had always disliked Marcia and was likely glad to get her off her hands. Aunt Polly meant to find a trail somewhere, no matter how many times they threw her off the scent.

Meanwhile, for Marcia the sun was shining again with some of its old brightness. The terrible self-renunciation was over, and familiar faces actually were smiling upon her and wishing her joy. She felt the flutter of her heart in her throat beneath the string of pearls and wondered if, after all, she might hope for a little happiness of her own. She could climb no more fences or wade in gurgling brooks, but mightn't there be other equally happy things? A bit of the pride of life had settled upon her. The relatives were coming with pleasant words and kisses, and the blushes on her cheeks were growing deeper. She almost forgot David in the excitement.

A few of her girlfriends ventured shyly near. They put out cold fingers in salute with distant, stiff phrases belonging to a grown-up world.

Only Mary Ann acknowledged their former bond as playmates when she leaned down and whispered with a giggle: "Say, you didn't need to envy Kate, did you? My! Ain't you in clover! Say, Marsh," she added wistfully, "do invite me fer a visit sometime, won't you?"

Now Mary Ann wasn't on the same social standing with the Schuylers; if it hadn't been for a distant mutual relative, she wouldn't have been invited to the wedding. Marcia had never liked her much, but now, with an uncertain future, it seemed pleasant and homelike to think of a visit from Mary Ann. So she nodded and said kindly, "Sometime, Mary Ann, if I can."

Mary Ann squeezed her hand, kissed her, blushed, and giggled herself out of the way of the next guest.

Everyone went into the dining room and sat around the long table. It was Marcia's timid hand that cut the bridal cake, and the whole room watched her. Seeing the pretty color come and go in her excited cheeks, they wondered why they never noticed before how beautiful Marcia was becoming. A handsome couple they'd make! And they looked from Marcia to David and back again, trying to fathom the mystery.

The truth about Kate and Captain Leavenworth was gradually stealing about the company. The minister had told it in his sad, gentle way. Just the facts. No gossip. Naturally everyone bristled with questions, but the minister didn't say much.

"I really don't know," he said graciously, and few dared ask further. Perhaps the minister, wise from experience, had asked as few questions as possible so as not to know too much before undertaking this task for his old friend the squire.

And so Kate's marriage went into the annals of the village, at least so far as that morning was concerned, quietly and with little exclamation before the family. The squire and his wife controlled their faces. As he talked with his friends, the squire's usually pleasant face seemed more austere, but his wife conversed with her customary poise and never gave cause for conjecture as to her true feelings.

Some dared to offer their surprised condolences. To them the stepmother replied that of course the outcome of events had been a sore trial to the squire and all of them, but they were delighted at the happy arrangement that was made. She glanced contentedly at the child-bride.

It was a revelation to the whole village that Marcia had grown up and was so lovely. But dismay filled the town gossips. They felt cheated; here was a fine scandal they failed to discover in time and spread abroad.

The bride sat in her finery like some wild rose caught as a sacrifice. But everyone admitted she might have done far worse. David was a good man, with prospects far beyond most young men of his time. Moreover, he was known to have a brilliant mind, and the career he'd chosen, that of journalism, in which he was already making his mark, promised to be lucrative as well as influential.

It was all very hurried at the last. Madam Schuyler and Dolly the maid helped Marcia off with the satin and lace, and she was soon out of her bridal attire and struggling with the intricacies of Kate's traveling outfit.

Marcia was no longer Marcia, but Mrs. David Spafford. She felt the new name almost at once. It gave her a sense of masquerading, pleasant enough for now, but with a dim foreboding of nameless dread and emptiness for the future, like all masquerading which must end sometime. And when a person removes the mask, how sad not to find one's real self again; it is worse still for a person who may never remove the mask but must grow to it and be it from the soul.

All this Marcia felt only faintly, of course. She was young and lighthearted naturally, and the excitement and pretty things about her were only pleasant.

For Kate's friends to stand around her, joking with her as they might have with Kate, and to feel their admiring glances and hear their envious references to her handsome husband, almost intoxicated her for a moment. Her cheeks grew rosier as she tied on Kate's pretty poke bonnet, whose nodding blue flowers had been brought over from Paris by a friend of Kate's. It seemed a shame Kate shouldn't have her things after all. The pleasure died out of Marcia's eyes as she carefully looped the soft blue ribbons under her round chin and drew on Kate's long gloves. Kate's outfit was certainly becoming to Marcia, for she had that complexion that looks good with any color, though in blue she wasn't at her best.

When Marcia was ready, she stepped back from the mirror with a frightened gaze about the room.

Now that the last minute had come, there was no one to understand her feelings or help her. Even the girls were standing there to say the last formal farewell and exclaim in astonishment over Kate's romantic disappearance. They were Kate's friends, not Marcia's, and they were bidding Kate's clothes good-bye for want of the original bride. Marcia's friends were too young and shy to do more than stand back in awe and gaze at their schoolmate so suddenly promoted to a life that yesterday seemed years away for any of them.

So Marcia walked alone down the hall, until a small, wrinkled hand was laid on her gloved one. Her true friend, the minister's wife, walked down the stairs arm in arm with the bride. Marcia's heart warmed again with gratitude for her friend. Yet all she said was, "My dear!" But her touch and her gentle voice comforted Marcia.

The older woman stood at the edge of the steps, with her white hair shining in the morning and her kind husband just behind her during the farewell, and Marcia felt happier because of her motherly presence.

The guests were out on the piazza enjoying the bright summer morning. David stood beside the open coach door, a carriage lap robe over his arm and his hat on, ready. He and the squire were talking, and they knew everyone was watching them. They laughed and talked with studied pleasantness, though there seemed to be an undertone of sadness that the most obtuse guest couldn't fail to detect.

Harriet, as a flower girl, stood on the lower step ready to fling posies before the bride as she stepped into the coach. And the little boys, to whom a wedding merely meant a delightful increase in opportunities, stood behind a pillar munching cake, more of which protruded from their bulging pockets.

Marcia, with a lump in her throat that threatened tears, slipped behind the people, caught the two little stepbrothers in her arms, and smothered them with kisses, amid their loud protestations and the laughter of those who stood about. But the little skirmish hid the tears, and the bride returned decorously to where her stepmother stood awaiting her with a smile of complacent—almost completed—duty on her face. She'd carried off a trying situation in a most creditable manner and knew she'd won the respect of every woman present. That meant a great deal to Madam Schuyler.

The stepmother's arms were around her, and Marcia remembered how kind they had felt when they first clasped her years ago; she was kissed then and told to be a good little girl. She had always liked her stepmother. Now, as she said good-bye to the only mother she'd ever known, who was a true mother to her in many ways, her young heart almost gave way. She longed to hide in those arms and stay under the wing of one who'd led her well along life's path.

Perhaps Madam Schuyler felt the clinging of the girl's arms about her, and her heart rebuked her that she'd let such a young, inexperienced girl go out into the world so suddenly this way. At last she stooped and kissed Marcia again and whispered, "You've been a good girl, Marcia."

Afterward, Marcia cherished that sentence among memory's dearest treasures, as though she'd fulfilled her stepmother's first command given on the night when her father brought home their new mother.

Then the flowers were thrown on the pavement to brighten it for the bride. She was handed into the coach behind the white-haired coachman, and by his side was Kate's fine new hair trunk. Ah! That was a bitter touch! Kate's trunk! Kate's things! Kate's husband! If only it had been her own small, moth-eaten trunk that had belonged to her mother and filled with her own things—and if only he'd been her own husband! Yet she wanted no other than David—if only he could have been her David.

Then Madam Schuyler, still troubled, stepped over and whispered, "David, you'll remember she's young. You'll deal gently with her?"

David nodded his head solemnly and answered, "I'll

remember. She won't be troubled. I'll care for her as I would for my own sister."

And Madam Schuyler turned away half satisfied. After all, was that what a woman wanted? Would she be satisfied to be cared for as a sister?

Then gravely, with his eyes almost not seeing her, the father kissed his daughter good-bye. David climbed into the coach, the door was shut, and the white horses arched their necks and stepped away amid a shower of rice and slippers.

Chapter 7

*F*or some distance the way was lined with people they knew, standing about the driveway and outside the fence, grouped along the sidewalk, to watch the coach pass by. To all, the bride's face was a surprise. They almost expected to see another coach following with the other bride.

Marcia nodded brightly to those she knew and threw flowers from the great nosegay Harriet had handed her. She felt for a few minutes like a girl in a fairy tale, riding in this fine coach in grand attire. She stole a look at David. He certainly looked like a prince, but grave lines were already settling about his mouth. Would he always look that way? Would he ever laugh and joke again as he used to do? Could she make him happy sometimes and help him forget?

They rode through the village in front of the store and post office where Marcia had bought her chintz three days earlier, then turned up the road she'd come with Mary Ann. How long ago that seemed! How light her heart was then and how young! All of life was before her with its delightful possibilities, and now it seemed to have closed, and she was someone else. She longed to jump down and run away from the coach and David and the new clothes that weren't hers—away from the new life planned for someone else that she must live now. She must always be a woman, never a girl anymore.

They drove out past Granny McVane's and into the country. The tall corn rustled as they passed, and the cows looked up from their munching in the pasture. The old schoolhouse came in sight with its worn playground and dejected summer air.

Marcia searched for the window by which she used to sit and eat her lunch in winters and the tree she would sit under in summers. She saw the path she and Mary Ann would take down to the brook. She searched them all out and bid them good-bye with her eyes. Then the road wound around through a maple grove, and the school was lost to view.

They passed the Westons' south meadow where Hanford was plowing. Marcia could see him wiping the perspiration from his brow, and her heart warmed to him now that she was going away forever.

Hanford caught sight of the coach and watched, thinking to see Kate sitting in the bride's place. He wondered if the bride would notice him and turned a deeper red under his heavy coat of tan.

The bride did notice him. She smiled the sweetest smile the boy had ever seen on her face, the smile he'd dreamed of as he thought of her at night standing under the stars all alone by his father's gatepost, whittling the crossbar of the gate. For a moment he forgot it was the bridal party, forgot the stern-faced bridegroom, and saw only Marcia—his girl-love. His heart stood still, and a bright light of response filled his eyes. He took off his wide straw hat and bowed her reverence. He would have called to her, and tried three times, but his dry throat gave forth no utterance. When he looked again the coach had passed, and only the flutter of a white handkerchief came back to him and told him the beginning of the truth.

Then the boy's face paled under the tan. He tottered to the roadside and sat down with his face in his hands to try to comprehend the meaning, while the old horse dragged the plow wherever he would in search of tender grass.

What could it mean, and why did Marcia occupy that place beside the stranger, obviously the bridegroom? Where was her sister? Would there be another coach presently, and was this man then not the bridegroom but merely a friend of the family? Of course, that must be it. He got up and staggered to the fence to look down the road, but no one came by except the jogging old gray and carryall, with Aunt Polly grim and offended and Uncle Joab meek and depressed beside her. Could he have missed the bridal carriage when he was at the other end of the lot? He thought to call out to Uncle Joab and inquire, but he was timid and held back until it was too late.

But why had Marcia wafted that strange farewell with its sense of the final? And why did he feel so strange and weak in his knees?

She was to help his mother next week at the quilting bee—surely she hadn't gone away to stay. He got up and tried to whistle and turn the furrows evenly as before. But his heart was heavy, and he couldn't understand the feeling that kept telling him Marcia was gone out of his life forever.

At last his day's work was done, and he could hasten to the house. Without waiting for his supper, he "slicked up," as he called it, and went at once to the village, where he learned the bitter truth.

Mary Ann told him. Mary Ann, the plain, the awkward, who secretly admired Hanford Weston as she might have an angel and who as little expected him to speak to her as if he'd been one. She stood by her front gate in the dusky summer evening, the halo of her unusual wedding finery upon her; she'd taken advantage of being dressed up to make two or three visits since the wedding and so prolong the holiday. The light of the sunset softened her plain features and gave her a gentler look than was her wont. Was it that and an air of loneliness akin to his own that caused Hanford to stop and speak to her?

She couldn't keep it in long. It filled her so that she could hardly think or speak of anything else. To think of Marcia taken in a day, gone from their midst forever, gone to be a grown-up woman in a new world! It was as strange as sudden death and almost as terrible and beautiful.

Tears formed in her eyes and in the boy's eyes as they spoke about the one who was gone, and the dusk hid the sight so that neither knew, but each felt a subtle sympathy with the other.

Before Hanford started home alone under the burden of his first sorrow, he took Mary Ann's slim, bony hand in his and said stiffly, "Well, good night, Miss Mary Ann. I'm glad you told me."

And Mary Ann responded with a deep blush under her freckles, "Good night, Mr. Weston, and—call again!"

Some sympathy lingered with the boy as he went on his way, and he wasn't without a certain sort of comfort. And Mary Ann climbed to her room in the loft with something new to dream about.

Meanwhile, the coach drove on, and Marcia passed from her childhood home into the world of men and women, changes, sorrows, and joys.

David spoke to her kindly now and then. Was she comfortable? Would she prefer to change seats with him? Were the cushions right? Did she forget anything? He seemed anxious to have this part of the journey over and asked the coachman frequent questions about the horses and their speed. Marcia thought he longed to escape the painful reminder of what he'd expected to be a joyful trip, and she pitied him; but she also felt an undertone of hurt for herself. She found such pure delight in this charming ride with the beautiful horses in this luxurious coach that she couldn't bear to spoil it with the thought that only David's sadness and pain had made it possible for her.

Constantly, as the scene changed, she had to restrain herself from crying out with joy over the beauty and calling David's attention. Once she pointed out a bird just leaving a stalk of goldenrod, its touch causing the spray to bow and bend. David looked with unseeing eyes and smiled absently. Marcia felt she might as well have been talking to herself. He wasn't even the old friend and brother he used to be. She sighed and wished this might have been only a happy ride ending at home and a longer girlhood without this wall of trouble Kate had put up in a night for them all.

The coach came at last to the town where they were to stop for dinner and a change of horses.

Marcia looked with interest at the houses, streets, and people. Two girls about her own age with long hair braided down their backs walked with their arms linked as she and Mary Ann had often done. She wondered if any sudden changes might be coming to them as had to her. They turned and looked at her curiously, enviously it seemed, as the coach drew up to the tavern and she was helped out with ceremony. Doubtless they thought of her as she'd thought of Kate last week.

She was shown into the dim parlor of the tavern and seated in a stiff haircloth chair. Before a high gilt mirror set on glass knobs like rosettes, she smoothed her windblown hair and looked back at her reflection with startled eyes. Even her face seemed changed. She knew the bonnet and hair arrangement were becoming, but she felt unacquainted with them and wished for her own modest braids and plain bonnet. Even a sunbonnet would have been welcome and made her feel more like herself.

David didn't see how pretty she looked when he took her to the dining room ten minutes later. His eyes were looking into the hard future, and he was steeling himself against others' glances. He must be the model bridegroom in the sight of all who knew him. His pride bore him out in this. He had acquaintances the whole way home.

They were expecting the bridal party, for David had arranged a fine dinner for his bride. Fine it was, with the best cooking and table service the mistress of the tavern could command and with many touches unfamiliar to Marcia and therefore interesting. It was all lovely play till she looked at David.

David ate little, and Marcia felt she must hurry through the meal for his sake. Then, when the carryall was ready, he put her in, and they drove away.

Marcia's intuition told her how many things were thought of for the comfort of the one who was to have taken this journey with David. Gradually the thought of how terrible it was for him and how dreadful of Kate to have brought this sorrow upon him overcame all other thoughts.

Sitting quietly, grasping the faded roses little Harriet had given her, Marcia let the tears come, though in silence. If David hadn't been weighed down with his own sorrow, he might have noticed long before he did the sad young face beside him. But she turned away to keep him from seeing. They must have driven for half an hour through a dim wood before he caught sight of the tear-wet face and realized at once other troubles were in the world beside his own.

"Why, child, what's the matter?" he said, turning to her with grave concern. "Are you so tired? I'm afraid I've been very dull company," he added with a sigh. "You must forgive me."

"Oh, David, don't," said Marcia, putting her face into her hands and crying now, regardless of the roses. "I don't want you to think of me. It's dreadful for you. I'm so sorry for you. I wish I could do something."

"Dear child!" he said, placing his hand on hers. "Bless you for that. But don't be troubled about me. Try to forget me and be happy. This trouble isn't for you to bear."

"But I must bear it," said Marcia, sitting up. "She was my sister, and she did an awful thing. I can't forget it. How could she do it? How could she leave a man like you for that—"

Marcia stopped, her brown eyes flashing fiercely as she thought of Captain Leavenworth's hateful look at her that night in the moonlight. She shuddered and hid her face in her hands again and cried with the fervor of her young, undisciplined soul.

David didn't know what to do with a young woman in tears. Had it been Kate, his alarm would have vied with a fine sense of his own power to comfort. But even the thought of comforting anyone but Kate was now bitter. Must he always remember his pain at every turn? He drew a deep sigh and looked helplessly at his companion. Then he did a hard thing. He tried to justify Kate, as he'd been trying all morning to justify her to himself. And the deepest sting of his sorrow was that Kate could have done this thing! His peerless Kate!

"She cared for him," he breathed the words as if they hurt him.

"She should have told you so before, then. She shouldn't have let you think she cared for you—*ever*!" said Marcia fiercely.

The plain truth was bitter to the man to hear, although he'd felt it ever since they discovered the bride's flight.

"Perhaps there was too much pressure on her," he said lamely. "Looking back, I can see times when she didn't second me in hurrying the marriage as warmly as I could have wished. I laid it to her shyness. Yet she seemed happy when we met. Did you—did she—have you any idea she was planning this for long, or was it sudden?"

The words were out now. Had she meant to torture him this way all along, or had she yielded to a sudden impulse that perhaps she'd already repented of? He looked at Marcia with almost pleading eyes; she so wished she could tell him what he wanted to know. Yet she couldn't help him; she knew no more than he. She steadied her own nerves and tried to tell all she knew or surmised and reveal Kate in her true character before him. Not that she wished to speak ill of her sister; only that she would be true and give him a chance to escape some of the pain if possible, by seeing the real Kate as she was at home without varnish. Yet she reflected that those who knew

Kate's shallowness well still loved her in spite of it and always bowed to her wishes.

Gradually their talk subsided into deep silence once more, broken only by the jog-trot of the horse or the stray note of some bird. The road wound into the woods with its fragrant scents of hemlock, spruce, and wintergreen, then out into an open, sunny way.

The strain of the day's excitement and its sorrow were telling on the two travelers. The horse plodded monotonously on along the dusty road. With the drone of insects and the glare of the afternoon sun, drowsiness soon overcame Marcia, and her head nodded until she was fast asleep.

David noticed that she slept and pulled her head against his shoulder so she might rest more comfortably. Then he settled back to his own pain, deeper when he thought how different it would have been if the head resting against his shoulder had been golden instead of brown. Then he, too, fell asleep, and the old horse, slowing down and finding no urging voice behind her, stopped at last in the shade of an apple tree. She ate the tender grass growing beneath the generous shade and nipped at an apple or two hanging within reach. Then she, too, stood there dozing.

A farmer, trundling by in his empty hay wagon, stopped and looked curiously at them. Then he drew up his team and came and prodded David in the chest with his long hickory stick.

"Wake up there and move on," he called as he jumped back into his wagon and took up the reins. "We don't want no tipsy folks around these parts." With a loud clatter he rode on.

David, whose strong temperance principles had marked him somewhat in his own neighborhood, roused and flushed over the insinuation and started up the lazy horse. But he was soon lost in his own troubles, which returned upon him doubly sharp as new sorrow does after a brief sleep.

But Marcia slept on.

Chapter 8

It was late in the evening when they reached the town and David saw the lights of his neighborhood gleaming in the distance. He was glad it was late, for now no one would meet them that night. His friends might think they'd stopped overnight on the way or been detained.

As David drew near the house, he felt he may have been wrong in carrying out his marriage as if everything were all right. It would be too great a strain on him to live in that house without Kate and come home every night and not find her there to greet him. Oh, if he might turn even now and flee from it, out into the wilderness somewhere, and hide himself from humankind, where no one would know or ever ask him about his wife!

He groaned as the horse drew up to the door. And beside him the sleeping girl who was his wife reminded him he couldn't go away; he must stay and face life's responsibilities which he'd taken upon himself and bear his pain. It wasn't the fault of the girl he married. She truly grieved for him, and he felt deeply grateful for the great thing she did to save his pride.

He leaned over and touched her shoulder gently to awaken her, but her sleep was deep and healthy, the sleep of exhausted youth. She didn't rouse or even open her eyes but murmured half audibly, "David has come, Kate—hurry!"

Guessing what must have passed the night he arrived, David stooped and gathered her tenderly in his arms. He felt a bond of kindness far deeper than brotherly love. It was a bond of common suffering, and by her choice she'd made herself his comrade in his trouble. He would at least save her from what suffering he could.

She didn't awaken as he carried her into the house or when he took her upstairs and laid her gently on the white bed prepared for the bridal chamber.

The moonlight stole in at the small-paned windows and fell across the floor, showing every object in the room plainly. David lit a candle and set it upon the high mahogany chest of drawers. The light flickered and played over the sweet face, and Marcia slept on.

David went downstairs and settled the horse. Then he returned, but Marcia hadn't stirred. He looked at her a moment helplessly. It didn't seem right to leave her this way, and yet it was a pity to disturb her sleep; she seemed so weary. It had been a long ride and the day filled with unwonted excitement. He felt it himself, and what must it be for her? Clumsily he untied the blue ribbons and pulled the poke bonnet out of her way. The luxuriant hair, unused to the confinement of combs, fell about her sleep-flushed face. Contentedly she nestled down, a half smile on her lips, the dark lashes lying on her rosy cheeks, one youthful hand on which gleamed the new wedding ring—which wasn't hers—resting on her chest, rising and falling with her breath. A lovely bride!

David, stern, true, pained, and appreciative, suddenly awakened to what a dreadful thing he'd done.

Here was this lovely woman, her womanhood not yet unfolded from the bud but lovely in promise even as her sister had been in truth. He'd taken her charms, her dreams, her woman's ways, her love—her very life—as ruthlessly and thoughtlessly as if she were a wax doll and put her in a home where she couldn't be what she ought to be, because the home belonged to another. Thrown away on a man without a heart! That was what she was! A sacrifice to his pride! There was no other way to put it.

It frightened him to think of his promises. "Love, honor, cherish"—yes, he promised those. And in a way he could perform them, but not as the wedding ceremony meant, not as he'd have performed them if the bride were Kate, his choice. Oh, why had this awful thing come upon him!

And now his conscience told him he'd done wrong to take this girl away from joy that might have been hers and sacrifice her to save his own sufferings, to keep his friends from knowing that the girl he was to marry had jilted him.

As he stood before the lovely, defenseless girl, her beauty and innocence arraigned him. He felt that God would hold him accountable for the act he had so thoughtlessly committed that day, and a burden of responsibility settled on his sorrow. He groaned aloud. For a moment his soul rebelled. Why couldn't he have loved this sweet, self-sacrificing girl instead of her fickle sister? She might perhaps have loved him in return, but now nothing could ever be! Earth was filled with darkness, and life henceforth meant renunciation and one long struggle to hide his trouble from the world.

But the girl he selfishly drew into his sorrow mustn't suffer more than he could help. He must try to make her happy and keep her as much as possible from knowing what she missed by coming with him. His stern resolve, a half prayer, went on record before God that he would spare her as much as he knew how.

Lying there asleep and thus defenseless, she appealed to him. Asking nothing, she yet demanded all from him in the name of true chivalry. How readily she gave up all for him! How sweetly she said she'd fill the place left vacant by her sister, just to save him from pain and humiliation!

A desire to stoop and kiss her face came to him, not for affection's sake, but reverently, as if to give her before God some fitting sign that he knew and understood her act of self-sacrifice and wouldn't presume upon it.

Slowly, as though he were performing a religious ceremony, a sacred duty, David bent over her, bringing his face to the gentle sleeping one. Her sweet breath fanned his cheek. His soul, awakened by his thoughts, gave homage to her sweetness. He kissed her lips, his bride, yet not his bride. Kissed her for the second time. That thought came to him with the touch of the warm lips and startled him. Was there some significance that he'd met Marcia first and kissed her by mistake instead of Kate?

It seemed as if the sleeping lips clung to his and half responded to the kiss, as Marcia in her dreams relived the kiss she received by her father's gate in the moonlight. Only the dream man was her own and not another's. As David lifted up his head and looked at her gravely, he saw a faint smile illuminating her face, as if the sleeping soul within had felt the touch and answered the call.

With a deep sigh he turned away, blew out the candle, and left her with the moonbeams in her chamber. He walked sadly to a rear room of the house and lay down on the bed to contemplate his miserable state.

Meanwhile, Kate, the cause of this misery, had quarreled with her husband already because he wouldn't further some expensive whim of hers. She told him she was sorry she hadn't stayed where she was and married David as she'd planned. Now she sat sulkily in her room alone, too angry to sleep, while her husband smoked sullenly in the barroom below and drank frequent glasses of brandy to fortify himself against Kate's moods.

Kate was considering whether she was a fool to marry the captain instead of David. The romance was already gone. She wished for her trunk and her pretty clothes. Her father's word of reconciliation would doubtless come in a few days with the trunks.

After all, Kate was intensely satisfied in having broken all bounds and done as she pleased. It would have been more comfortable if David hadn't been so absurdly in earnest and believed in her so thoroughly. But it was nice to have someone believe in you no matter what you did, and David would always do that. It began to look doubtful if the captain ever would.

David would never marry, she was sure, and perhaps, by and by, when everything had been forgotten and forgiven, she might establish a pleasant relationship with him again and flirt with him. He loved so devoutly, and his great eyes were so handsome when he looked at one with his whole soul in them. Yes, it would be good to have a friend like that when her husband was off at sea with his ship. Now that she was a married woman, she would be free of such childish trammels as being guarded at home and never going anywhere alone. She could go to New York, and she'd let David know where she was; he'd come up on business and perhaps take her to the theater.

Of course, she'd heard David express views against theater-going, and she knew he was as much of a churchman, almost, as her father. But she was sure she could coax him to do anything for her, and she'd always wanted to go to the theater. His scruples might be strong, but she knew his love for her and thought it was stronger. She'd read in his eyes that it would never fail her.

Yes, she thought, she'd begin at once to make a friend of David. She'd write him a letter asking forgiveness and keep him under her influence. There was no telling what would happen with her husband off at sea so much. Besides, it would be wholesome for the captain to know she had another friend. He might be less stubborn.

What a nuisance the marriage vows had to be taken for life! It would be much nicer if they could be put off as easily as they were put on. Rather hard on some women, perhaps, but she could keep any man as long as she chose, and then—she snapped her pretty thumb and finger in the air to express her utter disdain for the man she chose to cast off.

In running away from her father's house and her betrothed bridegroom and in breaking the laws of respectable society, Kate apparently gave up all attempt at any principle.

So she sat down to write her letter, with a pout here and a dimple there, and as much pretty gentleness as if she were talking with her own bewitching face and eyes quite near his. She knew she could bewitch him if she chose, and she was in the mood just now to choose very much, for she was deeply angry with her husband.

She'd always been heartless when she pleased, knowing only her returning sweet smile was needed to bring her abused subjects fondly to her feet again. It didn't occur to her that this time she sinned not only against her friends but against heaven and God-given love, and that a time of reckoning must come to her—had come, indeed.

Kate never believed they'd be angry with her, her father least of all. She had no thought they'd do anything desperate. She expected the wedding put off indefinitely and the servants sent hither and yon in hot haste to uninvite the guests, upon some pretext of accident or illness. The matter would be left to rest until the village ceased to wonder and her real marriage with Captain Leavenworth could be announced.

She counted on David to stand up for her. She didn't understand how her father's righteous soul would be stirred to the depths of disgrace over her wanton action. Not that understanding would have deterred her in the least from doing as she pleased—only that she counted on too great power with all of them.

The letter sounded quite pathetic and penitent. She blamed her action wholly upon her husband and made herself out to be a poor, helpless, sweet thing, bewildered by so much love put upon her. And she hinted that perhaps after all she made a mistake not to keep David's love instead of a wilder, fiercer one. She ended by begging David to be her friend forever and left a slight impression with him that already shadows had crossed her path, causing her to feel his friendship might be needed someday.

The letter was calculated to drive David, in love as he'd been, half mad with anguish, even without his hasty marriage added to the situation.

And in due time, by coach, the letter came to David.

Chapter 9

Sunlight fell across the floor when Marcia awoke the next morning. For a moment she couldn't think where she was or how she came there. She looked at the unfamiliar walls, covered with paper decorated in landscapes—a hill in the distance with a tall castle among the trees, a blue lake in the foreground, and two maidens sitting pensively on a green bank with their arms linked. Marcia felt there was a story in it. She'd like to imagine the lives of those two girls when she had more time.

No pictures in the room marred those on the wallpaper, but the walls didn't look bare. Everything was new and stilted and needed a woman's hand to bring the little homey touches, but the newness delighted the girl.

She was stiff from the long ride, but her sleep refreshed her, and now she was ready to work. As she rose, she wondered how she got on the bed and the blue bonnet untied and laid on the chair beside her. Surely she couldn't have done it herself, or did someone carry her? David? Good, kind David!

A bird hopped on the window seat and then flitted away. Marcia walked to the window to look after him and was held by the sights outside. She glimpsed houses through vines and smoke rising from chimneys. She wondered who lived nearby and if there were girls who would prove pleasant companions. Then she remembered she was no longer a girl and must associate with married women from now on.

Suddenly the clock on the church steeple across the way warned her it was late, and with a sense of deserving reprimand, she hurried downstairs.

The fire was already lighted, and David had brought in fresh water. His intuition told him that a great deal was necessary. He was raised by three maiden aunts who thought a man was out of his sphere in the kitchen, so the kitchen was an unknown quantity to him.

Marcia entered the room as if she weren't certain of her welcome. She was coming into a world she barely understood.

"Good morning," she said shyly, and a lovely color stole into her cheeks.

David's conscience smote him again as her waking beauty intensified the impression from the night before.

"Good morning," he said gravely, studying her face as he might have studied some poor waif whom he unknowingly ran over in the night and picked up to resuscitate. "Are you rested? You were very tired last night."

"What a baby I was!" said Marcia deprecatingly, with a soft, merry laugh.

David was amazed to find she had two dimples located about where Kate's were, only deeper and gentler.

"Did I sleep all afternoon after we left the canal? And did you have hard work to get me into the house and upstairs?"

"You slept soundly," said David, smiling in spite of his heavy heart. "It seemed a pity to waken you, so I did the next best thing and put you to bed as well as I knew how."

"It was very good of you," said Marcia, coming over to him with her hands clasped earnestly, "and I don't know how to thank you."

There was something quaint and old-fashioned in her way of speaking, and it struck David pitifully that she should be thanking her husband, the man who pledged to care for her all his life. Everywhere he turned his conscience reproached him.

They presently sat down to a fine breakfast with plenty of bread and fresh butter from the best butter maker in the county, the eggs laid the day before and the bacon browned just right. Marcia knew how to make coffee, and the cream was as rich and yellow as it came from the cows at home. And the blackberries were as large and fine as those Marcia had picked a few days before to buy her pink sprigged chintz.

David watched her deft movements and was reminded at once that Marcia was defrauded of the loving, joyous interchange that would have been present if Kate were here. But even sharper came the thought that Kate had wanted it, had preferred another man's love to his, and hadn't anticipated these joys as he had. He was a fool. All these months he thought he and Kate held joys and hopes and tender thoughts of one another in common. And, behold, he was having these feelings alone, blind fool that he was! He sighed bitterly. Excited at getting her first breakfast on her own, Marcia heard and forgot to smile over the completed work. She could hardly eat what she'd prepared, for she felt David's sadness keenly.

Shyly she poured the amber coffee and passed it to David. She was pleased he drank it eagerly and passed his cup back for more. He ate little but seemed to approve of all she'd done.

After breakfast David went down to the office. He told Marcia he'd step over and tell his aunts of their arrival, and they'd probably come over during the day to greet her. He'd be back for dinner at twelve. He suggested she spend her time resting, as she must be weary yet. He hesitated, then went out and closed the door behind him.

A moment later he opened the door. "You won't be lonesome, will you, child?" he asked, troubled.

"Oh, no!" said Marcia brightly, smiling back.

She thought it kind of him to think of her. She was eager to investigate her new domain and enjoyed feeling she was mistress and might do as she pleased. Yet she stood by the window after he was gone and watched his easy strides down the street with a feeling of mingled pride and disappointment. She was going through a nice play, and David was handsome, and her young heart swelled with pride to belong to him. But after all, something was left out—a mysterious longing unsatisfied. What was it, and what caused it? David's sorrow?

She turned with a sigh as he disappeared around a curve in the sidewalk and was lost to view. Then casting aside the troubles trying to settle on her, she gave herself up to the morning's delight.

In a few minutes she put the kitchen to rights, washing the delicate sprigged china with its lavender sprays and buff bands and placing it carefully on the shelves behind the glass doors. Then she pushed the table back against the wall.

She didn't need to worry about dinner. A leg of lamb was cooked beautifully, along with half a dozen pies, their flaky crusts bearing witness to the aunts' culinary skills. They'd also brought a fruitcake, a pound cake, a jar of delectable cookies, and another of fat, sugary doughnuts, three loaves of bread, and a sheet of puffy rusks with their shining tops dusted with sugar. And the preserve closet was rich in preserves, jellies, and pickles. No, it wouldn't take long to get dinner.

Marcia peeped into the great parlor first, for her hopes and fears had turned toward that room while she washed the dishes.

The Schuylers were one of the few families in those days to possess a musical instrument, and it had delighted Marcia. She had a natural talent for music and spent many hours at the old spinet drawing tender tones from the yellowed keys. The spinet had been in the family for years, and the Schuyler girls were very proud of it. Kate could rattle off merry waltzes and rollicking tunes that made the feet of the sedate village maidens flutter in time to their melody. But Marcia's music was softer and more spiritual. She loved the dear old hymns and some of the classics.

"Stupid old things without any tune," Kate had called them.

But Marcia persevered in playing them until she could bring

out the beautiful passages in a way that at least satisfied her. Her one great desire had been to take lessons from a real musician and play the wonderful pieces the old masters composed. Few of these had come her way—a rather mutilated copy of Haydn's *Creation*, a copy of Handel's *Messiah*, and a few fragments of an old book of Bach's preludes and fugues. Many of these she couldn't play at all, but others she managed to pick out. A visit from a cousin who lived in Boston and told of the concerts given there by the Handel and Haydn Society had strengthened her interest in music.

Ever since she awoke that morning, she'd wondered if there was a musical instrument in the house. If not, she felt she'd miss the old spinet in her father's house more than anything else about her childhood home.

So with fear and trepidation, she entered the darkened room, where the careful aunts had drawn the thick green shades. The furniture stood about in shadowed corners, and every footfall seemed to disturb the room.

Marcia's bright eyes darted about, noting the great glass knobs that held the lace curtains with heavy silk cords; the round mahogany table, with its china vase of "everlastings"; the high, stiff-backed chairs decked in elaborate antimacassars of intricate pattern. Then, in the farthest corner, shrouded in dark coverings, she found what she was searching for. With joy she sprang to it, touched its polished wood with gentle fingers, and lovingly felt for the keyboard. It was closed. Marcia pushed up the shade to see better and opened the instrument cautiously.

It was a pianoforte in the latest pattern. Exclaiming with delight, she sat down and began to strike chords, timidly at first, then more boldly. The tone was sweeter than the old spinet or Squire Hartrandt's harpsichord. Marcia marveled at the volume of sound. It filled the room and seemed to echo through the empty halls.

She played soft little airs from memory and felt joy rising inside her. She'd never be lonely in the new life, for she'd always have this wonderful instrument to flee to when she felt homesick.

Across the hall were two rooms, the front one furnished as a library, with rows of books behind glass doors. Marcia looked at them in awe. Might she read them all? She resolved to cultivate her mind that she might be a fit companion for David. She knew he was wise beyond his years, for she'd heard her father say so. She stepped closer and, scanning the titles, recognized at once a few familiar books she'd read and reread: *Thaddeus of Warsaw, Scottish Chiefs, Mysteries of Udolpho, Romance of the Forest,* Baker's *Livy,* Rollin's *History, Pilgrim's Progress,* and a whole row of Sir Walter Scott's novels. She caught her breath. What a pleasure was opening before her! All of Scott! And she'd read only one!

With difficulty she tore herself away from the tempting shelves and went on to explore the rest of the house.

Behind David's library was a sunny sitting room, or breakfast room, or dining room as it would be called at the present time. In Marcia's time the family ate most of their meals in one end of the large, bright kitchen, that end furnished with a comfortable lounge, a few bookshelves, a thick ingrain carpet, and a blooming geranium in the wide window seat. But there was always the other room for company, for "high days and holidays."

Out of this morning room the pantry opened with its spicy odors of preserves and fruitcake.

Marcia was pleased as she looked about her. The house itself was part of David's inheritance, his mother's family homestead. Things were on a grand scale for a bride. Most brides began simply and climbed up year by year. How Kate would have liked it all! David must have considered her fastidious tastes and spent a great deal of money trying to please her. The piano must have been very expensive. Once more Marcia felt how David had loved Kate, and a pang went through her as she wondered however he was to live without her. Her young soul hadn't yet awakened to the question of how *she* was to live with *him*, while he mourned continually for one who was lost to him forever.

The rooms upstairs were pleasant, spacious, and comfortably furnished. Much of the furniture was old, having belonged to David's mother, and well preserved, something to be proud of having.

There were four rooms besides the one in which Marcia had slept: a front and back on the opposite side of the hall, a room just back of her own, and one at the end of the hall over the large kitchen.

She entered them all and looked around. The three beside her own in the front part of the house were all large and airy, furnished, and with high four-poster bedsteads and pretty chintz hangings. Each was immaculate. Cautiously she lifted the latch of the back room. David hadn't slept in any of the others, for the bedcoverings and pillows were plump and undisturbed. But here—to the back room—he had carried his heavy heart, as far away from the rest of the house as possible!

The bed was rumpled as if someone had thrown himself heavily down on it without undressing. Water stood in the washbowl, and a towel hung carelessly across a chair as if it had been hastily used. A newspaper lay on the bureau and a handkerchief on the floor. Marcia looked sadly about at the signs of occupancy, her eyes dwelling on each detail. Here David had suffered, and her loving heart longed to help him in his suffering.

But there was nothing in the room to keep her. Then she remembered the fire she'd left on the hearth, which must need replenishing, and turned to go downstairs.

Just at the door, something caught her eye under the edge of the chintz valance around the bed. It was the corner of an old daguerreotype, but for some reason Marcia was moved to stoop and pull it out. Then she saw it was her sister's saucy, pretty face that laughed back at her in defiance from the picture.

As if she had touched something red hot, she dropped it and pushed it with her foot far back under the bed. Then shutting the door quickly she went downstairs. Would it always be that way? Would Kate always blight her joy?

Chapter 10

*M*arcia's cheeks were flushed when David came home to dinner, for at the end she had to hurry.

As he stood in the kitchen doorway and smelled the steaming platter of green corn she was putting on the table, David suddenly realized he'd scarcely eaten anything for breakfast.

Also, he felt a certain comfort from the wistful sympathy in Marcia's eyes. Did he imagine it, or did she have a new look on her face and a more reserved bearing, less childish, more touched by the sad knowledge of life and its bitterness? It was just an idea, of course, something he just now noticed. He'd seen so little of her before.

Something stirred in her that she didn't understand, something awakened by the sight of her sister's daguerreotype lying where it must have fallen from David's pocket without his knowing as he slept. It put into tangible form the solid wall of fact that hung between her and any hope of future happiness as a wife. For the first time she, too, began to realize what she'd sacrificed in throwing her young life impetuously into the breach that it might be healed. But she wasn't sorry—not yet, anyway—only frightened and filled with foreboding.

The meal was a pleasant one, though constrained. David roused himself to be cheerful for Marcia's sake, as he would have done for any stranger. And the girl sensed and appreciated it, yet she didn't understand why it made her unhappy.

She was anxious to please him and kept asking if the potatoes were seasoned right, if his corn was tender, and if he wouldn't have another cup of coffee. Her cheeks were red with trying to be dignified when David finally finished his dinner and returned to the office. Two big tears came and sat in her eyes for a moment, but she held them back. She longed to get out of doors and run free in the old south pasture for relief. She didn't know how different it was from the ordinary young married couple's first dinner—so stiff and formal, with no gentle touches, no words of love, no glances that told more than words. And yet, child as she was, she felt the lack, though she didn't know what it was.

But training is a great thing. Marcia had been trained to be on the alert for the next duty and to do it before she gave herself time for any of her own thoughts. The dinner table was awaiting her attention, and company was coming.

She glanced at the hall clock. She had scarcely an hour before David's aunts were coming to spend the afternoon and stay for tea. He'd brought word at dinner.

She shrank from it and wished he'd decided to stay and introduce her. It would be a relief to have him for a shelter. Somehow she knew he'd have stayed if it were Kate. She wondered if she were growing selfish, because it hurt to find herself of so little account. And yet it was to be expected, and she must stop thinking about it. Of course, he had chosen Kate, and Kate would always be the only one to him.

It didn't take her long to put the dinner table in order and prepare everything for tea, and in doing her work Marcia thought about more pleasant themes. She wondered what Dolly and Debby, the servants at home, would say if they could see her pretty china and the nice kitchen. They were always fond of her, and naturally her new honors made her wish to have her old friends see her. What would Mary Ann say? What fun it would be to have Mary Ann there sometime. It would be almost like the days when they played house under the old elm on the big flat stone; only this would be real house with real sprigged china instead of bits of broken things.

Then she took up a song they sang in school.

Sister, thou wast mild and lovely,
  Gentle as the summer breeze,
Pleasant as the air of evening
  When it floats among the trees.

But the first words reminded her of her own sister and how little the song applied to her. How much better it would have been, she thought, and how much less bitter, if Kate had been that way and lain down to die. They could have felt about her as they did about the girl for whom that song was written.

The work was done and Marcia arrayed in one of Kate's simplest afternoon dresses when the brass knocker sounded throughout the house, startling her with its unfamiliar sound.

Breathlessly she hurried downstairs. The crucial moment had come when she must meet her new relatives alone. With trembling hand she opened the door, but only one person stood on the stoop, a girl of about her own age, perhaps a few months younger. She had red hair, a freckled face, and blue eyes dancing under the red lashes with repressed mischief. She wore a plain dress and a brown calico sunbonnet.

"Let me in quick before Grandma sees me," she demanded unceremoniously, entering at once before there was opportunity for invitation. "Grandma thinks I've gone to the store, so she won't expect me for a little while. I was jest crazy to see how you looked. I've been watchin' out the window all morning, but I couldn't glimpse you. When David came out this morning, I thought you'd sure be at the kitchen door to kiss him good-bye, but you wasn't. I watched every chance I could, but I couldn't see you till you ran out in the garden for corn. Then I saw you good, for I was out hangin' up the dish towels. You didn't have a sunbonnet on, so I could see real well. And when I saw how young you was, I made up my mind I'd get acquainted in spite of Grandma. You don't mind my comin' over this way without bein' dressed up, do you? There wouldn't be any way to get here without Grandma seeing me, you know, if I'd put on my Sunday clo'es."

"I'm glad you came!" said Marcia impulsively, feeling something like tears in her throat at the relief of delay from the aunts. "Come in and sit down. Who are you, and why wouldn't your grandmother like you to come?"

The strange girl laughed a mirthless laugh.

"Me? Oh, I'm Mirandy. Nobody ever calls me anything but Mirandy. My pa left Ma when I was a baby an' never come back, an' Ma died, and I live with Grandma Heath. An' Grandma's mad 'cause David didn't marry Hannah Heath. She wanted him to, an' she did everything she could to make him pay 'tention to Hannah—give her fine silk frocks, two of 'em, and a real pink parasol. But David—he never seemed to know the parasol was pink at all, for he'd never hold it over Hannah, even when Grandma made him walk with her home from church ahead of us. So when it came out that David was marrying and wouldn't take Hannah, Grandma got as mad as could be and said we never any of us should step over his doorsill. But I've stepped, I have, and Grandma can't help herself."

"And who is Hannah Heath?" questioned the dazed young bride. There was apparently more than a sister to consider.

"Hannah? Oh, Hannah's my cousin, Uncle Jim's oldest daughter, and she's getting on toward thirty somewhere. She has whitey-yellow hair and light blue eyes and is tall and real pretty. She held her head high for a good many years waitin' for David, and I guess she feels she made a mistake now. I noticed she bowed real sweet to Herman Worcester last Sunday and let him hold her parasol all the way to Grandma's gate. Hannah was mad as hops when she heard you had gold hair and blue eyes, for it did seem hard to be beaten by a girl of the same kind. But you haven't, have you? Your hair is almost black, and your eyes are brownie-brown. You're years younger than Hannah, too. My! Won't she be astonished when she sees you! But I don't understand how it got around about your having gold hair. A man that stopped at your father's house once told it—"

"It was my sister!" Marcia said and then blushed crimson to think how near she'd come to revealing the truth which mustn't be known.

"Your sister? Have you got a sister with gold hair?"

"Yes, he must have seen her," said Marcia confusedly. She wasn't used to evasion.

"How funny!" said Miranda. "Well, I'm glad he did, for it made Hannah so jealous it was funny. But I guess she'll get a setback when she sees how young you are. You're not as pretty as I thought you'd be, but I believe I like you better."

Miranda's frank speech reminded Marcia of Mary Ann and made her feel at home with her curious visitor. She didn't mind being told she wasn't up to the mark of beauty. From her point of view, she wasn't nearly as pretty as Kate, and her only fear was that her lack of beauty might reveal the secret and bring trouble to David.

But she didn't need to fear. Anyone watching the two girls, as they sat in the large, sunny room, would have smiled to think the homely, crude girl could suggest that the other bud of womanhood wasn't as near perfect beauty as a bud could be. There was always something childlike about Marcia's face, especially her profile, something deep and otherworldlike in her eyes that so distinguished her from other girls that the word *pretty* didn't apply. Surface observers might have passed her by when searching for prettiness, but not those who saw soul beauties.

But Miranda's time was limited, and she wanted to make as much of it as possible.

"Say, I heard you making music this morning. Won't you do

it for me? I'd just love to hear you."

Marcia's face lit up, and she led the way to the darkened parlor and folded back the covers of the precious piano. She played some tender little airs as she would have for Mary Ann. And the two young girls were there together, children in thought and feeling, half a generation apart in position, and neither recognized the difference.

"My land!" said the visitor. "If I could play like that, I wouldn't care if I had freckles and no father and red hair."

Looking up, Marcia saw tears in the light blue eyes and knew she had a kindred feeling in her heart for Miranda.

Suddenly the knocker sounded through the long hall again, startling both girls. Miranda tiptoed over to the front window and peeped out between the green slats of the Venetian blind, while Marcia hurried to close the piano.

"It's David's aunts," whispered Miranda. "I mighta known they'd come this afternoon. Well, I had first try at you anyway, and I like you real well. May I come again and hear you play? You go quick to the door, and I'll slip into the kitchen till they get in; then I'll go out the kitchen door and round the house out the little gate so Grandma won't see me. I must hurry, for I should have been back ten minutes ago."

"But you haven't been to the store," whispered Marcia in dismay.

"Oh, well, that don't matter! I'll tell her they didn't have what she sent me for. Good-bye. You better hurry."

So saying, she disappeared into the kitchen. And Marcia, startled by such easy morality, stood dazed until the knocker sounded again, this time a little louder.

And so at last Marcia was face-to-face with the Misses Spafford.

They entered, each with her knitting in a black silk bag, and greeted the flushed, perturbed Marcia with gentle, righteous inspection. She felt with the first glance that she would be tried in the fire and must pass through no easy ordeal. They were determined to sift her to the depths and know at once the worst of what their beloved nephew had brought upon himself. If they found anything wrong with her, they meant to be kind and loving with her, all the while taking it out of her. This was the unspoken understanding between them as they made their way to David's house that afternoon, and this was what Marcia faced as she opened the door.

She gasped a little, as any girl thus overwhelmed might have. She didn't tilt her chin defiantly as Kate would have. The thought of David came to support her, and she tried to play her part creditably. She didn't know whether the aunts knew her true identity or not, but she wasn't left long in doubt.

"My dear, we've long desired to know you. We've heard so much about you," recited Miss Amelia, with slightly agitated mien. She bestowed a cool, dutiful kiss on Marcia's warm cheek, chilling the girl like the breath of a funeral flower.

"Yes, it's indeed a pleasure at last to look upon our dear nephew's wife," said Miss Hortense quite precisely and kissed the other cheek.

At that moment the verse "Whosoever shall smite thee on thy right cheek, turn to him the other also" flitted through Marcia's mind. She was shocked at her own irreverence and tried to keep back a desire to laugh hysterically.

The aunts, too, were taken aback. She wasn't at all the girlish wife they pictured. David had tried to describe Kate to them once, and this young, sweet, disarming thing didn't in the least fit their preconceived ideas. How could they carry on their campaign against a certain kind of enemy when they came upon the field of action and discovered the supposed enemy had taken another, more bewildering form than the one for whom they prepared? They were silent, gathering their thoughts, and tried to fit their intended tactics to the present situation.

Meanwhile, Marcia helped them remove their bonnets and silk capes and place them neatly on the parlor sofa and then offered them chairs.

The two angular older women watched her graceful movements and marveled over her roundness and suppleness. They saw what a power youth and beauty could have over a man. She might even be worse than they feared; though if you could have heard them talk about their nephew's bride-to-be to their neighbors long before, you'd have supposed they knew her to be a model in every direction. But their stately pride required their outward loyalty at least. Now that loyalty was to be tried, and Marcia had two narrow, well-fortified hearts to conquer before her way would be smooth.

Madam Schuyler would have been proud of her pupil as alone and unaided she faced the trying situation and mastered it in a sweet, unassuming way.

They began their inquisition at once, as soon as they were seated and the preliminary sentences uttered. The gleaming knitting needles seemed to Marcia like so many swarming, vindictive bees, menacing her peace of mind.

"You look young, child, to have the care of such a large house as this," said Aunt Amelia, looking at Marcia over her spectacles as if she were expected to take the first bite out of her. "It's a great responsibility!" She shut her thin lips tightly and shook her head as if to say, "It's a great *impossibility*."

"Have you ever cared for a house?" asked Aunt Hortense. "David likes everything nice, you know. He's always been used to it."

Something in the tone and the set of the bow on Aunt Hortense's purple trimmed cap roused Marcia's spirit.

"I think I rather enjoy housework," she responded coolly.

This both surprised and mollified the aunts. They'd heard to the contrary from someone who lived in the same town with the Schuylers. Kate's reputation was widely known for being a spoiled beauty who didn't care to work and would do whatever she pleased. The aunts had entertained many forebodings from the few stray hints an old neighbor of Kate's had uttered in their hearing.

The talk drifted at once to household matters, as though the young bride must first undergo that part of the examination. Marcia took early opportunity to appease her visitors further by her warm praise of the supplies in the pantry. But the aunt's faces only registered a mild response to what was due. If she hadn't praised them, they'd have marked it against her, but it counted little with them, warm as it was.

"Can you make good bread?" Aunt Hortense flung out the question like a challenge, and the very set of her nostrils warned Marcia.

"Oh, yes, indeed. I can make beautiful bread. I just love to make it, too!" she answered with assurance and a ripple of laughter.

"But how do you make it?" questioned Aunt Amelia. "Do you use hop yeast? Potatoes? I thought so. Don't know how to make salt-rising, do you? That's to be expected."

"David has always been used to salt-rising bread," said Aunt Hortense with a grim set of her lips. "He was raised on it."

"If David doesn't like my bread," said Marcia with rising color and a nervous little laugh, "then I'll try to make some he likes."

"David was raised on salt-rising bread," said Aunt Hortense again as if that settled it. "We can send you down a loaf or two every time we bake until you learn how."

"I'm sure it's very kind of you," said Marcia, not at all pleased, "but I don't think that will be necessary. David has always seemed to like our bread when he visited at home. Indeed, he often praised it."

"David wouldn't be impolite," said Aunt Amelia after a suitable pause in which Marcia felt disapproval in the air. "It would be best for us to send it. David's health might suffer if he wasn't suitably nourished."

Marcia's cheeks grew redder. Bread was one of her stepmother's strong points, well infused into her young pupil. Madam Schuyler could never say enough to express her scorn of people who made salt-rising bread.

"My stepmother made beautiful bread," she said quite childishly. "She didn't think salt-rising bread was as healthy as that made from hop yeast. She disliked the odor in the house from salt-rising bread."

Now, indeed, the aunts exchanged battle glances. Four red spots flamed out in their four sallow cheeks, and eight shining knitting needles stopped. It was as they feared. Salt-rising bread was one of their tender spots, and they'd fight to the bitter end for it. They stared at her with four steely, spectacled eyes.

"And she so young, too! To be so out of the way!" was what their looks seemed to Marcia to say. She doubted her wisdom in expressing her sentiments regarding salt-rising bread.

The pause was long and impressive, and the bride felt like a naughty four-year-old.

At last Aunt Hortense took up her knitting again as if to say they'd finished and passed an irrevocable verdict on the culprit.

"People never stayed away from our house on that account," she said dryly. "I hope it won't be so disagreeable that it will affect your coming to see us sometimes with David."

Her icy manner suggested a long line of offended family portraits frowning down upon her.

Marcia's cheeks flamed crimson, and her heart nearly stopped beating.

"I beg your pardon," she said quickly. "I didn't mean to say anything disagreeable. I'm sure I'll be glad to come as often as you'll let me."

But Marcia wondered if that were true. Would she ever be

glad to go to the home of those severe-looking aunts? There were three. Perhaps the third one would be even more withered and harsh. Marcia shuddered slightly with the realization of a side of married life she'd never thought of before.

For a moment she longed for her father's house and the shelter of his loving protection, amply supported by her stepmother's capable, self-sufficient, comforting countenance. She feared she could never do justice to the position of David's wife, and David would be disappointed in her and sorry he accepted her sacrifice. She roused herself to do better and make no more blunders.

She praised the garden, the house, and the furnishings in eager, girlish words until the thin lips relaxed and the drawn muscles of the aunts' cheeks took on a less severe aspect. They liked to be appreciated and had taken pains with the house— for David's sake—not hers. They didn't want her thinking they did it for her sake.

David was to them a young god, and they wished to impress his young wife with his supremacy. They concluded long ago that no mere pretty young girl could appreciate David enough. They'd watched him from babyhood and pampered and petted and corrected him by turns, until if he hadn't had an angel's temperament, he'd have been spoiled.

"We did our best to make the house just as David would have wished it," said Aunt Amelia at last, a brief shadow of what answered for her smile crossing her face.

"We didn't at all approve of this big house or of David's setting up a separate place for himself," said Aunt Hortense, taking up her knitting again. "We thought it utterly unnecessary and uneconomical, when he might have brought his wife home to us. But he seemed to think you'd want a house to yourself, so we did the best we could."

From the martyrlike air in Aunt Hortense's words, Marcia felt herself to be the criminal, though she knew she was suffering vicariously. But she was suddenly thankful for being spared the trial of living daily under the scrutiny of these two and blessed David for his thoughtfulness, even though it wasn't meant for her. She went into pleased ecstasies once more over the house and its furnishings and ended with her pleasure over the piano.

Grim stillness fell on the room when she touched on that subject. The aunts plainly didn't approve of the piano. Marcia wondered if they always paused so long before speaking when they disapproved in order to show their displeasure. In fact, did they disapprove of everything?

"You'll want to be very careful of it," said Aunt Amelia, looking at the disputed article over her glasses. "It cost a good deal of money. Buying that was the most foolish thing I ever knew David to do."

"Yes," said Aunt Hortense, "you'll not want to use it much; it might get scratched. It has a fine polish. I'd keep it closed up except when I had company. You ought to be very proud to have a husband who could buy a thing like that. Not many have them. When I was a girl, my grandfather had a spinet, the only one for miles around, and it was taken great care of. The case hadn't a scratch on it."

Marcia had started toward the piano, intending to open it and play for her new relatives. But she halted midway across the room and returned to her seat after that speech. She felt she must just sit and hold her hands until time to get supper, while these dreadful aunts picked her apart, body, soul, and spirit.

At last she heard David's step and knew she might leave the room and put the tea things on the table.

Chapter 11

They got through the supper without any trouble, for the aunts brightened considerably at the supper table under David's genial influence. They came as near to worshiping David as one can a human being. David desired above all to blind their keen, I-told-you-so eyes and thus became his former cheerful self so they didn't notice how few loving references he made to his bride, who was decidedly in the background. The aunts, perhaps intentionally, wanted to show her a wife's true place—at least the true place of David's wife.

They'd allowed her to bring their things and help them on with capes and bonnets. And when they were ready to leave, Aunt Amelia put out a lifeless hand that felt in its silk glove like a dead fish in a net.

"Our sister Clarinda is desirous of seeing David's wife," she said to Marcia. "She asked us particularly to give you her love and tell you she wishes you to come to see her at the earliest possible moment. You know she's lame and can't easily get about."

"Young folks should always be ready to wait on their elders," said Aunt Hortense grimly. "Come as soon as you can—that is, if you think you can stand the smell of salt-rising."

Marcia's face flushed painfully, and she glanced quickly at David to see if he noticed what his aunt said. But David was already anticipating the moment when he'd be free to lay aside his mask and bury his face in his hands and his thoughts in sadness.

So the aunts went home in the early twilight, each with her

bonnet strings tied precisely, her lace gloves drawn smoothly over her bony hands, and her little knitting bag over her right arm. They walked up the shaded, elm-domed street, knowing that an air of former greatness still hovered about them wherever they went.

Marcia's heart sank as she cleared off the supper things. Was life always to be this way? Would she always be inspected by those two grim women, who seemed to possess nothing warm or loving or womanlike?

She felt as if she were standing outside a married life and looking on as one might gaze on a panorama. It was all new and painful, and she was a central figure expected to act through all the pictures. She glanced over at David's pale, grave face, set in its sadness, and a sharp pain pierced her heart. Would he ever get over it? Would life ever be more cheerful than it was now?

He spoke to her occasionally, in a pleasant, abstracted way, and lit a candle for her when the work was done, saying he hoped she'd rest well, that she must still be weary from the long journey. And so she went up to her room again.

She didn't go to bed at once but sat down by the window staring out on the moonlit street. The church across the way had held a meeting, and the people were filing out, calling pleasant good nights and going their various ways home. The moon was still bright and cast sharp shadows.

Marcia longed to get out into the night. If she could have gone downstairs without being heard, she'd have slipped out into the garden. But downstairs she could hear David pacing back and forth like some hurt, caged thing. Steadily, dully, he walked from the front hall back into the kitchen and back again. There was no escaping his notice. Marcia felt she might breathe freer in the open air, so she leaned out of her window and looked up and down the street, thinking. At last she bent her dark head on the window seat and wept alone.

The next morning at breakfast, David told her of the festivities planned in honor of their homecoming. He spoke as if they were a great trial they both must pass through to have any peace and expressed his gratitude again for her willingness to come with him and go through it.

Marcia had the impression, after he left for the office, that he felt she came merely for these few days of ceremony and was dismissed afterward, her duty done, to go home. A lump rose in her throat, and she suddenly wished very much it were so. If so, how much she'd enjoy queening it for a few days— except for David's sadness. But already, in spite of herself, she was starting to resent something in that sadness. It was a heavy burden she saw dimly would be harder to bear as the days passed. She hadn't yet begun to think of the time before her in years.

They were to go to the aunts' for tea that evening, and after tea David's old friends—rather, David's aunts' old friends— were coming to meet them. The aunts had planned this, but it seemed they hadn't counted her worthy to be told the plans and only divulged them to David. Marcia didn't think a little thing could annoy her so much, but she found it vexed her more as she worked.

With the beds made, the rooms in order, and the summer breeze blowing the green tassels on the window shades, Marcia went softly down like some half-guilty creature to the piano. She opened it and was soon lost in delight at the sounds her fingers brought forth.

She'd been playing perhaps half an hour when she became conscious of another presence in the room. She glanced up with a start. Peering into the shadowy room lighted only from the window behind her, she made out a head looking in at the door, the face almost hidden by a sunbonnet. She soon recognized her visitor from the day before but, for some reason, was annoyed to hear Miranda's voice.

"Morning!" she curtsied, coming in as soon as she perceived she was seen. "At it again? I been listening some time. It's as pretty as Silas Drew's harmoniker when he comes home evenings behind the cows."

Marcia drew her hands from the keys. Miranda's abrupt tone seemed out of harmony with her pensive mood this morning. She scarcely knew what to say and felt her reverie spoiled.

But Miranda was too full of her own errand to notice the clouded face and cool welcome. "Say, you can't guess how I got here. You're going over to the Spafford house tonight, ain't you? And a lot of folks'll be there. Of course we all know about it; it's been planned for months.

"My cousin Hannah Heath has an invite. You can't think how fond Miss Amelia and Miss Hortense are of her. Well, she was talking about what she'd wear. She had three frocks made last week, all frilled and fancy. She don't want to let folks think she's down in the mouth about David. She'll likely make up to your face a whole lot and pretend she's the best friend you've got in the world. But don't be too sure of her friendship. She's smooth as butter, but she can slap you in the face if you don't serve her purpose. She's given me many a one." The pale eyes snapped in unison with the color of her hair. "You see, I heard her talking to Grandma, and she said she'd give anything to know what you were wearing tonight."

"How curious!" said Marcia. "I don't see why she'd care," she added with cool indifference and a touch of haughtiness. Marcia knew she belonged to an old and honored family and had a trunk full of clothes that could vie with any Hannah Heath could display.

Miranda admired her manner and wished silently she could convey that coolness for her cousin Hannah to see.

"H'm!" giggled Miranda. "Well, she does! If you were going to wear blue, she'd put on her green. She's got one that'll kill any blue that's in the same room with it, and she looks real fine in it, too. So when she said she wanted to know so bad, Grandma said she'd send me over to know if you'd accept a jar of her fresh piccalilli, and mebbe I could find out about your clothes. The piccalilli's on the kitchen table. I left it when I came through. It's good, but there ain't any love in it." Miranda laughed sharply and returned to her subject again.

"You needn't be a mite afraid to tell me about it. I won't tell it straight. I'd just like to see what you're going to wear so I can keep her out of her tricks for once. Is your dress blue?"

Now the trunk upstairs contained a good amount of the color blue, for Kate was her bonniest in blue, and the particular dress made for this first significant gathering was blue. Marcia had accepted the fact as unalterable. The dress's mission must be fulfilled, however much she might wish to wear something else. But as Miranda spoke, the thought of rebellion crossed her mind. Why must she do as Kate? If she accepted the sacrifice of living Kate's life for her, she might at least live it in the most pleasant possible way. Surely she should be allowed to settle the dress matter for herself if she was old enough to be trusted away from home.

Kate had made a sweet rose-pink silk tissue. Madam Schuyler frowned on it as frivolous, and she didn't think it becoming to Kate. She had a fixed theory that people with blue eyes and golden hair should never wear pink or red. But Kate as usual had her own way and, with her wild rose complexion, looked like the wild rose itself in spite of blue eyes and golden hair.

Marcia knew from the minute the lovely pink thing entered the house that it was the very thing to set her off. Her dark eyes and hair made a charming contrast with the rose, and her complexion was even fresher than Kate's. She was suddenly eager to wear the frilly thing and outshine Hannah Heath beyond any chance of further trying. There were other dresses in the trunk. Why should she be confined to the stately blue one marked out for this occasion?

With sudden inspiration Marcia answered calmly, as if these tumultuous clothes possibilities hadn't been whirling through her brain in that second's hesitation: "I haven't quite decided what I'll wear. It's not important, I'm sure. Let's go and see the piccalilli. I'm very obliged to your grandmother, I'm sure. It was very kind of her."

Somewhat awed, Miranda followed her hostess into the kitchen. She couldn't reconcile this girl's face with her stately airs, but she liked her and told her so.

"I like you," she said fervently. "You remind me of one of Grandma's flowers, bright and independent and lively, with a spice and a color to 'em, and Hannah makes you think of one of them tall spikes of gladiolus all fixed up without any smell."

Marcia tried to smile over the doubtful compliment. Something about Miranda reminded her of Mary Ann. *Dear* Mary Ann! For suddenly she realized everything reminding her of her childhood, left behind forever, was dear. If she could see Mary Ann at this moment, she'd throw her arms about her neck and tell her she loved her. Perhaps this feeling made her gentler with Miranda than she might have been.

When Miranda was gone the precious play hour was gone, too. Marcia had only time to dash into the parlor, close the instrument, and rush to get dinner ready. But as she worked other thoughts occupied her. She was adjusting to her new environment and found many unexpected things to make it hard.

Here, for instance, was Hannah Heath. Why did there have to be a Hannah Heath, and what was she to her? Kate might feel jealous, indeed, but not she, not the unloved, unreal wife of David. She'd rather pity Hannah that David hadn't loved her instead of Kate, or pity David that he hadn't. But somehow she didn't and couldn't. Hannah Heath had become a living, breathing enemy to be met and conquered.

Marcia felt her fighting blood and the Schuyler in her rising. However little there was in her wifehood, its name at least was hers. The tale Miranda told was enough, if it were true, to put any woman into battle array. Marcia was puzzling over the question that has burdened every woman since the fatal day Eve made her great mistake.

David was silent and distracted at the dinner table. Absorbed in her own problems, Marcia didn't feel left out by it. She was trying to determine whether to blossom in pink or be crushed and set aside into insignificance in blue or choose a happy medium and wear another color. She ventured a timid little question before David went away again: Did he, would he, that is, was there anything, any word he'd like to say to her? Would she have to do anything tonight?

David looked at her in surprise. Why, no! He knew of nothing. Just speak pleasantly to everyone. He was sure she knew what to do. He always thought her well behaved. She had manners like any woman. She needn't feel shy. No one knew of her peculiar position, and he felt reasonably sure the story wouldn't soon get around. Her position would be thoroughly established before then. She needn't feel uncomfortable. He looked down at her, thinking he'd said all that was expected, but he felt the trouble in the girl's eyes and asked her gently if there was anything more.

"No," she said slowly, "unless, perhaps, I don't suppose you know what it would be proper for me to wear."

"Oh, that doesn't matter in the least," he replied promptly. "Anything. You always look nice. Why, I'll tell you—wear the dress you had on the night I came." Then he suddenly remembered the reason why that was a pleasant memory to him and that it wasn't for her sake at all, but for the sake of one who was lost to him forever. His face contracted with sudden pain, and Marcia, cut to the heart, read the meaning and felt sick and sore, too.

"Oh, I couldn't wear that," she said sadly. "It's only chintz. It wouldn't be nice enough, but thank you. I'll be all right. Don't trouble about me."

She forced a weak smile to send him from the house and keep him from knowing he hurt her. His words recalled the vision of her standing at the gate in the moonlight looking from the portal of her maidenhood into the vista of her womanhood. It seemed then so far away and bright and was now upon her in sad reality. If only she could have caught his sentence about the dress to her heart with joy and known he said it because he, too, had a happy memory about her in it, as she felt her dream man would!

She spread the available dresses on the bed. David's suggestion, while impossible, had given her an idea. There was a soft sheer white muslin with Kate's daintiest embroidering and edged with fine lace frills. Quaint and girlish, it was the sweetest and simplest in Kate's elaborate wardrobe. Yet from an artistic point of view, it was perhaps the most elegant.

Marcia dressed early, for David said he'd be home by four o'clock and they'd start as soon afterward as he could get ready. His aunts wished to show her the old garden before dark.

She hesitated over how to arrange her hair. She rebelled at Kate's style. It didn't suit her face or her feeling. It made her seem unlike herself, or unlike the self she ever wished to be. It suited Kate, but not her. Suddenly she pulled her hair down from the top of her head and loosened its rich waves about her face, then twisted it softly behind, low on her neck, falling over her delicate ears. She was following instinct, not fashion, but conformed enough to the day's styles to keep from looking odd. Marcia couldn't help but notice it was more becoming than the style she'd worn for her wedding.

She put on the sheer white embroidered frock and, as a last touch, pinned about her throat the bit of black velvet with a single pearl that had been her mother's. It was the bit of black velvet she had worn the night David came. She was glad to follow his suggestion at least in that.

She'd just finished dressing when she heard David's step on the walk. He came in out of the sunshine and saw the girl in the shadow of the hall waiting shyly for him. Startled, he passed his hand over his eyes and looked at her again. She was beautiful. Even in the midst of his sadness he had to admit it. He smiled at her and felt another pang of condemnation for taking this beauty from some other man's lot perhaps and using it to shield him from the world's exclamation about his own lonely life.

"You've done it admirably. I don't see anything left to be desired," he said in his pleasant voice that used to make her heart flutter with pride that her brother-to-be was pleased with her. It fluttered now but with a wider sweep to its wings and a longer flight ahead of the thought.

The young wife accepted the compliment demurely. Then she folded her white muslin cape about her shoulders, put on the new lace gloves, and tied the white strings of a shirred gauze bonnet with tiny rosebuds beneath her chin.

Once more the bride was the center of attention, stared at by townspeople; only this time she walked on brick pavement, not oak stairs, and most of the eyes that observed her were sheltered behind green jalousies. Nonetheless, she was conscious of them as she accompanied David. Her eyes rested on the ground or glanced at things in the distance when they weren't lifted to her husband's face at some word he spoke. Just as she imagined in her girlish thoughts that her sister would do, so she did. And after what seemed an interminable walk, though it was only four village blocks, they arrived at the Spafford house.

Chapter 12

"This is your aunt Clarinda!"

The harshly spoken pronoun Aunt Hortense used held a challenge. Marcia felt she wished to remind her that her old life and relatives had passed away, and she had nothing now but David's. She shrank from looking, expecting to find the third and older aunt much sourer than the other two. But she finally raised her eyes to meet a gentle face set in a soft white cap with white ribbons flying. Though the old lady leaned on a crutch, she gave the impression she'd fairly flown in her gladness to welcome her new niece. Her face shone with the light of a repressed nature set free as she gazed upon the young woman. And Marcia felt herself folded in loving arms in an embrace her own repressed, loving nature returned with heartiness. At last she'd found a friend!

They walked out into the garden almost immediately, and Aunt Clarinda insisted upon hobbling along beside Marcia, though her sisters protested it would be too hard for her that warm afternoon. Marcia felt the kind eyes on her when she talked and knew at least one aunt was satisfied with her as a wife for David. Her eyes would travel from David to Marcia and back again to David, and when they met Marcia's, they held no disparagement in them.

The walk through the old garden was tiresome, for it was laid out in the ways of the past generation and bordered with much funereal box. Amelia and Hortense took the new member of the family through every path and told her how each spot was associated with some event in the family history.

Occasionally they paused solemnly to impress the new member of the house, and Amelia wiped her eyes with her carefully folded handkerchief.

Marcia felt very much like laughing. She was sure that if Kate had been obliged to pass through this ordeal, she would have giggled out at once and said some shockingly funny thing that would have horrified the aunts beyond forgiveness. The thought of this nerved her to keep a sober face. She wondered what David thought of it all. But when she looked at him, she didn't wonder anymore; he stood like one waiting for a dull ceremony to end. He didn't even see how it must strike the girl who was going through it all for him, for his thoughts were drifting on the tide of sorrow against the rocks of the might-have-been.

They went in to tea presently, just when the garden was its loveliest with a tinge of the setting sun. Marcia longed to run up and down the paths like a child and call to them to catch her if they could.

By sharp contrast, the stately house was dark and gloomy.

"You're coming up to my room for a few minutes after supper," whispered Aunt Clarinda to Marcia as they passed into the dark hall.

The supper table was lighted by an old silver candelabra whose wavering flames cast a grotesque shadow on the different faces. Beside her plate the young bride saw an ostentatious plate of puffy soda biscuits; involuntarily her eyes searched the table for the bread plate.

Almost at once Aunt Clarinda passed the bread with a smile to Marcia. With an answering smile she took a generous slice and instantly heard the other two aunts exclaim in chorus: "Oh, don't pass her the bread, Clarinda. Take it away, sister, quick! She doesn't like salt-rising! It's unpleasant to her!"

Then with blazing cheeks the girl protested that she wished to keep the bread, that they were mistaken; she hadn't said it was obnoxious to her but had merely given them her step-mother's opinion when they asked. They must excuse her for her apparent rudeness, for she hadn't intended to hurt them. She presumed salt-rising bread was very nice; it looked beautiful. This was a long speech for Marcia to make before so many strangers. David looked at her with troubled eyes, wondering what it all meant, and she felt she should do anything to save him from more suffering or annoyance.

He said little. He seemed to perceive there'd been an unpleasant prelude to this and perhaps knew from former experience it was best to change the subject. He launched into a detailed account of their wedding journey.

Marcia was grateful to him, for when she took the first brave bite into the very puffy, very white slice of bread, she decided it was much worse than what had been baked for their homecoming. It not only justified her stepmother's opinion, but it was also sour. She imagined whole calendars full of such suppers with the aunts and this bread and shuddered inwardly. Could she ever learn to like or even tolerate it? She doubted it. Then she swallowed and realized she'd accomplished the impossible once; she could again. But she must eat slowly; otherwise she might have to eat a second slice!

David was kind and roused himself to help his helper. Perhaps something in her girlish beauty and helplessness for his sake appealed to him. At least his eyes sought hers often with a tender interest to see if she was comfortable. And one time, when Aunt Amelia asked if they stopped anywhere for rest on their journey, his eyes sought Marcia's with a twinkling reminder of their roadside nap.

"Once, Aunt Amelia," he answered. "No, it wasn't a regular inn. It was quieter than that. Not many people stopping there."

Marcia's merry laugh almost bubbled forth, but she suppressed it just in time, horrified to think what Aunt Hortense would say. But after David said that, her heart felt a little lighter, and she took a big bite from the salt-rising and smiled as she swallowed it. There were worse things in the world, after all, than salt-rising. And smothering it in Aunt Amelia's peach preserves made it quite bearable.

Aunt Clarinda took her to her room after supper and left the other two sisters with their beloved idol, David. In their stately parlor lit with many candles in honor of the occasion, they talked quietly with him. Their hushed voices suggested condolence with his misfortune of marrying out of the family and disapproval with the married state in general. How their hard, loving hearts would have been wrung if they'd known the truth! And, strange anomaly, how much deeper their antagonism would have been toward Marcia! Just because she dared to think herself fit for David, belonging as she did to her renegade sister, Kate.

But they didn't know, and for this David was profoundly thankful. Those weren't the days of rapid transit, telegraph, and telephone, or even much letter writing; otherwise the story would probably have reached the aunts even before the bride and bridegroom arrived home. As it was, David hoped to keep his tragedy from his aunts' ears forever. Patiently he answered their questions concerning the wedding, questions intended to show whether David received his due respect and whether the family he so greatly honored felt the burden of that honor sufficiently.

Upstairs in her old-fashioned room, Aunt Clarinda took Marcia's face in her two wrinkled hands and looked into her eyes. "Dear child! You look just as I did when I was young. You wouldn't think it of me now, would you? But it's true. I might not have become such a dried-up old thing if I'd had somebody like David. I'm so glad you've got David. He'll take good care of you. He's a dear boy. He's always been good to me. But you mustn't let the others crush the roses out of your cheeks. They crushed mine out. They wouldn't let me have my life the way I wanted it, and the pink in my cheeks went back into my heart a good many years ago. But they can't spoil your life, for you've got David, and that's worth everything."

Then she kissed her on the cheeks and let her go. But that one moment gave Marcia a glimpse into another life and connected her with Aunt Clarinda in loving sympathy.

When they came into the parlor, the other two aunts looked up with a quick, suspicious glance from one to the other and then gazed disapprovingly at Marcia. They rather resented her prettiness. Hannah had been their favorite, and Hannah was beautiful in their eyes. They wanted no other to outshine her. Of course they'd be proud enough to hear their neighbors say their nephew's wife was beautiful.

After a chilling pause in which David was wondering anew at Marcia's beauty, Aunt Hortense asked, as though it were omitted from the former examination, "Did you ever make a shirt?"

"Oh, plenty of them!" said Marcia, so relieved she fairly bubbled. "I think I could make a shirt with my eyes shut."

Aunt Clarinda beamed at her. She'd never succeeded in making a shirt right. It was one thing her sisters had against her. Anyone who couldn't make a good shirt was deficient. She'd tried year after year, ripping out gusset, seam, and band, after putting them on upside down or inside out. But she delighted that the new girl, who was going to take her old self's place in her heart and live out all the beautiful but lost things, had mastered this one great accomplishment in which she'd failed so supremely.

But Aunt Hortense wasn't pleased. True, it was to her one of seven virtues a young wife should possess, and she'd carefully instructed Hannah Heath for a number of years back, while Hannah bungled out a couple for her father. But Aunt Hortense was sure if Hannah ever became David's wife, she herself might still make most of his shirts. That had been her happy task ever since David wore a shirt, and she hoped to continue until she left this mortal clay. Therefore, Aunt Hortense wasn't pleased, even though David's wife wasn't lacking, and though she imagined telling her neighbors the next day how many shirts David's wife had made.

"Well, David won't need any for some time," she said grimly. "I made him a dozen before he was married."

Marcia reflected that it seemed impossible to enter the good graces of either Aunt Hortense or Aunt Amelia. Amelia then took her turn at a question.

"Hortense," said she, with an ominous inflection in the word, "have you asked our new niece what name she desires us to call her?"

"I have not," said Hortense solemnly, "but I intend to do so immediately." Then both pairs of steely eyes were leveled at the girl.

Marcia suddenly faced a question she hadn't considered, and David started upright from his position on the haircloth sofa. She saw the pain and perplexity in his face, and her own courage gathered to brave it out in some way. The color flew to her cheeks and rose slowly in David's through heavy veins that swelled in his neck, but his lips were white. He felt that a moment had come he couldn't bear to face.

Then, with a slight hesitation and a sweet look, Marcia answered. And though her voice trembled, her eyes looked bravely into the battalion of steel ones.

"I'd like you to call me 'Marcia,' if you please."

" 'Marcia'!" Aunt Hortense snipped the word out as if with scissors of surprise.

But Aunt Amelia's mouth relaxed, and she heaved a relieved sigh. "Marcia" was much better than "Kate," more classical, more to be compared with "Hannah," for instance.

"Well, I'm glad!" she allowed herself to remark. "David has

been calling you 'Kate' till it made me sick, such a frivolous name and no sense in it either. 'Marcia' sounds quite sensible. I suppose 'Katherine' is your middle name. Do you spell it with a *K* or a *C*?"

But the knocker sounded on the street door, sparing Marcia the torture of a reply. She dared not look at David's face, no doubt expressing pain, and hoped the subject wouldn't come up again.

The guests were arriving. Old Mrs. Heath and her daughter-in-law and granddaughter came first.

Hannah was beautiful. She knew how to manage her shapely hands with their long white fingers and carry her height gracefully. Her hair was arranged on top of her head in puffs, ending in ringlets that strayed over her temple, ears, and neck. She wore a green silk dress—green enough to take away the heart from anything blue. The bride realized with a pang that the color might have been worn with an unkind purpose. Nevertheless, Hannah fascinated Marcia. She resolved to think the best of her and befriend her if possible. Why, after all, should she be blamed for wanting David? Wasn't he to be admired and desired? It was unwomanly, of course, that she'd let it be known, but perhaps her relatives were more to blame than she was.

Hannah chose to be effusive and condescending to the bride. She gave the impression she and David had been like brother and sister all their lives and that she might have been his choice if she'd chosen but was glad he'd found someone to console him. She didn't say this in so many words, but Marcia found that impression left after the evening was over.

With sweet dignity Marcia received her introductions, given in Aunt Amelia's most commanding tone: "Our niece, Marcia!"

"Marshy, Marshy!" the bride heard old Mrs. Heath murmur to Miss Spafford. "Why, I thought 'twas to be Kate!"

"Her name is Marcia," said Aunt Amelia in a most satisfied

tone. "You must have misunderstood."

Marcia caught a questioning look in Mrs. Heath's eyes, bright but not friendly.

She wished David were beside her and looked across the room at him. His face had recovered its usual calmness, though he looked pale. He was talking on his favorite theme with old Mr. Heath: the newly invented steam engine and its possibilities. He'd forgotten everything else for the time, and his face was animated as he tried to answer William Heath's arguments against it.

Marcia would have given a good deal to slip in beside David on the sofa and listen to the discussion. She wanted to know how he'd answer this man who could be so insufferably wise. But she had other work, and her attention was brought back to her own uncomfortable part by Hannah Heath's voice.

"Come right ovah heah, Mistah Skinnah, if you want to meet the bride. You must speak verra nice to me, or I shan't introduce you at all."

A tall, lanky man with stiff, sandy hair was making his way around the room. His small mouth was puckered a little as if he might be going to whistle, and a fuzz of sandy whiskers made a hedge down either cheek; otherwise he was clean shaven. He didn't look brilliant, and he certainly wasn't handsome, but he seemed to have an inoffensive desire to please. Introduced as Mr. Lemuel Skinner, he bowed low over Marcia's hand, said a few embarrassed sentences, and turned to Hannah Heath with relief. In his eyes Hannah was evidently a shining light.

But she'd turned her back on him now, leaving him to Marcia's mercies, and was engaged in talking to a younger man. "Harry Temple, from New York," Lemuel explained to Marcia.

That young man had large, lazy eyes and heavy dark hair with a discontented look on his face and a looseness about his lips that Marcia didn't like, though she had to admit he was handsome. Something about him reminded her of Captain Leavenworth, and she instinctively shrank from him. But Harry Temple wanted to talk to Marcia and so managed to draw her into a corner of the room away from others. Marcia wasn't flattered by the man's attentions and, in fact, wanted to be at the other end of the room listening to the conversation.

She listened as intently as she might between sentences, and her keen ears caught a word or two of what David was saying. She didn't care so much about the new railroad project, though it was interesting enough, as she wanted to watch and listen to David.

At first Marcia didn't hear some of the pretty things Harry Temple was telling her. But after a time she realized she must have made a good impression, and the flush in her cheeks deepened. She talked little.

He asked if she weren't bored with this little town and bemoaned her lot when he learned she hadn't much experience there. Then he asked if she'd ever been to New York and told of its attractions. He mentioned some concerts and immediately gained Marcia's attention. She responded eagerly to his words. Seeing he'd interested her at last, he kept on, and what he didn't know he fabricated. He'd been about the world and gathered enough superficial knowledge to do this. Thus he used a few musical terms and brought before Marcia's vivid imagination the performance of Handel's *Creation* given in Boston and of certain musical events to be attempted soon in New York.

He admitted he could play a little on the harpsichord. When he learned Marcia could play also and possessed a piano, he invited himself to play it.

Marcia found to her dismay she seemed to have invited him to come some afternoon when her husband was away. She only said politely she'd like to hear him play and expressed her great delight in music. He'd done the rest, but somehow it happened, and she didn't know what to do.

It troubled her, and she turned again toward the other end of the room. Almost everyone's attention was riveted upon the group discussing the pros and cons of the railroad, and David was at the center.

"Let's go over and hear what they're saying," she said eagerly.

"Oh, it's all stupid politics and arguments about that ridiculous railroad scheme. You wouldn't enjoy it," answered the young man. He saw in Marcia a beautiful young soul, the only one who'd really attracted him since leaving New York, and he wished to enjoy himself.

That she was married didn't matter to him. He felt secure in his own attractions. He always whiled away the time with whomever he chose, so why should a simple village maiden resist him? And this was an unusual one, he noticed.

Nevertheless, he was obliged to stroll after her, for she also suddenly realized they were in their corner a long time and saw Aunt Amelia's cold eyes fastened upon her.

"The farmers would be ruined!" Mr. Heath was saying. "Why, all the horses would have to be killed, because they'd be wholly useless if this new fandango came in, and then where would a market for wheat and oats be?"

"Yes, I've heard some say the hens wouldn't lay because of the noise," ventured Lemuel Skinner.

"I tell you, Dave," Mr. Heath added, "it can't be done. It's impractical. Why, no car could advance against the wind."

"They told Columbus he couldn't sail around the earth, but he did it!"

Stillness engulfed the room, for Marcia's clear voice had answered Mr. Heath's excited tones. She didn't know she was going to speak aloud. She was used to speaking her mind sometimes with her father but seldom with others around.

Now she was confused to think what she'd done.

The aunts, Amelia and Hortense, were shocked. A woman shouldn't speak on such subjects. She should be silent and leave such topics to her husband.

"Deah me, she's strong-minded, isn't she?" said Hannah Heath to Lemuel.

"Quite so!" murmured Lemuel.

But Marcia wasn't without consolation, for David flashed an approving look at her and made room for her beside him on the sofa. It was almost like belonging to him for a minute or two. Marcia felt her heart glow with something new and pleasant.

Mr. Heath drew his heavy brows together and looked at her grimly over his spectacles, poking his bristly underlip out in astonishment. He was bewildered to be answered by a gentle, pretty woman, all frills like his own daughter. He was used to considering a young woman like a kitten, and suddenly the kitten had lifted a velvet paw and struck him squarely in the face. He felt claws in the blow, too, for a truth behind her words set the room to mocking him.

"Well, Dave, you've got your wife well trained already!" he said laughing, concluding it was best to smile on the defeat. "She knows just when to come in and help when your side's getting weak!"

They served cake and raspberry vinegar then, and in a little while everyone went home. It was late, and the lights in most houses were out or burning dimly in upper stories. The guests' voices sounded subdued in the misty waning moonlight air. Marcia could hear Hannah Heath's voice ahead giggling to Harry Temple and Lemuel Skinner, as they walked on each side, while her father, mother, and grandmother came more slowly.

David drew Marcia's hand inside his arm and walked with her quietly down the street, hushing their steps instinctively so they might seem more removed from the others. They were both tired from the unusual excitement and strain, and each was glad of the other's silence.

But when they reached their own doorstep, David said, "You spoke well, child. You must have thought about these things."

Marcia felt a sob of joy rising in her throat. Then he wasn't angry with her and didn't disapprove as the two aunts had.

Aunt Clarinda had kissed her good night and murmured, "You're a bright girl, Marcia, and you'll make a good wife for David. You'll come soon to see me, won't you?"

That made her glad, but David's words were so good and unexpected she could hardly hide her happy tears.

"I was afraid I was forward," murmured Marcia in the shadow of the front stoop.

"Not at all, child. I like to hear a woman speak her mind— that is, if she has any mind to speak. That can't be said of all women. There's Hannah Heath, for instance. I don't believe she'd know a railroad project from an essay on ancient art."

After that the house seemed pleasant as they entered it, and Marcia went up to her rest with a lighter heart.

But she didn't know she impressed all who saw her that night as being beautiful and wise.

The aunts wouldn't express it even to each other—for they felt duty bound to discountenance her boldness in speaking out before the men and making herself so prominent by joining in their discussions. But each in spite of her convictions felt a deep satisfaction that their neighbors saw what a beautiful, bright wife David selected. They even felt triumphant over their favorite Hannah and thought secretly that Marcia compared well with her in every way. But they wouldn't have told this even to themselves, no, not for worlds.

So the gossipy town slept, and the young bride became a part of its daily life.

Chapter 13

*A*fter that, Marcia found life more familiar and interesting and her daily household duties pleasant.

Many other gatherings were held in honor of the bride and groom, with teas and evening calls, and Marcia became better acquainted with the people and grew to like some of them. Still, she felt it was pain and weariness to David.

But she was young, and it was only natural for her to enjoy her sudden promotion to matron and the attention paid her. It was a wonder her head wasn't turned, living as she did to herself, with no one to confide in. For David withdrew to such an extent she didn't like to trouble him with anything.

Only two days after the evening at the old Spafford house, David came home to tea with ashen face and haggard eyes. He scarcely tasted his supper and said he'd lie down, that his head ached. Marcia heard him sigh deeply as he left the room. That afternoon the post had brought him Kate's letter.

Sadly Marcia put away the tea things, for she couldn't eat anything either. She went up to her room and sat looking out into the quiet, darkening summer night, wondering what added sorrow had come to David.

David's face was pale the next morning. He drank a cup of coffee feverishly, then took his hat but paused at the door. He came back and said he wouldn't go if Marcia wouldn't mind taking a message for him. His head felt bad. She only needed to say he was detained and tell the man to go on with things as they'd planned. Marcia was ready at once to go.

She delivered her message in a straightforward manner with

a touch of matronly dignity, which added to her charm. She smiled openly in friendship, leaving the clerk and typesetters eager to serve their employer's wife. They watched her as she walked gracefully down the street and then returned to their work.

Harry Temple also watched her as she left the office. Stepping from the store where he'd been lingering, he crossed the street to intercept her as she turned the corner.

"Good morning, Mrs. Spafford," he said. "Are you going to your home? Then our ways lie together. May I walk beside you?"

Marcia smiled and tried to be gracious, but she wanted to enjoy the day alone and not talk.

Harry mentioned receiving a letter from a friend in Boston who'd heard a great chorus rendered recently. He wasn't sure of the composer's name because he read the letter hurriedly. He saw she was more interested in music than anything he said, racked his brains for all the music talk he'd ever heard, and made up what he didn't know, which wasn't hard to do, for Marcia was fairly ignorant on the subject.

At the door they paused. Marcia was wondering how David felt and longed to do something for him, while Harry Temple was admiring her features, the dainty chin, the curve of her cheek, the sweep of her eyelashes.

"I haven't forgotten my promise to play for you," he said lightly, watching to see if the rose flush would steal into her cheek and the deep light into her eyes. "How about this afternoon? Will you be at home and free?"

But Marcia didn't welcome him as he'd hoped. Instead, a troubled look came into her eyes.

"I'm afraid it won't be possible this afternoon," said Marcia. "That is—I expect to be at home, but—I'm not sure of being free."

"Ah! I see!" He raised his eyebrows. "Someone else more

fortunate than I is coming?"

Marcia didn't understand his insinuation, but the color rushed into her cheeks. She instinctively felt something unpleasant in his tone, something below her standard of morals or culture. She didn't know what it was but felt she must protect herself.

"Oh, no," she said quickly, "I'm not expecting anyone at all, but Mr. Spafford had a severe headache this morning, and the sound of the piano might make it worse. I think it would be better for you to come another time, although he may be better by then."

"Oh, I see! Your husband's at home!" he said. "I understand perfectly. I'll come some other time," he added with a peculiar smile, then left quickly.

Marcia was still troubled as she saw him round the corner. She went inside, stood at the dining room window, and gazed out on the Heaths' hollyhocks behind the picket fence, wondering what he could have meant and why he smiled in that hateful way. She didn't like him or think she'd like to hear him play. Something about him reminded her of Captain Leavenworth, and now that she saw it, she didn't care to have him about.

With a sigh she turned to fix a dinner she feared wouldn't be eaten. When it was finished and steaming on the table, she went and tapped on David's door. A voice hoarse with emotion and weariness answered.

"Dinner's ready. Isn't your head any better, David?" The caressing in his name wrung David's heart. If it were his Kate calling him, his heart would leap with joy! His headache would disappear, and he'd be with her in an instant.

For Kate's letter had its desired effect. Her wrongdoings, her crowning outrage of his noble intentions, were forgotten in the one little plaintive appeal she breathed in a minor wail throughout that treacherous letter, treacherous alike to her husband and to the one who still loved her. As Kate did with everyone, she blinded him to her faults and put herself in the light of an abused maiden in a predicament through no fault of her own.

David's anger was sometimes hot enough to erase the mist of fantasy Kate had woven about herself and let him see her as she was. At such times David confessed she must be heartless. Bright as she was, she couldn't have been so easily persuaded into running away with a man she didn't love. He'd never found it so easy to persuade her against her will. Did she love him? Had she truly loved him, and was she suffering now?

His soul writhed in agony to think of her as the wife of another against her will. If only he might rescue her. If only he might kill that other man! Then he confronted the thought of murder. Never before had he felt hatred for a human being.

Then his heart would soften toward him as he felt how the other must have loved his little wild rose! And his mind would whirl with mingled emotions, and he'd pause and pray for steadiness to think and know what was right.

Around and around he argued through the long morning hours, always ending abruptly with the thought that he could do nothing but bear it. Kate, after all, the Kate he loved with his whole soul, had done it and must therefore be to blame. Then he'd read her letter over, burning every word of it on his brain, until the piteous minor appeal tortured him and he'd try again to unravel the snarl and bring peace.

Like a sound from another world came Marcia's voice, its sweetness reminding him of that other lost voice.

And in the midst of his torture, his physical self answered gently that he didn't want any dinner; his head was no better; he was grateful for her thinking of him; and he'd take the tea she offered if it wasn't too much trouble.

Marcia hurried to the kitchen again and prepared a tray, not even glancing at the dinner table ready for its guest. Back she went to his door, an eager light in her eyes, as if she'd obtained audience to a king.

He opened the door this time and took the tray from her with a smile of ashen hue that fell like a pall upon Marcia's soul. She fled from it to her room, where she flung herself on her knees beside her bed and buried her face in the pillows. There she knelt, unmindful of the dinner waiting or the bright day shining. She didn't know whether she prayed or wept. Her heart was crying out for this cloud of sorrow to be lifted from David.

She might have knelt there until night if she hadn't heard a knock on the front door. She smoothed her rumpled hair, dashed some water on her eyes, and ran down.

It was the clerk from the office with a letter for her. The post chaise had brought it that afternoon, and he thought she'd like to have it at once since it was postmarked from her home. Would she tell Mr. Spafford when he returned—he took it for granted David was out of town for the day—that everything was going all right at the office during his absence and the paper was ready to go to press?

After he left, Marcia flew up to her room to read the letter, which she could tell was from Mary Ann. Never had Mary Ann's handwriting looked so pleasant. A letter was rare, and this one to Marcia in her distressed state seemed like a miracle. It began in Mary Ann's abrupt way and recalled the world of her home since she'd gone. A few days had passed, scarcely even weeks; yet it seemed half a lifetime to the girl thrust so suddenly into womanhood without the love and close companionship that usually make desolation impossible.

The letter began:

Dear Marsh,

I expect you think it odd of me to write so soon. I ain't much on writing, you know, but something happened right after you left and has kept right on happening that I feel I'd like to tell you. Don't mind my mistakes. I'm thankful you ain't the schoolteacher, or I'd never write as long as I'm living, but anyhow I'm going to tell you about it.

The night you went away, I was standing down by the gate under the old elm. I had on my best things yet from the wedding and hated to have the day over and have to put on my old calico tomorrow morning again and wash dishes just the same. I couldn't bear to have the world just the same now you was gone.

Well, I heard someone coming down the street, and who do you think it was? Why, Hanford Weston. He came right up to the gate and stopped. I don't know's he ever spoke two words to me in my life. Well, he stopped and spoke, and he looked so sad, seemed like I knew what he was feeling sad about, and I told him all about you getting married instead of your sister. He looked at me like he couldn't move for a while, and his face was as white as that marble man in the cemetery over Squire Hancock's grave. He grabbed the gate real hard, and I thought he was going to fall.

I felt awful sorry for him. Something came in my throat like a big stone, and my eyes got all blurred with the moonlight. He looked real handsome. I just couldn't help thinking you ought to see him.

By and by he got his voice back, and we talked a lot about you. He told me how he used to watch you when you was a little girl. You used to sit in the church pew across from his father's, and he could just see your big eyes over the top of the door. He says he always thought he'd marry you when he grew up. Then when you went to school and was so bright, he tried hard to study so you'd think him good enough for you. He owned up he was a bad speller and tried to do better, but it didn't come natural. So he thought maybe if he was a good farmer, you wouldn't mind about the spelling. He hired out to his father for the summer and was trying to be the kind of man 'twould suit you.

Then when he was plowing and planning what kind of house he'd build, here comes the coach and you in it! He said he thought the sky and fields was all mixed up and his heart was going out of him. He couldn't work anymore and started out to see what it meant.

He told it more like poetry, Marsh, the kind in our reader about Lord Ullin's daughter. I didn't know Hanford could talk like that. His words were pretty but kind of sorrowful. And it come over me you ought to know. You're married, of course, and can't help it now, but 'tain't every girl has a boy care for her like that from the time she's a baby with a red hood on, and you ought to know 'bout it, fer it wasn't Hanford's fault he didn't have time to tell you. He's just been living fer you fer a number of years, and it's kind of hard on him.

'Course you may not care, being you're married and have a fine house and lots of clo'es of your own and a good time. It seems, though, as if somebody ought to comfort him. I'd like to try if you don't mind. He does seem to like to talk about you to me, and I feel so sorry for him I guess I could comfort him a little, for it seems as if it would be the nicest thing in the world to have someone like you that way for years, just as they do in books. Only every time I think about comforting him, I think he belongs to you and it ain't right.

So, Marsh, you just say if you're willing for me to try to comfort him a little and make up to him fer what he lost in you, being as you're married and fixed so nice yourself. I know I ain't pretty like you and can't hold my head proud and step high as you always did, even when you was little, but I can feel, and perhaps that's something. Anyhow, Hanford's been down three times to talk about you to me, and if you don't mind, I'm going to let him come some more. But if you mind the leastest little bit, say so. Things are mixed in this world,

*and I don't want to trample any other person's feelings, much
less you who've always been my best friend and always will be
as long as I live, I guess.*

*It's lonesome here without you, and I hope you won't forget
me. If it wasn't for comforting Hanford, I shouldn't care much
for anything. I can't think of you a grown-up woman. Do you
feel different? I s'pose you wouldn't climb a fence or run
through the pasture lot for anything now. I wish I could see
you. And now, Marsh, I want you to write right off and tell
what to do about comforting Hanford, and if you've any message to send him, I think it would be real nice. I hope you've got
a good husband and are happy.*

> *From your devoted and loving schoolmate,*
> *Mary Ann Fothergill*

Marcia laid down the letter and buried her face in her
hands. To her, too, had come a thrust which must search her
life and change it. So while David wrestled with his sorrow,
Marcia entered upon the knowledge of her own heart.

Something in Mary Ann's revelation of Hanford Weston's
feelings toward her touched her immeasurably. If Hanford had
come to her and told her of his love before she left, she'd have
turned from him in dismay, almost disgust, and told him they
were both children, so how could they talk of love? She could
never have loved him. She'd have felt it instantly, and her
mocking laugh might have helped save him from sorrow. But
now, with miles between them and solemn marriage vows separating them forever, her own youth locked up until eternity
perhaps set it free, and no hope of a girl's bright dreams, could
she turn from even a schoolboy's love without passing tenderness, such as she'd never have felt if she hadn't come away from
it all? Told in Mary Ann's blunt way, with her crude attempts
at pathos, it reached her as it couldn't otherwise.

With her own new view of life, she could sympathize better

with another's disappointment. Perhaps her own loneliness gave her pity for another. Whatever it was, Marcia's heart turned toward Hanford Weston with gratitude. She felt she'd been loved, even though it was impossible for that love to be returned, and whatever happened she wouldn't go unloved to the end of her days.

Suddenly, out of her perplexing thoughts, she realized what was lacking in her life. She'd never felt it and probably wouldn't have now if she hadn't thus stepped into a place beyond her years. As she read and reread that letter, she felt as if she lived years that afternoon, changing her life from then on. She wasn't sorry she couldn't go back and live out her girlhood and have it crowned with Hanford Weston's love. Not at all. She knew he could never be anything to her, but she thought he could have given her something, in his clumsy way, that now she could never have from any man, since she was David's, and David couldn't love her that way, of course.

Concluding this, she arose and wrote a letter giving Mary Ann Fothergill all right, title, and claim to Hanford Weston's affections, past, present, and future. In it she sent him a message to smooth his ruffled feelings, with her pretty thanks for his youthful adoration; to comfort his sorrow with the thought it must have been a hallucination, that someday he would find his true ideal he'd only thought he had found in her; and to send him on his way rejoicing with her blessings and good wishes for a happy life.

As for Mary Ann, for once she received Marcia's love; for homesick Marcia felt more tenderness toward her than ever before. And her loving messages set Mary Ann in a delighted flutter as she laid plans for comforting Hanford Weston.

Chapter 14

David slowly recovered his poise. But the fact remained there was nothing he could do. At times the wretched truth rose to the surface, that Kate was at fault; having done the deed she should abide by it and not try to bind him. But he couldn't often think this way. Most of the time he mourned for the lovely girl he'd lost.

As for Marcia, she came and went unobtrusively, making things comfortable for David, though he scarcely noticed. At times he roused himself to be polite to her and amuse her, as if she were visiting him as a favor and he felt duty bound to pass the time pleasantly. But she troubled him so little that he usually forgot her. Whenever they were invited to a public function, he told her apologetically, as though she must be as bored as he, and regretted it was necessary to go to carry out their mutual agreement.

Marcia was delighted at every chance to go out and find something to drive away her new thoughts. But she covered her pleasure and dressed herself in the clothes made for her sister, hating them secretly, and was always ready when he came for her. David had nothing to complain of in his wife, as far as outward duty was concerned, but he was too busy with his own heart's bitterness to recognize it.

One afternoon, on a day when David had gone out of town and didn't expect to return until late in the evening, Marcia heard a knock at the door.

The knock had something womanish in it, she thought, and she wondered, smoothing her hair, if it could be the aunts making their fortnightly afternoon penance visit. She glanced into the parlor, hoping all was right, and was relieved she'd closed the piano. The aunts would consider it a breach of housewifely decorum to allow a moment's dust to settle upon its sacred keys.

But the aunts weren't standing on the stoop. Harry Temple was, smiling and bowing with assurance of his own welcome.

Marcia wasn't glad to see him and felt a sudden unreasoning alarm.

"You're all alone this time, sweet lady, aren't you?" he asked with easy nonchalance, as he entered the hall without invitation.

"Sir!" said Marcia, half frightened, half wondering.

But he smiled at her and closed the door himself.

"Your good man is out this time, isn't he?" he smiled again.

Marcia didn't return the smile. Why did he speak as if he knew where David was and seemed to be pleased he was away?

"My husband isn't in at present," she said guardedly. "Did you wish to see him?"

She was beautiful as she stood there in the wide hall, and he felt a strong desire to take her in his arms and tell her so. But he feared, from something he saw in her eyes, that she might run away too soon. So he only smiled and said his business with her husband could wait until another time; meanwhile, he'd called to fulfill his promise to play for her.

She took him into the darkened parlor and offered him the stiffest haircloth chair. But he walked straight over to the instrument and, with none of her reverence, flung back the coverings, threw open the lid, and sat down.

He ran his fingers over the keys as though he were at home among them, light little airs dripping like dew from a glistening grass blade. Marcia sensed butterflies and buzzing bees and flowers dancing on delicate stems, with a blue sky filled with the sound of lily bells. The music he played was what would be styled "popular" today, for this man was master of nothing except having a good time. He played quick jingles that to the puritanic-bred girl suggested only a glad heart bubbling over. But he meant for it to make her heart flutter and her foot beat time to the tripping measure. In his world, feet were attuned to lively music.

But Marcia stood quietly a little away from the instrument, her eyes bright with the melody and her hands clasped, absorbed with the music. Unknowingly, Marcia was standing where the light from the window fell across her face and every expression as she followed the music was visible. The young man gazed, almost as pleased with the lovely face as Marcia was with the music.

At last he drew a chair near his own.

"Come and sit down," he said, "and I'll sing to you. You didn't know I could sing, too, did you? Oh, I can. But you must sit down, for I couldn't sing right when you're standing."

He ended with his fascinating smile, and Marcia sat down shyly. She drew the chair a little back from where he'd placed it, however, and sat up quite straight and stiff with her shoulders erect and her head up. She'd forgotten her distrust of the man in what seemed to be his wonderful music. It was all new and strange to her, and she couldn't know how little there really was to it. She liked best the kind that made her think of the birds and the sunny sky, rather than the wild, whirly kind.

She meant to ask him to play the first tune again, but he struck up a Scottish love ballad. The melody intoxicated her, and her face shone with pleasure. She hadn't noticed the words, except that they were of love, and she thought with pain of David and Kate and how the pleading tenderness might have been his heart calling to hers not to forget his love for her.

But Harry Temple mistook her expression for interest in

him. With his eyes still on hers, as a cat might mesmerize a bird, he changed into a minor tune of heartbroken love. Its sadness brought tears to Marcia's eyes and deep color to her burning cheeks, while the music throbbed out her own half-realized loneliness and sorrow. The sounds seemed to paint a picture of what she'd missed out of love and set her sadness flowing tangibly.

The last note died away in an impressive diminuendo, and the young man turned toward her. His eyes were full of longing, his voice gentle, persuasive, as though the song had come a little nearer.

"And that's the way I feel toward you, dear," he said and reached out his hands to hers, lying forgotten in her lap.

But his hands had scarcely touched hers before Marcia sprang back, knocking over the chair.

Clasping her hands tightly behind her, she stood there frightened but alert.

Ah, but he was used to shy maidens and not put off. A little coaxing, a little gentle persuasion, a little boldness—that was all he needed. He'd conquered hearts before—why not this unsophisticated one?

"Don't be afraid, dear. There's no one around. And surely there's no harm in telling you I love you and letting you comfort my poor broken heart that I found you too late—"

He had arisen and with a passionate gesture put his arms about Marcia and before she could know what was coming had pressed a kiss upon her lips.

But she was aroused now with every bit of anger inside her. Every sense of right and justice inherited and taught rushed forward. Horror and rage filled her that such a dreadful thing should come to her. With no time to think, she raised her hands and beat him in the face, mouth, cheeks, and eyes with all her might, until he turned, blinded. Then she struggled away, crying, "You're a wicked man!" and fled.

Through the hall she ran to the kitchen and, flinging wide the nearest door, down the garden walk, past the dahlias, pumpkins, and corn, through the berry bushes at the lower end of the lot, and behind the currant bushes. She crouched a moment looking back to see if she were being pursued. Then, imagining she heard a noise from the open door, she scrambled over the low back fence as the comb in her hair unfastened and the waves of dark hair fell about her shoulders wildly.

She was in a field of wheat now, and the tall shocks stood about her, thick and close, touching her with their bent stalks as she passed. Ahead of her looked like an endless sea to cross before she reached another fence and a bare field, then another fence and the woods. There seemed no refuge but the woods. The woods were home to her. She loved the tall shadows, the whispering music in the upper branches, the quiet places underneath, the hushed silence. She hurried to the woods as she would have flown to the minister's wife at home and buried her face in her lap and sobbed out her horror and shame. Breathlessly she sped, without looking behind her, over the next fence and still another.

She forgot she was wearing Kate's special sprigged muslin and that it might tear. She forgot she was a matron and mustn't run wildly through strange fields. She forgot someone might be watching her. She forgot everything except that she must get away and hide her shamed face.

At last she reached the shelter of the woods and, with one wild, furtive look behind her, flung herself onto the lap of mother earth, burying her face in the soft moss at the foot of a tree. There she sobbed out her horror and loneliness, until her heart seemed to shudder.

At first she couldn't think clearly. Her brain was confused with the magnitude of what had happened to her. She tried to go over it and see if she might have prevented anything. She blamed herself for listening to the foolish music after her own suspicions were aroused. But how could she dream any man in his senses would do such a thing? Not even Captain Leavenworth would stoop to that, she thought. She knew so little of the world, and her world had been kept so sweet and pure.

She turned cold at the thought of her father's anger if he heard about this strange young man. She felt sure he'd blame her for allowing it. He tried to teach his girls to exercise judgment and discretion, and surely she must have failed in both, or this wouldn't have happened. Oh, why hadn't the aunts come that afternoon! Why hadn't they arrived before that man came! Yet if they'd come after he was there. . . !

How disgusting he seemed to her with his smirky smile and slender fingers! How utterly unfit beside David was he to breathe the same air. David, her David—no, Kate's David! Oh, pity! What a pain the world was!

She found nowhere to turn for comfort. For what would David say, and how could she ever tell him? Would he find out? What would he think? What would the aunts think? Ah! That was worse than all, for even now she could see Aunt Hortense's head tilt and Aunt Amelia's lips tighten. How dreadful if they found out! They wouldn't believe her, unless perhaps Aunt Clarinda might. She didn't look wise, but she seemed kind and loving. If it weren't for the other two, she might have fled to Aunt Clarinda. If only she could flee to her father's house!

How could she ever play on that dreadful piano again? She would always see that hateful, smiling face sitting there and how he looked at her. Then she shuddered and sobbed harder than ever. And mother earth, true to all her children, received the poor child with open arms. There she lay upon the resinous pine needles, sheltered at the foot of the tall trees. The winds blew sweetly from the buckwheat fields in the valley about her, and the birds sang softly overhead until she fell asleep.

Meanwhile, recovering from his rebuff and left alone in the

parlor, Harry Temple looked about him with surprise. Never in his short, brilliant career as a heartbreaker had he met with the like, and this from a mere child! She must have been playing and would come back soon with mischievous eyes and beg his pardon.

But even as he sat down to wait for her, something told him she wouldn't come. Something besides mischief was in the sharp raps whose tingle even now his cheeks and lips felt. The house, too, had grown strangely still as though no one else were in it. She must have gone out. Perhaps she was really frightened and would tell somebody! How awkward if she returned with one of those grim aunts or that solemn husband. Perhaps he'd better decamp while the coast was still clear. She didn't seem to be returning, and there was no telling what the little fool might do.

Suddenly feverish in his haste to get away, he compelled himself to walk slowly, nonchalantly out through the hall. Quiet as a thief he opened and closed the front door and reached the front steps—but not so quietly that an alert ear didn't hear the latch falling into place and a boot scraping on the path, or so invisibly or quickly that a pair of keen eyes didn't see him.

When Harry Temple went to the Spafford house that afternoon, with his dauntless front and conceited smile, Miranda was picking raspberries along the fence that separated the Heath garden from the Spafford garden.

Harry Temple was too new in town not to excite comment among the young girls wherever he went, and Miranda was always looking out for anything new. Not for herself! No, Miranda never expected anything from a young man for herself, but she was interested in what befell other girls.

So Miranda, behind the berry bushes, watched Harry Temple saunter down the street and saw with surprise that he stopped at the house of her new admiration. Now Miranda felt pleased that although Marcia was a married woman, she should have attention from others; she also felt some triumph over her cousin Hannah that he hadn't stopped to see her.

She picked berries as near the Spafford parlor windows as possible, delighting in the music that tinkled through the green shaded window, for Miranda liked the lively dance music. She fancied that her idol was playing. But then she heard a man's voice, and her picking stopped short insomuch that Mr. Temple's liquid tenor mingled with her grandmother's strident tones, calling to Miranda to "be spry there, or the sun'll catch you 'fore you get a quart."

All at once the music ceased, and in a minute or two Miranda heard the Spafford kitchen door thrown violently open and saw Marcia rush out.

She was too surprised to call out. She watched as Marcia flew between the rows of currant bushes, saw the comb fall from her hair, saw the flush on her cheek and the fire in her eye, saw her mount the first fence. Then suddenly a protective feeling rose within her.

Glancing toward her grandmother's window to be sure no one else saw the flying figure, she picked with all her might; but what went into her pail, whether raspberries or green leaves or briars, she didn't know. Her eyes followed the figure through the wheat, and she picked faster toward the lower end of the lot where runty old sour berries grew, if any. Once hidden behind the tall corn between her and her grandmother's vigilant gaze, she hastened to the end of the lot and watched Marcia. She watched her as she climbed the fences and held her breath at the daring leaps from the top rails, expecting to see the delicate muslin catch on the rough fence and send her to the ground senseless.

It was like a theater to Miranda, watching the beautiful girl in her flight, the long dark hair in the wind, the graceful untrammeled bounds. She watched with unveiled admiration until the dark green-blue wood swallowed her up. Then slowly her eyes traveled back over the path Marcia had taken, back through the meadow and the wheat, to the kitchen door left standing wide. Slowly, painfully, Miranda set herself to understand it. Something happened! That was flight with fear behind it, fear that forgot everything else. What happened?

Miranda was wiser in her generation than Marcia. She put two and two together. Her brows darkened, and a cunning look entered her honest blue eyes. She crept with catlike quickness along the fence to the front. There she stood like a red-haired Nemesis in a sunbonnet, with irate red face, confronting the unsuspecting man as he sauntered forth from the unwelcoming roof where he'd whiled away a mistaken hour.

"What you been sayin' to her?"

It was as if a serpent had stung him, unexpected, direct. He jumped aside and turned deadly pale. She knew her chance arrow struck the truth. But he recovered himself almost immediately when he saw what a harmless-looking creature attacked him.

"Why, my dear girl," he said, "you startled me! I'm sure you've made some mistake!"

"I ain't your girl, thank goodness!" snapped Miranda. "And I guess by your looks there ain't anybody 'dear' to you but yourself. But I ain't made a mistake. It's you I was asking. What you been in there for?"

Miranda's eyes blazed, and her stubby forefinger pointed at him like a shotgun.

The bold black eyes quailed for an instant. The young man's hand sought his pocket, brought out a piece of money, and extended it.

"Look here, my friend," he said. "You take this and say nothing more about it. That's a good girl. No harm's been done."

Miranda looked him in the face and with a sudden motion of her brown hand sent the coin flying on the stone pavement.

"I tell you I'm not your friend, and I don't want your money. I wouldn't trust its goodness any more than your face. As for keepin' still, I'll do as I see fit. I intend to know what this means, and if you've made her any trouble, you'd better leave town, for I'll make it too unpleasant for you to stay here!"

With a stealthy glance about him, the young man hurried down the street. He wanted no more parley with this loud, avenging girl. His fear returned to him in double force, and he glanced at his watch and quickened his pace almost to a run as though he'd suddenly remembered an engagement. Miranda, scowling, stood and watched him disappear around the corner. Then she turned back and picked raspberries with a diligence that would have astonished her grandmother, if she hadn't for the last hour been engaged with a visiting neighbor in a room at the other side of the house, where they were overhauling a fellow church member's character.

Miranda picked on but couldn't decide what to do. From time to time she glanced anxiously toward the woods and then at the lowering sun in the west. She considered going after Marcia, but a wholesome fear of her grandmother held her back.

At length she heard a firm step coming down the street. Could it be? Yes, it was David Spafford. How did he come so soon? Miranda had heard, as neighbors hear and know things, that David took the stage that morning, presumably on business to New York, and wasn't due back for several days. She'd wondered if Marcia would stay all night alone in the house or go to the aunts. But now here was David!

Miranda looked over the wheat, half expecting to see the flying figure returning in haste, but the parted wheat waved on.

David Spafford let himself in his house and searched for Marcia. The business that took him away in the morning, which he hadn't expected to finish before late that night, was partly transacted at a little tavern where the coach horses were changed that morning. He met there unexpectedly the two men he was going to see, who were coming straight to his town. So he turned back with them and came home. They were attending to other business in town, while he came home to tell Marcia they'd eat supper with him and perhaps spend the night.

He went upstairs and knocked timidly at her door, but no answer came. He thought she might be asleep and knocked louder. Finally he opened the door and peeped in, but he saw that quiet loneliness reigned there.

He went downstairs again and searched in the pantry and kitchen. The back door was stretched open as if thrown back in haste. He followed its suggestion and went out, looking down the brick path that led to the garden. Ah! Something gleamed in the sun with a spot of blue behind it: the bit of blue ribbon she had at her throat, with a tiny gold brooch, unclasped, sticking in.

Miranda caught sight of him coming and crouched behind the currants.

David searched the path on every side. A bit of branch was torn from a succulent, tender plant leaning over the path and lying in the way. It seemed another blaze along the trail. Farther down where the bushes almost met, a thread waved on a thorn. David hardly knew whether he was following these things or not. At any rate they weren't apparently leading him anywhere, for he stopped abruptly in front of the fence and looked both ways behind the bushes that grew in front of it. Then he turned to go back again.

Miranda held her breath.

Something touched David's foot in turning, and looking down, he saw Marcia's large shell comb lying in the grass. He picked it up and examined it. It was like finding fragments of a wreck along the sand.

All at once Miranda rose from her hiding place and confronted him, but not in the same way she had Harry Temple.

"She ain't in the house," she said hoarsely. "She's gone over there!"

David Spafford turned, surprised.

"Is that you, Miranda? Oh, thank you! Where do you say she went?"

"Through there, don't you see?" Again the stubby forefinger pointed to the rift in the wheat.

David gazed at the path in the wheat, but gradually it dawned on him that a distinct line ran through it where some-one must have gone.

"Yes, I see," he said, "but why would she go there? There's nothing over there."

"She went on further. She went to the woods," said Miranda, glancing around in case even now her grandmother might be upon her. "And she was scared, I guess. She looked it. Her hair come tumblin' down when she clum the fence, an' she just went flyin' over like some bird, didn't care a feather if she fell, an' she never once looked behind her till she come to the woods."

David's bewilderment was growing uncomfortable. His face showed a trace of alarm and the embarrassment one feels when a neighbor divulges news about a member of one's own household.

"Why, surely, Miranda, you must be mistaken. Maybe it was someone else you saw. I don't think Mrs. Spafford would be likely to run over there that way, and what in the world would she have to be frightened at?"

"No, I ain't mistaken," said Miranda, nettled at his unbelief. "It was her all right. She came flyin' out the kitchen door when I was picking raspberries and down that path to the fence and never stopped fer fence ner wheat ner medder lot but went into them woods there, right up to the left of them tall pines, and she—she looked plum scared to death 's if a whole circus menagerie was after her, lions an' elefunts an' all. An' I guess she had plenty to be scared at ef I ain't mistaken. That dandy Temple feller went there to call on her, an' I heard him tinklin' that music box, and it's my opinion he needs a wallupin'!

"You better go after her! It's gettin' late, and you'll have hard times finding her in the dark. Just you foller her path in the wheat and then make fer them pines. I'd hev gone after her myself, only Grandma'd make sech a fuss and hev to know it all. You needn't be afraid o' me. I'll keep still."

By this time David was alive to the situation and alarmed. He mounted the fence, glanced a "thank you" at Miranda, and disappeared through the wheat. Miranda watched him till she was sure he was heading for the right spot. Then, with a sigh of relief, she hurried into the house with her now-brimming pail of berries.

Chapter 15

As David made his way quickly through the rippling wheat, he experienced a series of emotions. For the first time since his wedding day, he forgot himself and his pain. What did it mean? Marcia frightened! At what?

Harry Temple at their house! What did he know of Harry Temple? Only that Hannah Heath introduced him and he was doing business in town. But why did Mr. Temple visit the house? David was sure he could have no possible business with him. Moreover, he now remembered seeing the young man standing near the stable that morning when he took his seat in the coach. He knew he must have heard his remark about not returning till the late coach that night or possibly the next day. He remembered as he said it that he'd unconsciously studied Mr. Temple's face and noted its weak points. Did the young man have a purpose in coming to the house during his absence? Anger rose inside him at the thought.

For the first time David saw himself as Marcia's natural protector—her husband. He saw a duty to her, aside from feeding and clothing her. He felt a personal responsibility and an actual interest in her. Out of the whole world, now, he was the only one she could look to for help.

It gave him a new feeling of possession and almost seemed pleasant. He forgot why he searched for Marcia in the first place and the two men who were probably at that moment preparing to go to his house. He forgot everything but Marcia and strode into the dark blue shadows of the wood and stopped to listen.

The hush was intense. No echoes of flying feet lingered down that pine-padded pathway. It was long since he'd had time to wander in the woods, and he wondered at their silence. The trees whispering above, the sky far away, the breeze quiet, the bird notes subdued—it seemed almost uncanny. He hadn't remembered the woods were like this. It struck him in passing that here would be a good place to bring his pain someday when he had time to face it again and wished to be alone with it.

He took his hat in his hand and stepped firmly into the vast solemnity as if he'd entered a great church when the service was going on, on an errand of life and death that gave excuse for profaning the holy silence. He went a few paces and stopped again, listening. Was that a sighing breath he heard or only the wind coughing through the waving tassels overhead? He summoned his voice. It was a great effort and sounded weak and feeble under the grandeur of the vaulted green dome.

"Marcia!" he called. "Marcia!" He realized it was the first time he'd called her by name or sought after her. He always said "you" or "child" or spoke of her in company as "Mrs. Spafford," a strange and far-off mythical person whose very intangibility separated her from him immeasurably.

He walked deeper into the forest, called again and yet again, and stood to listen. All was still about him, but in the far distance he heard the faint report of a gun. With a new thought of danger, he hurried deeper into the shadows. The gun sounded again more clearly. He shuddered and looked about in all directions, hoping to see the glimmer of her dress.

No wild beasts were likely so near the town, and yet they were seen occasionally—a stray fox and even a bear—and the sun was low. He glanced back, and the low line of the horizon gleamed gold at the sun's farewell for the night.

The gun again! Stray shots were known to kill people wandering in the forest. He was growing nervous now and went this way and that calling, but still no answer came. He started thinking he wasn't near the clump of pines Miranda spoke of and moved to the right. Then he turned to look back where he entered the woods, and there she lay, almost at his feet!

She slept as soundly as if she were lying on a velvet couch, with one round white arm under her cheek. Her face was flushed with weeping, and her lashes still wet. Her tender, sensitive mouth still quivered slightly as her breath caught, and her dark hair floated about her.

Coming upon her suddenly, the man stopped, awed by her beauty. He stepped softly to her side and, bending down, observed her, first to make sure she was alive and safe, then searching to know every detail of the picture before him because it was his. He had not only a right but a duty to possess and care for it.

She might have been a statue or a painting as he looked at her and noted the lovely curve of her flushed cheek. But when his eyes reached the firm brown hand and the slender finger on which glistened the wedding ring that wasn't really hers, something pathetic in the wet lashes and the sad, beautiful figure touched him. He stooped down gently and put his arm about her.

"Marcia, child!" he said in a low, almost crooning voice, as one might wake a baby from its sleep. "Marcia, open your eyes, and tell me you're all right."

At first she only stirred uneasily and slept on. But he raised her and, sitting down beside her, put her head on his shoulder and spoke gently. Then Marcia opened her eyes, bewildered, and, with a start, pushed back and stared at David, as if to be sure it was he and not that dreadful man from whom she'd fled.

"Why, child! What's the matter?" said David, brushing her hair back from her face.

Marcia scarcely knew him; his voice was so strangely sweet and sympathetic. She made one effort to speak, but her lips quivered, and the tears fell again. She covered her face with her hands and shook with sobs. How could she tell David what happened, now, when he was kinder than ever? He would become grave when she told him, and she couldn't bear that. He'd likely blame her, too, and how could she endure more?

But he drew her to him again and laid her head against his coat, trying to smooth her hair with his hand. Soon the tears subsided, and she pulled back from him.

"Indeed, I couldn't help it, David," she faltered, trying to smile.

"I know you couldn't, child." His answer was kind, and his eyes smiled at her as never before. Her heart leaped with surprise. It was so good to have David care. She hadn't known how much she wanted him to speak to her as if he saw her and thought a little about her.

"And now what was it? Remember that I don't know. Tell me quick, for it's growing late and damp, and you'll take cold out here in the woods with that thin dress on. You're chilly already."

"I'd better go at once," she said, willing to put off telling him as long as possible, if not altogether.

"No, child," he said, pulling her back, "you must rest before taking that long walk. You're weary and excited, and it'll do you good to tell me. What made you run off here? Are you homesick?"

He scanned her face, fearing that the sacrifice he accepted so easily was too much for the victim. It comforted him to have Marcia with him, to help him hide his sorrow from the world. He didn't know before that he cared.

"I was frightened," she said, looking down.

She tried to keep her lips and fingers from trembling, for she was afraid to tell him everything. But though the woods were growing dusky, he saw the fingers fluttering and gathered them in his own.

"Now, child," he said in that tone even his aunts obeyed,

"tell me all. What frightened you, and why did you come up here away from everybody instead of calling for help?"

Brought to bay, she lifted her eyes to his face and told him the story briefly, beginning with the night she first met Harry Temple. She said as little about music as possible, because she feared that the mention of the piano might be painful to David. But she made the whole matter plain in a few words so he could fill in between the lines.

"Scoundrel!" he murmured, clenching his fists. "He ought to be strung up!" Then he said gently again, "How frightened you must have been! You were right to run away, but it was dangerous to run out here! He might have followed you!"

"Oh!" said Marcia. "I never thought of that. I only wanted to get away from everybody. It seemed so dreadful that I didn't want anybody to know. I didn't want you to know. I wanted to run away and hide and never come back!"

"You mustn't talk that way," he said gently. "What would I do if you did that?" He laid his hand softly on her head.

It was the first time anything like a personal talk had passed between them, and Marcia was thrilled. His words were like heavenly comfort to her wounded spirit.

She stole a shy look at him and wished she dared say something, but no words came. They sat for a moment in silence, each sensing comfort in the other's presence and each clasping the other's hand with clinging pressure, yet neither fully aware of it.

The sun's last rays, lying for a while at their feet on the pine needles, slipped away. The world was suddenly in gloom, and the place where the two sat was almost dark. David noticed it first and, all at once, remembered his expected guests.

"Child!" he said. But he didn't release her hand or neglect to speak tenderly. "The sun has gone down, and here I've forgotten to tell you. We have guests for supper tonight—two gentlemen who are very distinguished in their lines of work. We have business together, and I must hurry. They're probably at the house already. Let's go as fast as possible."

"Oh, David!" she said. "And you had to come out here after me and have stayed so long! What a foolish girl I've been and what a mess I've made! They may be angry and go away, and I'll be to blame. I'm afraid you can never forgive me."

"Don't worry, child," he said pleasantly. "It couldn't be helped and isn't your fault at all. I'm only sorry these two men will delay me from hunting up that scoundrel Temple and recommending he leave town on the earliest stage. I'd like to give him what Miranda suggested, a good 'wallupin',' but perhaps that wouldn't be dignified."

He laughed as he said it, a hearty laugh with its old ring. Marcia felt happy at the sound. How wonderful if he'd be like that with her all the time!

He helped her to her feet and, taking her hand, led her out into the open field where they could walk faster. As he walked he told her about Miranda waiting for him behind the currant bushes. They laughed together, making the way seem shorter.

David had drawn Marcia's arm within his and, noticing that her dress was thin, pulled off his coat and put it firmly about her despite her protest. Thus warmed, comforted, and cheered, Marcia hurried back over the path she'd taken in such fright a few hours before.

When they could see the village lights twinkling below them, David told her about the two men who would be their guests. So interesting was his brief story that Marcia hardly knew they were home before David was helping her over their own back fence.

"David! The kitchen light is on! Do you suppose they've gone in and are getting their own supper? What shall I do with my hair? I can't go in with it this way. How did that light get there?"

"Here!" said David, fumbling in his pocket. "Will this help?"

He brought out the shell comb he'd picked up in the garden.

In the fading moonlight David watched her coil her long wavy hair and then gave his approval of the effect before they went in. They were just behind the tall sunflowers, whispering. Marcia hated to go in and end their closeness and fun, but she knew the sweet evening hour couldn't last. Then they took hands, stole up to the kitchen window, and looked in. The door stood open as both had left it that afternoon, a candle was burning on the shelf over the table, and the teakettle was singing on the crane above the hearth; but no one was in the kitchen. They crept into the room, each fearing the aunts had come and discovered their lapse. A light was shining in the front of the house, and they could hear voices—two men discussing politics. They listened longer but heard nothing else.

David in pantomime outlined the plan, and Marcia, understanding, slipped up the back stairs to freshen up after her nap in the woods. Then David opened and shut the kitchen door with a lot of noise and hurried in to greet his guests, who suspected nothing.

A bit earlier, good fortune had favored Miranda. The neighbor had stayed longer than usual, so Miranda slipped into the kitchen and picked over the berries quickly. While she did so, she could watch for David and Marcia through the pantry window that overlooked the hills and the woods. She wanted to see the drama to its close, with the rescue of the princess. The talk in the sitting room continued, so Miranda took the opportunity to be off again.

She ran down behind the currants and, standing on the fence between the corn, looked out across the wheat. But she saw no sign of anyone coming out of the woods.

She wondered if Harry Temple shut the front door when he left. But David went in that way, and he'd have closed it, of course. Still, he left in a hurry; maybe she should go and look. She didn't want her grandmother to catch her, so she stole along like a cat close to the dark berry bushes, and the gathering dusk hid her. She thought she could see from the front of the fence whether the door was closed. But people were coming up the street. She'd wait until they passed before she looked over the fence.

Two men were walking slowly, in earnest conversation. Each carried a carpetbag and seemed weary.

"This must be the house," said one. "He said it was exactly opposite the Seceder church. That's the church, I believe. I was here once before."

"There doesn't seem to be a light in the house," said the other. "Are you sure? Mr. Spafford said he was coming directly home to let his wife know about our arrival."

"A little strange there's no light. It's dark now, but I'm sure this must be the house. Maybe they're in the kitchen and not expecting us so soon. Let's try anyhow," said the other, setting down his carpetbag on the stoop and lifting the brass knocker.

Miranda debated for a moment. Not for nothing had she stood at Grandma Heath's elbow for years watching their neighbors' movements and interpreting what they meant. She hurried to a sheltered spot and climbed the picket fence separating the Heath garden from the Spafford side yard. Before the brass knocker sounded through the empty house the second time, Miranda had crossed the side porch, thrown her sunbonnet on a chair in the dark kitchen, and walked noisily to the front door.

She flung the door open, saying in a breezy voice, "Just wait till I get a light, won't you? The wind blew the candle out."

Not a particle of wind was blowing that soft September night, but that made little difference to Miranda. She was part of a play and acting her best. If her impromptu part was a little irregular, it was at least well intended and boldly presented.

Miranda found a candle on the shelf and, stooping to the smoldering fire on the hearth, blew and coaxed it into flame enough to light it.

"This is Mr. Spafford's home, isn't it?" asked the old gentleman Miranda heard speak first on the sidewalk.

"Oh, yes, indeed," said the girl glibly. "Jest come in and set down. Here, let me take your hats. Jest put your bags right there on the floor."

"You are—are you—Mrs. Spafford?" asked the man.

"Oh, landy sakes, no, I ain't her," said Miranda, laughing. "Mis' Spafford had jest stepped out a bit when her husband come home, an' he's gone after her. She didn't expect her husband home till late tonight. But you set down. They'll be home real soon now. They'd oughter been here before this. I s'pose she went further 'n she thought she'd go when she stepped out."

"It's all right," said the other gentleman. "No harm done, I'm sure. I hope we won't inconvenience Mrs. Spafford coming so unexpectedly."

"No, indeedy!" said Miranda. "You can't ketch Mis' Spafford unprepared if you come in the middle o' the night. She's allus ready for comp'ny." Miranda's eyes shone. She felt she was getting on well doing the honors.

"Well, that's very nice. I'm sure it makes a person feel at home. I wonder if she'd mind if we went up to our room and washed our hands. I'd like to be more presentable before we meet her," said the first gentleman, who looked weary.

"Why, that's all right. 'Course you ken go right up. Jest you set in the keepin' room a minnit while I run up 'n be sure the water pitcher's filled. I ain't quite sure 'bout it. I won't be long."

Miranda seated them in the parlor with great gusto and hurried up the back stairs. She wasn't sure which room would be called the guest room and whether the two strangers would occupy separate rooms or one together. At least it would be safe to show them one till Marcia returned. She peeped into her room and knew it instinctively before she caught sight of a cameo brooch on the pincushion and a rose-colored ribbon neatly folded lying on the foot of the bed. That question settled, she thought any other room would do and chose the large front room across the hall with its high four-poster bed. After lighting the candle on the bureau, she went down to invite the guests upstairs.

Then she dashed back into the kitchen to get supper for them and have everything ready when Marcia came so there'd be no bad breaks. She raked the fire and filled the teakettle, swinging it from the crane. Then she searched where she thought such things should be, found a tablecloth, and set the table. Her hands trembled as she took out the sprigged china from the corner cupboard. Perhaps this was wrong, and she'd be blamed for it, but at least it was what she'd have done if she were mistress of this house and had two nice gentlemen for tea.

Grandmother Heath rarely let her handle her sprigged china, so Miranda felt the joy and daring of it even more. Once a delicate cup slipped and rolled over on the table and almost reached the edge. A little more and it would have rolled off onto the floor and been shattered into a dozen fragments, but Miranda caught it in her apron.

She took pleasure in setting the table. She was doing it to please and surprise someone she adored, not because she'd been ordered to, and she was having an adventure. Miranda had longed for adventure all her life and thought it had come.

She slipped into the pantry and found what she needed: cold ham, cheese, pickles, seedcakes, gingerbread, fruitcake, preserves and jelly, bread, and raised biscuits. Then she went down to the cellar and found the milk and cream and butter. She'd just finished the table and set out the teapot when she heard the two men coming downstairs. They went into the parlor and sat down, remarking that their friend had a pleasant home, and then plunged into a political discussion again.

Miranda felt they were safe for a while. She stole into the

darkness to look for signs of the couple. A screech owl hooted across the night. Soon she heard subdued voices above the soft swish of the parting wheat and saw them coming. She slid quickly over the fence into the Heath backyard and crouched in her old place behind the currant bushes. She saw David help Marcia over the fence and watched them till they passed up the walk to the light of the kitchen door. Then she turned and disappeared to her own home, knowing the reckoning in store for her. She carried, however, an air of triumph as she entered.

"Where you been, Miranda Griscom, and what on airth you been up to now?" her grandmother greeted her as she lifted the latch of the kitchen door.

Her grandmother never mentioned the Griscom name unless she meant business. She hated the name because of the man who had broken her daughter's heart. Grandma Heath felt Miranda was an out-and-out Griscom without a streak of Heath in her. The Griscoms all had red hair. But Miranda lifted her chin high and felt like a princess in disguise.

"Been huntin' hens' eggs down in the grass," she said, taking the first excuse that came into her head. "Time to get supper?"

"Hens' eggs? This time o' night an' dark as pitch. Miranda Griscom, you ken go up to your room an' not come down till I call you!"

It would have been a dire punishment if Miranda hadn't been thinking of other things, for the neighbor had been asked to tea and she'd hear the latest village gossip at the table. Besides, her disgrace was apparently to be made public. But Miranda didn't care. She hurried to her attic window, which looked down on the dining room windows of the Spafford house. No one thought to close the shades. So she could watch the supper she prepared being served and let her mouth water over the doughnuts, currant jelly, and quince preserves, and pretend she was a guest. And thus she forgot the supper she was missing downstairs.

Chapter 16

$\mathcal{D}$avid apologized to his guests for his absence when they arrived. At first he wondered whom they referred to as "the maid," until he remembered Miranda and blessed her silently for her kindness. It was more than he'd expect from any member of the Heath household. He recalled Miranda's honest face among the currant bushes when she said, "You needn't be afraid of me. I'll keep still." She evidently figured out the truth and filled in the breach without divulging a word. He resolved to show his gratitude in some way.

If the girl, sitting supperless in the dark, had known his thought, her lonely heart would have beaten happily. But she didn't, and virtue had to bring its own reward in a sense of duty done. Then, too, the adventure added spice to her otherwise monotonous life, so she wasn't sad as she sat there imagining what the Spaffords thought and said when they found the house lighted and supper ready.

Marcia was the most astonished when she slipped downstairs from freshening up and found the table set. She couldn't keep from laughing to herself at the array of dishes filled with food from her pantry. But she was puzzled. Who would have set the table so oddly? The best china was laid out, but so many little bits of things were in separate dishes. Half a mound of currant jelly shimmered on a large china plate, while a fresh mound of quince jelly quivered in a common dish. Every available inch on the table was covered. It wouldn't do to call the guests to a table like that. What would David say?

Swiftly, Marcia weeded out some things and rearranged

those remaining, and then she made the tea. Before David had time to worry, she stood in the parlor door, shy and sweet, with brilliant color in her cheeks.

His little comrade, David thought. Again her beauty struck him as he stood to introduce her to the guests. He saw open admiration in their greeting and wondered what they'd have thought of Kate, wild-rose Kate with her graceful bewitching ways. A tinge of sadness crossed his face, but something suggested to him that Marcia was even more beautiful than Kate, more like a bud. He wondered why he'd never noticed how her eyes shone. He gave her a pleasant smile as they passed into the hall, which set the color flaming in her cheeks again.

David seemed different somehow, and that isolated feeling she'd had ever since she came here to live was gone. David was there, and he understood, at least a little. And they had something—even though it was only a few minutes in a lonely wood and his gentle words—to call their very own. At least that didn't belong to Kate, never was hers, and couldn't have been borrowed from her. Marcia sighed happily as she took her seat at the table.

The talk ran to Andrew Jackson and his last message to Congress. The older man expressed grave fears that a mistake had been made in policy and the country would suffer.

Governor Clinton was mentioned and his policy discussed. But all this talk was familiar to Marcia. Her father was interested in public affairs and had raised her to listen to discussions and think about such matters for herself. When she was little, her father had her read the whole paper out loud to him, as he lay back in his chair with his eyes closed and his shaggy brows drawn thoughtfully into a frown. Sometimes, while she read, he'd burst forth with a tirade against this or that man or set of men who opposed his views, and he'd pour out a lengthy reply to little Marcia as she sat patiently, waiting to continue her reading.

When she grew older, she was proud of being her father's political confidante and could talk on such matters as intelligently and as well as, if not better than, most of the men who came to the house. Kate was too full of her own plans, and Madam Schuyler too busy with household affairs to bother with politics and newspapers, so Marcia was always the one called on to read when her father's eyes were tired. As a result, she was far beyond other girls her age in knowledge of public affairs.

Well she knew what Andrew Jackson thought about the canal system and improvements in general. She knew which men in Congress were opposed to or in favor of certain bills. All through the struggle for improvements in New York State she was an eager observer. The minutest detail of the Erie Canal project had interested her, and she was never without her own little private opinion in the matter, which, however, seldom found voice except in her eager eyes.

Therefore, Marcia sat behind her sprigged china teacups and poured tea, taking in all that was said. At last the conversation neared what seemed to her the most important subject in the country then—a railroad run by steam.

Nothing was too great for Marcia to believe. Her father was inclined to be conservative in vast improvements. He'd favored the Erie Canal, though he feared it would be impossible to carry out such a project. Marcia in her girlish mind had rejoiced when it was completed and news arrived that many packets were traveling day and night on the waterway. She felt a sense of triumph to think men could study these big schemes and plan everything, then against great odds complete their project and prove to unbelievers it wasn't only possible but practicable.

Marcia longed for progress. She felt that if she were a man with money and influence, she'd venture into the world and get people to do the things the country needed. Progress was the keynote of her upbringing, and she found herself teeming with energy she doubted could ever be used to further her rising ambitions. She wanted to see the world alive and busy, the great cities connected with one another; to have free access to cities and libraries, pictures, and wonderful music. She desired to meet men and women who were making history, writing, speaking, and doing things that molded public opinion.

Reforms of all sorts would further her ambitions for the country. Why didn't people want a steam railroad? Why did they say it could never succeed, that it was impossible; that the roads couldn't be strengthened enough to bear such weight and constant wear and tear? Why did they object to every suggestion inventors and thinking men offered? Why did her dear father, who was so far ahead of his times in many ways, shake his head and say he feared it would never be in this country, at least not in his day; that it was impractical? Even in her young mind she had posed some of these questions, but now, in her exposure to a broader world, they came to mind more often.

Marcia ate bits of her biscuit absently and left her tea untasted till it was cold. The younger of the two guests was talking. His name was Jervis. Marcia thought she'd heard the name somewhere but hadn't placed him yet.

"Yes," he said, "it's coming sooner than they think. Oliver Evans said good roads were all we could expect one generation to do. The next must make canals, the next might build a railroad run by horsepower, and perhaps the next would run a railroad by steam. But we won't have to wait so long. We'll have steam moving railway carriages before another year."

"What!" exclaimed David. "You don't mean it! Do you have any foundation for such a statement?" He leaned forward, his eyes shining.

Marcia watched him and felt proud she belonged to him. She looked at the other men whose eyes were fixed on David with great interest.

The older man observed the scene a moment and then explained: "The Mohawk and Hudson Company has just engaged Mr. Jervis as chief engineer of their road. He expects to run that road by steam!"

He finished his fruitcake and preserves under the astonished gaze of his host and hostess.

David and Marcia both turned toward Mr. Jervis, who smiled in affirmation.

"But won't it be like all the rest—no funds?" asked David. "It may be years before it's really started."

"The contract is let for the grading," Mr. Jervis said. "In fact, work has already begun. I expect to begin laying the track by next spring, perhaps sooner. As soon as the track is laid, we'll show them."

David reached out and grasped the hand of the man who had the will and apparently the means of accomplishing this great thing for the country.

"It'll make a wonderful change in the whole land," David said, his face glowing.

Marcia was seeing a side of his nature she hadn't known—the man, the thinker, the writer, the former of public opinion, the idealist. She'd seen him in the light of her sister, a young man of promise, but that was all. Now she saw something more earnest, and at once she realized he was a man like her father.

His eyes suddenly met hers. He seemed to share his thought with her and smiled. He felt at once that she could and would understand his feelings about this great new enterprise and be glad, too. Some of his loneliness left. Kate would never have been interested in these things. He didn't expect such sympathy from her. She was something beautiful and separate from his world, and as such he adored her. But it was pleasant to have someone who could understand and feel as he did. Just then he wasn't thinking of his lost Kate.

Marcia felt the glow of warmth from his smile and returned it, and the two visitors knew they were among friends who understood and sympathized.

"Yes, it will make a change," said the older man. "I hope I live to see at least part of it."

"If you succeed, many others will follow. The land will soon be a network of railroads," David said.

"We'll succeed!" Mr. Jervis said.

"Now tell me about it," said David, as a child asks for a story.

The talk launched into a description of the proposed road, the roadbed, the manner of laying the rails, their thickness and width, and the way of bolting them to the heavy timbers underneath. Mr. Jervis took knives and forks to illustrate and then showed by plates and spoons how they were fastened down.

Marcia was fascinated, and David asked a question now and then, took out his notebook, and wrote down some things. The two guests were eager and clear in their answers. They wanted the information to be accurate and complete, and they wanted David to write it up.

"The other day I saw a question in a Baltimore paper," the older man said. "It was sent in by a subscriber: 'What is a railroad?' The editor's reply was, 'Can any of our readers answer this question and tell us what a railroad is?' "

The company laughed heartily over the uninformed unbelievers who seemed willing to remain ignorant of the march of improvement.

David finally laid down his notebook. "I have a great deal of faith in you and your skill, but I don't see how you'll overcome the obstacles. How, for instance, will you overcome the inequalities in the road? Our country isn't flat or even like those abroad where the railroad's been tried. We have sharp grades, and a lot of curves will be necessary."

Mr. Jervis had pushed his chair back from the table, but now he pulled it up again sharply and moved the dishes eagerly back from his place. Once again the engineer requisitioned the dishes and cups as he showed a crude model, in china and cutlery, of an engine he proposed to have constructed. He thus illustrated his own idea about a truck for the forward wheels that would move separately from the back wheels and enable the engine to conform to curves more readily.

Marcia, aglow, watched the outline of history to come, without realizing the little model before her, made from her teacups and saucers, would be the model for all the future engines of the railroads.

Finally the chairs were pushed back, but the talk continued. Marcia cleared the dishes quietly from the table. She could hear every word even while in the kitchen washing the china. They talked about Governor Clinton again and his attitude toward the railroad. They spoke of Thurlow Weed and others whose names were familiar to Marcia from the papers she'd read to her father. And they said that recently on the Baltimore and Ohio Railroad, Peter Cooper had experimented with a little locomotive and beaten a gray horse attached to another car.

Marcia smiled as she listened. But with her interest in the march of civilization, other thoughts mingled—of David and his connection with it all. He'd write about it and be identified with it. He was brave enough to face any new movement.

Few temperance papers were being published in those days, but David's was one of them. He'd already faced several unpleasant circumstances as a result. He wasn't afraid of sneers or sarcasm or of being called a fanatic. He'd taken such a stand that even those who were opposed had to respect him. Marcia felt great pride in him tonight.

Later, after the guests talked themselves out and took their candles to their rooms, David smiled again. In his mind's eye he saw the country's future and, for this one night at least, promised not to dream of the past and so bid her good night.

She went up to her white chamber and lay down on the pillow, fragrant with lavender blossoms, dreaming of tomorrow. She thought she was riding in a strange new railroad train with David's arm about her and Harry Temple running at his best pace to catch them, but he couldn't.

Miranda, at her window, watched the evening hours. She wondered why they stayed in the dining room so late and didn't go into the parlor for Marcia to play the "music box," as she called it. Why did a light glow so long in that back chamber over the kitchen? Did they put one of the guests there? Surely not. Perhaps that was David's study, and he was writing. But Miranda slept and ceased to wonder long before David's light was extinguished.

She guessed right though. David was sitting up to write while the inspiration was upon him. When he finally lay down, it was with a weary body and a mind free from any intruding thought of himself and his troubles.

He'd written an article that would appear in his paper in a few days and must convince doubters a railroad was at last an established fact among them. He needed to ask the engineer one or two points in the morning, but in reviewing the article, he felt deeply satisfied with his work. He loved to write and was glad to feel that delight again. Since his marriage he'd thought it was gone forever. But perhaps in time it would return to console him, and he could do greater things in the world because of his suffering.

As he was drifting off to sleep, a thought of Marcia entered his mind. She had something comforting about her and helpful in her smile. There was more to her than he'd supposed. She wasn't just a child. Her face glowed as the men talked of the projected railroad. She almost seemed to understand as they described the proposed engine with its movable trucks.

She would be a companion who'd be interested in his

pursuits. He'd hoped to teach Kate to understand his lifework and perhaps help him some, but she was by nature a brightly colored bird, always on the wing. He wouldn't have wanted her to be troubled with deep thoughts. Marcia seemed to enjoy such things. What if he'd take pains to teach her, read with her, and help cultivate her mind? It would at least occupy the leisure hours and be something to interest him and keep away the awful pall of sadness.

How sweet she had looked asleep in the woods with the tears on her cheek! She was a dear little girl, and he must take care of her and protect her. That scoundrel Temple! What were men like that made for? He must settle him tomorrow.

And so he fell asleep.

Chapter 17

Harry Temple sat in his office the next morning with his feet on the table and his chair tilted back against the wall. He had letters to write that should go out with the afternoon coach. He had at least three men he should see immediately for his employers' sake, and his office wasn't in good order. But his feet were elevated comfortably on the table, and he was deep in the pages of a story of the French court's loves, hates, and intrigues.

Annoyed, he looked up as the office door opened. His annoyance changed to apprehension when he saw his visitor. The chair legs dropped suddenly to the floor, along with his own feet.

A startled look of inquiry crossed Harry's face, and for an instant his complacency was shaken. But perhaps his alarm was unnecessary. Marcia was probably too frightened to tell her husband what had happened. He noticed the broad shoulder, lean body, keen eye, and grave posture and thought he wouldn't care to fight the man.

David Spafford stood calmly for a full minute, staring into Harry's face, with a growing contempt that needed no words to express it.

Harry felt the color rise in his cheeks, and his soul quaked for an instant. Then his customary conceit arose, and he tried to stare down the other's piercing gaze. Though it lasted only a minute, it seemed at least five to him. He offered him a chair, but it went unnoticed.

David looked at the man and knew him for what he was. At

last he spoke in a tone too courteous to be contemptuous, but it humiliated the listener even more than contempt.

"It would be good for you to leave town at once."

That was all. The listener felt a tone of command. His wrath rose and beat itself against the cool exterior of the visitor's gaze in a brazen look that could have faced a whole town of accusers.

"I don't understand you, sir!" he said. "That's an extraordinary statement!"

"It would be good for you to leave town at once."

The command was clear. Harry's eyes blazed.

"Why?" he asked with that impertinent tilt to his chin that usually angered his opponent in an argument. Once he could break that iron self-control, he felt he'd have the upper hand. He could easily persuade David Spafford everything was all right if he caught him off his guard and made him angry. An angry man could do little but bluster.

"You understand very well," replied David with a steady voice and unswerving gaze.

"Indeed! Well, this is most extraordinary. What are you accusing me of?"

"Nothing your own heart doesn't accuse you of."

His gaze held more than human indignation now—pity and a sense of shame for another soul who could lower himself to do unseemly things.

The blood crept into Harry's cheeks again. A new, uncomfortable sensation was stealing over him: a sense of sin—no, not that; rather, the feeling he'd made a mistake, perhaps. He was never hard on himself even when the evidence was clearly against him. It angered him to feel humiliated. What a fuss to make about a little thing! What a tiresome cad to care about a little flirtation with his wife! He wished he'd let the pretty baby alone. She was no finer than many others who'd accepted his advances with pleasure. He stiffened his neck.

"My heart accuses me of nothing, sir. Your words are an insult! I demand satisfaction for your insulting language, sir!"

Harry Temple had never fought or even seen a duel, but that was the language in which a challenge was usually delivered in the novels he read.

"It's not a matter for discussion!" said David, ignoring the other's blustering words. "I know what happened yesterday afternoon and tell you again that it would be good for you to leave town at once. I have nothing further to say."

David turned and walked toward the door. Harry stood, ignored, angry, crestfallen, and watched him.

"You'd better ask your informant about her part in the matter!" he hissed.

David turned back with a look of scorn.

Harry withered under that glance and regretted the false words. He felt his own small soul.

"I knew you were a knave, but I didn't suppose you were also a coward. A man who is not a coward will not blame a woman, especially an innocent one. You, sir, will leave town this evening. Any business further than you can settle between this and that I will see properly attended to. I warn you, sir, that it will be unwise for you to remain longer than the evening coach."

David's tones were courteous, his eyes commanding, his face determined. Harry couldn't reply or face his accuser. And before he realized it, David was gone.

He stood by the window and watched him walk swiftly down the street. Spafford's last words were true, he admitted; it was wise for him to leave town. But he rebelled at the idea. Business matters were in such chaos that it would be awkward for him to meet his employers and explain his desertion at that time. And several homes in the town, with their varied attractions, were open to him whenever he chose. He'd been leading a lazy, pleasant life here, wholly trusted and wholly disloyal to the trust. No uneasy overseers troubled him, not even his own conscience, and he was dined and smiled upon with lovely, languishing eyes. He didn't care to go, even though he'd decried the town as dull and monotonous.

But on the other hand, things had occurred—not the unfortunate little mistake of yesterday, of course, but other more serious things—that he'd hardly care to have exposed, especially through Spafford's paper. He'd seen other sinners brought to a bloodless retribution in those columns with that writer's sarcasm and wit. He didn't care to be humili-- ated in that way. He was convinced the man meant what he said, and from what he knew of his influence, Spafford would leave no stone unturned till he made the place too hot to hold him. Only Harry knew how easy that would be, for no one else knew how many "mistakes" he'd made; and he didn't know how many were not known by those who could harm him.

He stood a long time clinking sixpences and shillings together in his pocket and scowling down the street after David disappeared from sight.

"Blame that little pink-cheeked, baby-eyed fool!" he said at last, turning on his heel with a sigh. "I might have known she was too goody-goody. Such people ought to die young before they grow up to make fools of other people. Bah! Think of a wife like that with no spirit of her own. A baby!"

Nevertheless, in his secret heart, he knew he honored Marcia and felt a true shame that she had seen his tarnished soul.

Then he looked around on his papers representing a whole week's hard work and maybe more before they were all cleared away. How much easier to get up a good excuse and leave this to some poor drudge who'd be sent here in his place! He scanned the desk again, and his eyes lighted on his book. He'd left the heroine in an exciting crisis and sat down to his story again. At least nothing demanded his attention this moment.

If he went, he'd toss some things into his carpetbag and pretend to be summoned to see a sick and dying relative, a long-lost brother, something. It would be easy to invent an excuse when the time came. Then he could leave directions for his remaining things to be packed if he didn't return.

And why bother with the letters? Let them wait for his successor. His employers could suffer for his negligence as long as he finished his story. Besides, it wouldn't do to let that cad think he'd frightened him. He'd pretend he wasn't going, at least during his hours of grace. So he read his book.

To those who came into the office on business, he professed an unusually busy morning and scheduled appointments with them for the next day. This satisfied him as the morning wore away, and he was left to his book. At noon he strolled to his boardinghouse for his usual dinner, having come within a few pages of the end.

After a leisurely dinner he sauntered back to the office again, pleased. He'd passed David Spafford in front of the newspaper office and given him a most elaborate and friendly bow in the presence of four or five bystanders. David's look spoke volumes and convinced Harry to do as ordered—not, of course, because he was ordered to do so, but because it would be easier. In fact, he decided he was weary of this part of the country. He returned to his book.

Midafternoon he finished the last pages. He stood up hastily then and considered what to do. He glanced around the room, searched for a few papers, and took some daguerreotypes of girls from a desk drawer. Then, with another glance around, he walked out and locked the door.

He paused at the corner, undecided about his direction. He didn't need to go to his boardinghouse yet, for the afternoon was only half over, and he wished his departure to appear unpremeditated. A daring thought came to mind. He'd walk past David Spafford's house and let Marcia see him, if possible.

He'd show them he wasn't afraid. He even contemplated going in and explaining to Marcia that she had made a great mistake; he was only admiring her, meant no harm in anything he said or did yesterday, and was grieved she mistook his meaning for an insult. But it was a bit too much for even his bold nature, so he simply strolled by the house.

When he was directly opposite, he raised his eyes, bowed, and smiled. He didn't see anyone, though, for Marcia caught sight of him as she was coming out on the stoop and fled into her own room with the door buttoned. There she watched unseen from behind her curtain, but he made the bow as complete as though a whole family were greeting him from the windows. Marcia thought he must see her and felt frozen to the spot; she stared wildly through the curtain with trembling hands and weak knees till he passed.

Pleased, the young man walked on, knowing that at least three prominent citizens saw him bow and smile; they would be witnesses, against anything David might say to the contrary, that he was on friendly terms with Mrs. Spafford.

Hannah Heath was sitting on the front stoop with her knitting. She often sat there in the afternoon, with some domestic-appearing task, smiling at passersby and luring many in to talk with her. Grandmother Heath would have made some sharp remarks to Miranda about how long it took to finish the stocking, but she seldom did to Hannah.

Now Hannah, easily conquered, wasn't such a great favorite with Harry as Harry was with Hannah. But this afternoon was different. Hannah's appearance on the stoop was opportune and gave him an idea. He'd linger there with her. Fortune may favor him again, and David Spafford would pass by and see him. He'd have one more opportunity to stare at him in defiance before obeying. David gave him the day for doing what he would, and he'd make no move until the time was over and the evening coach departed. But he knew he'd bring down retribution then. In just what form that retribution would come, he wasn't quite certain, but he knew it would be severe.

So when Hannah smiled at him, Harry stepped across the mud in the road and went to sit beside her. He toyed with her knitting and held one of her plump white hands, while Hannah pretended not to notice.

Thus he sat about five o'clock, when David walked by and bowed gravely to Hannah, apparently without seeing Harry. Harry's eyes followed the tall figure in an insolent stare.

"What a dough-faced cad that man is!" he said. "No wonder his little pink-cheeked wife seeks other society. Handsome baby, though, isn't she?"

Hannah pricked up her ears. Her loss of David was too recent not to cause jealousy of his pretty young wife; she almost hated her already. And her upbringing with Grandmother Heath's sarcastic gossip had prepared her to see meaning in any insinuation.

She looked at him keenly, then dropped her gaze. "You shouldn't blame anyone for enjoying your company."

She glanced at him slyly to see how he took this, but Harry was an old hand against such scrutiny. He only shrugged his shoulders as if to shed any blame.

"And what's the matter with David?" asked Hannah. She watched him mount his own steps and remembered how often she thought he was destined for her. That he chose someone else made her almost desire revenge.

Harry lingered longer than intended. Hannah begged him to remain for supper, but he declined. When she pressed him he looked troubled and said he was expecting a letter in the afternoon coach. A dear friend, a beloved cousin, was lying very ill, and he might be summoned at any moment to his bedside. Hannah said some comforting little words in a caressing voice and hoped he'd find the letter saying the cousin was better. Then he hurried away.

At his boardinghouse it was easy to say he was called away. He rushed up to his room and threw some necessities into his carpetbag, scattering things around the room to help the impression he must leave quickly. When he was ready he looked at his watch. The evening coach left in half an hour. He knew its route well. It started at the village inn, where a crowd always gathered, and traveled down the old turnpike, stopping here and there to pick up passengers. Perhaps David Spafford would be in the crowd and witness his obedience to the command. He set his lips and decided to deny his adversary that satisfaction at least.

He'd have to sacrifice his supper, and he could smell the frying bacon coming up the stairs. But it would help the illusion, and he could perhaps get something on the way when the coach stopped to change horses.

He rushed downstairs and told his landlady he must start at once, since he must see a man before the coach left. She had no chance to suggest he leave her a deposit on the board he already owed her. He may have hurried for that reason also, for it always bothered him to pay his bills; he had so many other ways of spending his money.

So he caught a ride in a farm wagon heading toward the crossroads. When it turned off, he walked a little way until another wagon came along. Then he traversed several fields at a breathless pace and caught the coach just as it was leaving the crossroads, the last stopping place anywhere near the village. He climbed up beside the driver and, still breathless, detailed to him how he had received word that his cousin was dying. A messenger had come cross-country on horseback and delivered it just before the coach started.

After answering the driver's minutest questions, he sat back and reflected on his course. He was off, and he wasn't seen or questioned by a single citizen. By tomorrow night, his story, as he told it to the driver, would be fully known and circulated through the place he'd just left. The stage driver was one of the best means of advertisement. It was right to give him the details.

After he satisfied his curiosity about the young man and his reasons for leaving town so hastily, the driver waxed eloquent on the one theme occupying his spare moments: the railroad. Whether the sentiments were his own or borrowed from others, he uttered them with force and conviction. Many travelers sat and listened, viewing the subject from the coachman's standpoint.

A little later, Tony Weller, called by someone "the best beloved of all coachmen," voiced much the same sentiments in the following words: "I consider that the railroad is unconstitutional and an invader o' privileges. As to the comfort, as an old coachman I may say it, vere's the comfort o' sittin' in a harm-chair a lookin' at brick walls and heaps o' mud, never comin' to a public 'ouse, never seein' a glass o' ale, never goin' through a pike, never meetin' a change o' no kind (hosses or otherwise), but always comin' to a place, ven you comes to vun at all, the werry picter o' the last.

"As to the honor an' dignity o' travelin'," Weller said, "vere can that be without a coachman, and vat's the rail, to sich coachmen as is sometimes forced to go by it, but an outrage and an hinsult? As to the ingen, a nasty, wheezin', gaspin', puffin', bustin' monster always out o' breath, with a shiny green and gold back like an onpleasant beetle; as to the ingen as is always a pourin' out red 'ot coals at night an' black smoke in the day, the sensiblest thing it does, in my opinion, is ven there's somethin' in the vay, it sets up that 'ere frightful scream vich seems to say, 'Now 'ere's two 'undred an' forty passengers in the werry greatest extremity o' danger, an' 'ere's their two 'undred an' forty screams in vun!' "

But such sentiments as these didn't trouble Harry Temple.

He didn't care whether the present century had a railroad or traveled by foot. He wouldn't lift a finger to help or hinder. As the talk continued, he was considering how and where he might get his supper.

Chapter 18

The weather turned cold and raw that fall almost in one day. The trees that were green or yellowing in the sunshine put on their autumn garments of defeat, flaunted them for a brief hour, and dropped them early in despair. The pleasant woods, to which Marcia had fled, became a mass of finely penciled branches against a wintry sky, except for one group of tall pines standing high above the rest and defying even snowy blasts.

Marcia could see those pines from her kitchen window. Sometimes as she worked, if her heart was heavy, she'd look out at them and recall the day she laid her head down beneath them to sob out her trouble and awoke to find comfort. Somehow the memory of that little talk with David grew into vast proportions in her mind, and she cherished it.

Letters from home had arrived. Her stepmother wrote a stiff, not unloving, letter, full of injunctions to be sure to remember this and not do that and on no account to let any relative or neighbor persuade her from the ways in which she was brought up. She was attempting to do as many mothers do, when they see the faults in the child they've brought up, to try to bring them up over again. At some of the sentences, a wild homesickness overcame Marcia. Some little homely phrase about one of the servants or the mention of a pet hen or cow would bring tears to her eyes, and she felt she must throw away this new life and run back to the old one.

School had started at home. Mary Ann and Hanford would be taking the long walk back and forth together twice a day to the old schoolhouse. She half envied them their happy, care-free life. She thought of the shy courting she'd often seen between scholars in the upper classes. Sometimes when she was going to sleep, she pictured their walks to and from school and their sober talk. Not that she ever looked back to Hanford Weston with regret—she always knew he wasn't for her. And perhaps, even as early as that in her new life, if she'd had a choice of returning to her girlhood and being as she was before Kate ran away or staying here in the new life with David, she likely would have chosen to stay.

Squire Schuyler also sent occasional letters. He wrote of politics and sent many messages to his son-in-law, which Marcia handed to David at the tea table to read and which seemed to soften him and bring a sweet sadness into his eyes. He loved and respected his father-in-law. It was as if he were bound to him by the love of someone who had died. Marcia thought of that every time she handed David a letter and watched him read it.

Sometimes little Harriet or the boys printed out a few words about the family cat or the neighbors' children, and Marcia laughed and cried over the poor little attempts at letters and longed to have the eager, childish faces of the writers to kiss.

But in all of them was no mention of the bright, beautiful, selfish girl around whom the old home life used to center and who seemed now, judging from the home letters, to be worse than dead to them all.

But since the afternoon in the woods, a new and pleasant conversation had sprung up between David and Marcia. True, it was confined mainly to discussions of the new railroad, the possibilities of its success, and the construction of engines, tracks, and the like. David was constantly writing up the sub-ject for his paper and often read his articles aloud to Marcia when they were finished. She listened with breathless admira-tion, sometimes contesting a point ably, with the old vim she'd used in discussing the newspaper with her father. But mainly she agreed with every word he wrote and was always eager to understand down to the minutest detail.

He always seemed pleased at her praise and, while she put away the tea things, wrote on with a contented expression as though he'd passed a high critic and needn't fear another. Once he looked up with a quizzical expression and made a jocose remark about "our article," taking her into a sort of partnership with him in it. That set her heart to beating happily, until it seemed as if she were really, in some part at least, growing into his life.

But their companionship was a shy, distant one, more like a brother and sister separated all their lives and just beginning to get acquainted. And always a sadness was settled about the lines of David's mouth and eyes. They sat around one table now, the evenings when they were at home, for there were still occasional teas at their friends' houses. And one night a week was kept religiously for a formal supper with the aunts, which David kindly acquiesced in—more for his aunt Clarinda's sake than for that of the others—whenever he wasn't detained by actual business.

Then, too, the weekly prayer meeting was held at "early candlelight" in the old, shadowed church. They always walked down the twilighted streets together, and Marcia felt a sweet solemnity about that walk. They never said much to each other on the way. David seemed preoccupied with holy thoughts, and Marcia walked softly beside him as if he were the minister, looking at him proudly now and then. David was often called upon to pray in meeting, and Marcia loved to listen to his words. He seemed more intimate with God than the others, who were mostly old men and prayed with long, rolling sentences that put the whole community down into the dust and ashes before their Creator.

Marcia enjoyed the hour spent in the church, with the

flickering candlelight forming shadows on the wall and among the tall pews. The old minister reminded her of the one she'd left at home, though he was more learned and scholarly. And when he read the scripture passages, he took off his spectacles and lay them across the great Bible, saying, "Let's pray!"

Then a soft stir and hush were heard as the people bowed for prayer. Marcia sometimes joined in the prayer in her heart, uttering shy petitions; they were vague and indefinite and mostly concerned the days when she was troubled and homesick and felt David belonged wholly to Kate. Always her clear voice joined in the slow hymns that were given line by line to the worshipers.

Marcia and David would go out from that meeting down the street to their home with the hush upon them that must have been upon the Israelites of old after they went to the solemn congregation.

Once David came in earlier than usual and caught Marcia reading the *Scottish Chiefs*. While she jumped guiltily to be found thus employed, he smiled indulgently.

"Get your book, child, and sit down," he said after supper. "I have some writing to do, and after it's done I'll read it to you."

After that, Marcia often held a book in her hands in the long evenings when they sat together, instead of some useful employment, and so her education progressed. Thus she read Epictetus, Rasselas, *The Deserted Village*, *The Vicar of Wakefield*, *Paradise Lost*, *The Mysteries of the Human Heart*, Marshall's *Life of Columbus*, *The Spy*, *The Pioneers*, and *The Last of the Mohicans*.

She was asked to sing in the village choir. David sang a pure high tenor there, and Marcia's voice was clear and strong as a blackbird's with the plaintive sweetness of the wood robin's.

Hannah Heath was also in the choir and watched her every move, but of this Marcia was unaware until Miranda informed her.

She scarcely credited it, until one Sunday, a few weeks after

Harry Temple's departure, Hannah leaned forward from her seat among the altos and whispered quite distinctly before the service, so that those around could hear: "I've just had a letter from your friend Mr. Temple. I thought you might like to know his cousin got well, and he's gone back to New York. He won't be returning here this year. On some accounts he thought it was better not." She said it pointedly, with double emphasis on "your friend" and "some accounts."

Marcia felt her cheeks glow, much to her vexation, and tried to control her whisper to seem kind as she answered indifferently enough.

"Oh, indeed! But you must have made a mistake. Mr. Temple is a very slight acquaintance of mine. I met him only a few times and know nothing about his cousin. I wasn't even aware he went away."

Hannah raised her eyebrows and replied, quite loudly now, for the choir leader had stood up already with his tuning fork in hand, and one could hear it faintly twang. "Indeed," she said, using Marcia's own word, and added coldly, "I should have thought differently from what Harry himself told me."

Something in her tone deepened the color in Marcia's cheeks and caused it to stay there during the entire morning service as she puzzled over what Hannah could have meant. It rankled in her mind the whole day. She longed to ask David about it but couldn't get up the courage.

She couldn't bear to revive the memory of what seemed to be her shame. It was at the minister's donation party that Hannah, in a green plaid silk and tiny black velvet jacket, planted another thorn in her heart.

She selected a time when Lemuel was near and when Aunt Amelia and Aunt Hortense, who believed all young men in town were hovering about David's wife, sat on each side of Marcia, as if to guard her for their beloved nephew. He was discussing politics with Mr. Heath and never noticed, so blind he was in his trust of her.

"I've had another letter from New York, from your friend Mr. Temple." Hannah said it with the slightest possible glance over her shoulder to get the effect of her words on the faithful Lemuel. "He tells me he's met a sister of yours. By the way, she told him David used to be very fond of her before she was married. I suppose she'll be coming to visit you now she's as near as New York."

Two pairs of suspicious steely eyes flew like stinging insects to gaze upon her, one on each side, and Marcia's heart stood still for an instant. But she felt that here was her trying time, and if she'd help David and do the work for which she'd become his wife, she must protect him now from any suspicions or disagreeable tongues. By force of will she controlled the trembling of her lips.

"My sister won't likely visit us this winter, I think," she replied as coolly as if she'd had a letter to that effect that morning.

Then she deliberately looked at Lemuel Skinner and asked if he'd heard of the Baltimore and Ohio Railroad's offer of four thousand dollars in cash for the most approved engine delivered for trial before June 1, 1831, not to exceed three and a half tons in weight and capable of drawing, day by day, fifteen tons inclusive of weight of wagons, fifteen miles per hour.

Lemuel looked at her blankly and said he hadn't heard of it. He was engaged in thinking over what Hannah said about a letter from Harry Temple. He cared nothing about railroads.

"The second prize is thirty-five hundred dollars," stated Marcia eagerly, as though it were of the utmost importance to her.

"Are you thinking of trying for one of the prizes?" sneered Hannah, with a piercing look.

Now indeed the ready color flowed into Marcia's face. Her ruse was detected.

"If I were a man and understood machinery, I believe I would. What a grand thing it would be to invent a thing like an engine that would be of so much use to the world," she answered bravely.

"They're dangerous machines," said Aunt Amelia. "No right-minded Christian who wishes to live out the life his Creator has given him would ever ride behind one. I've heard boilers always explode."

"They're unnecessary!" said Aunt Hortense, as if that settled the question for all time and all railroad corporations.

But Marcia was glad for once of their disapproval and entered most heartily into a discussion of the pros and cons of engines and steam, quoting largely from David's last article for the paper on the subject, until Hannah and Lemuel moved slowly away. The discussion served to keep the aunts from inquiring further that evening about the sister in New York.

Then Marcia begged them to go with her into the kitchen and see the supply of good things brought to the minister's house by his loving parishioners. Bags of flour and meal, pumpkins, corn in the ear, eggs, and pats of butter were there, along with a wooden tub of doughnuts, baskets of apples and quinces, pounds of sugar and tea, barrels of potatoes, whole hams, a side of pork, a quarter of beef, and strings of onions.

Marcia watched the minister and his wife as they greeted their people. She wished she knew them better and might visit them and feel as much at home with them as with her own dear minister.

She avoided Hannah during the remainder of the evening. When the evening was over and she went upstairs to get her wraps, she'd almost forgotten Hannah and her ill-natured, prying remarks. But Hannah hadn't forgotten her. She came out from behind the bed curtains where she was searching for a lost glove and said she'd think Marcia would be lonely this first winter away from home and want her sister with her for a while.

But Hannah's presence always seemed to awaken Marcia's spirit.

"Oh, I'm not in the least lonely," she said, laughing. "I have many interesting things to do, and I love music and books."

"Oh, yes, I forgot you're fond of music. Harry Temple told me about it."

Again Marcia heard a hint of something more behind her words, aggravating her almost beyond control. For an instant a cutting reply reached her lips. Then she recognized how futile it would be, caught the words in time, and walked swiftly down the stairs.

Watching her come down, David saw the admiring glances of those standing in the hall below and took her under his protection with a certain pride in her youth and beauty he didn't at all realize. All the way home he talked with her about the new theory of railroad construction, contented in her companionship, while she, much perturbed, wondered how he'd feel if he knew what Hannah had said.

David fell into a deep study with a book and his papers about him after they reached home. Marcia went up to her quiet, lonely chamber, put her face in the pillow, and thought and wept and prayed. When at last she lay down to rest, she knew only to live day by day and help David all she could. At most she had nothing to fear for herself, except shame that she wasn't the first sister chosen, and she found to her surprise that was growing deeper than she'd supposed.

She wished as she fell asleep that her girlish dreams might have been left to develop and bloom like other girls' and that she might have had a real love—like David in every way; yet, of course, not David because he was Kate's. She longed for a man who'd meet her as David did that night when he thought she was Kate and speak to her tenderly.

One afternoon, weary with an uncommon round of burdens, David came home to rest and study some question in his library.

Finding the front door fastened and remembering he left his key in his other pocket, he walked around to the back door. Preoccupied with his thoughts, he passed through the kitchen and almost to the hall before the unusual sounds of melody reached his ears. He stopped for an instant amazed, then, remembering the piano, wondered who was playing. Perhaps some visitor was in the parlor. Being tired and dusty from the office, he didn't care to meet a visitor. So under cover of the music, he slipped into the door of his library across the hall and dropped into his armchair.

Softly and tenderly the music stole through the open door, like a psalm or chapter in the Bible sent to comfort an aching heart. He leaned his head back and let it float over him and rest him. Tinkling brooks and gentle zephyrs, waving forest trees and twittering birds, lazy clouds floating by, distant bells, lowing herds, music of the angels high in heaven—the soothing strain from each was extracted and brought to heal his broken heart. It fell like dew on his spirit.

Then, like a fresh breeze, came a new tune, grand and fine, calling him to better things. He didn't know it was a strain of Handel's music grown immortal, but his spirit recognized the higher call, commanding him to follow. Straightway he felt strengthened to go forward in the course he'd been pursuing. Old troubles lessened, while anguish fell away from him. He took a new lease on life.

Then she played by ear one or two of the old hymns they sang in church, touching the notes tenderly and almost making them speak the words. It seemed like a benediction. Suddenly the playing ceased, and Marcia remembered it was nearly suppertime.

He met her in the doorway with a new look in his eyes, of

high purpose and exultation. He smiled at her. "That was good, child. I didn't know you could do it. You must give it to us often."

Marcia felt pleasure in his kindness, although she felt that the look in his eyes set him apart and above her and made her feel like the child she was. She hurried out to get supper, sensing pleasure and nameless unrest. She was glad of this much, but she wanted more, something to satisfy her soul.

Chapter 19

Life hadn't gone well with Mistress Kate Leavenworth. She hadn't succeeded in turning her father's heart toward her as she'd expected when she ran away with her sea captain. She wrote a cheery letter home, prettily taking for granted the forgiveness she thought unnecessary to ask. But in return a brief, harsh statement came from her father that she was no longer his daughter and must cease further communication with the family in any way, that she should never enter his house again and not a penny of his money would ever pass to her. He also informed her plainly that the trousseau made for her was given to her sister who was now the wife of the man she didn't see fit to marry.

At first Mistress Kate stormed over this letter, then wept, and finally sat down to frame epistle after epistle in petulant, penitent language. These epistles followed each other by daily mail coaches but still brought nothing further from her irate parent. And she was at last forced to face the fact she must bear the penalty of her own misdeeds—a lesson she should have learned much earlier in life.

The young captain, who had always made it appear he had plenty of money, spent his salary and most of his mother's fortune, which was left in his keeping as administrator of his father's estate. So he had little to offer the spoiled beauty, who simply wouldn't settle down to the inevitable and accept what she had brought on herself and others.

Day after day she fretted and blamed her husband until he wished her back from whence he took her; wished her back with the straitlaced man from whom he stole her; wished her anywhere except where she was. Her brightness and beauty seemed gone; she was a sulky child insisting upon the moon or nothing. She wanted to go to New York and be established in a fine house with plenty of servants and a carriage and horses, and the young captain hadn't the means for furnishing these accessories to an elegant life.

He had loved her as far as his shallow nature could love, and perhaps she'd returned it in the beginning. He wanted to spend his furlough in quiet places where he might enjoy his ideal honeymoon, bantering Kate's sparkling sentences, looking into her beautiful eyes, and touching her rosy lips with his own as often as he chose. But Mistress Kate had lost her sparkle. She wouldn't be kissed until she gained her point, her lovely eyes were full of disfiguring tears and angry flashes, and her speech scintillated with cutting sarcasms. Indeed, those biting comments were hard to bear in that they pressed home some disagreeable truths to the careless spendthrift. The rose had lost its dew and was making its thorns felt.

And so they quarreled through their honeymoon, and Captain Leavenworth wasn't sorry when a hasty, unexpected end came to his furlough, and he was ordered off with his ship for an indefinite time.

Even then Kate tried to get her way before he left and held on to her sullenness and blame until the last minute. So he hurried away without even one good-bye kiss and with her angry sentences ringing in his ears.

True, he repented somewhat on board the ship and sent her back more money than she could have expected under the circumstances. But he sent it without one gentle word, and Kate's heart was hard toward her husband.

Then with bitterness and anguish she sat down to think of the man she'd jilted. He would have been kind to her and given her all she asked and more. He would even have moved his business to New York to please her, she felt sure. Why was she so foolish? And then, like other sinners who at least see the error of their ways, she thought ill of a Fate that allowed her to make such a great mistake and pitied her poor self.

But she took her money and went to New York, for she felt that only there could she be happy and have some delightful taste of true living.

She took up residence with an old relative of her own mother's, who lived in a quiet, respectable part of the city and was glad to piece out her small annuity with the modest sum Kate agreed to pay for her board.

Soon Mistress Kate—with her beautiful face and the pretty clothes she provided at once for herself from the diminishing sum her husband had sent her, not thinking of tomorrow or the day when the board bills would be due—became well known. Daily the musty little parlor of the relative was filled with visitors, and every evening Kate held court, with the old aunt nodding in her chair by the fireside.

Neither did the poor old lady have an easy time of it, in spite of the promise of weekly pay. Kate laughed at the old furniture and old ways. She demanded new things and got them, until the old lady saw little hope of any help from the board money.

"I saw this in a shop downtown, Auntie," Kate was constantly saying, "and since I knew you needed it, I bought it. My board this week will just pay for it."

As always, Kate ruled, and the little parlor acquired an air of brightness. A few women of fashion took her up, and Kate launched herself on a lively life, her one object to have as good a time as possible, regardless of what her husband or anyone else might think.

One day, when Kate had been in New York about two months, she went on a drive with one of her new acquaintances, a young married woman of about her own age, who'd been given all in a worldly way that had been denied to Kate. They made some calls in Brooklyn and returned on the ferry, carriage and all, just as the sun was setting.

The view was marvelous. The water was a flood of pink, green, and gold; the sails of the vessels along the shore lit up resplendently; the buildings of the city beyond sent back occasional flashes of reflected light from a window glass or a church spire. It was a picture worth looking at, and Kate's companion was absorbed in it.

Not so Kate. She sat up straight, aware she looked pretty in her new dress with the fine lace collar she'd purchased the day before and her leghorn bonnet with its real ostrich feather. She enjoyed sitting behind the coachman, her elegant friend beside her, and being admired by the two ladies and the little girl who sat in the ladies' cabin and occasionally peeped curiously at her from the window. She drew herself up and let her soul "delight itself in fatness"—borrowed fatness, perhaps, but still the long desired. She told herself she had a right to it, for wasn't she a Schuyler? That name was respected everywhere.

A young man, fashionably attired, sauntered up to the carriage. He spoke to Kate's friend and was introduced. Kate felt he came because of her, and his bold black eyes told her as much.

"You say you spent the summer near Albany, Mr. Temple," said Kate presently. "I wonder if you happen to know any of my friends. Did you meet a Mr. Spafford? David Spafford?"

"Of course I did, knew him well," said the young man with a guarded tone. But a gleam of dislike and perhaps fear crossed his face at the name.

Kate was alert and analyzed that look. She parted her charming red lips and showed her sharp little teeth.

"He was once in love with me," said Kate, wrinkling her nose and laughing in a way that would have cut David to the heart.

"Indeed!" said Harry. "I don't wonder. Isn't everyone when they see you, Madam Leavenworth? How kind of your husband to stay at sea so long and give us other poor fellows a chance to say pleasant things."

Then Kate pouted her pretty lips and tapped the delighted Harry with her carriage parasol across his hand that had taken familiar hold of the carriage beside her arm.

"Oh, you naughty man!" she exclaimed. "How dare you! Yes, David Spafford and I were quite good friends. I almost gave in at one time and became Mrs. Spafford, but he was too good for me!"

She uttered this truth in a mocking tone, and Harry saw her lead and followed. Here was a possible chance for revenge. He was ready for any. He studied the lady. What did that face remind him of? Had he ever seen her before?

"I'd judge him a little straitlaced for your lively ways," he responded gallantly, "but he's like all the rest, fickle. He's married. Have you heard?"

Kate's face darkened with something hard and cruel, but her voice was soft as a cat's purr. "Yes," she sighed, "I know. He married my sister. Poor child! I'm sorry for her. I think he did it out of revenge, and she was too young to know her own mind. But they'll have to bear the consequences of what they've done. Isn't it a pity that has to be, Mr. Temple? It's dreadful the innocent must suffer. I've been quite anxious about my sister."

She lifted her large eyes swimming in tears, and he didn't perceive the insincerity in her purring voice just then. He was thanking his lucky stars he was saved from any remarks about young Mrs. Spafford, whom her sister seemed to love so deeply. How fortunate he didn't speak! He tried to say some comforting nothings and was delighted to see her face clear into smiles and her blue eyes look into his. By the time the boat touched the New York side, the two felt well acquainted, and Harry Temple promised to call soon, which promise he lost no time in keeping.

Kate's heart had grown bitter against the young sister who took her place and against the man who so easily solaced himself. She couldn't understand it. She resolved to learn what Mr. Temple knew about David and if he were happy. She desired the lifelong devotion of every man who came near her, and have it she would or punish him.

Harry Temple, meanwhile, was reflecting upon his chance meeting that afternoon and wondering if he mightn't yet have revenge on the man who'd humbled him, perhaps with this woman's help.

After some thought he sat down and penned a letter to Hannah Heath, scattering devoted sentences throughout, which caused her eyes to sparkle and a smile of anticipation to frame her lips. When she heard of the beautiful sister in New York and her former relations with David Spafford, her eyes narrowed, and she frowned. Harry Temple drew a word picture of Mrs. Leavenworth. Gold hair! Ah! Hannah had heard of gold hair before and in connection with David's promised wife. Here was a mystery, and Hannah resolved to look into it. It would at least be interesting to note the effect of her knowledge on the young bride next door.

Meanwhile, the acquaintance of Harry Temple and Kate Leavenworth progressed rapidly. Seeing the lady a second time proved more interesting than the first, for now her beautiful gold hair added to the charm of her attractive face. Harry delighted in beauty, and a blond was more fascinating to him than a brunette. Kate dressed bewitchingly, and her manner was charming. She knew how to assume childlike airs but wasn't afraid to look him boldly in the eyes, and the light in her own seemed to challenge him.

Here was a delightful new study. A woman fresh from the country, having the appeal of innocence, almost as childlike as her sister, yet with none of her prudishness. Kate's eyes held latent wickedness in them, or he was mistaken. She didn't drop her lids and blush when he looked into her face but stared him back, daring, as though she'd go quite as far as he. Moreover, with her he was sure he needn't feel the same compunctions as with her younger sister who was obviously innocent; for whether Kate's boldness was from lack of knowledge or lack of innocence, she plainly could protect herself.

So Harry settled into his chair with a smile of pleasant anticipation on his face. He not only had the prospect of a possible ally in revenge against David Spafford, but he had the promise of an unusually delightful flirtation with a woman worthy of his best efforts.

Almost at once it began, with pleasant banter and compliments.

"Lovelier than I thought, my lady," said Harry, bowing low over the hand she gave him and brushing her pink fingertips with his lips in a way that signified he was her slave.

Kate blushed and smiled, for though she'd held her own little court in the village where she was brought up and queened it over the young men who flocked about her willingly, she wasn't used to the flattery that breathed from Harry Temple in every word and glance.

He stood back and observed her a moment to see if she was offended with his salutation, and saw as he expected that she was pleased. Her cheeks had grown rosier, and her eyes sparkled as she responded with gracious words.

Then they sat down and faced one another. A good woman would have called his look impudent—insulting. Kate returned it with an unwavering look and recklessly accepted the challenge. Playing with fire, these two were, and with no concern for the fearful results that might follow. Both knew the danger and liked it better for that. A long silence ensued. The game was opening on a wider scale than either had ever played.

"Do you believe in affinities?" asked the devil, through the man's voice.

The woman colored and showed she understood his deeper meaning. Her eyes dropped for an instant, and then she looked up and faced him provokingly.

"Why?"

He admired her with his gaze and waited, lazily watching the color play in her cheeks.

"Do you need to ask why?" he said at last, looking at her significantly. "I knew you were my affinity the moment I saw you, and I hoped you felt the same. But perhaps I was mistaken." He searched her face.

She kept her eyes upon his, returning their full gaze, as if to hold it from going too deeply into her soul. "I didn't say you were mistaken, did I?" asked the rosy lips.

Something in the curve of cheek and chin and sweep of dark lash over velvet skin reminded him of her sister. She'd sat thus, though utterly unaware, while he was singing, when he had that overwhelming desire to kiss her. If he kissed this lady, would she slap him in the face and run into the garden? He thought not. Still, she was brought up by the same father and mother in all likelihood, and it was better to go slow.

He reached forward, drawing his chair nearer, and then took one of her small, unresisting hands, gently, that he mightn't frighten her, and smoothed it thoughtfully between his own. He held it in a close grasp and looked into her face again.

She meanwhile watched her hand, as though something apart from her, a sort of distant possession for which she wasn't responsible.

"I feel that you belong to me," he said, looking into her eyes with a languishing gaze. "I've known it from the first moment."

Kate let her hand lie in his as if she liked it. "And what makes you think that, audacious sir? Didn't you know I'm married?" Then she swept her gaze up at him again and smiled, showing her dainty, treacherous teeth.

She was so pretty and tempting then that he desired to kiss her on the spot, but he thought he'd rather lead her further first. He was succeeding well. She had no mind to be afraid.

"That makes no difference," he said smiling. "That another man has won you first and has the right to provide for you and be near you is my misfortune, of course. But it makes no difference. You're mine! By all the power of love you're mine. Can any other man keep my soul from yours? Can he keep my eyes from looking into yours or my thoughts from hovering over you or—" He hesitated and looked at her, while she watched him, holding her breath and half inviting him. "Or my lips from drinking life from yours?" He stooped quickly and pressed his lips upon hers.

Kate gasped and pulled back. The aunt nodding over her Bible in the next room hadn't heard—she was nearly deaf— but for an instant the young woman felt that all the shades of her worthy patriarchal ancestors were scurrying around and away from her in horror. She came of too good Puritan stock not to know she was treading in the path of unrighteousness. Nevertheless, it was a broad path, easy and tempting. It promised to satisfy some of her untamed impulses.

She didn't look offended. She only pulled back to catch her breath and consider. The wild beating of her heart and the tumult of her cheeks and eyes were part of a new emotion.

"But I didn't say you might," she cried with a bewildering smile.

"I beg your pardon, fair lady. May I have another?"

His face was so near her own that she didn't see the evil triumph lurking there. She reached another corner in her life, and here she might turn back. She half knew this, yet she toyed with the opportunity, and it was gone. The new way seemed so alluring.

"You'll first have to prove your right!" she said with that pretty commanding air that had conquered so many times.

And so they continued through the evening, playing with edged tools.

A friendship thus begun—if such an unworthy intimacy may be called by that dear name—boded no good for either of the two, and that evening marked a decided turn for the worse in Kate Leavenworth's career.

Chapter 20

*D*avid found it necessary to travel, possibly having to stay away for several weeks. He told Marcia in the evening when he came home from the office, as he would have told his clerk. It merely annoyed him to start out in the early winter, leave his business in others' hands indefinitely, and go among strangers. He didn't see Marcia's face pale or her hand move quickly to her heart.

Even she didn't realize all it meant to her. This quiet life in the big house, with only David at intervals to watch and speak to occasionally, and no one to open her true heart to, was lonely. And many times when she was alone at night, she wept bitter tears—why, she didn't know. But now when she knew it would cease, and David was leaving her for a long time, perhaps weeks, her heart tightened. Tears almost came to her eyes, but she hurried over to the hearth for the teapot, busying herself there till they were under control again. When she returned to her place at the table, she was able to ask David some ordinary question about the journey, keeping her true feeling hidden.

He was to start the next evening if possible. Something important about railroading was coming up in Congress. He needed to be present to hear the debate and see and interview influential men. It meant a great deal to the success of the new enterprises for him to go and learn about them and write them up; his heart was in them and could do it best. He was pleased to be selected for this. It lifted him for a time above himself and his troubles and caused him to feel he had a worthwhile work, a chance to help unroll the secret possibilities of the universe.

Marcia understood and was proud and glad for him, but her own heart, beating in such perfect sympathy with the work, felt lonely and left out. If only she could have helped, too!

David had no time to take Marcia to her home to stay during his absence. He spoke of it regretfully as he was about to leave and asked if she'd like to get someone to escort her by coach to her father's house until he could come for her. But she held back the tears by sheer force and shook her head. She'd considered that question in the still night hours. She imagined meeting the home village with its kind and unkind curiosity; hearing their covert whispers as to why her husband didn't come with her; why he'd left her so soon after the honeymoon; why—a hundred things. She even thought of Aunt Polly and her acrid tongue and decided that whatever happened she didn't want to go home.

The only other alternative was to go to the aunts. David expected it, and the aunts spoke of it as if nothing else were possible. Marcia preferred to remain alone in her own house, with her beloved piano. But David wouldn't consent, and the aunts were scandalized at the suggestion. So to the aunts went Marcia, and they took her in with the hope that she might get the same good from the visit that the sluggard in the Bible is bidden to find.

"We must do our duty by her for David's sake," said Aunt Hortense, with pursed lips and folded hands that seemed aching to reconstruct the new niece.

"Yes, it's our opportunity," said Aunt Amelia with a snap. "Poor David!"

And so they laid out their plans for their sweet young victim, who unknowingly was coming to one of those tests in life whereby we are tried for greater things and perfected in patience and sweetness.

It began with the first breakfast. At supper the night before, she was company; but when morning came, they felt she must be counted as one of the family. They examined her thoroughly regarding housekeeping. They asked about her recipes for pickling and preserving. They put her through a catechism of culinary lore. Always after her most animated account of her careful training in this or that housewifely art, she looked up with wistful eyes that longed to please. But she was met only by the hard, set lips and steely glances of the two mentors who regretted that she hadn't been taught their way, which was so much better.

Aunt Hortense went so far as to suggest that Marcia write and tell her stepmother how much better it was to salt the water for boiling potatoes before putting them in. She was highly offended by Marcia's girlish laugh bubbling up involuntarily at the thought of teaching her stepmother anything about cooking.

"Excuse me," she said, sobering at the aunt's grim look and frightened at what she'd done. "I didn't mean to laugh. But it seemed so funny to think of my telling Mother how to do anything."

"People are never too old to learn," remarked Aunt Hortense, "and one should never be too proud when there's a better way."

"But Mother thinks there is no better way, I'm sure. She says it makes potatoes soggy to boil them in salt. Her rule is, all that grows below the ground should be salted after it's cooked, and all that grows above the ground should be cooked in salted water."

"I'm surprised your stepmother would hold such superstitious ideas," said Aunt Amelia.

"One should never be too proud to learn something better," Aunt Hortense said grimly.

Marcia retreated in dire consternation at the idea of these three notable housekeeping gentlewomen coming together.

But she felt triumph in the thought that it would be hard to down her stepmother.

Marcia was given a few light duties to "make her feel at home," but in reality, she knew, it was because the aunts felt she needed their instruction. They asked her if she'd like to wash the china and glass. So, regularly after each meal, a small wooden tub and a cloth were brought in with hot water and soap. She was expected to handle the costly heirlooms under the scrutiny of their worshiping owners, who evidently watched each process with strained nerves lest any bit of treasured pottery should be cracked or broken.

The girl would have been no girl if she didn't chafe under this treatment. To hold her temper steady and sweet under it was almost more than she could bear.

And during long afternoons it was sometimes decreed they should knit.

Marcia was used to taking long walks at home, however, over the smooth crust of the snow to her beloved woods, where she delighted to wander among the bare, creaking trees. But it would be a dreadful thing in the aunts' opinion for a woman, and especially a young one, to walk in the woods alone, in winter, too, and with no object whatever in view but a walk! What a waste of time!

Marcia found two places of refuge during the weeks that followed. One was home. How sweet that word sounded to her! How she longed to go back there, with David coming home to his quiet meals three times a day and with her own time to herself to do as she pleased. With housewifely zeal that was commendable in the aunts' eyes, Marcia insisted on going down to her house every morning to see that all was right, guiltily knowing she meant to hurry to her beloved books and piano.

To be sure, the empty house was cold and cheerless. She dared not make up fires and leave them, and she dared not stay too long or the aunts would feel hurt by her absence. But she longed to be back there by herself, away from that terrible supervision, living her glad little life and thinking her thoughts untrammeled by primness.

Sometimes she curled up in David's big armchair and cried. After that she took a book and read until the chills creeping down her spine warned her she must stop. Even then she ran up and down the hall or took a broom and swept vigorously to warm herself and then went to the cold keys and played a sad little tune. All her tunes seemed sad while David was gone.

The other place of refuge was Aunt Clarinda's room. She went there after supper, to the old lady's delight. Then the other two occupants of the house were left to themselves and might unbend from their rigid surveillance for a little while. Marcia often wondered if they ever did unbend.

Aunt Clarinda had a large, padded rocking chair in her room, and each evening Marcia laughingly took the little old lady in her arms and placed her comfortably in it, after a pleasant struggle on Aunt Clarinda's part to put her guest into it. It seemed to please the old woman mightily. Then when she was conquered, she always sat meekly laughing, a fine pink color in her soft peachy cheeks, with the candlelight from the high shelf throwing sparkles in her old eyes that always seemed young.

"That's just as David used to do," she said.

Then Marcia pulled up the mahogany stool covered with the worsted dog that Aunt Clarinda had worked when she was ten years old. Snuggling at the old woman's feet, she exclaimed, "Tell me about it!" And they settled down to solid comfort.

A letter arrived from David after he was gone a little over a week. Marcia hadn't expected to hear from him. He'd said nothing about writing, and their relations scarcely made it necessary. Letters were an expensive luxury in those days. But when the letter was handed to her, Marcia's heart pounded, the color flew into her cheeks, and she sped home on feet swift as a bird's wings.

The postmaster's daughter looked after her and remarked to her father: "My, but don't she think a lot of him!"

Straight to the cold, lonely house she flew and sat down in his big chair to read it.

It was a pleasant letter, beginning formally, *"My dear Marcia,"* and asking after her health. It brought back a little of the unacquaintedness she felt when he was at home, which was swept away partly by her knowledge of his childhood. But it continued quite happily telling about his journey and describing the places he saw and the people he met on the way; he detailed every incident as only a born writer and observer could do, until she felt as if he were talking to her. He told her about the men he met who were interested in the new project. He told of new plans and described his visit to the foundry at West Point and the machinery he saw.

Marcia read it all breathlessly, in search of something, she didn't know what, that wasn't there. When she finished without finding it, an aloofness and a disappointment welled up in her throat. She sat back to think about it. He was having a good time and wasn't lonely. He had no longing to be back in the house with everything running as before he left. He was out in the big glorious world with progress and meeting men who were making history.

Of course he didn't dream how lonely she was and how she longed, if for nothing else, just to be back here alone and do as she pleased and not be watched over. If only she might steal Aunt Clarinda to live here with her while David was away! But that wasn't to be thought of, of course. Soon she mustered courage to be glad of her letter and read it again.

That night she read the letter to Aunt Clarinda, and together they discussed the great inventions and the changes in the land. Aunt Clarinda was a little beyond her depth in the conversation, but Marcia did most of the talking. The dear lady made an excellent listener, with a pat here and a "Dear me! You don't say!" there and an occasional "Bless the boy! What great things he expects! I hope he won't be disappointed."

That letter lasted them many days until another arrived. This time it came from Washington, with descriptions of public men and public doings and a word picture of the place that made it seem much like any other place, even if it was the capital of the country. And once there was a sentence Marcia treasured: *"I wish you could be here and see everything. I know you'd enjoy it."*

Another letter arrived later beginning, *"My dear little girl."* Nothing else in it warmed Marcia inside; it was all about his work. But she carried it many days in her heart. It thrilled her to think of those beginning words. Of course it meant only that he thought of her as a girl, his little sister she was to have been. But the words had a kind of ownership that was sweet to Marcia's lonely heart. She realized she was always looking for something that would make her feel she belonged to David.

Chapter 21

After David was in New York about three weeks, he happened one day to pass the house where Kate Leavenworth was living.

Kate was standing listlessly by the window gazing into the street. She was cross and felt a great depression settling over her. The flirtation with Harry Temple was beginning to pall upon her. She wanted new worlds to conquer, to meet more people, senators, and statesmen, and have plenty of money to dress as became her beauty and to be admired publicly.

She half wished for her husband's return and considered making up with him in order to go to Washington and enjoy society there. Why run away with a naval officer if one couldn't benefit from it? She was a fool. Here she was almost to the last penny, and so many things she wanted. No word had come from her husband since he sent her the money at sailing. She felt a bitter resentment toward him for urging her to marry him. If she'd only married David, she'd be living a life of ease now, with plenty of money and nothing to do but what she pleased. She'd have no anxiety, for David would have done just what she wanted.

Then suddenly she looked up, and David walked by in front of her! He was engaged in a deep conversation with a tall, nice-looking man. He didn't know Kate was in New York and passed the house unaware of the eyes watching him.

Kate's face grew pale and her limbs weak, but she strained against the window to watch the retreating figure of the man who had almost been her husband. How well she knew the familiar outline. How fine and handsome he appeared now! Why didn't she think so before? Were her eyes blind, or had she been under some strange enchantment? Why hadn't she known her happiness lay in the way marked out for her? Well, at least she knew now.

She sat all day by the window and watched. She professed to have no appetite when pressed to come to the table, though she consumed the tray of tasty items brought to her. Her eyes were fixed on the street until the sun went down and dusk sifted through the streets, but she saw no sign of him again or heard his footsteps. Then she hurried up to her room, which also faced the street, and there, wrapped in blankets, she sat in the frosty air, waiting and listening. And while she watched she thought bitter, feverish thoughts.

She heard Harry Temple knock and knew he was told she wasn't feeling well and had retired early. She watched him pause on the stoop as if considering what to do with this unexpected time on his hands. Then she saw him saunter up the street and wondered idly where he'd go and what he'd do.

It grew late, even for New York. One by one the lights in the houses along the street went out, and all was quiet. She withdrew from the window, weary with excitement, and lay down on the bed, but she couldn't sleep. The window was open, and her ears were on the alert. Eventually she heard the distant echo of feet ringing on the pavement. Someone was coming. She sprang up. She felt sure it was he. Yes, there were two men. They were coming back together. She could hear their voices. She imagined she heard David's long before it was possible to distinguish any words. She leaned far out of her upper window till she could discern dim forms under the starlight.

Then just as they were under the window, she distinctly heard David say, "There's no doubt we'll win. The right is on our side, and it's the march of progress. Some of the best men in Congress are with us. And now that we're to have your influence, I don't feel afraid of the issue."

They passed by rapidly, like men on a long day's jaunt hurrying home to rest. Kate understood little in the sentence. She had no more idea whether the subject of their discourse was railroads or the last hay crop. The sentence meant only one thing to her: David kept company with the great men of the land, and his position would have given her a standing above the one she now occupied. Tears of defeat ran down her cheeks. She'd made a bad mistake and saw no way to rectify it. If her husband died—and it might be, for the sea was often treacherous, and of course there were all sorts of possibilities— but even then there was Marcia!

She set her teeth into her red lips till the blood came. She couldn't get over her anger at Marcia. It wouldn't have been so bad if David had remained hers, ready to fly to her if others failed. Her self-love was wounded, and she mistook it for love of David. She imagined she loved him after all and Fate had played her a mad trick and tied her to a husband she hadn't wanted.

Then out of her worn imagination a plan emerged. She thought of her intimacy with Harry and her newfound power. Could she exercise it over others as well as Harry Temple? Could she lead back this man who once loved her, to bow at her feet again and worship her? If so, she could bear the rest. She longed to see David grovel at her feet, to hear him plead for a kiss from her and tell her once more how beautiful she was and how she fulfilled his soul's ideals. She stayed by the open window with the icy night air blowing on her, but her cheeks burned in the darkness, and her eyes glowed like coals of fire. The blankets slipped away from her throat, and still she heeded not the cold but sat with hot clenched hands scheming with the devil's own strategy.

In time she lit a candle and brought out her writing materials. But she sat and thought awhile before she finally wrote a hastily scrawled note, signed and sealed it, and, blowing out her candle, lay down to sleep.

> *Dear David,*
>   *I've just heard you're in New York. I'm in great distress and don't know where to turn for help. For the sake of what we were to each other in the past, will you come to me?*
>   *Hastily, your loving Kate*

She didn't know where David was but felt reasonably sure she could find out his address in the morning. A small boy living next door could ferret out almost anything for money. Kate had employed him more than once as an amateur detective in cases of minor importance. So, with a bit of silver and her letter, she found him and explained carefully that the letter was to be delivered only to the man to whom it was addressed. She named several places where he might be found and hinted that more silver was forthcoming when he brought her an answer to the note. With a detailed description of David, the sharp-eyed boy set out, while Kate returned to her room to dress for David's arrival. She felt sure he would be found and come at once.

The previous night's icy wind, blowing on her exposed throat and shoulders, had given her a severe cold, but she ignored that. Her eyes and cheeks shone with fever. She knew she was entering a dangerous, unholy way. The excitement of it stimulated her. She didn't care for anything, right or wrong, sin or sorrow, only to win. She wanted to see David at her feet again. That alone would satisfy this insatiable longing in her, this wounded pride of self.

When she was dressed, she stood before the mirror and surveyed herself. She knew she was beautiful and defied the mirror to tell her anything else. She raised her chin in haughty challenge to the unseen David to resist her charms. She would make him forget Marcia, his home, his staid Puritan notions, and all else he held dear but her. He should bend and kiss her hand as Harry had, only more warmly, for instinctively she felt his was the purer life and therefore his surrender would mean more.

She'd arrayed herself in black velvet, without a touch of color or white. From her rich gown her slender throat rose, like a stem on which nodded the tempting flower of her face. No enameled complexion could have been more striking in its vivid reds and whites, and her mass of gold hair made her seem more lovely than she really was, for in her face was love of self, alluring but heartless.

The boy found David, as Kate thought he would, in one of the quieter hostelries where men of letter would stop when in New York. David read the letter and came at once. His heart beat wildly, excluding all other thoughts except that she was in trouble, his love, his dear one. He forgot Marcia and the young naval officer and everything but her trouble. Before he reached her house, the sorrow grew in his imagination into some great danger from which he must protect her.

She received him alone in the room where Harry Temple first called. A moment later Harry himself knocked and inquired after Mistress Leavenworth's health; he was told she was very much engaged at present with a gentleman and couldn't see anyone. Harry scowled and set himself at a suitable distance from the house to see who came out.

David's face was pale as death when he entered. She stood and posed—not at all the picture of broken sorrow he expected from her note—and let the sense of her beauty reach him. There she stood with the look on her face he'd pictured to himself many times when he had thought of her as his wife. It was a look of alluring, compelling love. He had thought she would meet him thus when he came home to her from his daily business cares. Now she was there, looking that way, and he stood here, so near her, and yet a great gulf fixed between! Heaven and hell were met together, and he had no power to change either.

He didn't come over to her and bow low to kiss the hand as Harry had—as she thought she could compel him to do. He only stood and looked at her with the pain of anguish beyond her comprehension, until the look would have burned through to her heart—if she'd had a heart.

"You're in trouble," he spoke hoarsely, as if murmuring an excuse for having come.

She melted at once into a lovely sorrow, her mobile features taking on a wan cast enlivened only by her glowing cheeks.

"Sit down," she said. "You were so good to come to me, and so soon." And her voice was like lily bells in a quiet churchyard among the headstones. She offered him a chair.

"Yes, I'm in trouble. But that's slight compared to my unhappiness. I think I'm the most miserable creature on earth."

And with that she dropped into a chair and hid her glowing face in a lace-bordered handkerchief, suppressing a well-timed sob.

Kate had wisely calculated how she could reach David's heart. If she'd looked up then and seen his pale look and the tense grasp of his hands that only the greatest self-control kept quiet on his knee, perhaps even her mercilessness would have been softened. But she didn't look and felt her part well taken. She sobbed quietly and waited.

"Will you tell me what it is and how I can help you?" his hoarse voice asked again.

He longed to take her in his arms like a little child and comfort her, but he mustn't. She was another's. Perhaps that other had been cruel to her! His clenched fists showed how terrible the thought was.

But the bowed figure in black only wept and said, "I'm so unhappy! I can't bear it any longer."

"Is—your—husband unkind to you?"

"Oh, no—not exactly unkind—that is, he wasn't very nice before he went away," she said, "and he went away without a kind word and left me hardly any money—and he hasn't sent me any word since—and Fa–Father won't have anything to do with me anymore—but—but—it's not that I mind, David. I don't think about those things at all. I'm so unhappy about you. I feel you don't forgive me, and I can't stand it any longer. I've made a frightful mistake, and you're angry with me—I think about it at night."

The voice grew lower, and the sentences broken by sobs told better than words the distress the sufferer wished to convey.

"I've been so wicked—and you were so good and kind—and now you'll never forgive me—I think it will kill me to keep on thinking about it—" she said, her voice trailing off into tears again.

David sprang to his feet.

"Kate," he cried, "my darling! Don't talk that way. You know I forgive you. Look up, and tell me you know I forgive you."

She almost smiled her triumph beneath her sobs in the lace border, but she looked up with real tears on her face; even her tears obeyed her.

"David!" she cried, standing and clasping her hands. "Can it be true? Do you really forgive me? Tell me again."

Now she stood close to the man who was wild with tumult inside. Her golden head was near his shoulder where it had rested more than once in times past.

He looked down at her, his arms folded tightly, and said, "I do."

With her pleading blue eyes, like two jewels of light now, she looked up, questioning if she might go one step further. Her breath came quick and soft.

She lifted her tear-wet face like a flower after a storm and whispered, "If you really forgive me, then kiss me, just once, so

I may remember it always."

It was more than he could bear. He caught her to himself and pressed his lips upon hers in one tortured kiss. It was almost as if wrung from him against his will.

Then suddenly he realized what he'd done as he held her in his arms, and he put her from him gently, as a mother might put away the precious child she was sacrificing tenderly, in agony but finally. Then he stood a moment looking at her, while she almost sparkled her pleasure at him through the tears. She felt she had won.

But gradually the silence grew ominous. She realized he wasn't smiling.

His mien was like one who looks into an open grave and gazes for the last time at a dear one's remains. He didn't seem like someone who had yielded a moral point and was ready now to serve her.

She grew uneasy under his gaze. She moved forward and put out her hands, inviting, yielding, as only such a woman could do.

The spell that bound him seemed broken. He fumbled for a moment in his waistcoat pocket and brought out a large roll of bills. Placing it on the table, he picked up his hat and turned toward the door.

"Where are you going?" she asked in a voice that sounded strange to her.

He turned and looked at her again, and she knew the look meant farewell. He didn't speak. Her whole being rose for one more mighty effort.

"You're not going to leave me—now?"

"I must!" he said, and his voice sounded harsh. "I've just done something I'd feel like killing any other man for, if I were your husband. I must protect you from yourself—from me. You must be kept pure before God if it kills us both. I'd gladly die if that could help you, but I'm not even free to do that. I belong to someone else."

Then he turned and was gone.

Kate's hands fell to her sides, stiff and lifeless. The bright color faded from her cheeks, and a cold horror took possession of her. "Pure before God!" She shuddered at the name. She sank to the floor with her face buried in the chair, and the waters of humiliation rolled over her. She'd failed, and for one brief moment she saw her own sinful heart as it was.

But the devil was there. He whispered David's last sentence to her: "I belong to someone else!"

Until then, in Kate's mind, Marcia was a negative factor in the affair. She was annoyed and angry at her as one whose ignorance and impertinence had brought her into an affair where she didn't belong. But now she realized Marcia must be reckoned with. Marcia the child, who was for years her slave and did her bidding, was standing in her way. And she hated her with a sudden vindictive hate that would have killed without flinching if the opportunity had come at that moment. Kate, with her uncontrolled nature, was at the mercy of any passing passion. Hate and revenge took up residence now.

She stood up, brushing her tumbled hair back. She was too agitated to notice someone had knocked at the front door and been admitted. So when Harry Temple walked into the room, he found her standing with her hands clenched together and tears flowing down her cheeks unchecked.

Now a woman in tears, when he hadn't caused them, was Harry's opportunity. He had ways of comforting that were as unscrupulous as they generally were ineffective, and so with tenderness he took Kate's hand and held it, calling her "dear." He spoke soothing words, smoothed her hair, and kissed her flushed cheeks and eyes. It was all very pleasant to Kate's hurt pride, so she let him continue for a while.

At last he said, "Now tell me all about it, dear. I saw Lord Spafford trail away from here looking like death, and I come here and find my lady in a fine fury. What's happened? If I'm not mistaken, the insufferable cad has been badly hurt, but it seems to have ruffled the lady also."

It helped to think David was suffering, for she wanted him to suffer. He'd shamed and humiliated her. She never realized that what shamed her was that he thought her better than she was.

"He is offensively good. I *hate* him!"

The man's face grew bland with satisfaction.

"Not so good, my lady, but that he has been making love to you, if I'm not mistaken, and he with a wife at home." The words were said quietly, but they carried more of a question than the tone conveyed. The man wanted evidence against his enemy.

Kate colored uneasily and dropped her lashes.

Harry studied her face and then went on cautiously, "If his wife weren't your sister, I'd say that one might punish him well through her."

Kate gave him a hard, scrutinizing look. "You have some score against him yourself."

"Perhaps I have, my lady. Perhaps I, too, hate him. He is offensively good, you know."

Silence stood in the room for a full minute while the devil worked in both hearts.

"What did you mean by saying one might punish him through his wife? He doesn't love his wife."

"Are you sure?"

"Quite sure."

"Perhaps he loves someone else, my lady."

"He does."

"Perhaps he loves you, my lady."

She was silent, but he needed no other answer.

"Then, indeed, the way would be even clearer—if his wife were not your sister."

Kate looked at him, with a sense of his meaning dawning in her eyes.

"How?"

"In case his wife left him, do you think my lord would hold his head so high?"

Kate still looked puzzled.

"If someone else won her affection and persuaded her to leave a husband who didn't love her and was bestowing his heart," he hesitated, and his eye traveled to the roll of bills still lying where David had left it, "and his gifts," he hazarded, "upon another woman—"

Kate grasped the thought at once, and an evil glint showed in her eyes. She could see what an advantage it would be to her to have Marcia removed from the situation. It would break one more cord of honor binding David to a code she hated now, because its existence shamed her. Nevertheless, unscrupulous as she was, she couldn't see how this was a possibility.

"But she is offensively good, too," she said as if answering her own thoughts.

"All goodness has its weak spot," sneered the man. "If I'm not mistaken, you've found my lord's. It's possible I might find his wife's."

The two pairs of eyes met then, filled with an evil light. It seemed as if they were permitted to look into the pit, see the possibilities of wickedness, and exult in it. Their lurid thoughts played in their faces. All the passion of hate and revenge rushed upon Kate in a frenzy.

"You needn't stop because she's my sister."

He felt he had her permission and glanced at her in admiration for the depths to which she could go undaunted. Here was evil courage worthy of his teaching. She seemed to him beautiful enough and daring enough for Satan himself to admire.

"And may I have the pleasure of knowing I would by so doing serve my lady in some way?"

She dropped her shameless eyes and murmured, "Perhaps." Then she looked full in his eyes as if to say they understood one another.

"Then I shall feel well rewarded," he said, bowing low, and bid her good day and went out.

Chapter 22

David stumbled out the door and down the street. His one thought was to get to his room at the tavern and shut the door. He had an important appointment that morning but forgot it completely, and he passed two or three men he knew without seeing them.

He reached his room and, fastening the door, fell on his knees beside the bed. Not even when Kate played him false on his wedding morning did he feel the pain that now cut into his soul. Mingled with it now was the consciousness of sin. He had sinned against heaven, against honor and love, against all that was pure and good. He was like any evil man. He had yielded to sudden temptation and taken another man's wife in his arms and kissed her! That the woman had been his by first right and that he loved her; that she invited the kiss, indeed, pleaded for it—his sensitive conscience told him in no way lessened the offense. He had also caused the one he loved to sin. He was a man and knew the world. He should have shielded her from herself.

Yet, as he went over and over the whole scene, his soul cried out in agony, and he felt his weakness even more. He'd failed and acted like any coward.

Through the shame her words echoed as she pleaded with him to kiss her. She wanted a kiss of forgiveness and begged for it as for her life. How could he refuse? Then he tried to prove to himself that the kiss and the embrace were justified, that he did no wrong in God's sight. And always, after this confused arguing, he ended with the terrible conviction he had sinned.

Sometimes Marcia's sweet face and troubled eyes appeared to him as he wrestled alone, as if she longed to help him. Again the thought pierced him that he'd harmed this gentle girl also. He'd tangled her into his own spoiled web of life and been disloyal to her. She was pure and true and good. She gave up everything to help him, and he forgot her. He promised to love, cherish, and protect her! That was another sin. He couldn't love and cherish her when his heart belonged to someone else.

Then he thought of Kate's husband, that treacherous man who stole his bride and left her sorrowing and penniless in a strange city. Why hadn't he been calmer and questioned her before he went? Perhaps she was in need. It comforted him to think he'd left her all the money he had with him, enough to keep her from want for a while. But perhaps he was wrong to give it to her. He had no right to give it!

He groaned aloud at being helpless to help her helplessness. Wasn't there some way he could find out and help her without doing wrong?

The heavens seemed like brass, and no answer came to his appeal. He didn't want to face life. He'd been tried and failed. Yet though he knew his sin, he had an intolerable longing to commit it again. Frightened at his own weakness, he prayed for help with renewed energy. It was like the prayer of Jacob of old, the crying out of a soul that wouldn't be denied. All day long the struggle continued and far into the night.

At last a peace began to settle upon David's soul. Things confused by his passionate desires cleared. Self dropped away, and sin, conquered, slunk out of sight. Right and wrong were once more clearly defined in his mind. However wrong it might or might not be, he was here in this situation. He'd married Marcia and promised to be true to her. He was doubly cut off from Kate by her act and by his. That was his punishment—and hers. He mustn't seek to lessen it even for her, for it was God-sent. His path and hers mustn't cross. If she were to be helped in any way from any trouble, he wasn't permitted to be the instrument. He had shown his unfitness for it that morning. It was his duty to cut himself off from her forever. He mustn't even think of her anymore. He must be as true and good to Marcia as possible.

The peace that came with conviction brought sleep to his weary mind and body.

When he awoke it was almost noon. He remembered the missed appointment of the day before and the journey to Washington he'd planned for that day. Startled, he looked at his watch and found he had only a few hours to make up for yesterday's negligence before the evening coach left for Philadelphia. His first waking thoughts of business kept him from rehearsing the painful events, as if some guardian angel were protecting him. He arose and hurried out into the busy world.

Late in the afternoon he found the man he was to have met the day before and convinced him to help the new enterprise. He was standing on the corner saying the last words before the two separated, when Kate drove by in a friend's carriage, surrounded by parcels. She'd gone shopping, spending the money David had given her on silks and laces and jewelry, and now she was returning in high spirits.

The carriage passed near David, who stood with his back to the street. She could see his animated face as he smiled at the other man, who looked as if he might be someone of note. The momentary glance didn't reveal David's haggard expression or the lines under his eyes, and Kate was angered to see him so unconcerned and unmindful of his pain from yesterday. Her face darkened with spite, and she resolved to make him suffer more for forgetting her.

But David was in the way of duty, and he didn't see her, for his guardian angel was hovering close at hand.

As autumn wore on and winter set in, Harry's letters became

less frequent and less intimate. Hannah was troubled and, after consulting with her grandmother, decided on an immediate trip to the metropolis. Meanwhile, Miranda had listened to these consultations at the latch hole, duly reporting quotations to her adored Mrs. Spafford.

"Hannah's gone to New York to find out what's become of that Harry Temple. She thought she had him fast, an' she's been holdin' him over poor Lemuel Skinner's head like thet there sword hangin' by a 'air I heard the minister tell about last Sunday, till Lemuel, he don't know but every minute's gone'll be his last. You mark my words, she'll hev to take poor Lem after all, an' be glad she's got him, too—and she's none too good for him neither. He's ben faithful to her ever since she wore pantalets, an' she's been keepin' him off 'n on an' hopin' an' tryin' fer somebody bigger. It would jes' serve her right ef she'd get that fool of a Harry Temple, but she won't. He's too sharp for that ef he *is* a fool. He don't want to tie himself up to no woman's aprun strings. He rather dandle about after 'em all an' say pretty things, an' keep his earnin's fer himself."

Hannah reached New York the week after David left for Washington. She wrote to Harry to let him know she was coming and made plain she expected his attention exclusively while there. He smiled blandly as he read the letter and her intentions between the lines. He told Kate about her that evening when he called and how he'd heard she was an old flame of David's.

Kate's jealousy was immediately aroused, and she wanted to meet Hannah Heath. She felt some triumph that she'd scorned and flung aside the man this woman had "set her cap" for, even though another woman was now in the place neither had.

Hannah visited a cousin in New York who lived in a quiet part of the city and didn't go out much. But for reasons they knew best, both Kate Leavenworth and Harry Temple elected to see a good deal of her while she was in the city. Harry was pleasant and attentive, but not more to one woman than to the other. Hannah, watching him jealously, decided that at least Kate wasn't her rival in his affections, so Hannah and Kate became quite friendly.

Kate could make much of her women friends when she chose, and in this case she chose. It occurred to her it would be good to have a friend in the town where her sister and David lived. She opened her heart to Hannah, and Hannah, discreetly and without wasting her scanty store of love, entered; and the friendship was sealed.

They hadn't known each other many days before Kate confided to Hannah the story of her own marriage and her sister's, embellished, of course, as she wished. Astonished and curious over the tragedy next to her very home, Hannah became friendlier than ever and hated more cordially than ever the young and innocent wife who had stepped into the vacant place and thus made her own hopes and ambitions impossible. She wanted to put down the pert young thing for daring to be there and be pretty, and now she felt she had the secret for doing so.

As the visit continued and it became apparent to Hannah she wasn't the only woman in the world to Harry Temple, she hinted to Kate she'd likely marry soon. She even told her she'd left home to decide the matter and had only to say the word and the ceremony would come off. Kate questioned eagerly and, seeing her opportunity, asked if she might come to the wedding. Hannah, flattered and recognizing a chance for triumph and revenge, assented with pleasure. Afterward, as Hannah had hoped and intended, Kate carried the news of the impending decision and probable wedding to Harry Temple's ears.

But Hannah's hint had no effect on the redoubtable Harry. Two days later he appeared, smiling and congratulating her; he deplored the fact she'd be lost in a certain sense to his friendship, although he hoped always to be considered as a little more than a friend.

Hannah covered her embarrassment under a calm, condescending exterior. She blushed appropriately, said some sentimental things about hoping their friendship wouldn't be affected by the change, and told him how much she'd enjoyed their correspondence. But she gave him to understand it was mere friendship, of course, from her viewpoint, and Harry indulgently allowed her to think he'd hoped for more and was grieved but consolable over the outcome.

They waxed sentimental at the parting. But when Harry was gone, Hannah wrote a touching letter to Lemuel Skinner, causing him to feel he was treading on air as he walked the prosaic streets of his town where he'd gone about during Hannah's absence like a lost sheep.

She wrote,

> *Dear Lemuel,*
>
> *I'm coming home. I wonder if you'll be glad.* (Artful Hannah, as if she didn't know!)
>
> *It's very delightful in New York, and I've been having a delightful time since I came. Everybody has been pleasant, but—*
>
> *" 'Mid pleasures and palaces though we may roam, still, be it ever so humble, there's no place like home. A charm from the skies seems to hallow it there, which, go through the world, you'll not meet elsewhere. Home, home, sweet home! There's no place like home."*
>
> *That's a new song, Lemuel, that everybody here is singing. It's written by a young American named John Howard Payne who's in London now acting in a great playhouse. Everybody is wild over this song. I'll sing it for you when I come home.*
>
> *I'll be at home in time for singing school next week, Lemuel.*

*I wonder if you'll come to see me at once and welcome me. You
can't think how glad I'll be to get home again. It seems as
though I've been gone a year at least. Hoping to see you soon,
I remain*

*Always your sincere friend,
Hannah Heath*

And thus Hannah smoothed out her path before her. Soon
after inditing this epistle, she bid good-bye to New York and
went home resolved to waste no further time in chasing will-
o'-the-wisps.

When Lemuel received that letter, he took a good look at
himself in the mirror. He'd served more than seven years for
Hannah, with little hope of reward. He was ten years older
than she, and already his face was showing it. He examined
himself critically and was pleased to find with hope shining in
his eyes he wasn't as bad looking as he feared. Though his
Sunday best wasn't shiny yet, he ordered a new suit of clothes
from the village tailor. If he didn't win now, he never would
and so resolved to do his best.

On the journey home, during the coach's jolts over rough
roads, Hannah Heath planned two campaigns—one of love
with Lemuel and one of hate with Marcia Spafford. She possessed knowledge she felt would help her in the latter and
often smiled as she laid her neat plans for destroying the
bride's complacency.

That night the fire in the Heath parlor glowed, and the candles in their silver holders flickered across Hannah's face as she
dimpled and smiled and flirted with Lemuel. But Lemuel
needed no pity. He wasn't afraid of Hannah. He understood
every foible of her shallow nature. He knew his time had come
at last, and he was getting what he wanted; for Lemuel had
admired and loved Hannah in spite of the dance she'd led him
in and other men she'd let come between them.

Hannah wasn't home many days before she called on Marcia.

Marcia had just seated herself at the piano when Hannah appeared from the hall, entering unannounced through the kitchen door as was the old neighborly custom. Vexed, Marcia left the piano and led Hannah to the sunny morning room that was bare of music or books. She didn't like to visit with Hannah in the parlor. Somehow her presence reminded her of Harry Temple's evil face as he stooped to kiss her.

"You know how to play, too, don't you?" Hannah said. "Your sister plays beautifully. Do you know the new song 'Home, Sweet Home'? She plays it with such feeling and sings it so that one would think her heart was breaking for her home. You must have been a united family." She said it with scrutiny in her voice and eyes.

"Sit down, Miss Heath," said Marcia coolly. "Did you have a pleasant time in New York?"

Hannah wasn't sure if the question was an evasion. Marcia's childlike manner disarmed suspicion.

"Oh, delightful, of course. Could anyone have anything else in New York?" she said, laughing.

"I suppose you saw all the wonderful things of the city," Marcia said, her eyes shining. "I'd enjoy being in New York a little while. I've heard of so many new things. Were any ships in the harbor? I've always wanted to go on a great ship. Did you have an opportunity to see one?"

"Oh, dear me, no!" said Hannah. "I wouldn't have cared in the least for that. I'm sure I don't know if any ships were in or not. I suppose there were. I saw a lot of sails on the water, but I didn't ask about them. I'm not interested in dirty boats. I liked visiting the shops best. Your sister took me around everywhere. She's most charming. You must miss her greatly. You were a sly little thing to cut her out."

Marcia's face flamed crimson with anger and amazement.

Hannah's dart had hit the mark, and she was watching her victim keenly.

"I don't understand you," said Marcia with girlish dignity.

"Oh, now don't pretend to misunderstand. I've heard all about it from headquarters. But then I don't blame you. David was worth it," she said with a sigh. If she'd ever cared for anyone besides herself, that one was David Spafford.

"I don't understand you," Marcia repeated, drawing herself up with all the Schuyler haughtiness she could muster, till she resembled her father.

"Now, Mrs. Spafford," said the visitor, looking into her face and watching every expression as a cat would watch a mouse, "you don't mean to tell me your sister wasn't at one time very intimate with your husband."

"Mr. Spafford has been intimate in our family for a number of years," Marcia said proudly. "But as for my having 'cut my sister out,' as you call it, you certainly have been misinformed. Excuse me. I think I'll close the kitchen door. It's causing a draft in here."

Marcia left the room with her head up and her color under control; when she returned, her head was still up, and her face wore a distant expression. Hannah felt she hadn't gained much after all. But after Hannah's departure Marcia climbed upstairs to her cold room and wept bitter tears on her pillow.

After that first visit Hannah never found the kitchen door unlocked when she came to make a morning call, but she made the most of every opportunity to torment her gentle victim. She'd had a letter from Kate. Had Marcia? How often did Kate write her? Did Marcia know how fond Harry Temple was of Kate? And where was Kate's husband? Would he be ordered home soon? These annoyances were almost unbearable sometimes, and Marcia worked hard to maintain her sweet disposition.

People looked at Lemuel with new respect. He had finally

won where for years they considered him a fool for hanging on. The added respect brought added self-respect. He took on new manliness. Grandmother Heath felt he wasn't so bad after all, and perhaps Hannah might as well have taken him at first. Altogether the Heaths were pleased, and preparations began at once for a wedding in the near future.

And still David lingered, held here and there by a call from first one man and then another and by important events in Congress. He seemed suited for the work.

Once he was called back to New York for a day or two, and Harry Temple happened to see him as he arrived. That night he wrote a friendly letter to Hannah—Harry was by no means through with Hannah—and casually remarked that David Spafford was in New York again. He supposed now that Mrs. Leavenworth's evenings would be occupied and society would see little of her while he remained. The day after Hannah received that letter was Sunday.

The weeks had gone by rapidly since David left home, and now spring was coming. The grass was green, and the willow tree by the graveyard gate was covered with tender green shoots. The foliage was out, fluttering its new leaves in the sunshine, as Marcia walked from the old stone church with the two aunts and opened her sunshade. Her movement brought a rustle from David's last letter where it lay near her heart, and not even Hannah Heath's presence behind her could cloud her joy.

However prim and faultfinding the two aunts might be in the seclusion of their own home, in public no two could have appeared more adoring than Amelia and Hortense Spafford. They hovered near Marcia and liked to show how close their relationship was with their new niece, of whom they were prouder than they'd have admitted. In their best black silks and fine lace shawls, they walked beside her and talked almost eagerly for them. They wished it understood that David's wife was worthy of appreciation, and they were more conscious than she of the many admiring glances in her direction.

Hannah Heath encountered some of those glances and saw jealously for whom they were meant. She hurried forward to greet Marcia.

"Good morning, Mrs. Spafford. Isn't that husband of yours home yet? Really! Why, he's quite deserted you. I call that hard for the first year, and your honeymoon scarcely over yet."

"He's been called back to New York again," said Marcia, annoyed. "He says he may be at home soon, but he can't be sure. His business is rather uncertain."

"New York!" Hannah exclaimed loudly. "Not again! There must be some great attraction there." Then, glancing at Marcia, she added, "I suppose your sister is still there!"

Marcia felt her face crimson and the tears start from angry eyes. She felt a sudden impulse to slap Hannah. What if she did? What would the aunts say? The thought of the stir she might make roused her sense of humor, and a laugh bubbled up instead of the tears. Hannah saw only eyes dancing with fun, though the cheeks were red. By her expression Marcia knew Hannah was baffled, but she couldn't get away from the disagreeable suggestion she'd made.

Yes, David was in New York, and Kate was there. Not for an instant did she doubt her husband's nobleness. She knew David would be good and true. She knew little of the world's wickedness and never thought of any blame, as other women might, in such a suggestion. But a great jealousy sprang up that she never dreamed existed. Kate was there, and he might see her, and his old love and disappointment would be recalled. Was she hoping he'd forget it? Was she claiming something of him in her heart for herself?

She longed to get away and think it over, but the solemn Sunday must be observed. She must fold her church things, put on another dress, and come down to the oppressive Sunday dinner, hear Deacon Brown's rheumatism discussed or listen to the morning's sermon compared with one preached twenty years ago by the former minister, now long dead, on the same text.

It was hard to concentrate with these other thoughts rushing through her brain. When Aunt Amelia asked her to pass the butter, she handed her the sugar bowl instead. Her aunt looked as shocked as if she'd broken the great-grandmother's china teapot.

Aunt Clarinda claimed her after dinner and carried her off to her room to talk about David, so that Marcia had no chance to think even then. She looked into the shadowed eyes and wondered why the girl looked so sad. She thought it was because David stayed away so long, and thus she kept her with her the rest of the day.

When Marcia went to her room that night, she fell to her knees beside the bed and tried to pray. She felt more lonely and heartsick than ever before. She didn't know what the great hunger in her heart meant. It was terrible to think David had loved Kate. Kate never loved him in return in the right way. Marcia felt sure of that. She wished she might have had the chance in Kate's place.

Then all at once she realized *she* loved David. It wasn't just a love that could come and keep house for him and save him from the criticisms and comments of others. Rather, it was a love that somehow demanded to be loved in return, that was mindful of every feature of his countenance. The knowledge overwhelmed her. She cared for nothing else just now, only knowing she loved David. David could never love her, of course, not in that way, but she would love him. She'd try to shut out the thought of Kate from him forever.

And so, hovering between what was bitter and sweet, she fell asleep with David's letter clasped close over her heart.

Chapter 23

*M*arcia went down to her house early the next morning. She'd hoped for a letter, but none had come. She felt torn between trying to ignore the hateful things Hannah Heath had said and reproaching herself for what she thought was an unseemly feeling toward David, who loved another and could never love her. It wasn't part of her life's dream to love someone who belonged to another. Yet her heart was his, and she realized everything belonging to him was dear to her.

She sat in his place at the table, then touched his desk and the books he used before he left. She went up to his room and laid her lips for an instant on his pillow, but she drew back with her heart pounding, ashamed of her emotion.

Finally she knelt beside his bed and prayed, "Oh, God, I love him! I can't help it!" as if apologizing for herself. Then she felt the sweet pain of love drift through her. Her love came through sorrow and wasn't as she'd have chosen it. It brought no hope of happiness in the future, except that of loving in secret and doing for the one she loved, with no thought of returned affection.

Then she walked downstairs, imagining how it would be when David returned. She wondered if he'd come back. It wasn't part of the spirit of her contract with David to give him this wild, sweet love he'd expected Kate to give. He hadn't wanted it. He'd wanted a wife in name only.

She had no desire for her dear woods in these days. She tried it one day in spring, slipping over the back fence and through the plowed field where the sea of silver oats had surged, up the hillside into the woods. But they reminded her so much of David that her heart ached. She wondered if the hillside or the sky didn't seem as joyous because she was getting old. She stooped to pick a handful of spring flowers, but they gave her no pleasure, and soon she dropped them and walked soberly to the house.

On this morning she didn't even care to play. She went into the parlor and touched a few notes, but her heart was sad. Life was growing too complex.

The previous week a letter had arrived from Harry Temple. It startled her, for she feared it was some bad news about David, coming as it did from New York and being written in an unfamiliar hand.

It was a plea for forgiveness, indicating the writer had experienced only repentance and sorrow since he saw her last. He set forth his case in a masterly way, with touching facts of his childhood and lonely upbringing with no mother to guide. He told her that her noble action caused him to revere her more; in short, she made a new creature of him by refusing to return his kiss that day and leaving him with such a severe rebuke. If all women were so good and true, men would be a different race, he felt. Now he looked up to an angel and could never be happy again on this earth until he had her written word of forgiveness. With that he could live a new life. She must rest assured he'd offer only reverence to a woman again.

He added that his action wasn't intended to insult her; he was merely expressing his natural admiration for such a true spirit and was innocent of any evil intention. He closed his epistle, clearing himself and assuring her he could have made her understand it that day if she hadn't left so suddenly and he hadn't been called away to his dear cousin's dying bed.

This contradictory letter troubled Marcia. She was sharp enough to see that his logic was faulty and that the two pages of his letter didn't hang together. But one thing was plain to her: He wished her forgiveness. The Bible said one must forgive, and surely it was right to let him know she did, though when she thought of the fright he gave her, it was hard to do. Still, it was right, and if he was so unhappy, perhaps she'd better let him know.

She'd rather wait until David returned to consult him, but the letter seemed so insistent that she finally wrote a stiff little note, in formal language: *Mrs. Spafford sends herewith her full and free forgiveness to Mr. Harry Temple and promises to think no more of the matter.* She wanted to consult someone. She almost thought of taking Aunt Clarinda into her confidence but decided she might not understand. So she finally sent off the brief missive, and her troubled thoughts wandered after it more than once.

She was standing by the window, looking out into the yard puzzling over this again, when she heard a loud knocking at the front door. She started, half frightened, for the knock sounded through the empty house so insistently, as if trouble were coming. She felt nervous as she walked down the hall.

It was only a barefoot boy. He'd ridden an old mare to the door and left her nosing at the dusty grass. He brought her a letter, and again her heart beat rapidly. Who could be writing to her? It wasn't David. Why did the handwriting look familiar? It couldn't be from anyone at home. Father? Mother? No, it was no one she knew. She tore it open, and the boy jumped on his horse and was off down the street before she realized he was gone.

Dear Madam,

I bring you news of your husband and, having met with an accident, I'm unable to come further. You'll find me at the Green Tavern two miles out on the corduroy road. As the business is private, please come alone.

A Messenger

Marcia trembled so that she sat down on the stairs. A sudden weakness swept over her like a wave, and the hall grew dark around her as though she were going to faint. But she was strong and well and had never fainted. So in a moment she rallied and tried to think.

Something had happened to David. Something dreadful perhaps, and she must go at once to find out. Still, it must be something mysterious, for the man said it was private. Of course that meant David wouldn't want it known. David intended for the man to come and tell her by herself. She must go at once and get rid of this awful suspense.

It was a good day for the message to come, for she'd brought her lunch, expecting to do some spring cleaning. David had been expected home soon, and she liked to make a bustle of preparation as if he might come any day, for it kept her cheerful.

Having resolved to go, she got up at once, closed the doors and windows, put on her bonnet, and went out down the street toward the old corduroy road. It frightened her to think what might be at the end of her journey. Possibly David himself, hurt or dying, and he'd sent for her this way so she might break the news gently to his aunts.

As she walked along she conjured various troubles that might have come to him. Now and then she tried to take a cheerful view, telling herself David might have needed more important papers he didn't want everyone to know about and sent by special messenger for her to get them. Then her face brightened, and her step grew more brisk. But always came the dull thud of the possibility of something more serious.

Her heart beat so fast sometimes that she was forced to lessen her speed to catch her breath. For though she was going through town and must walk somewhat soberly lest she call attention to herself, her nerves and imagination were running ahead and waiting impatiently for her feet to catch up at every turn.

At last she came to the corduroy road—a long stretch of winding trail overlaid with logs that made an unpleasant path. Most of the way was swampy and bordered in some places by thick, dark woods. Marcia sped on from log to log. She wasn't afraid of the loneliness, only of what might be at the journey's end.

But suddenly, in the densest part of the wood, she sensed footsteps echoing hers, and a chill ran through her. She turned her head, and there, wildly gesturing and running after her, was Miranda!

Marcia was annoyed and impatient to be on her way. But she wondered what the girl could want and stopped to wait for her.

"I thought—as you was goin' 'long—my way," Miranda said, puffing, "I'd jes' step along beside you. You don't mind, do you?"

Marcia thought if she said she did, Miranda might suspect something. So she tried to smile and ask how far the girl was going.

"Oh, I'm goin' to hunt fer wild strawberries," said the girl, clattering a big tin pail.

"Isn't it early yet for strawberries?"

"Well, mebbe, an' then ag'in mebbe 'tain't. I know a place I'm goin' to look anyway. Are you goin' 's fur's the Green Tavern?"

Miranda's bright eyes looked her through, and Marcia's truthful ones couldn't evade. She scanned the girl's homely face, filled with a kind of blind adoration, and suddenly yearned for counsel. She was reminded of Miranda's helpfulness when she ran away to the woods and her care in guarding the matter so no one ever heard of it. An impulse came to her to confide in Miranda. She was a girl of clear common sense and might help with advice. At least she could get comfort from telling her trouble.

"Miranda," she said, "can you keep a secret?"

The girl nodded.

"Well, I'm going to tell you something, just because I'm anxious and feel as if it would do me good tell it."

She smiled, and Miranda answered the smile with satisfaction and without surprise. Miranda had come for this, though she didn't expect it to be so easy.

"I'll be mum as an oyster," said Miranda. "You jest tell me anything you please. You needn't be afraid Hannah Heath'll know a grain about it. She an' I are two people. I know when to shut up."

"Well, Miranda, I'm very troubled. I've just had a note from a messenger my husband has sent asking me to come out to that Green Tavern you were talking about. He was sent to me with some message and has had an accident so he couldn't come. It kind of frightened me to think what might be the matter. I'm glad you're going this way, because it keeps me from thinking about it. Are we nearly there? I never went out this road so far before."

"It ain't fur," said Miranda. "I'll go right along in with you, then you needn't feel lonely. I guess likely it's business. Don't you worry."

"No, I guess that won't do, Miranda, for the note says it's private and I must come alone. You know Mr. Spafford has important matters to write about, railroads and such, and sometimes he doesn't care to have anyone get hold of his ideas before they appear in the paper. His enemies might use them to stop the plans for the great improvements he's writing about."

"Let me see that note!" demanded Miranda. "Got it with you?"

Marcia hesitated. Perhaps she shouldn't show it. Yet the note contained only what she'd already told the girl, and she felt sure she wouldn't breathe a word after her promise. She handed Miranda the letter, and they stopped a moment while she slowly spelled it out. Miranda was no scholar. Marcia watched her face eagerly, as if to gather a ray of hope from it, but was puzzled by Miranda's look. A kind of satisfaction spread over her countenance.

"Would you think from that David was hurt—or ill—or— or killed or anything?" She asked the question as if Miranda were a wizard.

"Naw, I don't reckon so!" said Miranda. "Don't you worry. David's all right somehow. I'll take care o' you. You go 'long up and see what's the business, an' I'll wait here out o' sight o' the tavern. Likely's not he might take a notion not to tell you ef he see me come along with you. You jest go ahead, and I'll be on hand when you get through. If you need me fer anything, you jest holler out 'Randy!' good and loud, an' I'll hear you. Guess I'll set on this log. The tavern's jest round that bend in the road. Naw, you needn't thank me. This is a real pretty mornin' to set an' rest. Good-bye."

Marcia hurried on, glancing back with relief at her protector in a calico sunbonnet and seated on a log with her tin pail beside her. She arrived at the tavern with almost a smile on her face, though her heart was beating wildly when a girl led her into a big room at the right of the hall.

As Marcia disappeared around the bend in the road, Miranda stole along the edge of the woods till she stood hidden behind a clump of alders. There she could peer out and watch Marcia until she reached the tavern and passed safely by the row of lounging, smoking men and on through the doorway. Then Miranda looked in all directions and dashed across the road, mounting the fence and running through two meadows and the barnyard to the kitchen door of the tavern.

"Mornin', Mis' Green," she said to the slovenly woman who sat by the table peeling potatoes. "Mind givin' me a drink o' water? I'm terrible thirsty and seemed like I couldn't find the spring. Didn't thare used to be a spring 'tween here an' town?"

"Goodness sakes! Randy! Where'd you come from? Water!

Jes' help yourself. There's the bucket jes' from the spring, an' there's the gourd hanging up on the wall. I can't get up—I'm that busy. Twelve to dinner today, an' only me to do the cookin'. Lindy, she's got to be upstairs helpin' at the bar."

"Who all you got here?" questioned Miranda as she took a draught from the old gourd.

"Well, got a gentleman from New York fer one. He's real pretty. Quite a beau. His clo'es are that nice you'd think he was goin' to court. He's that particular 'bout his eatin' I feel flustered. Nothin' would do but he hed to hev a downstairs room. He said he didn't like goin' upstairs. He don't look sickly, neither."

"Mebbe he's had a accident an' lamed himself," suggested Miranda. "Heard o' any accidents? How's he come? Coach or horseback?"

"Coach," said Mrs. Green. "Why do you ask? Got any friends in New York?"

"Not many," responded Miranda, "but my cousin Hannah Heath has. You know she's been up there fer a spell visitin', an' they say there was lots of gentlemen in love with her. There's one in particular used to come round a good deal. It might be him come round to see ef it's true Hannah's goin' to get married to Lem Skinner. Know what this fellow's name is?"

"You don't say! Well, now it might be. No, I don't rightly remember. Seems it was something like Church or Chapel. Lindy could tell ye, but she's busy."

"Where's he at? Mebbe I could get a glimpse o' him. I'd jest like to know ef he was coming to bother Hannah."

"Well, now. Mebbe you could get a sight of him. There's a cupboard between his room an' the room back. It has a door both sides. Mebbe ef you was to slip in there you might see him through the latch hole. I ain't usin' that back room fer anythin' but a storeroom this spring, so look out you don't stumble over nothin' when you go in, fer it's dark as a pocket.

You go right 'long in—I reckon you'll find the way. Yes, it's on the right-hand side o' the hall. I've got to set here an' finish these potatoes er dinner'll be late. I'd like to know real well ef he's one o' Hannah Heath's beaux."

Miranda needed no second invitation. She slipped through the hall and storeroom and in a moment stood before the closet door. Softly she opened it and stepped in, lifting her feet cautiously, for the closet floor seemed full of old boots and shoes.

It was dark, and only one slat of light stabbed the darkness coming through the irregular shape of the latch hole. She could hear voices speaking in low tones on the other side of the door. Gradually her eyes grew accustomed to the light, and one by one objects took shape in the shadows: a white pitcher with a broken nose, a row of bottles, a bunch of seed corn with the husks braided together and hung on a nail, an old coat on another nail.

Miranda dropped down on her knees beside the crack of light. She pressed first her eye and then her ear to the small aperture. She could see only a table directly in front of the door about a foot away on which were quills, paper, and a large horn inkstand filled with ink. Someone evidently had been writing, for a page was half done, and the pen was laid down beside a word.

The latch hole's limits made it impossible for Miranda to make out any more. She pressed her ear to it and could hear a man's voice talking in low insinuating tones, but she could make out little of what was said. She was losing time. Miranda meant to find out who was in that room and what was going on. She felt a righteous interest in it.

Her eyes could see in the dark closet now. The door had a big button. She put her hand on it and tried to turn it. It was tight and squeaked a little. She stopped, but the noise seemed to have no effect on the evenly modulated tones inside. She moved the button again, holding the latch firmly in her other hand to keep the door from flying open. At last the button was turned entirely away from the door frame, and the lifted latch swung free in Miranda's hand.

The door opened outward. If it were allowed to go, it would probably strike the table. Miranda let it open a crack. She could hear words now, and the voice reminded her of something unpleasant. The least little bit more she dared open the door, and she could see, as she expected, Marcia's bonnet and shoulder cape as she sat at the other side of the room. This then was the room of the messenger who had sent for Mrs. Spafford so imperiously.

The next thing was to discover the messenger's identity, though Miranda had her suspicions. The night before she saw a man lurking near the Spafford house when she went out in the garden to feed the chickens. She had watched him from behind the lilac bush, and when he finally went away, she followed him some distance until he turned into the old corduroy road and was lost in the gathering dusk. She'd seen the man before, so she had reason for braving her grandmother and hunting wild strawberries out of season.

With the caution of a forest creature, Miranda opened the door an inch farther and pressed her eye to the latch hole again. The man's head was in full range of her eye then, and her suspicion proved true.

When Marcia had entered the big room minutes earlier and the heavy oak door closed behind her, her heart seemed about to choke her. She tried with all her might to be calm. She would know the worst now.

On the other side of the room in a large armchair, with his feet extended on another and covered by a traveling shawl, a man reclined. Marcia moved toward him and then stopped with horror.

"Mr. Temple!"

"I know you're astonished, Mrs. Spafford, that the messenger should be one so unworthy. Let me say at the beginning that I'm more thankful than I can express that your letter of forgiveness reached me before I had to start on my sorrowful commission. I beg you to sit down and be as comfortable as you can while I explain further. Pardon my not rising. I've met with a bad sprain caused by falling from my horse on the way and could barely reach this place. My ankle is swollen so badly that I can't step on my foot."

Marcia, her face pale, moved to the chair he indicated near him and sat down. The one thought his speech conveyed to her came through those words "my sorrowful commission." She needed to sit down, for her legs would no longer bear her up, and she felt she must immediately know what was the matter.

"Mrs. Spafford, may I ask you once more to speak your forgiveness? Before I tell you what I've come for, I long to hear you say the words 'I forgive you.' Will you give me your hand and say them?"

"Mr. Temple, I beg you to tell me what is the matter. Don't think any further about that other. I meant what I said in the note. Tell me! Is my husband—has anything happened to Mr. Spafford? Is he ill? Is he hurt?"

"How can I bear to tell you? It seems terrible to put your love and trust in another human being and then suddenly find—but wait. Let me tell the story in my own way. No, your husband isn't hurt physically. Illness and death even aren't the worst things that can happen to a mortal soul. It seems cruel to me, as I see you sitting there so young and beautiful, that I must hurt you by what I have to say. I have the purest motive in telling you a sad truth about one who should be nearest and dearest to you on the earth. But before I begin, I pray you'll tell me you forgive me for all I have to say. Put your hand in mine and say so."

Marcia listened to this torrent of words with a choking sensation in her throat and fear gripping her heart. Some terrible thing had happened. Her senses refused to name the possibility. Would he never tell? Why did he want her hand in forgiveness? Of course she forgave him. She couldn't speak, and he kept urging.

"I can't talk until I have your hand as a pledge that you'll forgive me and not think unkindly of me for what I'm about to tell you."

He must have seen how powerfully he stirred her up, for he continued until, wild with fear, she stumbled toward him and laid her hand in his. He grasped it and thanked her profusely. He looked at the cold little hand in his own.

"Mrs. Spafford, you're good and true. You've saved me from a life of uselessness, and your example and high noble character have inspired me. It seems poor gratitude to turn and stab you in the heart. Ah! I cannot do it, and yet I must."

Marcia pulled her hand sharply away and held it to her heart. She felt her brain reeling with the strain. Harry Temple saw he must go on at once or he'd lose what he'd gained. He had meant to keep that little hand and touch it gently with a comforting pressure as his story continued, but it wouldn't do to frighten her, or she might be alarmed.

"Sit down," he begged, reaching out and drawing a chair near his own.

But she stepped back and dropped into the one she'd first taken.

"You know your husband has been in New York?" he began. She nodded.

"Did you never suspect why he's there and why he stays so long?"

A cold vise gripped Marcia's heart. She paled but said nothing, only looked steadily into the false eyes that glowed at her like two coals of fire that would scorch her soul and David's to a horrid death.

"Poor child, you can't answer. You've trusted perfectly. You thought he was there on business connected with his writing. But didn't it occur to you what a long time he's been away and that—that there might also be some other reason he hasn't told? But you must know it now, my child. I'm sorry to say it, but he was keeping it from you, and those who love you think you ought to know. Let me explain.

"Soon after he reached New York, he met a woman he used to know and admire. She's very beautiful and, though married, is still much sought after. Your husband, like the rest of her admirers, soon lost his heart completely and his head. Strange he could so easily forget the pearl of a woman he left behind! He went to see her and showed his affection for her in every possible way. He gave her large sums of money. In fact, to make a long story short, he's lingering in New York just to be near her. I hesitate to speak the whole truth, but he's surely done what you can't forgive. You with your lofty ideas—Mrs. Spafford—he's cut himself off from any right to your respect or love.

"And now I'm here today to offer to do all in my power to help you. From what I know of your husband's movements, he'll likely return to you soon. You can't meet him knowing that the lips that will salute you have been pressed upon the lips of another woman, and that woman *your own sister,* dear Mrs. Spafford!

"Ah! Now you understand. Your lips quiver! You have reason to understand. I know you can't think what to do. Let me think for you."

His eyes were glowing, his face animated. He was using all his persuasive power, and her gaze was fixed upon him as though mesmerized. She couldn't resist his eloquence. She could only look on, frozen with horror.

He felt he'd almost won, and with demoniacal skill he phrased his sentences.

"I'm here to help you and for no other reason. In the stable are horses harnessed and a comfortable carriage. My advice to you is to fly from here as fast as these fleet horses can carry you. Where you go is for you to say. I'd advise going to your father's house. I'm sure that will please him best. He's your natural refuge at a time like this. If you shrink from appearing before the village gossips in your town, I'll take you to the home of a dear old friend of mine, hidden among the quiet hills. You'll be cared for royally and tenderly for my sake and can work out your problem in the way that seems best to you. I'm planning to take you there tonight. We can easily reach there before evening if we start at once."

Marcia started to her feet in horror.

"What do you mean?" she stammered. "I could never go anywhere with you, Mr. Temple. You're evil, and you're lying! I don't believe one word of what you've said. My husband is noble and good. If he did any of those things you say he did, he had a reason for it. I'll never distrust him."

Marcia was holding her head up high now. She looked the man in the eye until he quailed, but still he sought to hold his power over her.

"You poor child!" he said in a gentle, forbearing voice. "I don't wonder in your shock and horror that you feel as you do. I anticipated this. Sit down and calm yourself and let me tell you more about it. I can prove everything I've said. I have letters here—"

He swept his hand toward a pile of letters lying on the table. Miranda, from the closet, noted the position of those letters.

"All I've said is true, I'm sorry to say, and you must listen to me—"

Marcia interrupted him, her eyes blazing, her face excited. "Mr. Temple, I shall not listen to another word you say. You're a wicked man, and I was wrong to come here at all. You deceived me, or I wouldn't have come. I must go home at once." With that she started toward the door.

Harry Temple flung aside the shawl that covered his ankle, rose quickly, and stepped in front of her, forgetting his invalid role.

"Not so fast, my pretty lady," he said, grasping her wrists fiercely in his hands. "You won't escape so easily. You won't leave this room except in my company. Don't you know you're in my power? You've spent nearly an hour alone in my bed-chamber. What will your precious husband have to do with you after this is known?"

Chapter 24

Miranda saw her time coming and was prepared. Like a flash she pushed open the closet door and grabbed the inkstand from the table. Before the two occupants of the room heard her or even realized she was near, she hurled it into Harry Temple's face. The inkstand itself was a light affair of horn and inflicted only a slight wound, but the ink splashed into his eyes, blinding him completely, as Miranda meant for it to do. She saw no other available weapon of defense.

Harry dropped Marcia's wrists and groaned in pain, staggering back against the wall and sinking to the floor. But Miranda didn't stay to see the effect of her punishment. She seized the frightened Marcia and dragged her toward the cupboard door, sweeping the pile of letters, finished and unfinished, into her apron as she passed. Then she closed the cupboard doors carefully behind her. Guiding Marcia through the dark storeroom to the hall and pushing her toward the front door, she whispered: "Go quick, 'fore he gets his eyes open. I've got to go this way. Run down the road fast as you can, an' I'll be at the meetin' place first. Hurry!"

Marcia's feet shook so that every step seemed about to slip. But she finally traversed the length of the porch with dignity, passed the loungers, and was out in the road. Then she ran.

Miranda, breathless but triumphant, went back into the kitchen. "I guess 'tain't him after all," she said to the woman who was putting the potatoes on to boil. "He's real interesting to look at though. I'd like to stop and watch him longer, but I must be goin'. I come out to hunt fer"—Miranda searched for

236

a suitable object before this country-bred woman who knew strawberries weren't ripe yet—"wintergreens fer Grandma," she added cheerfully, not sure if they grew around those parts, "and I must be in a hurry. Good-bye! Thank you fer the drink."

Miranda whizzed out the door, calling a good morning to one of the hostlers as she passed the barnyard, and was off through the meadows and over the fence like a bird.

Neither of the two girls spoke after they met but continued their rapid gait, until the end of the corduroy road was in sight and they felt comparatively safe.

"Wal, that feller certainly ought to be strung up an' walluped, now, fer sure," remarked Miranda, "an' I'd like to help at the wallupin'."

Marcia suddenly dissolved into hysterical laughter. The contrast from the tragic to the ridiculous was too much for her. She laughed until the tears rolled down her cheeks, and then she cried in earnest. Miranda stopped and put her arms about her as gently as a mother might and smoothed her hair back from her cheek.

"There now, you poor pretty flower. Jest you cry 's hard 's you wan' to. I know how good it makes you feel to cry. I've done it many a time up in the garret where nobody couldn't hear me. That old Satan, he won't trouble you fer a good long spell again. When he gets his evil eyes open, if he ever does, he'll be glad to get out o' these parts, or I miss my guess. Now don't you worry no more. He can't hurt you one mite. An' don't think a thing about what he said. He's a great big liar, that's what he is."

"Miranda, you saved me. Yes, you did. I never can thank you enough. If you hadn't come and helped me, something awful might have happened!" Marcia shuddered.

"Nonsense!" said Miranda, pleased. "I didn't do a thing worth mentioning. Now you jest wipe your eyes and chirk up.

We've got to go through town, an' you don't want folks to wonder what's up."

Miranda led Marcia up to the spring whose location had been known to her all the time, of course, and Marcia bathed her eyes and was soon looking more like herself. Now and then her lips still trembled a bit. But her companion talked cheerfully and tried to keep her mind from reviewing the morning's events.

When they reached the village, Miranda suggested they go home by the back street, slipping through a field of spring wheat and climbing the garden fence. She thought it best to keep out of her grandmother's sight for a while longer.

"I might 's well be hung for a sheep 's a lamb," she remarked as she slid in at Marcia's kitchen door in the shadow of the morning-glory vines. "I'm goin' to stay here a spell an' get you some dinner while you go upstairs an' lie down. You don't need to go back to your aunt's till near night, an' you can wait till dusk, an' I'll go with you. Then you needn't be out alone at all. I know how you feel, but I don't believe you need worry. He'll be done with you now forever, er I'll miss my guess. Now you lie down till I make a cup o' tea."

Marcia was glad to be alone and soon fell asleep, too weary to go over the awful occurrences of the morning now.

Miranda, coming upstairs with the tea, tiptoed in and looked at her. With no hope of attaining the beautiful things of life, Miranda loved unselfishly this girl who had what she didn't. And she longed to comfort and protect the sweet thing who seemed so ill prepared to protect herself. She leaned over the sleeper for a moment but was afraid of waking her. Then she took the cup of tea and tiptoed out again, satisfied. She had a task to do and was glad Marcia slept, for it gave her an opportunity to carry out her plans.

Downstairs in David's library, she opened the desk drawers until she found writing materials. She had a letter to write, and a letter, to Miranda, was a major achievement. She never expected to write another one again. She plunged into her subject at once.

The letter began:

Dear Mr. David,

She was afraid that sounded a little stiff but felt it was too familiar to say "David" as he was always called.

I ain't much on letters, but this one has to be writ. Something happened, and somebody's got to tell you about it. I'm most sure she won't, and nobody else knows 'cept me.

Last night 'bout dark I went out to feed the chickens, an' I see that Harry Temple skulkin round your house. It was all dark there, an' he walked in the side gate and tried to peek in the winders, only the shades was down an' he couldn't see a thing. I thought he was up to some mischief, so I followed him down the old corduroy road. It was dark by then an' I come home, but I was on the watchout this morning, an' after Mis' Spafford come down to the house, I heard a horse gallopin' by, an' I looked out an' saw a boy get off an' take a letter to the door an' ride away, an' pretty soon all in a hurry your wife come out tyin' her bonnet and hurryin' along lookin' scared.

I grabbed my sunbonnet an' clipped after her, but she went so fast I didn't get up to her till she got on the old corduroy road. She was awful scared lookin', an' she didn't want me much I see, but pretty soon she up an' told me she had a note sayin' there was a messenger with news from you out to the old Green Tavern. He had an accident an' couldn't come no further. He wanted her to come alone 'cause the business was private, so I stayed down by the turn of the road till she got in, an' then I went cross lots an' round to the kitchen an' called on Mis' Green a spell. She was tellin me about her boarders, an' I told her I thought mebbe one of 'em was a friend o' Hannah Heath's, so she said I might peek through the keyhole of the cubberd an' see. She was busy, so I went alone.

Well, sir, I jest wish you'd been there. That lying thing was jest goin' on the sweetest, as respectful an' nice a thankin' your wife fer comin, an' excusin' himself fer sendin' fer her and sayin' he couldn't bear to tell her what he'd come fer, an' pretty soon when she was scared es death, he up an' told her a awful fib 'bout you an' a woman called Kate, whoever she is, an' he jest poured the words out fast so she couldn't speak, an' he said things about you he shouldn't uv, an' you could see he was makin' it up as he went along, an' he said he had proof. So he pointed at a pile of letters on the table, an' I eyed 'em good through the hole in the door.

Pretty soon he ups and perposes that he carry her off in a carriage he has all ready and takes her to a friend of his, so she won't be here when you come home, 'cause you're so bad, and she gets up looking like she wanted to scream, only she didn't dare, and she says he don't tell the truth, it wasn't so any of it, and if it was it was all right anyway, that you had some reason, an' she wouldn't go a step with him anywhere.

An' then he forgets all about the lame ankle he had kept covered up on a chair pertendin' it was hurt fallin' off his horse when the coach brought him all the way, fer I asked Mis' Green—and he ketches her by the wrists and says she can't go without him, and she needn't be in such a hurry fer you wouldn't have no more to do with her anyway after her being shut up there with him so long, an' then she looked jest like she was going to faint, an' I bust out through the door an' ketched up the ink pot, it want heavy enough to kill him, an' I slung it at him, an' the ink went square in his eyes, an' we slipped through the closet an' got away quick 'fore anybody knew a thing.

I brought all the letters along, so here they be. I havn't read a

one, cause I thought mebbe you'd ruther not. She ain't seen 'em
neither. She don't know I've got 'em. I hid 'em in my dress.
She's all wore out with cryin' and hurryin', an being scared, so
she's upstairs now asleep, an' she don't know I'm writing. I'm
goin' to send this off 'fore she knows, fer I think she wouldn't
tell you fear of worryin' you. I'll look after her es well's I can
till you get back, but I think that feller ought to be strung up.
But you'll know what to do, so no more at present from your
obedient servant,

Miranda Griscom

After she sealed her packet to her satisfaction, with the
diminishing stick of sealing wax she found in the drawer,
Miranda slid out the front door and by a detour went to David
Spafford's office.

"Good afternoon, Mr. Stone," she said to the clerk.
"Grandma sends her respects and wants to know if you'd be
so kind as to back this letter fer her to Mr. David Spafford.
She's writin' to him on business, an' she don't rightly know
his street an' number in New York."

Mr. Stone wrote the address, and Miranda carried it to the
post office. Then she hurried back to Marcia.

In the same mailbag that brought Miranda's package to
David, a letter arrived from Aunt Clarinda. David's face lit up.
Her letters came so seldom that they were a rare pleasure. He
laid aside the thick package written in his clerk's hand. It was
doubtless some business papers and could wait.

Aunt Clarinda wrote in a fine old script that in spite of her
eighty years was clear and legible. She told about the beautiful
weather, that Amelia and Hortense were almost finished with
housecleaning, and that Marcia went to their house every day
keeping it in order. Then she added a paragraph that David,
knowing his aunt well, understood to be the *raison d'etre* of the
whole letter.

I think your wife misses you very much, Davie. She looks sort of peaked and sad. It's hard on her being separated from you so long this first year. Men don't think of those things, but it's lonely for a young thing like her here with three old women, and you know Hortense and Amelia never try to make it lively for anybody. I've been watching her, and I think if I were you, I'd let the business finish itself up as soon as possible and hurry back to put a bit of cheer into that child. She's paler than she ought to be.

David read it over three times in astonishment with mingled feelings he couldn't analyze.

Of course Aunt Clarinda didn't understand the situation and was mistaken. Marcia wasn't sighing for him, though it might be dull for her at the old house. He should have thought of that. A great burden settled upon him. He wasn't doing right by Marcia. She couldn't miss him, if indeed Aunt Clarinda was right and she was worried about anything. Perhaps something had happened to trouble her. Could that snake of a Temple have turned up again? No, he felt reasonably sure he'd have heard of that; besides, he saw him not long ago on the street at a distance. Could it be some beau at home whose memory troubled her? Or had she discovered what a sacrifice she'd made of her young life? Whatever it was, it was careless and cruel of him to have left her alone with his aunts all this time. He was a selfish man, he told himself, to have accepted her quiet little sacrifice of all for him.

He read the letter over again, and suddenly he wished Marcia *was* missing him. He'd tried to train himself that no one would ever care for him again, but now it seemed dear and desirable that his sweet young companion would like to have him back. He envisioned home as it had been, pleasant and restful, always with the food he liked and his wishes considered, and he felt condemned. He hadn't noticed or cared.

Did she think him ungrateful?

He read the letter over again, noting every mention of his wife in the account of daily life. He was searching for some clue that would give him more information about her. And when he reached the last paragraph about missing him, a tingle of pleasure shot through him at the thought. He didn't understand it. After all, she was his. If possible, he must help make up to her for what she had lost in giving herself to him. If the thought of doing so brought him unexpected satisfaction, he wasn't to blame in any way.

Since his encounter with Kate and the terrible night of agony, David had plunged into his business. Whenever a thought of Kate came, he banished it if possible; if it wouldn't go, he got out his writing materials and worked on an article in order to absorb his mind. Several times in the night he got up to write because he couldn't sleep and must think.

When he had to be in New York, he steadily kept away from the house where Kate lived and never walked through the streets without fully occupying his mind so he wouldn't chance to see her. In this way his sorrow was growing old without having been worn out, and he was regaining much of his former happiness and interest in life. Not so often now did Kate's vision come to trouble him. He thought she was still his one ideal of womanly beauty and grace and perfection, of course, and always would be, but she wasn't for him to think about anymore. He was becoming a strong, true man out of his sorrow. Now when he thought of Marcia with a certain sweetness, he could be glad and not resent it. Of course no one could ever take Kate's place—that was impossible.

So reflecting, with a pleasant smile on his face, he opened Miranda's epistle.

Puzzled and surprised, he began to read the strange chirography. As he read, his face darkened, and his brows pulled together in a heavy frown.

"The scoundrel!" he muttered as he turned the sheet.

His look grew anxious. He scanned the page quickly as if to gather the meaning from the crooked misspelled words without taking them one by one. But he had to go slowly, for Miranda had written more with haste than plainness. He held his breath when he thought of the gentle girl in that unscrupulous man's hands. A terrible fear gripped his heart. Marcia, so sweet and pure and good. A vision of her face as she lay asleep in the woods slipped between him and the paper. Why had he left her unprotected all these months? Fool that he was! She was worth more than all the railroads put together.

As if his own life hung in the balance, he read on, growing sick with horror. Poor child! What did she think? And how were his own sin and weakness discovered, or was it merely Harry Temple's wicked heart that evolved these stories? The letter smote him, and all at once it alarmed him that Marcia had heard such things about him. When he came to her trust in him, he groaned aloud, buried his face in the letter, and then raised it quickly to read to the end.

When he finished he stood up to pack his carpetbag and go home at once. Marcia needed him, and he felt a strong desire to be near her, to see her and know she was safe. It was overwhelming. He didn't know he could ever feel so strongly again. He must confess his own weakness, of course, and he would. She should know all and know she might trust him after all.

But in standing up he sent the other papers to the floor, and the bundle of letters Miranda enclosed in the packet scattered about him. He stooped to pick them up and saw his name in Kate's handwriting. Old association held his attention. Curious, fearful, and not wholly glad to see it, he picked up the letter. It was an epistle of Kate's, in intimate style, to Harry Temple and spoke of David in contemptuous terms. She even detailed to Harry an account of her triumph that miserable morning when he took her in his arms and kissed her.

Certain expressions in the letter revealed her wicked heart to David. He read one letter after another and saw how she plotted with this man to wreck her young sister's life for her own revenge. And as he did so, the vision of the woman he had loved and thought beautiful within as well as without crumbled into dust before him. When he looked up at last with a pale face and set lips, he found his soul was free forever from the fetters that had bound him to her.

He crossed to the fireplace and laid the letters among the embers, blowing them into a blaze, and watched until the fire devoured them, leaving only dead gray ashes. The thought came to him that was like his old love—burnt out. There hadn't been the right kind of fuel to feed it. Kate was worthless.

But he was alive, and, please God, he'd see better days. He'd go home at once to the young wife who needed him and whom now he might love as she should be loved. The thought was sweet to him as he threw his things into his bag and arranged for his trip home. He decided that if he ever returned to New York, Marcia would come with him.

Chapter 25

*M*arcia hurried down to her house early one morning, with the phantoms of the Green Tavern pursuing her. Once there she could only go over and over Harry Temple's dreadful words. She tried in vain to work. She walked into the library and picked up a book, but her mind wandered to David.

Sitting down at the piano, she played a few soft chords and sang an old Italian song someone had left at her old home years ago.

Dearest, believe,
Whene'er we part:
Lonely I grieve
In my sad heart—

With a sob her head dropped on her hands in one crash of discordant tones from the keys, while the sound died away in the vibrating strings. Absorbed in her thoughts, Marcia didn't hear the lifting of the side door latch and the quiet step of a foot. Her smothered sobs were mingled with the fading music, still audible to her fine ear.

David came by instinct to his own home first. He felt Marcia would be there. Now that he'd come and the morning sun flooded everything and made it all look so good, he felt he must find her before reestablishing his relationship with home. He passed through the kitchen, dining room, and hall, and by the closed parlor door. He never thought of her being in there with the door closed. He glanced into the library and saw the book lying in his chair as she'd left it, and it touched him with her presence. He went softly toward the stairs to find her. He'd stopped at a shop the last thing and bought a beautiful creamy shawl of China crepe, heavily embroidered and finished with long, silken fringe. He took it from his carpetbag and was carrying it in its rice paper wrapping so it wouldn't be crushed. Pleased at the present he brought her, he felt strangely shy about giving it to her.

Just then he heard a sound from the parlor, tender and plaintive. Marcia had conquered her sobs and was singing again. The words drew him toward the parlor door.

Dearest, believe,
  Whene'er we part:
Lonely I grieve
  In my sad heart:
Thy faithful slave,
  Languishing sighs,
Haste then and save—

Here the words trailed away again into a half sob, and the melody continued in broken chords that faded into the shadows of the room.

Aunt Clarinda was right: Something was wrong with Marcia. He felt troubled, almost jealous, and couldn't understand it. Who was Marcia singing this song for? That it was a true cry from a lonely soul, he believed. Was she feeling imprisoned in this lonely house with only a forlorn man whose life and love had been thrown away on someone else? Poor child! Could he make her forget the one for whom she was sighing and bring peace and interest in other things into her life? He wanted to make a new life for her. He had so unthinkingly torn her from her home nest and her future and compelled her to take up his barren life. He'd make it up to her if he could. Then he opened the door.

In the faint green light of noonday filtered through the shades, Marcia's color didn't show as it flew into her cheeks. Her hands grew weak and dropped onto the keys with a soft tinkle. She sprang up and took a step toward him, then clasped her hands to her heart and stopped shyly.

David entered the room and, anxious, stopped midway, too. For an instant they looked at one another. David saw a new expression on the girl's face. She seemed much older than when he'd left. The sweet round cheeks were thinner, and her mouth drooped a little. He longed to take her in his arms and kiss her, and the longing startled him. So many months he'd thought of only Kate in that way and then taught himself not to think of caring for Kate or any woman. He felt he was disloyal to himself, to honor, to Kate—no, not to Kate, for he had no call to be loyal to her. She'd never been loyal to him. Rather, he might have expressed it as loyalty to love for love's sake, love that is worthy to be crowned by a woman's love.

David walked toward her slowly, trying to be natural and regain his former manner with her. He extended his hand stiffly to shake hands as he'd done when he left, and timidly she placed hers in it. Yet as their fingers closed, a thrill of sweetness leaped from one to the other. Neither guessed the other knew, while they tucked it in their memories for closer inspection as to what it could mean. Their hands clung together longer than either intended, and they sensed something pleasant in being together again.

David thought it was because here was home and peace, and he was no longer anxious about Marcia now that he saw she was all right. Marcia knew it was better to have David standing there with his strong fingers about her trembling ones than to have anything else in the world. But she wouldn't have told him so.

"That was a sweet song you were singing," David said. "I hope you were singing it for me and that it was true! I'm glad I'm home, and you must sing it again for me soon."

It wasn't at all what he meant to say, and the words tumbled out so that he was almost embarrassed and wondered if Marcia would think he'd lost his mind in New York.

But she treasured every word and hugged them to her heart and carried them in her prayers.

They went to the kitchen and made dinner together like two excited children. They kept trying to return to their natural ways of doing and saying things but couldn't. Instead, they stumbled over their words, almost ran into one another as they tried to help each other, and laughed and blushed and stumbled again. When they both reached for the teakettle to fill the coffeepot and their fingers touched, each drew back and pretended not to notice but felt the contact sweet.

They were lingering over dinner when Hannah Heath came to the door. David was telling about some of his adventures, enjoying the expressions on Marcia's face as she listened to every word. They'd pushed their chairs back a little and were sitting there talking—rather, David was talking and Marcia listening.

Hannah stood for one jealous instant and saw it all; this was what she'd dreamed of for years for herself and David. In recent months she'd begun to wonder just what feeling might be between him and Marcia. Now more than ever she wanted to bring him face-to-face with Kate and read the truth for herself. She hated Marcia for that look of intense delight and sympathy on her face; for her right to sit there and hear what David said—some stupid stuff about railroads. She didn't see that she herself would have made a poor companion for a man like David.

As yet neither Marcia nor David had touched on the subjects that had troubled them. They were so happy in each other's company that they forgot.

But the pleasant conversation was broken up at once when Marcia's expression changed to one of alarm at the sight of Hannah standing in the doorway.

"Why, David, are you home at last?" asked Hannah. "I didn't know."

Indeed, that was scarcely true, for she'd watched him from behind Grandmother Heath's rosebush.

"Where did you come from last? New York? Oh, then you saw Mrs. Leavenworth. How is she? I fell in love with her when I was there."

Now David never took in Kate's married name. He knew it, of course. But in his happiness at getting home and his absorption in the work he'd been doing, the name "Mrs. Leavenworth" conveyed nothing to David's mind.

He stared blankly at Hannah and replied, "No, Miss Hannah, I had no time for social life. I was busy every minute I was away."

David never expected Hannah to say anything worth listening to and was so engrossed in his subject that he didn't notice she made no reply.

Hannah watched him curiously as he talked; his remarks, after all, were directed more to Marcia than to her. When he paused, she said with a sneer in her voice, "I never could understand, David, how you seem to have so much sense in other things but take up such impractical dreams as this railroad. Lemuel says it'll never run."

Hannah quoted her beloved with a proud bridling of her head as if the matter were settled once and for all. It was the first time she acknowledged to the world her relation to Lemuel. She wasn't averse to having David understand she felt other men existed besides him.

But David turned cheerful eyes on her. "Lemuel says? And how much does he know about the matter?"

"Lemuel has good common sense," said Hannah, "and he knows what's possible and what isn't. He doesn't need to travel all over the country on a wild-goose chase to learn that."

Now that she'd accepted him, Hannah didn't intend to let Lemuel be discounted.

"He hasn't long to wait to be convinced," said David thoughtfully, not noticing her tart tone. "Before the year is out, it will be a settled fact everyone can see."

"Well, it's beyond comprehension that you care, anyway," Hannah retorted. "Did you really spend all your time in New York on such things? It seems incredible. There certainly must have been other attractions."

Hannah's voice held insinuation, though smooth as butter, but David had long years of hearing her sharp tongue. He paid no attention. Marcia's color rose, however. She made a hasty errand to the pantry to put away the bread, and her eyes flashed at Hannah through the close-drawn pantry door. But Hannah didn't give up so easily.

"It's strange you didn't stay with Mrs. Leavenworth," she said. "She told me you were one of her dearest friends, and you used to be quite fond of one another."

Then it suddenly dawned upon David who Mrs. Leavenworth was, and a sternness spread over his face.

"Mrs. Leavenworth, did you say? Ah! I didn't understand. I saw her only once and that for only a few minutes soon after I first arrived. I didn't see her again." His voice was cool and steady.

Marcia was coming from the pantry, ready to defend if she could, and marveled at his coolness. Fear gripped her heart, yet she felt joy at David's words. He saw Kate only once. He knew she was there but stayed away. Hannah's insinuations were false. Mr. Temple's words were untrue. She knew it all the time, yet what sorrow they had given her!

"By the way, Marcia," said David, turning toward her with

a smile that erased the earlier sternness in his voice, "didn't you write me some news? Miss Hannah, you're to be congratulated, I believe. Lemuel's a good man. I wish you much happiness."

Thus David turned aside Hannah Heath's dart. Yet while she left the house with a smile and the sound of pleasant wishes in her ears, she carried a bitter, revengeful heart.

David was suddenly confronted with what he had to tell Marcia. He sat watching her as she moved back and forth from kitchen to pantry, and at last he stood beside her, taking her hands in his and looking down into her face. It seemed terrible to him to tell this to the innocent girl, just when he was anxious to win her confidence. But it must be told, and better now than later lest he be tempted not to tell it at all.

"Marcia!" He said the name tenderly, with an inflection he'd never used. It wasn't passionate, but it reached her heart and drew her eyes to his and the color to her cheeks. She thought how different his clasp was from Harry Temple's hateful touch. She looked up at him with trust and waited.

"You heard what I said to Hannah Heath just now about— your"—he paused—"about Mrs. Leavenworth." It was as if he wanted to set the subject of his words far from them.

Marcia's heart beat wildly, remembering what she had been told. Yet she looked bravely into his eyes.

"It was true what I told her. I met Mrs. Leavenworth only once while I was away. It was in her own home, and she sent for me, saying she was in trouble. She told me she was terribly distressed that I wouldn't forgive her. She begged me to say I forgave her. When I told her, she asked me to kiss her once to prove it. I was utterly overcome and did so, but the moment my lips touched hers, I knew I was doing wrong, and I put her from me.

"She begged me to stay, and I now know she was false from the first. She was only playing a part when she touched my heart until I yielded and sinned. I've learned that only recently, within a few days, and from words written by her own hand to someone else. I'll tell you all about it sometime. But I want to confess to you this wrong I've done and let you know I left her that day and have never seen her since. She'd said she was without money, and I left her all I had with me.

"I feel that all this was a sin against you. I want you to forgive me if you can, and I want you to know that this other woman, who was the cause of our coming together, is no longer anything to me. Even if she and I were both free as we were when we first met, we could never be anything but strangers. Can you forgive me now, Marcia, and can you ever trust me after what I told you?"

Marcia looked into his eyes and loved him more for his confession. Her whole countenance answered with her voice, "I can."

It made David think of their wedding day, and suddenly he realized that this dear womanly woman belonged to him. He marveled at her forgiveness.

"You've had some sad experiences yourself. Will you tell me all about it now?" He asked the question wistfully, still holding her hands in a firm, close grasp, and she left them nestling safely there.

"Why, how did you know?" Marcia asked, touched by his kindness and relieved she didn't have to open the story.

"Oh, a guardian angel whispered the tale," he said pleasantly. "Come into the room, where we can be sure no Hannah Heaths will trouble us." He led her into the library and seated her beside him on the sofa.

"But, Marcia," he said, his face sobering, "what's happened to you is no light matter to me. I've been in agony all the way home. I was afraid I might not find you safe and well after escaping such a terrible danger."

He drew the whole story from her bit by bit with gentle

questions. His face blazed with righteous wrath and darkened from knowing more as she continued to the end. He saw the twisted heart of the villain who had dared such a diabolical conspiracy and the inhumanity of the woman who had helped—no, instigated—the intrigue against her own sister. His new understanding of Kate's character was confirmed at the worst.

Marcia could only guess his deep feelings from his shaken countenance and the earnest way in which he folded his hands over hers.

"We should be deeply thankful to God for saving you," he said in low tones filled with emotion, "and I must be very careful of you after this. That villain will be searched out and punished if it takes a lifetime, and Miranda—what shall we do for Miranda? Perhaps we can induce her grandmother to let us have her sometime to help take care of us. We seem unable to get along without her. We'll see what we can do sometime in return for the great service she's rendered."

But the clock striking in the hall suddenly reminded David he must go at once to the office. So he hurried away, and Marcia set about her work with energy and a song of praise in her heart.

David had said he wouldn't have time to go to his aunts' that night, so she invited them to tea. She much preferred to have him to herself that first evening, but it would please them to come, especially Aunt Clarinda. Marcia didn't have time to prepare supper, but she stirred up a gingerbread and made some puffy cream biscuits to go with honey, fresh eggs, and peach preserves. She ran to Deacon Appleby's to get cream for her biscuits and ask Tommy Appleby to harness David's horse and drive over for Aunt Clarinda. Then she hurried down to invite the aunts, of whom Clarinda was especially thrilled.

It was a happy gathering that evening. David looked around the dining room with genuine boyish pleasure. It did his heart good to see Aunt Clarinda there. It never occurred to him she could come. He turned to Marcia with a light in his eyes that fully repaid her for the little trouble in carrying out her plan. He began to feel home meant something even though he'd lost the home of his dreams.

He talked a great deal about his trip, and in between the sentences, he caught himself watching Marcia, noting the curve of her round chin, the dimple on her left cheek when she smiled, the way her hair waved off from her forehead. He found a distinct pleasure in noting these things and wondered at himself. It was as if he suddenly were placed before some great painting and given the knowledge to appreciate art to its fullest or heard a marvelous piece of music and understood its gracious melodies and majestic harmonies.

Aunt Clarinda watched his eyes and was satisfied. Aunt Hortense watched his eyes jealously and sighed. Aunt Amelia watched his eyes and set her lips.

"He'll spoil her if he does like that," she told her sisters later. "She'll think she can walk right over him."

But Aunt Clarinda knew better. She recognized the eternal right of love.

They took the three old ladies home in the rising of an early moon, with Marcia walking on the sidewalk beside Aunt Amelia, while David drove the chaise with Aunt Clarinda and Aunt Hortense.

As he lifted Aunt Clarinda down and helped her to her room, David felt her hands tremble and press his arm. When he reached her door, he bent over and kissed her.

"Davie," she said, "she's a dear child! She's as good as gold. She's the princess I used to put in all your fairy tales. David, she's just the right one for you!"

"I believe she is, Aunt Clarinda," David answered, as if he were discovering a surprising, yet not unwelcome, truth.

They drove to the barn, and Marcia sat in the chaise in the

hay-scented darkness while David put up the horse by the cobwebby lantern light. Then he drew her hand through his arm, and they walked quietly back to the house.

What had come to him? David wondered. Joy welled up in his heart—a rift in the dark clouds of fate, a show of sunshine where he'd never expected to see the light again. Why was it so pleasant to have that little hand resting on his arm? Was it really pleasant, or was it only part of the rest of getting home again away from strange faces and uncomfortable beds?

They let themselves into the house as if they were walking into a new world together, and both were glad to be there again.

In her room Marcia stood before the mirror and looked at herself by candlelight. Her eyes were bright, and her cheeks burned red in the center like two soft, deep roses. She felt she hardly knew herself. She tried to be critical. Was she pretty? Would she be thought so if compared with Kate and Hannah Heath? Would a man—would David—if his heart weren't filled—think so? She decided not. She felt she was too immature. There was too much shyness in her glance and babyishness about her mouth. No, David could never have thought her beautiful, even if he saw her before he knew Kate. But perhaps, if Kate had been married first and away and then he had come to their home, if he knew no one else well enough to love—could he have cared for her?

Oh, it was a dreadful, beautiful thought. It thrilled through her till she hid her face from her own gaze. She suddenly kissed the hand that had rested on his sleeve and then reproached herself for it. She loved him, but was it right to do so?

As for David, he was sitting on the side of his bed with his chin in his hands. After reading those letters two short days ago, he thought all possibility of love and happiness had died.

But he found himself filled with pleasure over the look in a girl's soft eyes and the touch of her hand. And that girl was his wife. It was enough to keep him awake to try to understand himself.

Chapter 26

*H*annah Heath's wedding day dawned bright enough for a less calculating bride.

David didn't get home until half past three. He had to drive out to the starting place of the new railroad near Albany, where he needed to get a few points correct. The next day the Mohawk and Hudson Railroad—the first train drawn by a steam engine in the state of New York—was to take its initial trip.

His article about it, bargained for by a New York paper, must be on its way by special post as soon after the train started as possible. He must have everything accurate, including preparation technicalities, a description of the engine and coaches, details of arrangements, and so on, before he added the final paragraphs describing the actual start of the train. His article was finished, except for these few items.

He started early that morning on his long drive but was detained longer than he'd expected. Thus he arrived home with barely time to dress for the wedding and hurried in at the last moment with Marcia. They were the last guests to arrive. It was time for the ceremony, but the bride, true to nature, still kept Lemuel waiting. And Lemuel, true to the end, stood smiling and patient.

David and Marcia entered the large parlor and shook hands here and there with those assembled. A hushed air otherwise pervaded the room in anticipation of the ceremony.

Soon after their arrival, a woman in purple silk with gold hair walked downstairs and seated herself in a vacant chair close to where the bride was to stand, directly opposite David and Marcia. David was engrossed in a whispered conversation with Mr. Brentwood about the events of the next day and didn't notice her entrance, though she paused in the doorway and searched him out before taking her seat. Marcia, who was talking with Rose Brentwood, caught the vision of purple and gold and turned for an instant to see the scornful, sardonic glance of her sister. The color drained from her face.

Then Marcia summoned all her courage and braced herself for what was coming. She forced herself to smile in answer to Rose Brentwood's question. But all the while she was trying to understand why her sister's look hurt her. It wasn't the anger; she was prepared for that. It wasn't the scorn; she'd encountered that often. Was it the sardonic expression? Yes, that was the sting. She'd felt it so keenly as a little girl when Kate made fun of some whim of hers. But she couldn't see why Kate would find cause for fun now. It was almost as if she ignored Marcia's relationship to David in her scornful laugh and appropriated him for herself.

Marcia's color came back as if by force of her will. She would show Kate—or David at least—that she could bear all things for him. She'd play her part of wife well today. The happy two months since David returned from New York had made her feel almost as if she really was his and he hers. For this hour she'd forget it was otherwise. She'd look at him and speak to him as if he'd been her husband for years, as if the truest understanding lay between them—as, indeed, a certain pleasant sort did. She wouldn't let the dreadful thought of Kate cloud her expression for others to see. Bravely she faced the company.

But her heart under Kate's blue dress sent up a swift prayer pleading from a higher Power something she knew she didn't have in herself and therefore must find in Him who had created her. It was the most trustful, neediest prayer Marcia had ever uttered, and yet she spoke no words nor even closed an eye. Only her heart took the attitude of prayer.

The door upstairs opened in a businesslike manner, and Hannah's composed voice was heard giving a direction. Miranda told Marcia afterward that she had kept her standing at the window for an hour beforehand to see when David arrived and when they started over to the house. Hannah kept herself posted on what was going on in the room below as well as if she were down there. She knew where David and Marcia stood and told Kate exactly where to go. It was like Hannah that in the moment of sacrificing her long-cherished hopes, she'd planned a dramatic revenge to help carry her through.

At last the bride's rustle became audible from the hall, and even David and Mr. Brentwood heard and turned from their conversation. Hannah, cold and beautiful in her bridal array, was in the doorway when David looked up, and almost at once he saw the vision in purple and gold, like a saucy pansy, standing near her.

Kate's eyes were fixed on him with a bewitching smile of recognition, like a naughty little child in hiding who peeps out laughing over his elders' discomfiture. So Kate encountered David's astonished gaze. But no light of love shone in his eyes as she expected. Instead, in his face righteous anger blazed.

In spite of herself Kate was disconcerted. She felt that David was challenging her presence there, looking through her, searching her, judging her, sentencing her, and casting her out. Presently his eyes wandered beyond her through the open hall door and out into God's green world, and when they returned and next rested on her, his look had frozen into a stranger's glance.

Angry and ashamed, she bit her lips in vexation but tried to keep the smile. She hated him and vowed to make him bow before her smiles again.

David didn't see the bride to notice her, but the bride, unlike the one of the psalmist's vision whose eyes were on "her dear bridegroom's face," was looking straight across the room to observe David.

The ceremony proceeded, and Hannah played her part correctly and calmly. She knew she was giving herself to Lemuel Skinner irrevocably. Yet she also knew of the discomfiture of the girl-wife who sat across the room bravely watching the ceremony with pale cheeks.

Marcia didn't look at David. She stood with him in heart, suffering with him. She didn't need to look. Her part was to ignore and help cover.

They went through it well. Not once did Aunt Amelia or Aunt Hortense notice anything strange in the demeanor of their nephew or his wife. Aunt Clarinda wasn't there; she wasn't fond of Hannah.

As soon as the service was over and the relatives broke the solemn hush by kissing the bride, David turned and spoke to Rose Brentwood, making some smiling remark about the occasion.

Kate flushed angrily. If he'd spoken to Marcia, she'd have judged he did it out of pique, but a pretty stranger coming on the scene at this moment was trying. Then, too, David's manner was so indifferent, so natural. He didn't seem in the least troubled by seeing her.

David and Marcia didn't go up to speak to the bride at once. He stepped back into the window seat to talk with Mr. Brentwood and seemed to be in no hurry to follow the procession filing past the bride to congratulate her. Marcia remained quietly talking to Rose Brentwood.

At last David turned toward his wife with a smile, as though he knew she was there all the time and felt her sympathy. Her heart leaped up with new strength at that look, and her husband's firm touch as he drew her hand within his arm gave her courage. With a bright smile she walked with him to the front.

"I'd about given up expecting any congratulations from you," said Hannah sharply as they approached. She was evidently waiting for them.

"I wish you much joy, Mrs. Skinner," said David mechanically, scarcely feeling she'd have it, for he knew her dissatisfied nature.

"Yes," said Marcia, "I hope you'll be happy, as happy as I am!"

It was an impetuous, childish thing to say, and Marcia hardly realized what words she meant to speak until they were out, and then she blushed. Was she happy? Why was she happy? Yes, even in the present trying circumstances, she felt a deep happiness in her heart. Was it David's look and his strong arm under her hand?

Hannah shot a look at her, stung by the words. Did the girl-wife mean to flaunt her own triumphs in her face? Did she fully understand? Or was she trying to make them believe she was happy? Hannah was baffled anew by Marcia.

Kate turned on Marcia for an instant again with that sardonic look that pierced her sister's soul.

But Marcia was lost in another thought. Did she imagine it, or at her words to Hannah did David's arm press hers closer as they stood there in the crowd? The thought gave her greater strength.

Hannah turned toward Kate.

"David," she said, "you knew my friend, Mrs. Leavenworth!"

David bowed gravely but didn't extend his hand to take the one Kate offered in greeting. Instead, he laid it over Marcia's trembling one on his arm as if to steady it.

"We've met before," David said and, turning, left the room to make way for the Brentwoods who were behind him.

Hannah was so vexed with the way things were turning out that she all but ignored the Brentwoods. She flashed an annoyed look at Kate, whose returning glance seemed to blame Hannah.

Soon everyone gathered in the dining room and hall for Grandmother Heath's fried chicken and currant jelly, delicate soda biscuits, and fruitcake baked months before and ripened. At first David and Marcia felt they couldn't swallow a mouthful, but strangely enough they found themselves eating with relish, perhaps to encourage the other but almost enjoying it.

Kate was seated by Hannah on the other side of the dining room, toying with her food and watching the two incessantly with that scornful look. She was apparently waiting for David to put on his true character. She never doubted they were acting.

The wedding supper was over at last. The guests crowded out to the front stoop to bid good-bye to the happy groom and cross-looking bride, who seemed as if she left the festive scene reluctantly.

For a moment Marcia was separated from David, who stepped down on the grass and stood to one side to let the bridal party pass. The minister was at the other side. Marcia had slipped into the shelter of Aunt Amelia's black silk presence and wished she might run out the back door and home.

Suddenly a shimmer of gold and purple caught her gaze. There on the top step behind David, unseen by him, stood her sister.

Marcia's heart gave a quick thump and seemed to stop, then labored on. She stood still watching for David to turn and see Kate so she might look into his face and read there what was written.

Patting cushions and adjusting curtains to suit her, the adoring Lemuel put Hannah carefully into the carriage. In her last moment Hannah liked showing others what a slave her husband was.

The guests looked after the carriage, but Marcia watched David. Then, just as the carriage wound around the curve in the road and was lost from view, she saw him turn and knew at once she mustn't see his face as he looked at Kate. Closing her eyes for an instant, she spun around and fled upstairs to get her shawl and bonnet. There she took refuge behind the curtains, praying without knowing what she prayed and thankful she didn't see what yet she'd longed to see.

As David turned to go up the steps and search for Marcia, he was confronted by Kate's beautiful, smiling face, as radiant as when it first charmed him. He exulted, on seeing it, that it no longer did.

"David, you don't seem a bit glad to see me," pouted Kate, gazing into his face with her sky-blue eyes. They almost held a hint of tears.

He used to kiss them when she looked like that. Now he felt only disgust as some of the sentences in her letters to Harry Temple came to his mind.

His face was stern and unrecognizing.

"David, you're still angry with me! You said you'd forgive!"

The other guests had all gone into the house. David made no response. Undaunted, Kate spoke again.

"I have something very important to consult you about. I came here on purpose. Can you give me some time tomorrow morning?"

She wrinkled her face into dimples and tilted her head to one side. "You know you never could refuse me anything, David."

He didn't smile or answer the look. With a voice that recognized her only as a stranger, he said: "I have an important engagement tomorrow morning."

"But you'll put off the engagement."

"It's impossible!" said David. "I'm starting quite early to drive over to Albany. I must be present at the starting of the new steam railroad."

"Oh, how nice!" said Kate, clapping her hands. "I've wanted to be there, and now you'll take me. Then I—we—can talk on the way. How like old times that will be!" She flashed him an alluring smile.

"That, too, is impossible, Mrs. Leavenworth. My wife accompanies me!" he answered her clearly and with a curt bow left her and went into the house.

Kate was angry, and for her, that meant venting it on someone—the offender, if possible, or at least the one nearest the offender. She'd failed to win back the friendship of her former love. She'd hoped to enjoy his attention and bathe her heart in the wistful glances of the man she had jilted, perhaps even being invited to his house. She would have then contrived to have her own way, for a rich, adoring brother-in-law wasn't bad to have, especially when his wife was her own little sister whom she'd always dominated. She was tired of New York and at this season preferred the country. She could thus hoard her small income and save for the next winter, as well as finally enter into her father's good graces again through David and Marcia's forgiveness. But she'd failed.

Could he care for Marcia? That child! She must find out at once.

Quickly she searched the downstairs rooms and then hurried upstairs. Instinctively she went to the room where Marcia had hidden herself.

With that upward breath of prayer, Marcia was steady again. She was standing with her back to the door looking out the window toward her own home when Kate entered the room. Without moving she felt Kate's presence. The moment had come. She turned around, her face calm and sweet, with her bonnet—Kate's bonnet and Kate's fine lace shawl sent from Paris—grasped in her hands.

The sisters faced each other, and without a word understanding passed between them. Marcia suddenly saw herself standing there in Kate's rightful place, Kate's things in her hands, Kate's garments on her body, Kate's husband held by her. It was as if Kate charged her with these things, as she surveyed her from the tips of her slippers to the ruffle around her neck. And what scorn flamed from Kate's eyes, scorching her cheeks into crimson and burning her lips dry and stiff! Yet when Kate's eyes reached her face and charged her with the supreme offense of taking David from her, Marcia's eyes looked bravely back, her soul untouched by the fire. Something about the thought of David, like an angelic presence, seemed to save her.

The silence between them was so intense that the two could hear nothing else. It drowned the voices below, the footstep on the stair, as if they were not.

At last Kate spoke, angered even more by her sister's soft eyes that gazed back and refused to drop before her own. Her voice was cold and cruel, with nothing sisterly in it, nothing to remind either that the other had ever been beloved.

"Fool!" hissed Kate. "Silly fool! Did you think you could steal a husband as you stole your clothes? Did you suppose marrying David would make him yours, just as putting on my clothes seemed to make them yours? He'll never be a husband to you. He doesn't love you and never can. He'll always love me. He's as much mine as if I married him, in spite of your attempts to take him.

"Oh, you needn't pucker your baby mouth as if you were going to cry. Cry away. It won't do any good. You can't make a man yours any more than you can make somebody's clothes yours. They don't fit you any more than he does. You look horrid in blue, and you know it, in spite of all your prissing around. I'd be ashamed to be dressed that way and know every piece of clothes I had was made for somebody else.

"As for pretending you have a husband—it's a lie. You know he's nothing to you. You know he never told you he cared for you. I tell you he's mine, and he always will be."

"Kate, you're married!" cried Marcia, shocked. "How can you talk like that?"

"Married! Nonsense! What difference does that make? Hearts count, not marriages. Has your marriage made you a wife? Answer me that! Has it? Does David love you? Does he ever kiss you? Yet he came to see me in New York this winter and took me in his arms and kissed me. He gave me money, too. See this brooch? I bought it with his money. You see he still loves me. I could bring him to my feet with a word today. He'd kiss me if I asked him. He's weak as water in my hands."

Marcia's cheeks burned with shame and anger. She felt almost at the end of her strength. For the first time in her life, she felt like striking—striking her own sister. Horrified by her feelings and the rage that was tearing her soul, she looked up, and there stood David in the doorway, like some tall avenging angel!

Kate had her back that way and didn't see him at first. But Marcia's eyes rested on him, pleading, and his answered hers. From her sister's sudden calmness, Kate realized someone was near and, turning, saw David.

But he didn't glance at her. How much or how little he heard of Kate's loud tirade, he didn't let them know, and neither dared ask him, in case he didn't hear anything. His eyes were like steel toward everything but Marcia, and his tone held kindness and a sense of mutual understanding.

"If you're ready, we'd better go now, dear, hadn't we?"

How gladly Marcia followed her husband downstairs and out the door! She scarcely knew how she went through the formalities of getting away. As she looked back, it seemed as if David sheltered her from everything and said what was needed, and all she did was smile an assent. He talked calmly to her all the way home; told her Mr. Brentwood's opinion about the change the new railroad would make in the country's commerce; told her even though he must have known she couldn't listen.

Perhaps both were conscious of the bedroom window across

the way and a pair of blue eyes that might be watching them. David took hold of her arm and helped her up the steps of their own home as if she were some great lady. Marcia wondered if Kate saw that. In her heart she blessed David for this outward sign of their relationship. It covered her shame a little at least. She glanced up toward the next house as she went in and felt sure she saw a glimmer of purple move away from the window. Then David shut the door behind them and led her gently in.

Chapter 27

*H*e took her into the parlor and sat down, unnerving her with his gentle ways. The tears came involuntarily, and with his handkerchief he wiped them softly off her cheeks. He untied the bonnet that wasn't hers and flung it far into a corner of the room. Then he unfolded the shawl—Kate's beautiful thread lace shawl—from her shoulders and threw that into another corner. Marcia felt like laughing hysterically, but David's voice was steady and quiet.

"There now, dear," he said, calling her "dear" a second time. "That was an ordeal, and I'm glad it's over. It'll never trouble us that way again. Let's put it aside and never think about it anymore. We have our own lives to live. I want you to go with me tomorrow morning to see the train start if you feel able. We must start early, so you need a good rest. Would you like to go?"

Marcia's countenance answered for her as she smiled through her tears. All the while David talked, his hand was moving back and forth across Marcia's hot forehead and smoothing the hair. He talked quietly to calm her and give her a chance to regain her composure, mentioning a few necessary arrangements for the morning's ride.

Then he said, "Now, dear, I want you to go to bed, since we must start rather early. But first do you think you could sing me that song you were singing the day I came home? Don't, though, if you feel too tired."

Then Marcia sprang up and walked eagerly to the piano. There she began to play and sing the words she sang before when she didn't know he was listening.

> *Dearest, believe,*
> *Whene'er we part:*
> *Lonely I grieve*
> *In my sad heart—*

From behind the chintz curtains across the yard where she was shedding angry tears on her purple silk, Kate heard the dulcet tones of the piano, which might have been hers. And she heard her sister's voice and began to understand that she must bear the punishment for her own rash deeds.

The room had changed from dusk into quiet darkness while Marcia was singing, for the sun was almost down when they'd walked home. When the song was finished, David looked almost wistfully at Marcia for a moment. He hesitated as if he wanted to say something more and then thought better of it. At last he stooped and lifted her hand from the keys and led her toward the door.

"You must go to sleep at once," he said. "You'll need all the rest you can get."

He lit a candle for her and said good night with his eyes as well as his words. And Marcia felt as if she moved upstairs by some gentle, loving power that surrounded her and would always guard her.

Earlier Miranda had been sent over with a forgotten piece of bride's cake for Marcia. When she heard the piano, she stole discreetly to the parlor window, returned at once, and detailed for that unhappy guest, Mrs. Leavenworth, why she couldn't get in and would have to take it over in the morning.

"The window was open in the parlor, and they were in there, them two, but they was so plum took up with their two selves, as they always are, that there wasn't no use knockin' fer they'd never hev heard."

Miranda enjoyed making those remarks to the guest. Some keen instinct told her where best to strike her blows.

When Marcia had reached the top stair, she looked down, and David was smiling up at her.

"Marcia," he said in a tone that seemed half ashamed and half amused, "have you any—that is—things—you had before—all your own, I mean?"

Marcia understood at once, and her own shame about her clothes that weren't hers came back upon her with double force. She suddenly saw herself again standing before her sister's censure. She wondered if David had heard. If not, how did he know? Oh, the shame of it!

"Yes," she said, trying to think. "Some old things and one dress."

"Wear it then tomorrow, dear."

Marcia smiled. "It's very plain, only chintz, pink and white. I made it myself."

"Perfect! Wear it, dear. Marcia, one thing more. Don't wear any more things that don't belong to you. Not a thing. Promise me? Can you get along without it?"

"Why, I guess so. I'll try to manage. But I haven't any bonnet. Nothing but a pink sunbonnet."

"All right, wear that."

"It'll look a little odd, won't it?" she asked doubtfully.

"Never mind," he said. "Wear it. Don't wear any more of those other things. Pack them all and send them where they belong, just as quick as we get home."

David's voice held something masterful and delightful in it, and Marcia with a happy laugh took her candle and went up, saying, "All right!" She went to her room with David's second good night ringing in her ears and her heart so light she wanted to sing.

Marcia didn't go to bed at once. She set her candle on the bureau and pulled her old haircloth trunk out of the closet. It had been sent to her after she left home, but she'd scarcely looked in it. It had seemed as if her girlhood were shut up in it. Now she began searching wildly in it.

What a flood of memories rushed over her! Inside lay relics of her childhood and school days. She touched them tenderly but set them aside one after another on the floor, until down in the lower corner she found a roll of soft white cloth. It contained a number of white garments, half a dozen finished and several others cut out and barely begun. Every stitch was her own, with the first piece started when she was a little girl and her stepmother had taught her to sew. What pride she took in them! How pleased she was when allowed to put real tucks in some of them!

At different times as she sewed on them, she thought they'd be part of her own wedding trousseau. And then her wedding came upon her unawares, with the trousseau ready-made and everything belonging to someone else. She'd folded her own garments away and thought she'd never take them out again, for they seemed to belong to her dead self.

But now that dead self had suddenly come to life again. These hated things she'd worn for a year that weren't hers were to be put away, and, pretty as many of them were, she didn't regret a thread of them.

She laid the white garments out on a chair and decided she'd put on what she needed the next morning, rumpled or not. She even hunted out an old pair of her own stockings and laid them next to the other things. They were neatly darned as always, under her stepmother's supervision. Further search brought to light a pair of partly worn prunella slippers with narrow ankle ribbons.

Then Marcia took down the pink sprigged chintz she made a year ago and placed it near the other things, with a bit of black velvet and the quaint old brooch. She felt a little dubious about appearing on such a great occasion, almost in Albany, in a chintz dress and without a wrap. Wait! The white crepe shawl David had brought her—it was hers. She'd had no other good occasion to wear it. Now she pulled it out breathlessly. A white crepe shawl and a pink calico sunbonnet! Marcia laughed softly. But David had said to wear it.

Everything was ready for tomorrow. She even had the white lace gloves Aunt Polly had given her in a rare benevolent spirit.

Then, to complete the change, she searched out an old nightgown, plain but smooth and clean, and put it on. At last she lay down, thankful and happy, and fell asleep.

In the room below David was pondering, strange to say, the subject of dress. Some pride was involved, of course, since there usually is in the matter of dress. But the bonnet lying in the corner with limp blue ribbons and crushed blue flowers made the subject more prominent in his thoughts that night.

He was going over to close the parlor window when he saw it discarded in the corner. Though somewhat damaged, it held enough of its original aristocratic style to cause him to stop and think.

It was fine to suggest Marcia wear a pink sunbonnet; it sounded so picturesque. She looked lovely in pink, and a sunbonnet was pretty and sensible on anyone. But tomorrow was a great day. Many people would see David and scrutinize his wife closely. Furthermore, Kate might appear on the scene to jeer at her sister in a sunbonnet. In fact, when he considered it, he didn't want to take his wife to Albany in a sunbonnet. The outrageous words he'd heard Kate Leavenworth say to his wife still burned in his brain like needles of torture: revelation of the true character of the woman he once longed to call his own.

He examined the bonnet. What was the proper bonnet for a woman in his wife's position to wear? He never noticed one before except absentmindedly in front of him in meeting. This bonnet seemed made up of three component parts—a foundation; a girdle apparently to bind it together and tie on the head; and a decoration of straw, silk, and some kind of unreal flowers. He stooped down and picked it up with his fingertips, held it at arm's length as though it were contaminated, and examined the inside. It had another element in its construction, a sort of frill of something thin, like the foam of a cloud. He touched the tulle clumsily with his thumb and finger and then dropped the bonnet back into the corner. He thought for a moment and looked at his watch.

It was early enough to try, though of course the shop would be closed. But the village milliner lived behind her shop. He could rouse her easily; besides, he'd known her all his life. He slipped out the door, fastening it behind him, and hurried down the street.

The milliner's shop was closed, but a light was shining in the side windows. David was soon tapping at Miss Mitchell's side door. She opened the door cautiously, peeped over her glasses, and, seeing who it was, welcomed him with a bright smile.

"Come in, David," she said. "I'm right glad to see you! Sit down."

"I haven't time to sit down tonight, Miss Susan. I've come to buy a bonnet if you have one. I hope it isn't too late because I want it very early in the morning. It's for my wife. You see, she's going with me over to Albany tomorrow morning. We're going to see the new railroad train start, and she seems to think she hasn't a suitable bonnet."

"Going to see a steam engine start, are you? Well, take care, David, that you don't get too near. They say they're terrible dangerous things, and fer my part I can't see what good they'll be, fer nobody'll ever be willin' to ride behind 'em, but I'd like to see it start well enough. And that sweet little wife of yours thinks she ain't got a good enough bonnet? Land sakes!

What's the matter with her Dunstable straw, and what's become of that one trimmed with blue lutestrings, and where's the shirred silk one she wore last Sunday? They're fine bonnets and should last her a good many years yet if she cares fer 'em. The mice haven't got into the house and et them, hev they?"

"No, Miss Susan, those bonnets are all whole yet, I believe, but they don't seem to be just right. In fact, I don't think they're overly becoming to her, do you? You see, they're mostly blue—"

"That's so!" said Miss Mitchell. "I think myself she'd look better in pink. How'd you like white? I've got a pretty thing I made fer Hannah Heath, an' when it was done, Hannah thought it was too plain and wouldn't have it. I sent for the flowers to New York, and they cost a high price. Wait! I'll show it to you."

She took a candle, and he followed her to the dark front room ghostly with bonnets in various stages of perfection.

He knew at a glance it was superior to most of the bonnets produced in the village. Its foundation was of fine Milan braid, creamy white and smooth. It was trimmed with soft white taffeta ribbon on the outside. Around the face was a soft ruching of tulle, and in the tulle nestled a few delicate green leaves looking as if they were just plucked from a wild rose bank.

David was delighted. Somehow the bonnet looked like Marcia. He paid the price at once, declining to look at anything else. It was enough that he liked it and Hannah Heath hadn't. He'd never admired Hannah's taste. He carried it home, letting himself into the house, lit three candles, took the bonnet out, and hung it on a chair. Then he surveyed it critically, first from this side, then from that. He almost wished Marcia would hear him and come down. He wanted to see it on her but decided he was becoming boyish and should control himself.

The bonnet approved, he walked back and forth through the kitchen and dining room thinking. He compelled himself to review the afternoon's events and analyze his innermost feelings. In fact, after doing that he went further back and tried to find out how he felt toward Marcia. What had been growing in him unaware through the months that made his homecoming sweet, brightened every day since, and made this meeting with Kate a mere commonplace? What was this precious thing that nestled in his heart? Could he call it love? Surely! All at once his pulses thrilled with gladness. He loved her! It was good to love her. She was the most precious being on earth to him. What was Kate compared with her—Kate who showed herself cold and cruel and unloving in every way?

His anger flamed anew at those cutting sentences he'd overheard, taunting her own sister about the clothes she wore. Boasting he still belonged to her! She, a married woman! A woman who of her own free will left him at the last moment and went away with someone else! His whole nature recoiled against her. She'd sinned against her womanhood and might no longer claim from man the homage a true woman had a right to claim.

His heart went out to Marcia. He couldn't bear to think of her having to listen to that heartless tirade. And he was the cause of all this. He had allowed her to take a position that opened her to Kate's vile taunts.

Up and down he paced till the torrent of his anger spent itself and he could think more calmly. Then he went back in his thoughts to the time when he first met Kate and she bewitched him. He could see her heartlessness now. He met her first at a friend's house where he was visiting, partly on pleasure, partly on business. She'd devoted herself to him during her stay in a charming way, though now he recalled she had also been equally devoted to the son of the friend he was visiting.

When she went home she asked him to call, for her home was only seven miles away. He was so charmed with her that he accepted the invitation and rashly, he now saw, engaged himself to her, after being with her face-to-face only a few days. To be sure, he'd known of her father for years and took a good deal for granted because of her fine family. They corresponded after their engagement, which lasted nearly a year. In that time David saw her only twice, for a day or two at a time, and each time he thought her more lovely.

Her letters were marvels of modesty and shy admiration. It was easy for Kate to maintain her character on paper, though she had little trouble in making people love her under any circumstances. Now as he looked back, he recalled many instances when she'd shown a cruel nature.

Then, all at once, it occurred to him to be thankful to God for his experience. After all, to love with enduring love wasn't taken from him; for though Kate was snatched from him just at the moment of his possession, Marcia had been given to him. Fool that he was! He'd been blind to his own salvation. Suppose he'd been allowed to go on and marry Kate! Suppose her character had been revealed to him suddenly as her letters to Harry Temple revealed it—as it surely would have been, for such things cannot be hidden—and she was his *wife*! He shuddered. How he would have loathed her! How he loathed her now!

Strangely enough, realizing that fact gave him joy. He sprang up and waved his hands about in delight. He felt like shouting for gladness. Then he knelt beside his chair and uttered an audible thanksgiving for his escape and the joy he'd been given. Nothing else seemed a fitting expression of his feelings.

He had one other question to consider—Marcia's feelings. She was always kind and gentle and loving to him, as a sister might be. She was still very young. Did she know, could she understand, what it meant to be loved the way he was sure he could love a woman? And could she ever love him that way? She was so shy that he hardly knew whether she cared for him or not.

But one thought gave him unbounded joy: She was his wife. At least no one else could take her from him. He'd felt condemned for marrying her when his heart was heavy lest she'd lose the zest for life, but all that was changed now. Unless she loved someone else, surely his love could draw hers, and finally she'd be as happy as a woman could be.

Misgiving crossed his mind as he admitted Marcia might love someone else. True, he knew of no one, and she was so young she probably hadn't left her heart with anyone in her youth. Still, he'd heard of strong heart unions between those who loved from early childhood. Marcia's occasional sadness might be because of a youthful companion.

He suddenly longed to rush up and awaken her and find out if she could ever care for him. He scarcely knew himself. This wasn't the dignified self he'd lived with for twenty-seven years.

It was late when he finally went upstairs. He walked softly lest he disturb Marcia. He paused before her door, listening to know if she was asleep but hearing only katydids in the branches outside her window and tree toads in a nearby orchard. He tiptoed to his room but didn't light the candle; so no light shone in the back room of the Spafford house that night for any watching eyes to ponder.

David threw himself on the bed. He was tired, yet his soul seemed buoyant as a bird in the morning air. The moon was almost full and was casting long bars of silver across the rag carpet and white counterpane. Tomorrow it would be full, as it was the night he'd met Marcia down by the gate and kissed her.

For the first time he thought of that kiss without pain. It used to hurt him that he made a mistake and took her for

Kate. It seemed like a bad omen of what was to come. But now it filled him with joy. After all, he kissed the right one. Was he guided to her that night? And why didn't he see her sweetness sooner? How did he live with her nearly a year, watch her loving ministry, and not know his heart was hers? Why did he grieve over Kate for so long? Now since he'd seen her again, he had no regret in his heart that she wasn't his. Only a beautiful revelation of his love for Marcia had been wrought in him. How did it come about?

And the persistent little night singers answered him a thousand times: "Kate-did-it! Kate-she-did-it! Yes, she did! I say she did. Kate did it!"

Did angel voices reach him through his dreams and reveal what the insects voiced in their ridiculous colloquy? It was Kate herself who showed him how he loved Marcia.

Chapter 28

*T*he moon rose over the house and down toward its way in the west, and after its vanishing chariot the night stretched wistful arms. Softly the gray in the east tinged into violet and glowed into rose and gold. The birds awakened and told one another that the first of August was come and life was good.

The breath that came in the early dawn savored of new-mown hay, and the bird songs thrilled Marcia as if it were the day of her dreams.

She forgot her troubles, forgot even her wayward sister next door, and rose with a song in her heart. No matter what happened, she had this great day from which to date. David had asked her to go somewhere just because he wanted her to. She knew it from the look in his eyes when he told her, and she knew it because he might have asked a dozen men to go with him. He didn't need to take her today, for this wonder of machinery was distinctly an affair for men. It was a privilege for a woman to go. She felt it.

She dressed with trembling fingers and a light heart. Even the thought of wearing her pink calico sunbonnet on such a grand occasion couldn't spoil the day. In such a large crowd, her bonnet would hardly be noticed. If David was satisfied, why, what difference did it make? She hummed a tune that melted into the melody of the song she sang last night.

Then she smiled at herself in the mirror. She was fastening the brooch in the bit of velvet around her neck and thought of the day a year ago when she fastened that brooch. She'd wondered then how she'd feel if the next day were her own wedding day. Now as she smiled back at herself in the mirror, she felt all at once as if this was her wedding day. Somehow last night seemed to realize her dreams. A wonderful joy had descended on her heart. Maybe she was foolish, but wasn't she going to ride with David? She didn't long for the green fields and a chance to run wild through the woods now. This was better than those childish pleasures. This was real happiness. And to think it came through David!

She hurried to arrange her hair. She wanted to get downstairs and see if it was true or if she was dreaming. Would David look at her as he had last night? Would he speak that precious word "dear" to her again today? Would he lead her by the hand sometimes, or was that only because he knew she suffered from her sister's words? She clasped her hands over her heart and looked back at her face in the mirror.

"Oh, I love him, love him!" she whispered. "And it can't be wrong, for Kate is married."

But though she was up early, David came down before her. The fire was already lit and the kettle singing on the crane. He even pulled out the table, put up the leaf, and tried to put the dishes on it for breakfast. He was sitting by the hearth, impatient for her to come, with a bandbox by his side.

It was like another sunrise to watch their eyes light up as they saw one another. Their glances rushed together as though withheld from each other a long time, and over Marcia's face spread a rosy glow that made her long to hide it for a moment. Then she knew in her heart that her dream wasn't a dream. David was the same. Whatever this wonderful thing was that bound them together had lasted. She stood still in her contented bewilderment, looking at him, and he, enjoying the radiant morning vision of her, stood, too.

Again David longed to take her in his arms. But he was resolved to be careful and not frighten her. He must be sure it wouldn't be unpleasant to her before he let her know his great love. He mustn't take advantage of the fact that she was his.

And so their two looks met, both longed to come closer but held back, and a lovely shyness crept over Marcia's face. Then David remembered the bandbox.

He took up the box and untied it, fumbling in the tissue paper for the handle end of the thing. Where did they grasp bonnets anyway? He had no trouble with it the night before. Now he was almost afraid she might not like it. Hannah Heath had decided against it. It suddenly seemed impossible he bought a bonnet a pretty woman said wasn't right. Something must be wrong with it after all, though it had the requisite number of materials—one, two, three, four—like the despised bonnet he'd thrown on the floor—straw, silk, lace, and flowers.

Marcia stood there wondering what he was doing.

"I thought maybe this would do instead of the sunbonnet," he said at last, pulling out the bonnet by one string and holding it dangling before him.

"Oh!" exclaimed Marcia, catching it with her hands.

Her cheeks flushed with pleasure, and her eyes danced with joy.

"Oh, it's beautiful! It's so sweet and white and cool with that green vine. Oh, I'm so glad! I'll never wear that old blue bonnet again."

She walked over to the mirror and put it on. The soft ruching settled about her brown hair and made a lovely setting for her face. The green vine twined in and out under the round brim, and the ribbon sat in a bow beneath her chin.

She glanced at herself one more time in the mirror and then turned to David. In that glance she realized just how much she'd dreaded wearing her pink sunbonnet and how relieved she was to have a substitute.

Her look was shy yet with a little daring, as she said, "You—are—very—good to me."

He almost forgot his vow of carefulness but remembered when he got halfway across the room.

"Dear, *you* have been very good to *me*."

Marcia's eyes suddenly sobered, and half the glow faded from her face. Was it then only gratitude? She took off the bonnet and touched the bows tenderly as she laid it aside till after breakfast.

He watched her and misinterpreted the look. Was she disappointed in the bonnet? Wasn't it right after all? Had Hannah known better than he?

"Is there—is it—that is—perhaps you'd rather take it back and choose another. You know how to choose one better than I. There were others, I think. In fact, I forgot to look at any but this because I liked it, but I'm only a man—"

"No! No! No!" said Marcia, her eyes sparkling. "There couldn't be a better one. This is just exactly what I like. I don't want anything else. And I—like it all the better because you selected it," she added, lifting her face to his with a spice of her own childish freedom.

His eyes admired her.

"She told me Hannah Heath thought it was too plain," he added honestly.

"Then I'm sure I like it even more for that," said Marcia so emphatically that they both laughed.

Then the clock in the hall clanged out the hour, and David suddenly realized they must hurry.

In a dream, or perhaps on the borders of the morning, he'd had an idea. He told Marcia he must see about the horse now, but he also made a brief visit to his office clerk's home and another to the aunts. When he returned with the horse, he'd left things in such order that if he didn't return that evening, he wouldn't be greatly missed. But he said nothing to Marcia about it.

He laughed to himself as he thought of the sleepy look on

his clerk's face and the offended dignity in the ruffle of Aunt Hortense's nightcap all awry as she peered over the balusters to receive his early visit. The aunts prided themselves on being early risers. It hurt their vanity for anything short of sudden serious illness, death, or a fire to cause others to rise before them. Therefore, they didn't accept with good grace the message that David was planning another trip away from the village for a few days.

Aunt Hortense asked Aunt Amelia if she ever feared Marcia would have a bad effect on David by making him frivolous. Perhaps he'd lose interest in his business with all his careering around the country. Aunt Amelia agreed Marcia must be to blame in some way. Then, discovering they had a whole hour before their usual rising time, the two good ladies settled themselves with indignant composure to their interrupted repose.

Breakfast was ready when David returned. Marcia supposed he only went to harness the horse. She glanced out through the window to where the horse stood tied to the post in front of the house.

Marcia would scarcely have eaten anything in her excitement if David hadn't urged her to. She cleared the dishes away and then flew upstairs to arrange her bonnet in front of the mirror and don the creamy crepe shawl, folding it around her shoulders and knotting it in front. She put on her gloves, took her handkerchief, and came down ready to go.

But David no longer seemed in such haste. He made a great fuss fastening up everything. She wondered at his unusual care, for she thought everything was quite safe for the day.

She raised one shade toward the Heath house. It was the first time she'd permitted herself to think of Kate this morning. Was she still there? Probably, for no coach had left since last night, and the only other way was by private means. She looked up to the front corner guest room where the windows were open and the white curtains swayed in the morning breeze. No one seemed to be moving about in the room. Perhaps Kate wasn't awake. Just then she caught the flutter of blue muslin on the front stoop. Kate was up, early as it was, and was coming out.

A sudden misgiving seized Marcia. Many times when she was a child, her sister came and ate the piece of cake or sweetmeat that was given to her. Now she felt in some mysterious way Kate would contrive to take her newfound joy from her. She couldn't resist her—David couldn't resist her—no one could ever resist Kate. Her face paled, and her hand trembled so that she dropped the curtain she was holding up.

Just then she heard David's clear voice. It was louder than necessary and pitched as if he were calling someone upstairs, though he knew she was just inside the parlor where she'd gone to check the window fastening.

"Come, dear! Aren't you ready? We should have started already."

His voice carried a cheerful ring that belied his rather exacting words, and Marcia's heart leaped up to meet him.

"Yes, I'm all ready, dear!" she called back with a giddy laugh.

Of course Kate couldn't hear so far, but it pleased her to say it. The final word was unpremeditated. It bubbled up out of the depths of her heart and made the red rush back into her cheeks when she realized what she'd said. It was the first time she had ever used a term of endearment toward David. She wondered if he noticed it and if he'd think her bold or immodest for using it. She looked at him shyly, inquiring with her eyes, as she came out to him on the front stoop, and he smiled so at her she felt as if it were a caress.

Yet neither was conscious of this real byplay they were enacting for the benefit of the one in blue muslin across the way. How much or how little she heard, they couldn't tell. But it was satisfying to go through with it, since it was real and not acting at all.

David fastened the door and then helped Marcia into the carriage. They were both laughing happily like two children starting on a picnic. Marcia was serenely conscious of her new bonnet, and it was pleasant when David tucked the linen lap robe over her chintz dress so carefully. She was certain Kate couldn't identify it now at that distance, thanks to the lap robe and her crepe shawl. At least Kate couldn't see any of her own trousseau on her sister now.

Kate was sitting on the white seat, sheltered by the honeysuckle vine, and facing them on the stoop of the Heath house. They couldn't know whether she was watching them or not, and they didn't look up to see. She was talking with Mr. Heath, who, in his milking garb, was perking up some shrubs and plants that were trampled during the wedding festivities. But Kate must have seen a good deal.

David picked up the reins, smiled at Marcia, and touched the horse with the tip of the whip, causing him to spring forward and carry them swiftly a rod or two past the Heath house. That left only time for David to lift his hat politely, which might or might not have included Kate, and they were on their way together.

Marcia could scarcely believe she was here beside David, riding with him through the village and leaving Kate behind. She felt a passing pity for Kate. Then she looked shyly up at David. Would his cheerfulness pass when they were away, and would he grow sad again as soon as he was out of Kate's sight? She'd learned enough of David's principles to know he wouldn't think it right to let his thoughts stray to Kate now. But did his heart still turn that way in spite of him?

Through the town they sped, glad with every roll of the wheels that took them farther away from Kate. Each was conscious of that day a year ago when they rode together out through the fields into the country. Today was much like that other one, just as bright and warm, yet much more radiant to both! Then they were sad and fearful of the future. Their lives seemed in the past. Now they'd journeyed through the darkness and reached the brightness again. In fact, the future stretched before them that fair morning and looked bright as the day.

They were conscious of the blue sky, the soft clouds that hovered in haze on the rim of the horizon, as holding off far enough to spoil no moment of that perfect day. They noticed the waving grains and the perfume of the buckwheat drifting like snow in the fields beyond the wheat; the meadowlark and the wood robin's note; the whir of a locust; and the thud of a frog in the cool green pool. They saw the mated butterflies circling in the simmering gold air; the wild roses lifting fair pink petals from the brambly banks beside the road; the whispering pine needles in a wood they passed; the fluttering chatter of leaves and silver flash of the lining of poplar leaves, where tall trees stood like sentinels. They took note of a little brook that tinkled under a log bridge they crossed, then hurried on its way unmindful of their happy crossing. They even saw the dusty daisy beside the road. They were conscious of all these things, but mostly of each other, close, side by side.

That ride was so dear and over so soon. Marcia was just trying to get used to looking up into the light of David's eyes. She dropped her own almost immediately, for the truth she read in his was overpowering. Could it be? A thought came timidly to her heart and wouldn't be denied: *Can it be that he cares for me? He loves me. He loves me!*

David's eyes told the story his lips dared not risk yet. But eyes and hearts aren't held by the conventions that bind lips.

All too soon they turned into a road with other vehicles going in the same direction. Men and women in festive daywear laughed and talked expectantly and looked at one another as the carriages passed, all sharing a common purpose. Family coaches, farm wagons with kitchen chairs to accommodate the family, old one-horse chaises, carryalls, and even a stagecoach or two wheeled onto the old turnpike. David and Marcia settled into subdued quiet, their joy not expressing itself in the ripples of laughter that had rung out earlier in the morning when they were alone. They sought each other's eyes often, and in one of these exchanges, David noticed how extremely becoming the new bonnet was. He decided to risk letting her know. He wasn't shy about it now.

"Do you know, dear," he said, and a good many "dears" had slipped back and forth unannounced during that ride and not openly acknowledged either, "how becoming your new bonnet is to you? You look prettier than I ever saw you look, except once before." He kept his eyes on her face and watched the sweet color steal up to her eyelashes.

"And when was that?" she asked, glancing at him and laughing to hide her embarrassment.

"Why, that night at the gate, in the moonlight. Don't you remember?"

"Oh–h–h–h!" Marcia caught her breath. A feeling of joy passed through her that made her close her eyes lest the glad tears should come. Then her heart sang in earnest, *He loves me. He loves me. He loves me!*

He leaned a little closer to her.

"If so many people weren't looking, I think I'd have to kiss you now."

"Oh–h–h–h!" said Marcia, drawing in her breath again. Alarmed, she glanced at all the people driving around them. They were almost to the railroad now and could see the black smoke of the engine just beyond where it stood puffing and snorting on its track like some sulky animal that had been caught and chained and harnessed and was longing to leap forward and upset its load.

But though Marcia looked about in delightful alarm and sat a bit straighter in the chaise, she didn't move her hand away from where it lay next to David's underneath the lap robe. He put his own hand over it and covered it in his firm grasp. Marcia was almost faint with joy. She wondered if she were foolish to feel that way and if all love had this terrible element of solemn joy in it that made it seem too great to be real.

They had to stop a number of times to speak to people. Everybody knew David, it appeared. This man and that had a word to say to him—some bit of news he mustn't omit from his article; some new development in an influential man's attitude; some change of those who were to go in the coaches on this trial trip.

To all of them David introduced his wife, with pride in his voice as he said the words "my wife." And all of them stopped whatever business they had and stepped back to bow to the beautiful woman who sat smiling by his side. They wondered why they hadn't heard of her before and looked curiously, then enviously, at David and back in admiration at Marcia. It was quite a little court she held sitting there in the chaise beside David.

Men who have since won mention in the pages of history were there that day, and nearly all of them had a word for David Spafford and his lovely wife. Many of them stood for some time and talked with her. Mr. Thurlow Weed was the last one to leave them before the train was ready to start, and he laid an urging hand on David's arm.

"Then you think you can't go with us? Better come. Mrs. Spafford will let you, I'm sure. You're not afraid, are you, Mrs. Spafford? I'm sure you're a brave woman. Better come, Spafford."

But David laughed and thanked him again, as he'd thanked others, and said he couldn't go; he and his wife had other plans, and he must go on to Albany as soon as the train started.

Marcia looked up at him as he said this, wondering what it was, instinctively knowing that for her sake he was giving up this honor they all wished to put upon him. It would naturally have been exciting for him to take this first ride behind the new engine, the Dewitt Clinton.

Then, suddenly, like a chill wind from a thundercloud that steals up and clutches the little wildflowers before they can bind up their windy locks and duck their heads under cover, something happened that clutched Marcia's heart and froze the joy in her veins.

Chapter 29

A coach filled with people was approaching, and Marcia knew some of the friends and neighbors in it from their village.

Behind it plodded a horse with a strangely familiar gait drawing four people. Mr. Heath was driving and looking askance at the scene before him. He didn't believe an engine could haul a train any appreciable distance and thus came to witness the entire company of fanatics circumvented by the ill-natured iron steed that stood on the track ahead. Surrounding the engine were gaping boys and a flock of quacking ganders, living symbol of the people who came to see the thing start, so thought Mr. Heath. He told himself he was as much of a goose as any of them to have let this woman fool him into coming out here when he should be in the hayfield today.

Beside him, in shimmering blue with a wide, white lace bertha and a bonnet with a steeple crown wreathed about with roses, sat Kate. A blue silk parasol shaded her eyes from the sun, those eyes that sought to conquer, piercing through and beyond her sister and ignoring her.

Mrs. Heath and Miranda were along, but they didn't count, except to themselves. Miranda longed to see that wonderful engine in which David was so interested.

Marcia's bright bloom faded in an instant, and a frenzy seized her. She had a wild desire to get out of the carriage and run with all her might away from this hateful scene. To her the sky was suddenly clouded over, and the hum and buzz of voices seemed an unceasing babble.

David felt the arm beside his cringe and shrink back. Looking down he saw the fear on her face, and following her glance, his own face hardened into righteous anger. But he didn't say a word and gave no sign of seeing the oncoming carriage. He busied himself at once talking with a man who happened to pass the carriage. When Mr. Heath drove by to get a better view of the engine, David was so absorbed in his conversation that he didn't notice them.

But Kate wouldn't be so easily foiled. She had a great deal at stake and must win if possible. She got Mr. Heath to drive around to the end of the line of coaches, out of sight of the engine, and where there was little chance of seeing the train and its passengers—the only thing Mr. Heath cared about. From there Kate had an excellent view of David's carriage and would be within hailing distance if she had no further opportunity of speaking with him.

As Mr. Heath sat patiently behind the last coach, he thought it strange he had done what she asked. She didn't look like a woman who was timid around horses; yet she professed a terrible fear that the screech of the engine would frighten the staid old Heath horse.

Miranda, at that, insisted on changing seats, thus getting nearer the horse and the action. She didn't want to miss seeing the engine start.

At last, word to start was given. A man ran along by the train and mounted into his high seat with his horn in his hand ready to blow. The fireman ceased his raking of the glowing fire, and every traveler sprang into his seat and looked toward the crowd of spectators. The little ones whose fathers were in the train began to call good-bye and wave their hands, and one old woman whose only son was going as a train assistant sobbed out loud.

Every time the engine snorted, it let off steam and caused a horse in the crowd to balk and rear. He was right behind

Marcia. She turned her head and looked straight into his eyes, red with fear and frenzy, and felt his hot breath on her cheek. A man was trying in vain to hold him, and it seemed the horse would break free any minute and lunge at them.

Marcia uttered a frightened cry and clutched at David's arm. Turning, he saw instantly what was the matter, placed his arm about her, and guided his own horse out of the crowd and nearer the engine. That protecting arm steadied Marcia, as she watched the wheels begin to turn and the whole train start slowly on its way.

For that instant she forgot her trouble. David's arm was still about her, with a reassuring pressure in it. He seemed to forget that the crowd might see him, while the crowd, of course, was too busy watching something more wonderful.

Probably only one person saw David sitting with his arm around his wife—for he soon put it quietly on the back of the seat—and that person was Kate. She didn't come to this hot, dusty place to watch an engine creak along a track; she came to watch David and was vexed at what she saw. Here was Marcia flaunting her power over David directly in her face. Spiteful thing! She'd pay her back yet and let her know she couldn't touch the things that she, Kate, had put her own sign and seal upon.

So, at the last minute, Kate allowed poor Mr. Heath to drive around near the front of the train, saying that since David Spafford seemed to find it safe, she supposed she shouldn't hold them back for her fears. The irked and curious squire needed only a word to send him to a spot directly behind David's carriage. There Miranda could see quite well, and Kate could watch David and frame her plan of action as soon as the curtain fell on this ridiculous engine play over which everybody was wild.

And so, amid shouts and cheers and squawking geese trying to precede the engine like a white, frightened bodyguard down the track; amid the waving of handkerchiefs, the whoops of excited little boys, and the neighing of frightened horses, the first steam engine that ever drew a train in New York State started on its initial trip.

Then a great hush settled over the spectators assembled. The wheels were rolling, the carriages were moving, the train was actually going by them—what had been talked about so long was an assured fact. They were seeing it with their own eyes and would be witnesses of it to their acquaintances. They dared not speak or breathe lest something should happen and the great miracle stop. So they watched in silence until the train moved on between the meadows, slitted into the shadow of the woods, flashed out into the sunlight beyond again, and then was lost behind a hill. A low murmur grew into a shout of "Hurrah!" as the crowd faced one another and the fact of what they saw.

"She kin do it!" exclaimed Mr. Heath, who had watched the melting of his skeptical opinions in speechless amazement.

His words were the first intimation to the Spaffords of Kate's proximity. Marcia paled with sudden fear again. After many years of living with her sister, she knew that cruel nature and dreaded it.

David smiled at the squire's words and looked at Marcia for agreement in his smile. But seeing her face, he turned frowning toward those behind him.

Kate saw her opportunity. She leaned forward with a honeyed smile and, wily as the serpent, addressed her words to Marcia, loud and clear enough for all those around them to hear.

"Oh, Mrs. Spafford! I'm going to ask a great favor of you. I'm sure you'll grant it when you know I have so little time. I'm extremely anxious to get a word of advice from your husband on some pressing business matters. Would you kindly change places with me during the ride home and give me a chance to talk with him about it? I wouldn't ask it, but I must leave for New York on the evening coach and shall have no other opportunity to see him."

Kate's smile was roses and cream touched with frosty sunshine, and to onlookers nothing could have been sweeter. But her eyes were cold and cruel as sharpened steel and said to her sister as plainly as words could have spoken: "Obey my wish, my lady, or I'll freeze the heart out of you."

Marcia turned white and sick. She felt as if her lips had suddenly stiffened and refused to obey her when they should have smiled. What would all these people think of her and how was she behaving? For David's sake she should do something, say something, look something—but what?

While she was thinking this, with her heart freezing up into her throat, tears beating at the portals of her eyes, and time standing still, waiting for her leaden tongue to speak, David answered, without so much as a second's hesitation or the shadow of a sign he was angry.

"Mrs. Leavenworth, I'm sure my wife wouldn't wish to seem ungracious or unwilling to comply with your request, but as it happens, it's impossible. We're not returning home for several days. My wife has some shopping to do in Albany, and in fact we're expecting to take a little trip. A sort of second honeymoon, you know," he added, smiling toward Mrs. Heath and Miranda. "It's the first time I've had the opportunity to plan for it since we were married. I'm sorry I have to hurry away, but I'm sure my friend Squire Heath can give as much help in a business way as I could. Furthermore, Squire Schuyler is now in New York for a few days, as I learned in a letter from him that arrived last evening. I'm sure he can give you more and better advice than I could. I wish you good morning. Good morning, Mrs. Heath. Good morning, Miss Miranda!"

Lifting his hat, David drove away from them and straight over to the little wayside hostelry. There he was to finish his article to send by the messenger who was even then ready and mounted to go.

"My! Don't he think a lot of her though!" said Miranda, rolling the words as a sweet morsel under her tongue. "It must be nice to have a man so fond of you."

Miranda wished she had eyes in the back of her head. She'd seen a thing or two and heard scraps of her cousin Hannah's talk. But from the front seat under her bonnet she could only imagine how the guest behind her looked.

Marcia sat in the parlor of the little hostelry. David was writing hurriedly at the table, glancing up at her now and then and handing her the finished sheets for her criticism. She thought she saw the Heath wagon drive away toward home but wasn't sure. She half expected to see the door open and Kate walk in. Her heart was thumping so she could scarcely sit still, and the brightness of the world outside seemed to make her dizzy. She was glad to have the sheets to look over, for it took her thoughts off herself and her nameless fears. She wasn't quite sure what it was she feared, only that in some way Kate would have power over David to take him away from her. As he wrote, she studied the lines of his face and knew, as well as human heart may ever know, how dear his soul had become to hers.

David had little to write, so it was soon signed, approved, and sealed. He sent his messenger on the way and then, coming back, closed the door and went and stood in front of Marcia.

As though she felt some critical moment had come, she arose, trembling, and looked into his eyes with a question.

"Marcia," he said in a serious, earnest tone, putting her on an equality with him, not as if she were a child anymore. "Marcia, I've come to ask your forgiveness for the terrible thing I did to you. I allowed you, who scarcely knew what you were doing then, to give your life away to a man who loved another woman."

Marcia's heart stood still with horror. It had come then, the dreadful thing she'd feared. The blow was going to fall. He didn't love her! What a fool she'd been!

But the steady voice continued, though the blood in her neck and temples throbbed in such loud waves that she could barely understand the words.

"It was a crime, Marcia, and I've come to realize it more and more during this year that you've spent yourself for me without complaint. I know now, as I didn't in my careless, selfish sorrow, that I was as cruel to you, with your sweet young life, as your sister was cruel to me. You might already have given your heart to someone else; I never stopped to inquire. You might have had plans and hopes for your own future; I never even thought of it. I was a brute. Can you forgive me? Sometimes the thought of the responsibility I took upon myself has been so terrible to me that I felt I couldn't stand it. You didn't realize what it was then that you were giving, perhaps, but somehow I think you've begun to realize now. Will you forgive me?"

He stopped and looked at her anxiously.

Her shoulders sagged, and her face paled as if a blast had suddenly struck her and faded her sweet bloom. Her throat was hot and dry, and she tried three times before she could frame the words, "Yes, I forgive."

The words had no hope, no joy, and sudden fear enveloped David's heart. Had he done more damage than he knew? Had he broken the child's heart and she just realized it? What could he do? Must he conceal his love from her? Perhaps this was no time to tell it. But he must. He couldn't bear the burden of having harmed her and not also tell her how he loved her. He'd be careful and considerate; he wouldn't press his love as a claim, but he must tell her.

"And, Marcia, I must tell you the rest." For a moment his own words stayed on his lips and then tumbled over one another. "I've learned to love you as I never loved your sister. I love you more and better than I could ever have loved her. I can see how God has led me away from her and brought me to you. I can look back to that night when I came to her and found you there and kissed you—darling. Do you remember?"

He took her cold little trembling hands and held them firmly as he talked, his whole soul in his face, as if his life depended upon the next few moments.

"I was troubled at the time, dear, for kissing you and giving you the greeting I thought belonged to her. I rebuked myself for thinking since how lovely you looked in the moonlight. But afterward I knew my love belonged to you, and to you the kiss should have gone. I'm glad it was so, glad God overruled my foolish choice. Lately I've looked back to that night I met you at the gate and felt jealous that meeting wasn't all ours, that someone else's heartlessness has shadowed it for us. It gives me joy now that I took you in my arms and kissed you. I can't bear to think it was mistake. Yet glad as I am that God sent you down to that gate to meet me, and much as I love you, I'd rather die than feel I brought sorrow into your life and bound you to someone you can't love. Marcia, tell me truly— never mind my feelings! Can you ever love me?"

Then Marcia lifted her face, bright with tears of joy and a rosy smile and a deep light glowing in her eyes. But she couldn't speak; she could only look, till after a little while she whispered, "Oh, David, I think I've always loved you! I think I was waiting for you that night, though I didn't know it.

"And look!" she exclaimed, with a sudden thought.

She drew from around her neck a small locket hanging on a chain out of sight. She opened it and showed him a soft gold curl that she touched gently with her lips, as though sacred.

"What is it, darling?"

"It's yours," she said, disappointed he didn't understand. "Aunt Clarinda gave it to me while you were away. I've worn it ever since. And she gave me other things and told me all about you. I know everything, about the tops and the marbles and the spelling book, and I've cried with you because of the punishments you suffered, and—I—love it all!"

He'd fastened the door before he began to talk, but he caught her in his arms now, despite the shades that were up and swaying in the summer breeze.

"Oh, my darling! My wife!" he cried and kissed her lips for the third time.

The world was changed then for those two. They belonged to each other, they believed, as no two who ever walked through Eden had ever belonged. When they thought of the precious bond that tied them together, their hearts beat with a joy that nearly overwhelmed them.

A dinner of stewed chickens and white soda biscuits was served them, fit for a wedding breakfast. The maid had whispered to the cook that she was sure a bride and groom were in the parlor, for they looked so happy and seemed to forget anyone else was around. But it might have been ham and eggs for all they knew. These two were so happy that they looked only into each other's eyes.

When the dinner was over, they started on their way again, with Albany shimmering in the hot sun in the distance. David's arm slid from the top of the seat to circle Marcia's waist.

"This is our real wedding journey, dearest," he whispered, "and this is our bridal day. We'll go to Albany and buy you a trousseau, and then we'll go wherever you wish. I can stay a whole week if you wish. Would you like to go home for a visit?"

Marcia, with shining eyes and glowing cheeks, answered, "Yes, now I'd like to go home, just for a few days, and then back to our home."

And David, looking into her eyes, understood why she hadn't wanted to go before. She was taking her husband—her husband, not Kate's—with her now and might be proud of his love. She could go among her old comrades and be happy, for he loved her. He looked a moment, understood, and sympathized. Then, pressing her hand close instead of kissing her, for a wagon bearing a load of hay was approaching, he said, "Darling!" But their eyes said more.

Author Biography

Perhaps the work of Grace Livingston Hill is so enduring because her stories parallel the experiences in her own life. Born in Wellsville, New York, in 1865, she almost died during the first hours after birth. But her loving parents and their friends turned to God in prayer. She survived miraculously.

Likely inspired by her beloved Aunt Isabella Alden, who was also a published author, Grace Livingston Hill became known as "America's most beloved author." During her remarkable career, she wrote 147 books. And although she passed away in 1947, her romance novels live on today.

Also available from
BARBOUR PUBLISHING, INC.

Lo, Michael
A newsboy saves the life of an heiress—
opening doors of opportunity for himself.
ISBN 1-59310-675-0

Miranda
Miranda longs for the day
she'll see the man she loves.
ISBN 1-59310-678-5

Lone Point
Loss of fortune forces Maria to
reconsider her perspective on life.
ISBN 1-59310-676-9

The Witness
Paul Courtland is tormented by
the consequences of his choices.
ISBN 1-59310-680-7

Phoebe Deane
Phoebe is on the verge of
losing her last hope.
ISBN 1-59310-679-3

Available wherever books are sold.